HUMANS

Also by AG Claymore:

Humanity Ascendant

Human

Humans

Humanity

Ragnarok

Rebels and Patriots

Rebels and Patriots

Beyond the Rim

The Gray matter

The Black Ships

The Black Ships

The Dark Defiance

The Orphan Alliance

Counterweight

Asymmetry

Firebringer

Terra Cryptica

Prometheus Bound

Humans

Published by A.G. Claymore
Edited by Beryl MacFadyen
Copyright 2019 A.G. Claymore

Andrew Claymore asserts the moral right to be identified as the author of this work.

ISBN: 9798728510192

Get Free e-Novellas

free **stories**

When you sign up for my new-release mail list!

Follow this link to get started:
http://eepurl.com/ZCP-z

The Illusion of Control

Preoccupation
Susa, planetary capital of Tadmor.

"You hand the bastard an empire on a platter and what does he say?" Eth tossed down the last of his espresso and slammed the tiny mug on the counter. He paid no attention to the weapons fire coming from the intersection behind him. "Not half bad," he allowed. "I'll have another."

A slightly bluish hand darted up to snatch away the mug. Its owner, not caring the least about whatever the 'bastard' had said, did his best to refill the mug, though he dropped it once when a flurry of small arms fire impacted one of the carboncrete columns where he'd set up his stand.

"That's fine," Eth told him. "Don't bother cleaning it. Just fill it up again."

The hand placed the chipped mug back on the counter in front of Eth.

"So he says to me," Eth continued, looking with appreciation at the light brown layer of crema on top of the drink, *"Get your lazy arse over to Tadmor cause we gotta steal...* don't even recall the name of the damn thing." He poured the hot liquid down his throat as Gleb ran past behind him, arms flailing and a respectable plume of flames lighting up the back of his armor.

"The golden hunk of… shit, I suppose." He waved the empty mug airily as their shuttle emerged from an underground parking elevator, drifting his way on autopilot. "Supposed to help stop one of the dozens of private little wars, or so he thinks."

The shuttle suddenly exploded, sending combatants scrambling for cover. A large chunk flew past Eth's right hip, smashing away half of the small coffee stand. The stall-owner let out a rattling croak of terror.

Eth set the mug down on the remaining half of the counter and drew his sidearm, swinging it up into the face of a Tadmoran security officer who'd thought he was being sneaky.

"I came here to help you idiots avoid a war," he snapped at the officer, "and I've had nothing but trouble ever since!" He squeezed the trigger and a tiny sphere flew out from a chamber under the main rails.

It stuck to the left side of the officer's forehead and he went down, twitching uncontrollably, electrical arcs snaking around his body. The sphere snapped back into Eth's weapon and he holstered it again.

"Look, our ride's on its way," he said, leaning over to look down at the stand owner. He reached down with his left hand, fist bent back in the universal gesture of payment. The owner responded out of sheer habit.

"There's a little extra to cover damages," Eth told him. "Can't help but feel *partially* responsible for all this." He waved vaguely out to the debris field that had been a shuttle.

He turned and walked over to where Gleb was directing the rest of their small team of Humans. They were in a large landing where three broad sets of stairs converged before leading down to a mass-transit node.

"You got it?" he asked Gleb.

"Yeah, we got it," Gleb answered. "Glad to see you taking an interest in the operation..."

"Hey!" Eth spread out his hands. "I was showing confidence in your leadership!"

"And all this time I thought you were being a self-absorbed jackass in need of a caffeine fix."

"Yeah, well... it can be both. C'mon, you didn't even need me along for this."

"Whatever. Let's just get out of here before we have more company than we can handle. They still hang thieves here..."

"Tadmorans," Oliv scoffed, "couldn't hang a curtain!"

A deep, thrumming moan rumbled through their bones.

"Heavy response unit's here," Eth said.

They all dropped their weapons and knelt in a single line, helmets open and hands behind their heads. The Tadmoran heavy response team crested the top edge of the stairs and stopped in mild confusion.

"C'mon, fellas," Eth called up to them. "It's not like we've got all day, y'know."

The heavily armored officer with a centurion's glyph pulled out a couple of drone clips and the rest were broken out of their surprised immobility by his example.

The resulting flock of drones buzzed down to the waiting humans, each attaching first to one arm and then pulling it up to where they could get a grip on the second. By the time the security team had descended to the landing, the Humans were all restrained.

The centurion's helmet snapped open and folded itself out of sight. "Even as an elector, the Prince Mishak still resorts to petty thievery?" the officer sneered in a voice like a bubbling stream. "The empire will see how you hang for his crimes..."

3

Eth turned to look at Gleb and the two burst out laughing.

"Very mature, assholes!" Oliv muttered.

"What?" the centurion demanded. "What's so amusing about being hung?"

"Oh my gods!" Oliv started to chuckle. She shook her head at the officer. "You're doing this on purpose now, right?"

The centurion drew himself up to full height – the better to glare down menacingly. "You find it amusing to be hung?"

"Amusing's not the word I'd choose," she said, giggling. "Gratifying, maybe, for all concerned…"

The whole team roared with laughter now. Gleb was pressing his elbows ineffectively against his armored abdomen. "Stop it!" he wheezed. "My sides!"

"Enough!" the centurion shouted. He waved his team forward. "Get them loaded up!"

The Humans were hustled aboard the armored security shuttle, the centurion pinioning their drone clips to the ceiling with a touch of his wrist pad. Two officers brought the case containing the golden lump of misplaced meaning and secured it under a side bench.

Eth nodded across to Oliv and Gleb. "Wait till the ramp is closed." He turned to the centurion's quizzical glare and gave him a friendly grin.

The centurion turned to face him but the ramp had just clanged shut. Oliv stared intently at the large Tadmoran for a few seconds. His face suddenly went slack and he clattered to the deck.

The rest of the security force had fallen as well and Gleb let out a sigh. Eth wasn't sure whether it was from the effort of knocking out the rest of the crew or from the orders not to kill them.

Even though Gleb had been the first to start studying under Eth, Oliv had quickly proven a better student when it came to affecting matter with her mind. That was why she'd been tasked with knocking

4

out the centurion. They needed him to fall the right way and she'd shown far more finesse than her fellow student.

Of course, that didn't mean the big oaf wasn't free to fall on top of his left forearm.

Grunting, Eth jumped backwards, swinging from his restraints, back down to deliver a kick at the officer's shoulder. He tried again, and the Tadmoran rolled over, exposing his control pad.

"We're wasting time," Gleb grumbled. "I can just…"

"No!" Eth insisted. "None of us has fine enough control yet. If we smash the controller, then we're stuck here till another team arrives. I'll try with my foot, first."

"Yeah," Oliv mused, watching him scrape his armored toe across the control pad. "That's not gonna break it at all!"

"Just… let me…" Eth didn't finish his sentence. The clips all released, dumping the Humans to the deck.

"Oliv, get us moving," Eth ordered, rolling to his knees.

"You got it, boss." She clambered over the fallen Humans and unconscious Tadmorans.

"Let's hope Orbital Control doesn't pay too much attention to a police shuttle," she muttered.

"Don't worry," Eth called after her. "That's *my* job. By the time they notice we're not headed for the detention orbiter, we'll be back aboard the *Mouse*."

The Tadmorans might be willing to hang a few Humans, but a heavy cruiser in Mishak's service, along with a horde of those deadly dark-ships, was another matter entirely.

They didn't want that kind of trouble.

Peacemaker
The Dibbarra, *Tadmor System*

The arguing had died out, unfortunately.

Now both the Tadmorans and the Ninevans had turned their attention on Mishak and he wasn't ready.

Mishak had arrived before the Ninevan assault fleet and he'd dispatched Eth with a team to secure the golden… what the hell was it called again? Anyway, it had been stolen from Ninevah thousands of years ago and it was at the base of all ill feelings between the two fiefs, even today.

Mishak frowned down at the table. It wasn't the *entire* reason, of course. The lord of Ninevah wanted to advance at court and taking a second system was a very important first rung along the way. The golden *whatsit* was an important cultural icon… probably… but it served nicely as a pretext.

Tadmor was horrendously unprepared for the situation. They produced a range of products but nothing terribly lucrative. Textiles accounted for more than half of their GDP and the margin was slim.

Too slim to field more than a few obsolete frigates. Ninevah wasn't much better, but they were strong enough to swallow up Tadmor.

So why was Mishak even here? Why care if one little fight flared up and resolved itself quickly?

This was more about him than the combatants. This was to be an easy intervention. He'd show up with a sizeable force but he'd bring the dispute to an end without fighting.

As long as his Humans could hold up their end of the plan.

He almost sighed and that surprised him. It was a Human reaction, or was it? He searched his short-term memory, realizing the Ninevan admiral had just sighed.

It was amazing how little the Quailu attended to physical cues. As empaths, they didn't notice such things. Mishak had been mostly dismissive, until he'd started an illicit relationship with one of his Humans.

A holo notification popped up in front of him. Eth's team was on approach to the forward hangar bay. Mishak waved it away and stood. "Perhaps a break, my lords? We can reconvene in fifteen."

"And what could possibly be different from what has already been discussed?" Gobryas, lord of Ninevah demanded. "We've been more than patient, my lord."

"Indeed you have, my friend," Mishak assured him. "I only ask that you give me the chance to reward that patience properly." He left without a further word.

He entered the hangar as Eth and his team were descending the boarding ramp of... a Tadmoran security shuttle? "Where's my personal shuttle?"

"Ah," Eth sighed. "Well, lord, it's going to need a little work..."

"A little work?" Gleb blurted, his surprise clear as he set a large case down on the deck. "The fornicating thing blew up all over us!" He held up his right arm to show where the shrapnel had scored deep gouges in his armor.

"Alright," Eth conceded, "it's probably a lost cause but at least it got us down there in one piece without interference from Orbital Control."

This time, Mishak *did* sigh. He pinched the bridge of his nose, eyes shut. "At least tell me there's something useful in that box."

"My lord!" Gobryas' voice thundered across the hangar.

Mishak turned to see the Ninevan delegation moving toward him.

"We have given you the respect due to your exalted station," Gobryas said, voice lowering as he came close, "but it is time for us to carry on. Our cause is just and we intend to see it through."

As if to underscore his words, Gobryas' delegation had broken off and was now moving toward their shuttle. The Tadmorans, who'd followed their enemy down to the hangar, were making no corresponding move to their own shuttle.

Of course they weren't.

They were looking at defeat and they had to know it.

"We got it, lord," Eth assured him quietly.

That was a relief. Mishak was about to close the deal when Tashmitum glided into the hangar bay, accompanied by her personal secretary, four of her Varangians and two Scensors. The pungent aroma from the slowly burning chitinous projections on the Scensors' heads lent the moment a distinctly formal feeling.

"My dear." Mishak greeted her with a bow. "You're feeling better?"

"Much better," she said before turning to Gobryas. "I have heard much about *you*, my lord," she told him. "It's a pleasure to finally meet you face to face."

"Highness!" was all Gobryas managed in return. He bowed deep to cover his surprise at meeting such a high-born Quailu.

Mishak took a half step forward, wanting to strike while the other noble was distracted. "As you've said, Gobryas, your cause is indeed a just one. That is why I offer you this token of our esteem." He stepped to the side, gesturing to Eth, who knelt and opened the case.

Mishak frowned a little, though he didn't notice this time. His anger was clearly projecting, though.

"You're offering me sandwiches?" Gobryas asked, a hint of derision coming from his mind.

Eth was still staring down into the box. "Gleb," he said softly, "there was more than one box under the bench?"

"I'm thinking *yes*…"

"Go get it," Eth suggested, packing a great deal of urgency into his quiet words.

Gleb ran back into the shuttle. There was a loud crash followed by muffled curses and then he came running back out to place the box next to the first.

Eth opened it up and a buttery golden glint finally put Mishak's mind at ease. More or less. "Is that…"

"That," Eth stated in a flat tone, "most certainly *is*."

"From the fourteenth emperor of the Holy Quailu Empire," confirmed Gobryas in reverent tones. "It remained like that, even after his death so it was removed and gilded."

"He certainly seems to have died happy," Mishak mused.

"I doubt his empress had any complaints either," Gleb added, then offered a quick bow. "Begging your pardon, Highness."

Tashmitum waved off the apology, her amusement evident.

"We urge you to take your relic and return home in peace, my lord," Eth said. "Let old grievances remain in the past where they belong."

Gobryas brought his gaze back up to meet Mishak's. "I regret that I cannot. We have stated our intentions before the entire empire and can't simply walk away, having accomplished only half of our goal and without firing a single shot."

He brought his left palm up, flat and facing toward his right hand. He balled his right into a fist and hammered it into his left palm in an ancient gesture.

"The ram has touched the wall," he insisted. "We must continue."

He must increase his influence, Mishak thought. Taking a second world would do that.

"You are an intrepid lord, Gobryas," Tashmitum intervened. "Your true reasoning in this matter is subtle and you pursue your aims with a single-mindedness that we admire." She'd all but called him out on his desire to increase his standing at court.

"When my noble father passes to the next Universe, we shall find ourselves in need of wise council." She leaned forward. "I would like to think that I could call upon you when that time comes."

Gobryas drew himself up to full height, right hand above his hearts. "I would be honored to serve, Highness!" His pride, though mingled with surprise, proved the truth of his words.

Tashmitum turned to her secretary. "Sabitum, queue up a special dispensation for the Lord Gobryas. Upon our ascension to the throne, it shall give him leave to triple his allowed presence on Throne-World as well as the right to maintain a barge in the throne-room."

Gobryas was clearly thrilled.

"You understand, my friend," Mishak cut in, "that this must be contingent upon your keeping the peace?" He spread his hands. "I hope to join my wife on the Dais, when the time comes, but that's already complicated by my father's holdings.

"My fellow electors will be leery of an emperor who is also one of the most powerful lords in his own right. You will need to avoid the perception of being a system-hungry opportunist and I will need to explore ways of lightening my own... burden."

Gobryas was somewhat befuddled at that. He was probably trying to work out whether that was a threat or a promise. Mishak might have been hinting at giving away some systems...

Tashmitum judged the moment to perfection. "I'm sure you have much to prepare, my lord." She stooped to retrieve the golden phallus and handed it to Gobryas. She placed a guiding hand on his shoulder, steering him toward the Ninevan shuttle. "You will need to start preparing your eldest to look after your holdings, selecting retainers for Throne-World, shopping for a new residence there…"

As they walked away, Daon, lord of Tadmor, came stalking up. "You stole the sacred phallus and you gave it to… to… *that* fool?"

Mishak looked at him for a few moments. "That sums things up pretty nicely, I suppose."

Daon was visibly taken aback. "And he's to be an advisor at court?" He pounded his chest. "What do *I* get?"

Mishak gestured past the stolen security shuttle to where the curve of Tadmor filled half the view. "You get to keep *that*."

"I already *had* that," Daon spluttered.

"But you would have lost it by now, if I hadn't intervened." He suddenly stepped in close, forcing the Tadmoran noble back a pace.

"Your ancestor was a fool! I mean, who steals a golden penis? He gave the Ninevans a permanent *cassus belli* to justify any kind of aggression but completely neglected to prepare a defense against it.

"If we hadn't come here, you'd be just another penniless *emigre* noble, trying to think of a wealthy relation from whom you could beg shelter."

"I could offer my services as an advisor…"

Mishak cut him off with a sharp chopping motion. "Let me lay this out for you. Your decisions, and those of your forebears, have brought you to this sorry state.

"Gobryas and his ancestors have bided their time and, when the moment was right, launched their plans into action. He may not have taken your world but his decisions have brought the heirs-apparent into the matter and he's managed to avail himself of our influence."

"No small feat for a one system minor lord," Eth suggested.

It wasn't entirely proper for Eth to interject like that, or was it? Mishak paused. Would he think differently if Eth were a Quailu?

11

Nonetheless, it provided him with another point. He gestured back at Eth. "That man was grown to be a slave and he has more sense than *you've* shown. I take his advice. I won't be asking for *yours*."

He waved at the Tadmoran delegation's shuttle. "Go home and be grateful you've still got a planet to run."

Daon stalked into his shuttle and the ramp had barely closed when the Humans started laughing.

"You find the humiliation of a Quailu noble to be amusing?" Mishak demanded, wheeling on them.

'No lord," Eth said breathlessly. "It's just that we had that centurion, dirtside, telling us the empire would see how we hang and…" He chuckled.

Mishak had spent a lot of time among his Humans. He'd gotten drunk with them and he'd heard most of their jokes a hundred times. He understood where this was going.

He nodded at the empty case on the floor. "So, getting a chance to see how the empire was hung?"

It can be very isolating; the life of a noble and he'd been isolated further still by an overbearing father. Mishak had withdrawn to the point where he came to prefer the company of his Humans.

Humans couldn't read his thoughts and judge his insecurities. It seemed almost karmic that they'd provided him with the means to boost his confidence, defy his father and launch himself on the path to the imperial throne.

He enjoyed the rare moments when he could let down his guard and connect with them. Managing to elicit such an unrestrained gale of laughter from them was a very gratifying experience.

Still, some of them were changing. A few of their minds were closing to the empathic ability that all Quailu shared.

HUMANS

They served him loyally, but the Quailu were accustomed to seeing the secret heart of those over whom they ruled. On top of all the pressures of being the crown-prince, it was one more irritant.

Pacification
The Ishkur, *Bilbat System*

Kuri knelt and placed his hands on Sekandr's shoulders. "You must show courage. Our people will look to you in my absence."

The youngster drew himself up to his full height. "You will not be absent, Father," he insisted proudly. "You will be out there fighting our enemies!"

Not for the first time, Kuri wished he could send his family off-world until the matter was settled, but a noble who did not share in the risk he allowed to fall upon his people was no noble at all.

He gave Sekandr's shoulder one final squeeze and stood. He gestured his security detail toward an open portal. "Time to go," he said, not caring that the moment could have used a more memorable quote.

They passed through the portal and into a fast lighter that would take him to his waiting fleet. Well, half of it.

It was a dangerous plan and many of his councillors had argued against it. That, in itself, was probably a good recommendation, as most of them had seen very little combat.

It had been endorsed by Sin-Nasir, and Kuri was inclined to favor his opinions in this matter. Sin-Nasir had taken a medium-sized force to fight for Tir-Uttur when the Emperor was struggling to consolidate his position on the throne. He'd made a name for himself through his shrewd manipulation of both the enemy and the battlespace.

The trick was in the timing.

The lighter slid up to Kuri's flagship, an older cruiser design, but still a potent weapon in the right hands. He led the way up to the bridge, where Hunzu, his fleet-captain, was conferring with Sin-Nasir over a holo-channel.

14

By rights, Sin-Nasir should have been fleet-captain but he'd insisted on commanding the decoy fleet orbiting Bilbat. It was the point of greatest risk and, though Kuri had wanted it, he'd yielded to his general's relentless logic.

Sekandr was a fine young Quailu but he was still too young to claim his inheritance. If Kuri died today, even in a victory, he would leave Bilbat open to endless claims from neighboring lords.

There was no room for heroism in the fight to come.

"Lord," Hunzu greeted him. "Scouts report that the enemy have pathed away from their consolidation point sooner than we expected. The disarray shown there may have been deliberate. Their blockade, after all, has been remarkably well managed."

"They thought to catch us off guard?" Kuri asked. "We went to full alert as soon as we found them."

"Perhaps they think they're being clever," Sin-Nasir's holographic image suggested. "I've seen commanders use misdirection for its own sake rather than in pursuit of their mission. In any event, I'm moving my forces to a new orbit on the off-chance they're intending to drop-wash us."

The plasma released by an incoming ship when it dropped out of path-shaping could be incredibly destructive.

Kuri shuddered. Such an opening move against an orbiting force could be devastating for the planet beneath them. He had to remind himself that the inbound force was coming from the enemy blockade and wouldn't have time to build up much of a discharge on their way.

Still, it represented dangers...

"Path alert!" the sensor coordinator announced. "Multiple paths inbound, danger-close for the planet!"

Kuri's blood ran cold. "Main view!"

The image in the center of the bridge showed the enemy ships surrounding the planet with more appearing. It made no sense!

15

"What the hells?" Hunzu growled. "They're not even in formation, they just…"

"They just brought our entire economy to a screeching halt!" Kuri exclaimed. Those drops would have released enough plasma to generate electromagnetic pulses and their scattered arrival had clearly been intended to fry every bit of electronics on the surface of Bilbat.

"It's just a straight up fur-ball now," Kuri decided. No clever flank assault on a committed enemy attacking force. They'd made the civilians on the surface their priority target and now they'd pay for it.

"Get us in there," he ordered the fleet captain. "Micro-path the entire fleet to the side opposite from Sin-Nasir's force. One more set of EMPs won't do any further harm."

It was maddening to stand there while coordinates were passed to the other ships and path-drives were brought online. Down on Bilbat, every communications device, every shuttle, every harvester and ground transportation unit had ground to a halt.

Water would stop flowing through conduits, food distribution was effectively destroyed. Within two days, the riots and killing would start and young Sekandr would have his hands full trying to restore order.

One of the cable trays vibrated above Kuri as the ship began shifting the Universe to put Bilbat beneath them. That tray always did that and Kuri had refused to let engineering replace it. He couldn't put his finger on it but he found the rattling imperfection to be comforting for some reason.

The noise didn't end the way it usually did because the time between initiation and drop out were so close together this time. The curve of his home-world threw itself into view, dotted here and there with individual ships.

"They're trying to come together," the sensor coordinator advised.

"They can't hope to coalesce into a proper force now," Kuri said, "unless we stay together as a fleet and give them room on the far side. Captain Hunzu, break the fleet into its four sub-squadrons, if you please, and assign them each a quadrant."

"Aye, Lord."

"Don't let em regroup, Captain. Hunt them. Hunt them hard and we'll go for that big bastard." He reached up into the holo to select the cruiser that almost certainly represented the flagship.

"How many ships did they bring?" he demanded, whirling on the sensor coordinator.

"One cruiser, sixteen frigates and three hundred fifty two gunboats, lord," the coordinator replied.

"I believe they've pulled every ship from their blockade, lord," the intelligence officer advised. He was standing among the sensor team, still looking up at the displays as he addressed his lord. "If we beat them…"

"Then we don't have to worry about another immediate attack from their blockade while we're licking our wounds," Kuri finished the thought.

And we can finally send an envoy to ask the emperor for help, he thought, feeling the intelligence officer's agreement.

"Taking fire from their gunboats," tactical advised. "No damage. Secondary batteries are engaging."

Kuri fumed as he watched the enemy gunboats disappear from his display. None of it made a lick of sense. Why did they fiddle around with looking unready when they had to know Bilbat was already on high alert? Why waste time targeting the planetary economy in such a way when it left them so vulnerable to counter attack?

The Universe slid back into view.

"One of their ships at this location, sire," the sensor coordinator said. "All of our fleet have checked in and are recharging for pathing operations."

"Open a channel," Memnon ordered, waving to the center of the bridge's display area. "Put it right here."

A Quailu shimmered into view and bowed low. "The attack is underway, sire."

"Perhaps you could tell me why that is," Memnon suggested in a cold voice. "My orders, which were confirmed just before I pathed here, were to wait for my arrival. Why were they so eager to begin the destruction that they couldn't wait for my own participation?"

The holographic figure straightened but it had no answers.

"You have a signal-pair to keep you in touch with your master." Memnon pitched it as a statement of fact. "Transfer your feed to my bridge immediately."

The figure hesitated for the briefest instant before realizing who he would rather have angry with him. He turned to the side and, after a few seconds, an icon appeared next to his ghostly image.

Memnon activated it and the *Battle of Bilbat* was presented in all its glory. "What the hells am I looking at?" he growled.

They were supposed to punch their way in, destroy the biosphere, and fight their way back out.

"Reading no EM signatures of any kind from the surface, sire," the intelligence officer advised. "Estimate a massive, global EMP assault."

"Those silly bastards," Memnon ground out. His noble father continually berated him for his screw-ups, but he had to know what sort of idiots he had to work with out here.

There was a reason, after all, that these fools were still one-system minor lords and it sure as hells wasn't lack of ambition. These idiots had decided to change the plan and keep the planet for themselves and they were hoping to force Memnon into coming to their rescue.

"Ops… path status."

"Sire, the fleet stands ready, except for one frigate."

"Reason?"

"Cascade failure in their flash capacitors, sire. They require a half cycle to replace the affected units." The ops officer quailed under Memnon's anger. "Apologies, sire," he stammered. "A half cycle for the mechanical work and another quarter for charge-tempering."

"They'll have to shift for themselves," Memnon decided. "Tell them to make their way to the rendezvous point once they've effected repairs. We need to get in there before this goes completely off the rails."

He enlarged the view of the battle and selected the icon showing a large cruiser. "There's our target for drop-out. Match coordinates with the fleet and open a path."

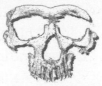

"Multiple path alerts!" the sensor coordinator yelled in alarm.

Kuri took a full step back from the holo-display as the red cones began to show where inbound plasma bursts were appearing. "Who are they?" He looked up to the color corrected image of the enemy cruiser just as it was smashed out of the sky by an incoming vessel.

The only cruiser the enemy had brought with them was now little more than a tumbling mass of plasma and wreckage. And a new cruiser, so new that its nanites still hadn't been scorched clean by solar winds, now lay along the axis of destruction.

"Crossed cipher keys," the intelligence officer said.

"Mishak?" Kuri was certain his couriers had all been intercepted, so how…

"Not on a red field, lord," the intelligence officer countered. "The Lord Mishak uses gray and his father uses black."

"Then who…"

"Incoming signal from that cruiser, lord."

Kuri gestured. "Route it here."

A figure appeared, wearing the newest model of combat armor, the type that cost a year's profits for a planet like Bilbat. "Well, my lord," the figure said tiredly, "this is a major fornicating mess if ever I've seen one.

"These fools thought they'd force my hand." The figure paused for a moment. "I suppose they *have*, though not in the way they'd expected. In any event, I owe you my deepest sympathies." The figure turned to wave a hand at someone who wasn't in the projection.

"I don't understand, my lord." Kuri stole a quick glance at Hunzu but found no help there. "We owe you much for your help."

"You shouldn't mistake my intervention for help," the figure advised.

"Gods!" the sensor coordinator shouted. "Artificial gravitational singularities just opened up in the atmosphere!"

Kuri was suddenly flushed with adrenaline, fear and rage. He wasn't alone. Everyone on the bridge suddenly turned their thoughts to the loved ones down on Bilbat. The planet's atmosphere was spiraling up into the singularities and there was no way to stop such weapons. Firing at a singularity weapon merely fed the beast.

They would burn themselves out, being mere shadows of their wild cousins, but not before rendering the entire planet incapable of supporting life. The state of panic reached a crippling stage by the time Memnon's missiles struck Kuri's flagship.

His last thought was of Sekandr.

Sneak & Peek
Sippar System, Outer Planets

"Full normalization," Hendy reported from the nav station with a grin. "We are one with the Universe again, bathing in the cool embrace of the local gas giant."

Eth rolled his eyes. "Let's not get all poetic, Hendy. We built a scout with a path drive. It was bound to happen sooner or later."

"Yeah," Noa agreed from the aft hatch, "but only by us. You really think those hard-charging Quailu would have bothered with something like this?" He rested a hand against one of the stanchions… caressed it, really.

It was a beautiful little ship and Eth was giving serious thought to breaking up the *Mouse* to build more like her. The *Scorpion* was the first of Noa's designs to have a path drive.

Building on his success with the smaller scout-ships, he'd gutted a captured frigate and rebuilt her around the original core, leaving just enough room for three pitch drives, an augmented emission management suite, weapon systems and crew spaces.

Named for the ceremonial sword worn by the Varangian Guard, the Scorpion carried a vicious sting, but her chief weapon was her ability to slip past an enemy's guard.

She was coated with the same carbon nanotubules that had made her smaller predecessors so difficult to spot but it was an advantage that came with a price. The *Scorpion's* hull was several times the size of the smaller scouts and the stellar and sensor radiation that bounced down between the microscopic carbon-tubules had to go somewhere.

That it didn't simply bounce back into space made her a ghost to the enemy, but that energy had to be contained and no system had yet been invented that could do so indefinitely.

"Take us deeper, Hendy. Find us a zone where the temperature is a hundred fifty above absolute zero." Eth turned to Gleb. "Open the interchange valves." He looked back to his own display, noting the new progress bar. "How long to charge the cryo-banks, Noa?"

"At one-fifty over absolute, I'd say about twenty minutes. We can probably squeeze a little more performance from those CB's but I'd rather test that in a non-combat environment."

"You see me arguing?" Eth demanded. "We don't have an abundance of choice. Half the empire is shooting at each other. The only reason it's not a full civil war is the lack of organization."

He turned. "Speaking of combat testing – Oliv, what's our weapon status?"

"They haven't malfunctioned and killed us all, if that's what you were wondering." She shuddered. "I don't mind testing them for the old gal, but hanging onto the damn things until we need to fire em off is creeping the hells outta me. What if one of those MA fields develops a sense of humor and goes rogue while we're executing a course change?"

Mass attenuation. The 'old gal' was the Lady Bau and she'd taken the Arbella system where a research team had been on the verge of bringing the new tech to market. She'd sensibly put a stop to broad commercialisation and restricted it to military use until the end of the current state of unrest.

Missiles, those using chemical thrust, were an ancient technology in an empire where micro gravity drives were readily available. One of those ancient missile designs, coupled with an MA field generator, suddenly opened an entirely new aspect in ship-to-ship combat.

The MA field could reduce the overall mass of the missile to a tiny fraction of its real value without reducing the effectiveness of the action/reaction of the propellant exiting the thrust nozzles. That required some very fine tuning of the field itself but it allowed a normal thrust profile.

The thrust, however, was concentrated on accelerating a much smaller mass. Mass attenuation or not, acceleration was still the result of force divided by the mass of the object.

Trying to intercept a missile when it's approaching your ship at a nearly relativistic velocity?

Good luck with that…

"Nobody seems crazy enough to attack her," Eth replied mildly, "and she wants them tested. Surely, you see her dilemma?"

In reality, at least half her reason for giving MA-equipped missiles to Eth for his new ship was in gratitude for having saved her life several times in the fight against Uktannu.

"Well, let's just hope one of those MA generators doesn't get frisky and *increase* the mass of the weapon," she muttered darkly, "or hadn't any of you geniuses considered that? A missile with the mass of a small moon sitting in the magazine compartment? You think our grav plating can keep up with that? We'd have to maintain course and velocity until it was repaired…"

"Hammurabi's ass fungus!" Noa burst out, eyes wide. "Can you imagine what we could do with a kinetic warhead? Would the math even support it?"

"Whoa!" Eth pointed an admonitory finger at the engineer. "No tinkering with those MA fields on our ship! When time permits, we'll find a nice little moon where you can set up a lab."

"This is why I don't sleep well," Oliv muttered.

"Missing your Quailu boyfriend?" Noa teased.

"That ended a while ago." She shook her head.

"Oh!" Noa scratched at the back of his neck, his ears red. "I, uh, didn't mean to…"

"It was never serious," she scoffed. "Just keep your hands off those weapons, alright?"

Eth chuckled as Noa scurried aft to engineering. "You're pretty good at getting people to do what you want, aren't you?"

"I have no idea what you mean," she replied with a grin. She nodded at her display holo. "You see the cryo-bank status?"

Eth turned back to his screen. *Just as she intended*, he thought with wry amusement. He'd already decided to hand this ship over to her, after this operation. He just wished she didn't keep proving what a good decision it was.

The cryo-banks were fully cooled.

"Alright," he said. "Cryo-banks are ready to go. Close the interchange valves and bring the emission management system online."

"Interchanges are closed," Gleb confirmed from the engineering console. Ship is rigged for quiet running."

"Very well," Eth acknowledged. "How long before we have to come back here and dump some heat?"

"Half a day, if we're just sitting quiet," Gleb replied without checking. "Maybe a third of that, though, if we're doing much acceleration."

"So, that would let us reach the planet and return, if we wanted?"

Gleb nodded. "Take us about an hour at full pitch on all three drives. We'd have about an hour on target before we had to disengage and return here."

Eth nodded. "Good to know. Hendy, take us up." He stood and walked over to the edge of the large holo-display that took up the center of the bridge.

"Let's see what all the fuss is about," he said quietly.

"We're clear," Oliv announced half a second before the holo populated the data-skeleton for the Sippar system with actual information.

"Color correct," Eth told the computer. "Adjust for Human visual range."

The blue-scale image hadn't been changed from this ship's earlier incarnation as a Quailu frigate. Eth had never even noticed until now. For some reason, when they were in a potentially hostile situation, he started noticing the small distractions.

The image changed to show a miniature solar system in true color. Eth drew a rough box around the main inhabited planet and its surrounding region. "Reset bounds," he commanded.

The image zoomed in.

Eth grunted. "Anyone here think that's a little bit odd?"

"Well," Oliv frowned up at the central holo, "some might think it a tad odd to send a massive assault force and just have it sit there, watching an almost insignificant defense force…"

"A bold strategy, Oliv," Gleb declared in a reasonable approximation of a sports announcer's voice. "Let's see if it works out for them."

"Belnut," Eth muttered, zooming in on one of the ship's flanks. "Wasn't aware Lord Belnut had any claims in the region." He zoomed the view back out. "Hendy, start taking us in closer – three drives at fifty percent. Gleb, keep an eye on our return parameters."

"Three drives at fifty percent," Hendy confirmed.

The display began to zoom in very quickly, leaving nothing in view in a matter of seconds. "Reset and pin view boundaries," Eth instructed the computer.

The image was restored to show the two opposing forces but their motion was artificially accelerated. With every passing second, the *Scorpion* was moving forward in time, as far as the image was concerned.

The gas giant had been just under two light-hours from their target. More than enough time for a battle to have happened, so they might be approaching a very different situation from the one that currently showed on the holo.

Ships were jockeying between echelons and shuttles scurried between the vessels of the attackers with what looked like reckless velocities.

But still, nothing was happening and they had a half-day-long approach.

Fighting in space lacked the immediacy of ground operations. It was surprising how often a decision to initiate action led to a long period of boredom. He raised an eyebrow.

If nothing was happening…

"Lieutenant, you have the bridge," Eth said, turning to her. "Haven't slept for twenty-three hours now. I'll be in my bunk if anything happens."

He knew he'd never be able to sleep, not while they were hurtling toward a hostile fleet with stealth as their main weapon. Still, he'd said he was going to his bunk, so he could hardly be seen wandering the corridors.

He climbed into his bunk, ordered a wakeup alarm and lay down for a long stretch of staring distractedly at the ceiling. There might even be a headache if he was lucky.

"Yeah," a voice said, "you got it rough, alright!"

Startled, Eth lurched back to a sitting position, his right hand reaching for the weapon he'd set aside before getting into his bunk. He frowned at the intruder.

"Ab? You're dead!"

"Ah! That must be why the back of my head seems to be missing," Eth's old mentor mused sarcastically. "Thanks, though, for the reminder. Never know when a fella might forget to stay dead, especially if most of my hippocampus is a stain on a Chironan sidewalk…"

"What…" Eth trailed off, squinting at his dead comrade.

"What am I doing here in your quarters?" Ab shrugged. "Someone's gotta tell you to get your head out of your ass! Being in charge is never easy." He held up a hand, palm toward Eth to forestall any interjection. "I know… believe me… I know I made it look easy but it's an endless ass-ache to have everyone looking to you for the answers."

"You ever wish you were just one of the team?"

"All the time, as far as you know."

Eth tilted his head quizzically. "As far as *I* know?"

"Well, *yeah*," Ab said, raising that damned eyebrow. "You didn't think I was a ghost, did you? I'm just a dream."

The alarm surprised him when it went off. At first, he thought it had mistaken his instructions and gone off almost immediately but he'd been sleeping for eight hours.

He rolled out of the bed, stretching his arms to work the kinks out of his shoulders. *If I'm going to get into my bunk, I should really remove my armor. Maybe that'll keep Ab from visiting.* He walked back to the bridge, hardly believing that nothing significant had happened yet. Still, if anything had changed, Oliv would have sent for him.

He walked onto the bridge, returning her nod.

"Forty light-minutes out," Oliv said, "and still no action. What the hells are they playing at?"

She turned to the helm. "Hendy, let's stop around ten light-minutes out." She cloned a smaller, secondary display and zoomed it

28

out by a factor of ten. "Sippar 2 is almost in conjunction with Sippar Prime. Put us just outside of 2's orbit. We'll peer over her shoulder."

The fleets continued with their pointless perturbations.

"Technically," Hendu hedged as he stabilized *Scorpion's* position near Sippar 2, "this puts us eleven and a half minutes out, but I doubt anyone will file a complaint."

"And they're still just batting their eyelashes at each other," Oliv mused.

Eth dismissed the small, cloned display. "Gleb, what kind of loiter time do we have if we stay here?"

"Nearly a half day."

Eth darted a surprised look at him.

"You gotta remember," Gleb said in response to the look, "that the one hour loiter time was after a full-pitch run. We came in here at half power and those engines are exponential cookers. At fifty percent pitch, you're gonna generate way less than half the heat you would at a hundred."

Eth understood the math involved; he'd even discussed it with Noa during the design of the latest ship, but he was still getting used to the whole heat-management side of these new ships. He nodded. "Keep track of when we need to make a run back to that gas giant, assuming a full-power run on all three drives. Put it up here." He pointed to a space above Sippar Prime.

A clock appeared, counting down from twenty-two hours and seventeen minutes.

Eth nodded again, gesturing at the clock. "This is good. Let's turn it into a table – loiter times before a return run at one hundred percent, seventy five and fifty."

"Hang on." Gleb's fingers flew through the air in front of his face. "There! How's that?"

The clock updated, showing the three options as well as listing the return location.

Eth walked around the data table, watching its interaction with the rest of the holo. "Computer, set text color to white with dark gray background." He waited for the update. "Reduce emissive factor by fifty percent."

He nodded as the text grew dimmer. "Perfect. Pin this display in the holo and make it standard operating procedure."

It gave him a measure of confidence, knowing exactly how much time he had to work with. "Quarter power, Hendy. Let's get close enough to pick their pockets."

"Something sure as hells doesn't add up here," Oliv said quietly.

"Yeah," Eth confirmed. "Something's missing. I can feel it."

She raised an eyebrow at him. "A feeling? Is this something you haven't shared with us?"

He shrugged. "Not sure. I don't think it's like *that*. It's just my subconscious, I think, showing better sense than my conscious mind." He nodded at the displayed fleets. There's a reason for that. I think it's meant to draw us in."

They watched in silence as the *Scorpion* drew nearer and nearer. Conversation faded as their unease grew. The loiter time ticked down, slowing to reveal roughly three quarters of a day when they came to a stop, just a few light-seconds out from the invaders.

"They're still just waiting," Oliv groused. "This is downright unsettling."

"Waiting for what?" Hendy turned to look at Eth. "Their victims are sitting right in front of them. What more can a glory-hungry Quailu want?"

"Us," Eth replied with calm certainty. "Our lord, to be specific." He turned to Gleb. "If we fire up the signal pair, what would it do to our countdown?"

Gleb frowned. "Initiating the link draws a shitload of power. Keeping it open is a heavy draw as well but it's the initiation that'll really hurt. We'd end up having to dump heat before we got halfway back to that gas giant."

He offered an apologetic shrug. "Sorry, sir. No way we can get away with opening a link while we're still sitting here."

"Sure there is," Eth countered, "'cause we're tossing the plan of going back via the outer planets. Bring the path drive online and then initiate the signal pair."

"Very well, sir," Gleb said, shaking his head in resignation. "If there's anything else we can do to increase our heat generation, just let me know…"

After a few minutes, a space to Eth's right began to shimmer and the decking changed color in a small space beneath the anomaly. A new layer of noise emitted from the shimmer and, suddenly, a Quailu stepped into view.

"Fleet-Captain Rimush." Eth inclined his head in polite acknowledgement.

"Lieutenant Commander." Rimush replied curtly. "Report."

"Something very odd, sir." Eth grabbed the clone icon for his main display and tossed it into the shimmering image of Rimush.

Rimush turned to the side, nodded and stepped out of sight.

Mishak appeared and Eth inclined his head much farther than he had with the fleet-captain. "Lord."

"What are we looking at?" Mishak demanded. "Is this a recording?"

"Live data, lord. I believe their true intent is to draw you here, though I can't imagine what their purpose might be. We've observed nearly ten standard hours of them sitting here like this and the gods only know how long this has been going on before we arrived."

Nonetheless...
The Dibbarra, *Kwharaz Sector*

Mishak looked away from the holo-image of Eth. "Someone wants us to go to Sippar."

"And we can't refuse," Tashmitum insisted. "Their overlord supports us at court. We can't simply ignore a threat to one of their systems."

"This *is* a trap," Rimush reminded them, tightly controlling his emotions.

'Which is why we don't simply blunder into it," Mishak confirmed.

"Lieutenant Commander," he turned back to the holo. "How much time do you have left before you lose stealth?"

"With the signal pair running, the path drive spooled up and a little room for maneuver, we've got just over an hour, lord."

"Then there's no time to waste," Mishak said, darting a glance at Rimush. "Spool up the fleet. We jump in five." He tilted his head back toward Eth. "You're three light-seconds away from the enemy. Those missiles from the Lady Bau can cross that distance without running out of fuel?"

The holo shrugged. "As I understand it, lord, the MA weapon will simply stop accelerating after the fuel runs out. Nonetheless, it will still have its accumulated velocity, even if the MA field generator cuts out. These weapons can cross three light-seconds in an extremely small time-frame.

"My concern is more about the detonation sequence. They claim to have developed processors fast enough to handle the high-speed impacts but we have our doubts."

"But at such a high velocity," Mishak countered, "wouldn't the kinetic impact do severe damage?"

Eth nodded. "It should. Hard to tell how it plays out in a real situation. It's why I've let my engineer install shaped osmium inserts inside the missile casings."

"Osmium?"

"Aye, lord. Densest thing we could find on short notice. Twice the density of lead." The holographic Human grinned wickedly. "Should make a nice kinetic insurance policy if our detonation sequences fail on us!"

Mishak made a deliberate effort to grin at his Human officer. "Well done! You'll be our insurance policy. I doubt we'll get out of there without a bit of killing. We're pathing in now. Shut down your pair node; that should cut your heat profile a bit. We'll re-establish comms on a standard secure link on drop-out. Three light-seconds is tolerable enough and I need you listening in on whatever happens."

"We'll be ready, lord." Eth shimmered out of sight.

"We stand ready, Lord," Rimush said. "General quarters has been declared throughout the fleet and coordinates have been passed and confirmed by all call-signs for a standard intervention posture."

"Very good, Fleet Captain. Initiate."

"What do you think their goal is here?" Tashmitum asked as the deck plates rumbled with the energy of transition. "Have we started a bad precedent by making a belligerent into a future councillor?"

"You think this might be a bald attempt to extort a promise of influence?" Mishak asked.

"Perhaps," she admitted. "I may have opened a book we can't close when I made that offer to Gobryas."

Mishak considered it for a moment. "I think you did what had to be done. That was a relatively small conflict. If we'd failed to find a peaceful resolution there, then how can the electors expect us to maintain peace in the rest of the empire?"

"Nonetheless," she countered, "we can't simply make every stubborn belligerent into an advisor. The throne room is crowded enough as it is. We'd have to issue regulations to reduce the size of courtier barges, update traffic control... It's not a road we should follow."

"I agree." Mishak was surprised to find his fists clenched in anticipation. He felt slightly guilty, being reminded of his heightened awareness of physical cues, given *who* had taught him. It wasn't something he could tell Tashmitum about.

"It's time to take off the velvet glove and show the iron fist," he continued. "It's time to start applying more violent means of negotiation."

They dropped out on a plane that separated the two opposing fleets, but aimed away from them so as not to accidentally destroy them with the plasma of their drop-wash.

Not that there was much drop-wash accumulation during the short hop from Kwharaz but it was best to start on a polite footing.

"Bringing the fleet around," Rimush said. "We'll be..."

"Multiple mass separations!" tactical announced, urgency radiating from the entire tactical station. "Hostile fleet is launching multiple missiles and kinetics!"

"Probable targets?" Rimush demanded, deadpan. His calm demeanor washed back against the excitement with the ease of long experience.

"Target is definitely the defending fleet," the tactical officer answered, calmer now and slightly embarrassed.

Mishak noticed an incoming comms icon from his scout and dragged it into a secure algorithm. The two ships compared encryption keys, a technology the family was known for, and Eth appeared.

"... Your pardon, lord," Eth said, then shimmered into a haze of fragments before stabilizing again. "I shifted our link to a rolling encryption," he explained. "It seemed necessary. I've got a feeling I can't shake that tells me standard methods won't be sufficient."

"Very well," Mishak replied, for lack of anything better to say. He was hardly going to complain about heightened security. "It would seem our arrival has kicked off the festivities."

"Indeed, Lord." The shimmering Human looked up for a moment. "The defenders were all but annihilated in the opening salvos." He looked back at Mishak. "I believe that whoever is making this point will be showing up very soon so he can drive it home."

As if on cue, a series of brilliant flashes heralded the arrival of another fleet. It was roughly the size of Mishak's force and, from the low intensity of the flashes, they'd also launched from a nearby system. One cruiser and fifteen frigates.

It seemed that Mishak wasn't the only one receiving reports from this system.

"Turning to meet the new fleet," Rimush announced.

The battle was already over. The defenders, brave but hopelessly outnumbered, were nothing more than a cloud of tumbling debris and bodies.

"Lord!" The tactical officer looked up at Mishak, consternation flowing off the officer like a wave hitting rocks. He made an adjustment to his controls and, taking liberties above his station, pre-empted Mishak's holo settings to display the cruiser leading the new fleet.

"What do you think you're..." Mishak trailed off into silence, forgiving the officer for his trespass as he stared at the cruiser's flanks.

"Your father?" Rimush guessed, his calm shattered, though he was working to master his emotions.

"No." Mishak shook his head, though he didn't notice. "He uses a black background. I use gray. There's no heraldry-record for crossed

36

encryption keys on a red background. No such sigil exists." *Perhaps Eth was right to use rolling encryption?*

"Incoming call-group," the comms officer said. "Initiated by the unidentified cruiser."

Mishak waited until Tashmitum was at his side. "Put them in the central holo," he ordered.

It got crowded. Almost thirty Quailu wavered into hazy existence. They sat in a large circle around the outer edge of the bridge's holo-space. One figure stepped forward.

"Hello, Brother," he sneered.

So, this is the backup heir? Mishak thought. His uncle had warned him, just before his death. Well, gloated about him might be a better description.

And here he was, putting on a show for his captains – the new guy, eager to score some quick points on his way up. He was doing this by ship-to-ship holo, most likely to prevent his feelings from being read.

Fortunately, Mishak had learned much from his Humans, one Human in particular.

"I'm sorry," Mishak said. "Have we met?"

The figure stalked around Tashmitum, leering at her. "Does it matter if we've met?" he demanded, coming to face Mishak. "We've met *now*. My name is Memnon."

"What an infernal piece of luck on your part," Mishak commiserated, determined to keep this interloper on the back foot. He was gratified to see Memnon's hands balling into fists. This *brother* was clearly eager to get an angry display out of him so he must try to beat him at his own game.

"I bring a message from our father," Memnon ground out. "May he outlive us all!"

Mishak watched as the assembled holograms repeated the phrase, with the exception of Eth, of course, who owed no allegiance to Sandrak.

They looked at him expectantly and Mishak let the moment draw out, savoring how uncomfortable it was getting. They seemed to expect, perhaps out of habit, that he would repeat the phrase but he was no longer just Sandrak's son. He was an elector now, his father's equal in title, if not in military muscle.

Finally, he relented. "I *also* hope he outlives each one of you," Mishak said cheerfully. "And I wish you luck in finding the recipient of this message that you bear from my father."

Memnon stared at him for a moment. "The message is for you," he said evenly.

Mishak waited again but not quite as long as the first time. He just wanted to accentuate the pitfalls Memnon kept walking into. Clearly, he'd not spent much time around their father. Sandrak had derived endless entertainment from making Mishak look foolish.

It was a humiliating way to teach your child but it *had* worked, after a fashion. "Look, Melvin…"

"Memnon!" His brother, unsettled by the awkward pause, blurted the correction before he could steady himself.

"Sure, if you prefer Memnon," Mishak conceded. "I don't want to be an interfering *bastard*, telling you how to deliver messages, but this is twice now that you've announced your task and, still, you haven't delivered your message, have you?

"What is it that my father wants me to know?"

Memnon seemed to get some of his bumptious swagger back but Mishak couldn't quite put his finger on why he thought that.

"You have been disinherited," Memnon said triumphantly. "His holdings will not come to you after his demise. May he outlive us all!"

Again, the assembled holographic figures mumbled their way through the phrase.

"Be careful what you wish for," Mishak advised the group of holograms. *We knew this day would have to come,* he thought. "As for your message, I assumed I would just get a notification from the King-of-Arms' office when my father got around to disinheriting me.

"Frankly, I'm surprised to see how long it took for him to take care of this for me," Mishak added. "Damned hard, trying to round up votes when you still stand to inherit a massive chunk of the empire in your own right."

He showed no reaction as his holographic brother took a half step backwards, head tilting down and to the side closest to Mishak in order to protect the primary arteries. Memnon had been expecting some kind of angry outburst at his news.

Had Sandrak given him reason for his expectation? *Water will find any crack,* he remembered from one of Marduk's endless lessons, *and, freezing, expose the weakness within.*

"My father," he continued, "knows that the other electors will be nervous of a candidate who has too many systems. An emperor should be first among equals, not an overbearing tyrant. They won't set us on the throne when Tir Uttur dies, may he outlive us all..." he paused while everyone repeated the phrase, "... if we're powerful enough to take away their freedoms and prerogatives.

"I'm sure my father told you all of this," Mishak said. "He wouldn't send you off to deliver this message without preparing you properly." *Of course he would, the old bastard!*

"*Our* father," Memnon said, snapping at Mishak's repeated bait, "is no longer any concern of yours, now, is he? You won't inherit from him."

"Be sure to convey my thanks," Mishak replied warmly, "but tell him he could have done it a little sooner. As for your parentage, I don't recall hearing that my father had taken a new wife," he said with a questioning tone and upward head-tilt, "several decades ago…"

"A lord of your father's stature, my love," Tashmitum added, "would never have been able to keep a marriage secret."

"Aye, lord," Eth's holograph chimed in. "He'd have had a *bastard* of a time trying to keep that under wraps."

Mishak would have slapped his Human officer down for that but he could see the un-solicited comment had hit home and he bit back his own anger. It was even more piquant, after all, coming from a former slave.

The Human obviously knew his lord wasn't just tweaking Memnon out of petty rivalry. Mishak wanted to push this new half-brother. He wanted to see where the cracks were and test his breaking-strain.

Memnon had probably arranged this entire incident, as he claimed, to deliver a message. If it were any different, he'd have attacked while he still had surprise on his side.

But could he be goaded into ignoring Sandrak's wishes?

"Do you know who your *real* mother was?" Mishak asked him, deliberately insinuating some hidden knowledge of the matter – knowledge Sandrak may have imparted to his elder, *acknowledged* son.

"My mother is Silpana," Memnon growled, "of Keeva."

"So you're Mot's brother?" Mishak blurted out in shock. *No wonder he's so annoying!*

"Mot?" Tashmitum asked. "Who is Mot?"

"A distant branch of the family," Mishak explained, trying to think of a way to turn his own shock back against Memnon. "My father wanted us to marry."

"Ah," Tashmitum sighed, giving off an aura of mischeif. "*She's* the one! That summer on Keeva, when you both discovered the pleasures of the flesh together?"

"Enough!" Memnon snarled.

"Hey, lighten up," Eth soothed. "It's nothing to be embarrassed about. It was just two young Quailu exploring each other's bodies, touching, tasting, inserting…"

This is it, thought Mishak, *I'm going to burst out laughing and spoil the whole thing. I've let Eth have too much leash here…*

"Shut up!" Memnon roared. "Or I swear by all the gods that I'll…"

"You'll what?" Mishak demanded. "You'll do us harm will you? Big talk for a messenger."

"I'll destroy the *Dibbarra*," he raged, "and take the rest of your ships for my own!"

That should be sufficient provocation, Mishak thought, *just barely.* "You might find it hard to turn your words into deeds."

"Look around you," Memnon said, bringing his anger under control. "I have brought many more ships than you, *brother*."

"Have you?" Mishak asked. "Perhaps I had a force here before, watching your waiting fleet."

"Then you would have saved your friends from destruction."

"Not true," Mishak countered. "It all happened so quickly. We could tell that you wanted me to come here but we had no idea you'd start the fight the moment my main force arrived."

"You're lying," Memnon stalked toward his brother. "You're lying because you know I'm about to kill you!"

"Perhaps a demonstration?" Mishak offered. He still didn't believe Memnon was angry enough to open fire but he'd said more than enough to justify Mishak's 'measured' defensive response.

He only hoped Memnon was stupid enough to think his brother was lying.

"I would be most grateful if you could arrange a demonstration," Memnon said, clearly not intending any gratitude.

"Excellent!" Mishak enthused. "Select five ships and I'll have them destroyed by the force that preceded me here."

"Five ships…"

"*Yours*, not mine," Mishak clarified.

Memnon was neatly cornered now. He'd made threats and a Quailu did not make idle threats. Mishak had every right to launch a limited defensive strike and still not be considered the aggressor. It was usually done as a warning and, though it could lead to an escalation of hostilities, Mishak didn't believe Memnon would push the matter.

He already seemed reluctant. Indeed, he hadn't even begun to choose the ships for Mishak to target. After a moment of hesitation, Memnon reached out and began selecting icons that only he could see. He cloned it and tossed it at his brother.

"All Belnut's ships?" Mishak commented when the display appeared in the central area, now visible to the other captains. He turned toward one of the holograms which was now quite agitated.

"Lord Belnut, I presume?" Mishak offered a half-bow. "You might want to find new friends. This one's kind of an ass."

"You have no right," Belnut yelled, but whether it was at Memnon or Mishak, no one could tell.

"Do you serve under Melvin?"

"I don't!"

"Just a coincidence, I suppose, that you're here. Still, your independence in this matter means that he can't designate your ships." Mishak turned back to Memnon. "As I said, pick any five of *your* ships."

Those fists clenched again. Memnon sent a new grouping, five of his frigates.

"That will do nicely," Mishak said, starting to feel the nerves now. If he fired on the ships, they might all end up in a fight and it would probably go badly for him because this was an elaborate bluff.

He was pretending to have far more power than his current forces represented.

Those damned missiles might also fail in any of a number of ways and leave them looking like idiots. He brought his feelings under control. There was nothing else he could do.

If the missiles failed, he'd look foolish and a fight would probably follow. Neither side could afford to walk away from an incomplete demonstration.

"Stand by, the process is rather complex, I'm afraid." He turned to Eth's holo. "Lieutenant Commander?"

"Sir?"

"You have the trace showing the five ships?"

"Aye, lord."

"Very well. Kill the bastards."

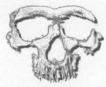

"Three missiles for each target," Eth said loudly, glad to be free of the holo-comms. "I want to make sure we get this done properly the first time. Tactical, make sure they're set to self-detonate if they run out of authorized targets. We don't want them falling into hostile hands."

"We're loaded," Oliv said, "and guidance is confirmed on all fifteen weapons. Ready to fire on your order."

"I want you to eject them but wait for a few seconds before engaging the motors," Eth decided. "We'll let 'em disperse first so they show as coming in from multiple angles. We want the enemy to think there are more than one of us out here, after all."

"I'll give them five seconds of drift. Should be enough to simulate a loose formation." Oliv made the adjustments. "Ready."

"All fifteen weapons – launch."

The deck shuddered and they could hear the hum of the mag-rails ejecting the weapons. Eth counted slowly to five.

"MA fields confirmed on all fifteen weapons we…"

There was no time left for further comment. The fifteen weapons weighed only a miniscule fraction of their usual mass, thanks to the MA field, and the field ended at the rocket nozzles. The propellant returned to full mass as it began its expansion, concentrating normal thrust on a nearly negligible mass.

"Gilgamesh wept!" Gleb whispered.

The five ships had each taken three strikes and the results were terrifying. The missiles had all penetrated before detonation and, frankly, it was anyone's guess as to whether the explosive warheads had detonated.

Given the speed of impact, the entirety of each weapon, including the dense osmium insert, was converted to impact plasma and it was trapped inside the frigates.

But only for a heartbeat.

Each of the five ships shattered outward in a brilliant white flash, tumbling parts spinning crazily on their way toward sister ships who began jockeying to get out of the way. Some of those ships were taking damage from impacts but most were able to avoid the debris.

"That was horrifyingly effective," Oliv whispered, a shudder in her voice.

"Hendy, move us to starboard." Eth ordered. "Take us halfway toward the larger moon. I don't want us sitting in the middle of all those inbound vectors, just in case someone is paying attention over there."

"They're blanketing the area around their fleet with short-range scanning energy," Oliv said. "Given the short time between our lord's orders and our strike hitting home, they must be thinking we're right up their backsides!"

"Good," Eth replied, "but I still don't want us sitting anywhere near the paths those missiles took." He stared at the enemy formation for a few moments. "The missiles really don't need those warheads, do they?"

Oliv looked up at the central holo, a mild frown on her face. "You never know when you might be in too close for the MA field to have much use." She overlaid her energy spectrum map. "Look at their scanning profile. They think we're close, really close. If we *were*, then those warheads would come in handy and those osmium inserts would be a hindrance during conventional acceleration."

Eth nodded. "Better make sure we keep a good supply of conventionals on hand." He looked down at his timer. Twenty minutes…

Mishak stood perfectly still. He'd started out that way from the shock of Eth's devastating strike, but now he was trying not to look surprised. *Can't just stand here like an idiot,* he realized.

Memnon was still projecting onto the *Dibbarra*'s bridge but he was looking to the side, gesticulating and shouting at his crew. Mishak turned to Eth's holo.

"Good shooting, Lieutenant Commander! Please convey my compliments to your captains." He'd noticed how the missiles had come in from several angles and he had no doubt the hostiles would eventually notice as well. It wouldn't hurt to reinforce the deception.

He also knew they'd have to dump their excess heat at some point, though he had no idea how long they had. "I imagine things got *heated*, when you were choosing which of your ships would have the honor?"

"Indeed, lord."

A timer appeared in front of Mishak, set for a very narrow viewing angle. *Nineteen minutes. Can I get rid of them in time? I'd better lay the groundwork for an unexplained path alert, one that preserves the illusion of a hidden fleet.*

"Lieutenant Commander, I'm sending you back to the rendezvous with dispatches. Detail your deputy to stay here with the rest of your force. This system will bear watching, for the time being. Prepare your ship for departure."

"Aye, lord."

"Memnon," he turned back to his distracted half-brother. "You have had your demonstration. I am required by custom to give you this chance to leave with your honor intact. You have taken fire bravely. Now will you leave this system without claim to revenge?"

Memnon shuddered with rage. Mishak could see it, even if he couldn't *feel* it. The hologram inclined its head, just barely enough for civil discourse. "We part on amicable terms," he rasped, looking anything but amicable. He looked to the left. "Bring the path drive online," he ordered as he shimmered out of view.

Mishak realized there was no way the two fleets of hostiles would clear the system in… eighteen minutes. The last of the holo-projected captains had disappeared, leaving only the Human. "Well done!" Mishak said judiciously.

Eth had pushed some boundaries – interjecting in the conversation with Memnon – but it had worked out well enough. *If he were Quailu, wouldn't I be rewarding him?*

"Your new ship has proven very effective. I'm giving you a free hand with the scouting division and your ship designs," he said, leaning in. "Path out when you're ready and… get to work… Commander!"

Eth raised an eyebrow and Mishak was pleased to notice it before hearing the guarded word of inquiry. "It's traditional to send back dispatches with the hero of the day and it's also traditional to promote the celebrated messenger."

Mishak waved a hand airily. "And I grow tired of having to add the extra syllables every time I say lieutenant. Your rank is effective immediately. Get back to the rendezvous and start building your new vessels."

The holo grinned. "Aye, lord!"

"Full normalization," Hendy announced.

"Area is secure," tactical added. "Our ships are the only ones here."

"Secure the path-drive," Eth ordered, "and extend the radiator arrays before we burn out the emission management system."

Noa approached Eth, stopping beside him to gaze at the holo of the current Human vessel complement. Their little fleet centred on the *Mouse*, a heavy cruiser they'd seized from Mishak's renegade uncle. There were also nine frigates, eight of the small scout-ships and the *Scorpion*.

The scout-ships were essentially unarmed but they were even harder to spot than the newer cousin he'd brought to the Sippar system. Their lack of a path-drive and missile-bank gave them a smaller profile, blocking fewer stars as the carbon nanotubule coated ships snuck up on their targets.

But, aside from observation, mine-laying or inserting boarding parties, they weren't good at fighting on their own. They still had their place but they'd also highlighted the need for something between a scout-ship and a main combat vessel.

"One might reasonably assume that an escort of four frigates is unremarkable for a cruiser," Eth observed, acknowledging Noa with a nod.

Noa, having just certified the *Scorpion*, his own design, for active duty a few days ago, grinned broadly. "One might be forgiven for thinking they're looking at a risibly small force," he said. "But, then, the dead are often viewed with more charity than the living…"

The engineer chuckled. "Gleb told me about you waving a hand for that Quailu guard to look at and then slapping him into the next month with the other…"

"Huh!" Eth reached up to stroke his chin. "That's kind of the same thing, isn't it? Am I becoming predictable?"

"Hells no!" Noa scorned. "Ain't nobody gonna see *this* coming. I just like when the Universe repeats itself, that's all. Proof that *nobody's* perfect…"

In the holo, five of the frigates were dissolving into blocks of nanites, ready for re-use. Two of them were already using those nanites to manhandle pitch-drives into place.

They'd had to sacrifice shuttles, but Eth would rather have Scorpion-class vessels than shuttles.

He was going to need some more sword names.

Reality Intrudes

Blockade
Mirsit Transit Point, Imperial Sovereign Territory

Fidrelt slid out of bed, yawning hugely. He went to the sink and threw a quick splash of water on his face before stepping into his armored EVA suit. He worked his way through a series of stretches to sort out the suit's fit before stepping out his door.

The guard stiffened to a position of respect as he passed, turning right to enter the bridge. "Report," he demanded curtly as his number two gave a stiff bow.

"No traffic in the last shift, Lord, with the exception of a few drop-washes out beyond the asteroid fields."

Hardly surprising, Fidrelt thought. His fleet's depredations here had led to a sharp reduction in traffic on the route and many of those who did pass this way took care to drop out as far from the regular area as possible.

The Mirsit Transit Point was hardly friendly to path travel in the first place but it at least allowed a decent pitch field to exist and that was more than you could say for the area surrounding it.

The Great Barrier was a collection of pulsar-wind nebulae that interfered with just about any useful energy field known to sentience. Path-fields collapsed and pitch drives fared no better. Few ships, aside

51

from those who bothered to equip themselves with old-fashioned reaction-thrust engines, ever escaped from the barrier.

Widely believed to be constructed by an ancient civilization of immense power, the Great Barrier had one opening that allowed pitch-fields to form. Ships passing into the resource-rich frontier zones had to stop here and proceed through on pitch alone.

And Fidrelt, though he was here at the behest of more powerful interests, was nonetheless enriching himself very nicely.

He'd already seized more ships than his own fief's entire economic fleet and he still had plenty of prize-crews left.

He settled into his command chair and began going over the reports from the previous shift. One of his frigate captains had complained of a glitch in the sensor suite. They were claiming that the system was dropping some of the stars from the background, essentially making a hole in the data-stream.

He flagged it for his sensor officer to look into and waved over one of his wardu servants. "Coffee," he ordered, giving the tall thin native a cuff on the ear-aperture for good measure.

Damned useless creatures. It's their fault I'm out here, he thought. *And, for the price I'm forced to pay…*

"Path alert!" the sensor officer called out. "Estimate fifteen signatures, lord!" His eagerness washed over the bridge. Fifteen ships would result in a lot of prize-money.

"All call-signs, hands to battle-stations," Fidrelt ordered. "Rig for combat!"

There was a series of flashes as the latest victims dropped out in the middle of the primary wash-dump. Fidrelt's helmet snapped itself together just as the tactical officer shouted his warning.

"They're warships, lord!" His voice transitioned from open air to the slightly tinny reproduction of Fidrelt's helmet speakers in mid-sentence. His blood began coursing with adrenaline and his mood

52

mingled with the rest of the bridge crew, amplifying the reaction to dizzying heights.

He felt like his head would explode and he nearly jumped out of his own skin when the communications officer's voice sounded in his helmet, advising him of an incoming call.

He stepped over to the central holo to find the prince-presumptive himself shimmering in front of him. "Lord Mishak," he said, fearing his voice sounded unnaturally high.

Mishak was clearly not on a ship rigged for combat. His helmet was down, which seemed a little dismissive, if Fidrelt was to be completely honest about it.

"Fidrelt," Mishak bowed politely. "What are you doing out here, interdicting traffic in HQE sovereign territory?" He turned away slightly before looking back. "And I see you've decided to spend money on new designs; how interesting!"

"My business is none of your... business," Fidrelt replied, deeply regretting his adrenaline-addled wits.

"Oh, but it is my business, Fidrelt. I've received complaints about ships seized out here." Mishak shook his head, a gesture that even the Quailu recognized.

"A bad business, Fidrelt. Investor confidence is taking a beating. Nobody wants to risk capital on a venture that stands a better-than-evens chance of being pirated."

"I'm no pirate," Fidrelt said indignantly. "I have a legitimate grievance against..."

"Not in HQE space, you don't," Mishak cut him off calmly.

Fidrelt's eyes darted from side to side. The carefully worded justification provided to him had proven to be flimsier than the clothing his slaves wore. He forced himself to accept the only remaining option.

That, after all, was why Memnon had given him the new ships.

"Trade, Fidrelt," Mishak insisted.

"Trade?"

"That's right. Trade. It's what the empire was built on. It's what all of our laws are designed to protect. It's why we have a military. Without it, we have nothing but decay and chaos." The hologram took an aggressive stride forward and Fidrelt actually yelped in alarm as he backpedaled two steps.

"Trade," the hologram insisted, "and you're buggering up a very important segment of the empire's trade. I'm giving you one chance to step back from this and return what goods you've stolen."

Fidrelt knew what would happen to his own economy if he shifted over to Mishak's side. "I regret, my lord, that we will not be able to reach an agreement." He drew himself up to his full height and even forced himself to take a step toward the prince. "If you persist, we will have to fight and you will not find me an easy opponent!"

He was even starting to believe himself! He could just imagine the tales folks would tell of how Fidrelt the Ferocious fought Prince Mishak to a standstill at the *Battle of Mirsit*.

Mishak sighed and raised a holographic hand. "Do you see this hand?"

Fidrelt frowned. "Yes, but what the hells does…"

"Multiple inbound traces detect… gods!" the sensor coordinator screamed, startling several years off the sensor officer's lifespan. Fidrelt himself had lost at least a few months. "We're down to three frigates and our cruiser!"

How? He wondered numbly. Most of the fleet gone in the blink of an eye? He looked at the boiling mass of wreckage.

"It came from nowhere," the sensor officer said, outraged at an enemy that showed such proficiency, "and the weapons are so fast our sensors were barely even aware of them."

His remaining ships were blessedly clear of the deadly debris, thanks to their position at the rear of his formation. He'd have to run for it and hope Memnon would understand. "Engineering, bring our path drive online and…"

An alarm sounded, followed closely by an opening appearing in the hull directly in front of him. Figures in armored EVA suits poured through, shoving the crew away from their stations. One figure, an alien skull painted on his faceplate in white, grabbed him and dragged him over to the small knot of captured Quailu.

That was when it finally gelled for Fidrelt. *How had the enemy gotten so close that their missiles only showed up when it was too late to do anything? How did they approach so close that they could just stroll onto his bridge and take over?*

That was no sensor glitch in the reports. That other ship was noticing starlight blocked by stealthy ships!

The alarm cut off and one of the aliens secured the ship from battle stations. The openings in the hull sealed themselves and the atmospheric cyclers quickly re-pressurized the cruiser.

No wonder Mishak had suddenly vaulted to prominence, Fidrelt realized as his helmet snapped open. He had managed to get his hands on some kind of stealth tech!

The alien's helmet retracted revealing what must have been one of Mishak's Humans. He had an ugly, flatish face and Fidrelt didn't care for the cut of his teeth. Too much of the meat-eater in these creatures, if he wasn't mistaken. He was also unreadable and Fidrelt shuddered in disgust.

If I can get my hands on their tech, he thought, *then the empire would be talking about the rise of Fidrelt, not this upstart Mishak!*

The Human ordered a course, full pitch, and Fidrelt, who'd been thinking of his future greatness, suddenly felt a pang of renewed alarm. The Humans had killed rather a large proportion of the crew, if his suit's data feed was correct, but they'd left the bridge-crew unharmed and he'd taken that as a good sign.

He'd hoped to get a chance to steal one of their stealthy ships and pull a skedaddle, but there seemed to be more than a little symbolism in the Human's current choice of destination.

He started as he realized the Human was standing beside him.

"You'll never guess," the Human said in a voice that was much higher than a Quailu's, "what we found on our way in to your position." He blew out a heavy breath, startling Fidrelt, both from the sudden noise and from the realisation that the alien was working to control emotions that Fidrelt couldn't sense.

He reached over to pull the power cell from the back of Fidrelt's suit. "Then again, I imagine you could come up with a pretty shrewd guess, couldn't you? I'd bet you've got a lot of these stored somewhere." He hefted the power cell.

And suddenly, his fate became clear.

"No!" the disgraced lord held up his hands toward the Human, disgusted at how quickly he'd resorted to begging this native mushkenu for mercy.

But self-loathing was a good deal more enjoyable than what he now knew awaited him.

"You don't understand," he began.

"Oh, I understand," the Human said, his voice chillingly quiet. "And there will be no last-second escape and rise to power for you! A monster like you given the power of our technology would be an abomination!"

Fidrelt was shocked. So much so that he momentarily forgot about his looming fate. Had the unreadable creature read him?

"We're in position," one of the Humans announced from the helm.

Fidrelt realized that, though he couldn't read the Human who'd taken his power cell, he *could* read most of the others, though he wished he couldn't. It was one thing to learn to live with your sins. It was quite another to see those sins reflected in the hearts of others.

"If it were up to me," his captor mused, "I'd shove you out there to die with all the ships' crews you murdered."

Fidrelt felt a flare of hope. He'd been certain he was about to die by the same method he'd been using to dispose of the captured ships' crewmen. Admittedly, it had been cruel of him, but they were mostly natives...

"You're making excuses for your behavior, aren't you?" the Human asked, startling him, reminding him that he might be able to read feelings.

A Human approached, sparing a glance for Fidrelt, and the Quailu shuddered at what he felt from him. Then the mind went blank again. *What manner of creatures are these that they can open and close their minds to a Quailu so completely?*

"Commander, there are hundreds of the poor bastards drifting around out there, not a single life-sign among them."

"Like I said," the Human, apparently a commander, turned to face Fidrelt, "if it were up to me, I'd have you all out there with your victims."

The other Human darted a look at the commander. "Sir? I'm no admiralty lawyer but I'm pretty sure it *is* up to you."

Fidrelt's blood ran cold. *He was toying with me?*

"Hey," the commander replied with a strange curl of his lips, "you're right!" He moved over to the forward hull.

"Noa, I want an airlock right here!"

"One minute," one of the Humans responded, leaning over a console.

After a few minutes, a flow of nanites came snaking along the bottom of an overhead cable-tray. Several plates of high-impact glazing dangled from the flow.

"Windows?" The commander chuckled. "Where did you find those, dare I ask?"

"Sneeze guards from the mess-hall," came a laconic reply. "They're stronger than most folks realize."

"Really?"

"We only need them to hold against a one-atmo difference."

Fidrelt realized he didn't want to die listening to a discussion about sneeze guards, not when he could be begging instead. "Please!" He sank to his knees, hands raised. "It wasn't my fault. We were only following orders!"

"Memnon's orders?"

"You don't know what he'd do if I ever defied him."

"What would he do?"

Fidrelt opened his mouth to answer but remembered, just in time, that telling this Human would have the same effect as pissing off Memnon. Either way his fief would be ruined and his daughter would inherit a stone-age world.

"So it's like that, is it?" The commander leaned close. "I have orders as well. Would you like to hear them?"

The Quailu was afraid to answer, positive or negative. He felt the results would be unpleasant.

"From the harmonized admiralty orders for house militaries, chapter five, para sixty-two, sub-section nine, suffer not a pirate to live." He straightened, raising his voice. "For they crush the lifeblood of the very empire herself and all warriors' hands must be set against them."

"But we're not pirates!" he protested desperately. "We only seized legitimate prizes of conflict…"

"In unaffiliated imperial territory?" the commander shouted over his protest. "And is that your idea of acceptable prisoner detention?" He waved in the direction of the small constellation of dead bodies.

"But they were just…" Fidrelt trailed off, just before ending the sentence with the word 'natives'.

The commander let a flare of rage escape. "Bring him."

Strong hands seized Fidrelt's arms. He was dragged over to the growing airlock, which had sneeze-guard windows on one side.

"Bridge crew first," the Human leader ordered.

Fidrelt watched in fascinated horror as they were herded into the chamber. Their terror bounced from mind to mind, amplifying as it went. They were going to die and they knew it.

That terror had fully claimed him. His mouth hung open in a silent scream as the opening flowed shut.

"These Quailu stand guilty of piracy," the Human leader declared. "They are convicted by the grisly aftermath of their crimes and they'll spend eternity among their victims." With a nod, he signaled to his engineer, who opened the hull side of the chamber.

Fidrelt could feel their pain, their sheer terror as their eyes, less robust than most species in the HQE, ruptured. Their hearing was next to go and, though he could feel that as well, he was mesmerised by the tendrils of intraocular fluid that extended from their eyes.

They would freeze, but not right away. The vacuum of space was a poor medium for heat transfer. Their immediate enemy was the pressure drop. One crewman, at least, had forgotten the survival drills and he'd held his breath. His lungs ruptured, releasing gas bubbles into his bloodstream and he doubled over in agony.

The nitrogen in their blood was turning back to gas, the bubbles stopping the flow and depriving their tissues of oxygen. The more they moved, the greater the pain in their muscles.

They were all struggling wildly in their panic, bumping each other out of the small chamber and into the void.

Where their victims awaited them.

Their minds were fading quickly, now that there was no oxygen, and Fidrelt's terror abated somewhat as the outer opening closed. He closed his mouth and tried desperately to think of some way out of this mess. *Do I know anything about Memnon they might be able to use?"* He knew the answer to that question even as he was thinking it.

Memnon wasn't stupid enough for that. Fidrelt had wasted precious seconds of life on the bastard. He was wasting it still…

Hands grabbed him and shoved him into the chamber. *Die well,* he told himself, forcing back the fear and coming to stand in front of the window. He would face this impudent Human executioner – show him how an awilu died.

The commander was opposite him on the safe side of the glass and he squinted, leaning down to look at something on the glass. "Is that Durian crisp-leaf?"

"Well the glass *did* come from their salad station," the engineer replied. "Worth a look when we're done here. Don't often see fresh crisp-leaf on a ship."

The portal flowed shut, cutting off the sound of their conversation, and Fidrelt stared in disbelief as the Human leader ignored him completely. He seemed to still be talking about food with his engineer. He mimed taking a bite of something as the outer hull began to open.

That was the last he saw. His eyes ruptured, scaring him more than hurting, but it at least brought on the agonized gasp that emptied his lungs before they could burst. He'd expected a searing cold in his lungs when he breathed in but there were no gasses to pull inside.

His eardrums hurt more than his eyes. Fidrelt gave a silent scream of agony, reaching up to touch the side of his head, noticing, just before passing out, that his skin had swollen from the evaporation of water in the cells.

Eth stood patiently in the holographic image of Mishak's bridge. He bowed his head when the Quailu approached him. "Lord."

"Another successful deployment!" Mishak offered him a grotesque version of a Human grin, which was an honor, considering the Quailu had minimal use for facial expression.

Eth returned the grin. "And four prizes taken," he added, hopefully. Though his Humans had done the taking, it was still up to their lord to decide what happened to them.

"I can use another cruiser," Mishak mused.

"And I could use more frigates," Eth ventured. "Word has it there's a new draft of Humans waiting for us at Kwharaz Station. I'd be able to fill out the crews on my six Scorpion-class ships and still have enough to crew three more."

"You don't want the cruiser instead?" Mishak asked.

Eth shook his head, flattering his lord by implying that he'd catch the gesture. "They don't suit our fighting style and they're a damned personnel sponge. Takes too many of our people and we'd rather sneak up and slit the enemy's throats while your cruisers are giving them an honourable, face-to-face beating."

Mishak nodded. "Very well, commander. I'll send over a team to take that cruiser off your hands before we return to my own territory."

"Very well, lord." Eth bowed his head again. When he looked up, the holo of the *Dibbarra* was gone.

The Multitasker
Mirsit Transit Point, HQE space

Eth stopped at the entry to the shower hall, head tilted to the side. *I suppose I've never taken a shower on this ship during path travel before,* he thought. The ceiling plates in the anteroom were vibrating, giving off a low-pitched thrumming sound. Some series of physical connections leading from the engine mounts had led here, transmitting a vibration that matched the resonant frequency of the moisture-resistant cladding.

He continued inside. Stepping up to a cubicle, he pushed his heels inward to start the retract sequence. He lifted his feet out of the foot-plates and stepped forward to struggle out of his under-armor suit.

He turned around and walked into the shower hall, tossing the suit through a hole in the bulkhead that led down to the ship's laundry unit. He nodded politely to the young crew-woman who was the only other person using the room and moved to the far end.

It wasn't exactly a written rule but the generally accepted practice was to give one another the maximum amount of room possible in the shower hall. It didn't always work out that way, especially in the later watches, when more crewmen were off duty, but you still didn't shower next to someone in an empty hall.

And you didn't look either.

That was a new one. Before they'd won their freedom, they'd openly ogled and propositioned one another. With no STD's and zero chance of procreation, sex was a casual, inconsequential pastime for many Humans.

He didn't think any of his species had done anything to reverse their steri-plants yet, but they were certainly experiencing an evolution in their attitudes. *If we actually are a species,* he thought, then smiled to himself.

Perhaps they were becoming one after all…

Attitudes toward sex didn't make a species, but they might be a potential indicator. It was taking on a new meaning for Humans.

He finished up and headed back out to the doorway, noticing that the woman had already finished. The air-curtain activated as he walked out, leaving him mostly dry. The fresh suit he grabbed from a shelf by the door would wick up the rest and feed it into his EVA suit for later use.

He walked back to the cubicle where he'd left his armor, noticing out of the corner of his eye that the crew-woman was struggling into her own fresh suit.

He dressed and stepped back into his suit's foot-plates. It finished flowing into place around his body just as the young woman strode past, her suit not bearing the color-coded bands of any of the ship's various divisions, and he realized who she was.

"Scylla!" he called, jogging out of the anteroom to catch up with her.

She stopped, turning to meet him with a distant smile. "Hello, commander. Can I help you?"

He grinned. "I was going to ask you the same thing. How are you adjusting to life on the ship?"

Scylla was the name Eve had given to the young woman they'd captured at Kwharaz Station. They still had no proof of where she'd come from, though they had a shrewd suspicion the Chironians, whom his team had exposed for having illegal copies of the Human genome, were behind it.

She'd been wearing a bomb intended for either Mishak, Sandrak or Marduk, the emperor's chief of staff. Eth had felt her presence on his way to a meeting of the three nobles and had managed to stop her but some kind of neural pre-conditioning had wiped her mind.

Since then, she'd been aboard the *Mouse,* developing a new persona like a newborn in an adult body.

"Well enough but I have no work to do and I'm pretty sure I'm the only one here who can say that."

"You feel ready for specialty training?"

"I think so. I'm getting tired of just wandering the corridors, soaking up the crew's sympathetic glances."

Eth nodded slowly, impressed by the calm confidence he felt from her. "Do you have a moment? There's something we should discuss in private."

"I'm not sure I'm quite ready for that yet," she countered calmly.

Eth reddened. "Whoa! I just mean…"

"It's alright, commander," she assured him, deadpan. "That was just a joke."

He stared at her. *Could at least smile if it's a joke, dammit!*

She looked at him for a moment, long enough to make the moment more uncomfortable. "Interactions have a steep learning curve," she finally announced, though Eth had already been thinking the same thing.

"It's difficult to gauge what's appropriate behavior for our species," she added.

Eth offered a wry smile. "You're not alone in that," he assured her. He gestured down the corridor. "Can you join me?" he asked. "In the ready room," he added hurriedly.

She nodded and turned to head forward. "I don't suppose there's a manual on interpersonal relationships among Humans?"

"I doubt any species has such a manual," he said with a frown.

"Of course they do," she insisted with quiet conviction. "They call them families."

Eth had no answer to that. He chewed it over all the way to the bridge but, when they reached the ready room door, he put it aside in favor of an issue he felt better equipped to deal with... Marginally...

He closed the door, giving them privacy from the bridge crew and sat opposite her at the large table. "I know you have no memories of it," he began cautiously, "but you were taken from Kwharaz Station by the Varangians."

"So you told me."

"I was taken as well and it changed me."

She frowned. "How were you changed?"

He hesitated, looked around the room. *I'm going to tell her,* he decided. Still, no Varangian had shown up with a gun to stop him from polluting the timeline. *Have they sent someone before? If so, I wonder how many times...*

"My perception, my understanding of the universe, of the *universes*, was altered. Where they took us both – it was outside of this universe. We were outside, looking back at ourselves, in a way. It stripped away the biological filter we use to view our existence."

He sensed shock in her mind.

"I've heard that before," she whispered, shuddering, terror creeping up from her amygdala.

Eth came around the table, turning her chair and kneeling to place his hands on her shoulders. "We're still here," he said, softly but firmly. "This universe is no less real for us now that we see it differently!"

She was shaking violently but she fixed her eyes on his, delved deep into what she found there, and found someone who'd been through the same ordeal. Gradually, the shaking subsided.

Eth could feel the fear abate but there was the same mistrust for the physical realm that he'd felt after his own journey. She'd remembered some of her experience, even though her mind had been blanked. *Maybe the mind is more resilient than the Chironians realize.* "How much do you remember?"

"A lot!" Her focus drifted away from his face. "I remember escaping from our Chironian handlers, at Kwharaz," she said. "I spent weeks living in the alleys, snatching scraps from the refuse conveyors behind the chop-shops…" She looked at him, her gaze sharper.

"I remember seeing you, wondering how you'd escaped. I didn't recognize you…" Her eyes darted left and right as she searched her mind. "The memory stops there, as if I fell asleep. Then I woke up screaming with a Varangian on the other side of the glass!" She shuddered again.

"Chironians?" Eth asked, knowing it wasn't as important as her own possible transformation, but the word had been shocked out of him. He'd given up on ever finding evidence of a Chironian involvement in the plot that had nearly killed his lord.

She nodded. "I was the only one meant to stay on the station, so they were acclimatizing me. The others were going to be sent to something called the Irth Project."

"What the hells is an Irth?"

She shrugged. "I don't know but that's where the other Humans were supposed to go."

Eth decided to come back to that later. "When I came back from my time with the Varangians," he said, watching her closely, "I was different. I'd discovered that I had new… abilities."

Her eyes were focused on his shoulder, her mind teasing at the tendrils of memories given up for lost. "Did your Varangian talk about dimensions with you?"

Eth nodded, though her eyes stayed on target. "The speech about a two-dimensional creature stepping out into our three-dimensional world and seeing itself in a new way?"

66

"And how," she added, "we would look like line segments if we happened to interact with that creature's two-dimensional universe." She looked up, into Eth's eyes. "That line segment is only a tiny fraction of our entire being. But what if a circle in that two-dimensional plane steps out to discover that he's actually a sphere and his wife is a cube?"

Eth grinned at her. "It would explain why she keeps changing her length!"

Another shrug. "No doubt he'd always thought of her as mysterious." She stared at him calmly, then gestured at her own body. "Effectively, what you see here is just another line segment."

Eth's head tilted slightly to the right. "You mean…"

"I mean," she cut in, touching her chest, "that this and this," she reached out to press her hand against Eth's chest, "are miniscule parts of what we really are. I understood this until I returned to Kwharaz Station and ran into a Chironian handler, which caused my mind to reset."

Despite the momentous words, Eth felt a quickening of his pulse at the touch, even with his EVA armor in the way. *Can you go any lower?* He excoriated himself. *She's practically an infant in an adult body!*

She smiled, the most emotion he'd ever seen on her face.

"So much is coming back to me now. Until this talk, I've been like an amnesia patient. An adult's mind but with no memories to give context to my world."

Can she read actual thoughts? Fornication! Can she read this right now or is she really good at reading faces?

She actually chuckled. "As I was saying, we are so much more…

"…than what our eyes show us."

Eth, still on one knee, spun in shock. Her voice had finished that sentence from behind him and he lost his balance, his left elbow stopping his fall by coming to rest on her seat.

The seat was empty and he was now looking up at her. She had been leaning down to finish her alarming sentence but now she straightened.

"How did you do that?" he blurted.

She opened her mouth, as if to respond, but then closed it again, frowning. "Give me a moment." She grimaced. "It's one thing to suddenly realize you know something incredible. It's quite another to put it into words."

She looked over his head for a moment, then nodded to herself. "If you stick your index finger through the two-dimensional universe," she began slowly, "it appears as a line to the other inhabitants." She extended her index finger and poked it downward.

She pulled it up, moved it to the left and poked down again. "If I do this, I seem to disappear and then pop up in a new place. That's all I'm doing. I'm moving this three-dimensional intersection of myself from one place to another." She offered her hand.

Eth took her hand and climbed to his feet. "And here I thought I was going to be the one telling *you* amazing things about the nature of our existence," he admitted ruefully.

"What amazing things?"

Eth shrugged. "Empathic abilities, telekinesis… Nothing big…"

She smiled. "I haven't tried moving things with my mind, but I can read thoughts."

Great! She knows how you've been reacting to her! He stiffened, realizing she could read that thought as well.

"It's alright," she assured him. "I haven't been in this body for very long but my brain has the same hard-wired instincts as any other

Human. I can plainly see it's an attractive physical form. You wouldn't believe what some of the crew think about doing to it."

"Ah, well…" Eth rubbed his hand on the back of his neck. "Some of the crewmen are used to an unrestrained way of life…"

"It's not just the men," she corrected. "And, frankly, you barely scratch the surface before you catch yourself. It's *far* more intriguing…"

"Hear that, dumbass?" Ab said in his mind. *"She likes us!"*

"Not now!" Eth hissed, darting his gaze to the right. *Now he's in my waking mind?*

"Very well," Scylla said calmly. "I hope you take no offense. As I said, I'm still finding my way through Human norms. I'll do a database search on the proper way to initiate a sexual encounter."

"Told you!" Abdu crowed.

"Just hold it!" Eth told Ab, realizing too late that Scylla might not understand to whom he was talking. *Can she hear him?* Then her words registered. "Wait, what?"

"Hear who?" she asked.

"Um, it's my…" He pointed a finger at his head. "… old…" He trailed off, dropping his hand and shaking his head. "It's complicated," he explained lamely.

"She can't hear me," Abdu declared. *"Turns out I'm more than just a thinly veiled symptom of your desire to have a father-figure in your life! I'm also a way for you to preserve some semblance of privacy in your inner dialogue!"*

"So," he began, and then realized he had nothing to follow 'so' with. He dropped his right arm on the table, fingers clenching nervously. He pressed his lips tightly together, mind racing for a way forward.

"You said your presence only represents a tiny fraction of who you are," he asked, desperate to steer the conversation back to safer ground. "Where is the rest of you?"

"Scattered across what we perceive as time. A two-dimensional circle perceives the third dimension as time. We do the same with the fourth."

She said it as if the last few minutes of weirdness hadn't even occurred.

"It's not really time, then?"

She looked at his face for a moment, lost in thought, then shook her head. "Not really but that perception is a comfort to us. It helps us to explain our existence."

She sat, the conventional way, and Eth sat in the chair next to her.

"So," he began slowly, "when you're spending *time* with me in this room, what you're doing is committing more of your fourth-dimensional self to me?"

She allowed a grudging nod. "Our biology puts its own spin on it, though, and it ends up as *time*."

"How long have you known you can… transpose yourself like that?"

"I don't know," she frowned. "I suppose I've been aware of it, at some level, since coming back from the Varangian visit but the Chironians were waiting for me. As soon as I set foot back on the station, one of them hit me with a control phrase and I was back under their programming. This was the first time I tried it."

"Oh!" Eth's eyes grew wide. "It felt like you'd been practicing."

"No, I just… remembered that I understand."

"How far can you move?"

She squinted, her focus wandering. "I don't think there's a limit. I think I could put myself on a planet on the other side of the galaxy, if

70

I wanted, but I'd rather not try, just yet. I don't want to get stuck in the middle of a moon or find myself in empty space because I got distracted at the last second."

"Well… wow!" Eth offered quietly, leaning back in his chair. "I have to warn you, most of our people aren't aware that some of us have any strange abilities. Too many know, actually, but the longer we can keep this quiet, the lower the chances the empire will decide we're a threat and try to wipe us out."

"You think they might?"

"If they decide we're too powerful?" Eth nodded. "They're already nervous that natives are killing Quailu. If they think we're moving entirely beyond their control…"

"So I should keep my mouth shut about all this?"

"You should." He grinned. "Except when you're trying to teach *me!*"

"Oooh! Can I watch when she's 'educating' you?"

Going Deep
The Deathstalker, *Heiropolis System*

"Cryo-banks fully charged for both the *Scorpion* and the *Last Thing You'll Ever See*," the engineering officer announced.

"Very well," Oliv acknowledged. "Close the interchange valves and disconnect the link to the scout-ship as well."

"Aye, ma'am. Valves are closed and the link is severed."

Oliv took a deep breath. "You're ready for this?"

Gleb shrugged. "Sure. It sounds like fun."

She shook her head. "Bring the emission management system online and start dropping us toward Heiropolis Prime, three-quarters pitch."

Gleb could have had his own Scorpion-class ship by now. In fact, he *did* have one. Eth was holding onto it, in the meantime, but he'd hand it over to Gleb the moment he got back. He'd already been commissioned and named for the command slot.

As long as he found a way to come back...

They'd found Human DNA in the debris from Memnon's five destroyed ships at Sippar. That was curious enough on its own, but it also meant there was a chance to slip someone into the enemy's forces unnoticed.

Gleb was a good candidate. As one of Eth's earliest and best students in what they were quietly referring to as *understanding*, he'd have an advantage over his adversaries.

It also made him almost too valuable to risk, but risk was a part of conflict.

"Still planning on the flagship?" she asked.

"If I'm going to find information," he said, "then I need to get close to the biggest source of information, and that'll be Melvin the Bastard."

"Better hope they have Humans on the flagship," she warned.

Gleb grunted. "I'll just claim I got stuck on an inter-ship shuttle transfer by mistake or… you know."

He chuckled at her rolled eyes. "Let's face it: there's bound to be a string of unexplained Quailu deaths on that ship over the next few days or weeks."

If Sandrak or Memnon had any idea the kind of danger represented by Humans, they certainly wouldn't be using them on their ships. They clearly had no idea, so Gleb should be able to move around on the enemy's vessels without attracting any notice.

"You'd better get down to the scout-ship," she said, putting a hand on his shoulder. "Make sure you come back, you jackass."

"Count on it," he told her on his way to the aft hatch. "As long as they don't offer me a better command, that is."

"Better than a Scorpion-class?" she called after him before continuing, talking now to herself. "He'll be back."

"Three light-seconds out," the helmsman advised. He brought them to a halt.

"*Scorpion* actual, this is the *Last Thing You'll Ever See*," Eve called. "I see we've stopped but I still don't have my cargo."

"He should almost be there," Oliv replied.

"Affirmative, I see him strolling across the hangar bay now. Seems a little casual, considering where we're taking him."

"I suppose he needs to stay in character," Oliv countered. "It's not like we're gonna play some kind of theme music or anything. Just get him inserted and then we'll pull out."

"Umm, *Scorpion* actual… you might want to reconsider your phrasing on that."

The bridge crew broke out in laughter. Oliv even treated herself to a chuckle. "Now that's the kind of send-off our Gleb would prefer!"

Gleb's suit closed up as the scout-ship pumped its atmosphere into storage. A green light pulsed in his HUD as the hull melted away to show a corresponding hole in the hull of Memnon's flagship.

"Stay sharp," Eve told him. She gave him a light punch on the shoulder. "Don't be a hero; get the skinny on what they're up to and get the hells out of there."

He rolled his eyes. She'd been like this during the entire approach. He appreciated her concern but it seemed like she was more concerned about this than *he* was. He was actually feeling the need to distract her from the dangers he would be facing.

"I thought there was supposed to be some *inserting* going on that involved me?" he hinted hopefully.

She snorted, nodding toward the hole in the hull. "That's all the inserting you'll be doing today, hotshot. Come back in one piece and we'll talk."

With a disappointed sigh that was only half-feigned, he turned and stepped into an unpressurized engineering space inside the hull of Memnon's ship. He activated a small programmable-logic-control unit on his chest and a block of spare nanites followed him in from the scout-ship.

He waved to Eve before the hulls closed up and then moved over to a pressure bulkhead and activated the next control in the PLC menu. The nanites flowed up to create an airtight chamber around him, the ship's pressure bulkhead forming the inner wall.

"Point of no return," he said calmly, though, with Eve now gone, he had no way of leaving this ship. He opened the charging valve on his oxygen storage and pressurised the small chamber.

He opened his helmet and leaned his head against the pressure-bulkhead. He could feel a consciousness but it was quickly fading. Finally, certain nobody was in the corridor on the other side of the bulkhead, he activated the final command on the controller, opened a hole in the panel and stepped through.

The hole closed up as he started walking. He didn't bother picking a direction for any particular reason, he just started moving in the direction he'd been facing. One of the surest ways to get caught was to stand around looking lost.

He kept moving along the outermost corridor until he reached the cross aisle just forward of the engine room. He turned in and started across to the far side of the ship, planning to work his way to the centerline and then move to the next deck.

He was hoping to see Humans before running into any Quailu. He wanted to get an idea of how they fared aboard Memnon's ships so he could adjust his own attitude accordingly. He had nearly reached the forward cross aisle, just aft of the officer's galley, when a Quailu petty officer rounded the corner.

"You there," he called out peremptorily. "With me!" The petty officer turned and headed back for the galley.

Gleb could feel his anger at how long the Human was taking to catch up. He reminded himself to let normal, expected feelings emanate from his mind.

"Get this coffee-service up to the ready room," he commanded, giving Gleb a slap on the side of the head for emphasis, "and be quick about it or you'll miss a sleep shift!"

"Yes, petty officer," he replied meekly. He treated himself to a feeling of servile fear and the Quailu, convinced that the matter was well in hand, left without another word.

Gleb stepped over to the trolley and checked to see that the large carafe was actually full. He got the thing moving with a rattle of steel mugs, careful to keep his mind numb.

He took the ramp up to the command deck and passed the guards at the main bridge hatch as though he didn't even exist. The ready room was hard on his right and Memnon was in there with several of his captains.

"Heiropolitans," Memnon sneered as Gleb pushed his trolley up against the starboard wall. "One of the wretched creatures tried to corner me and start a conversation but I shot him in the liver."

A scattering of sycophantic chuckling broke out. Everyone in the room was holding a tight rein on their feelings.

"Too bad *they're* not transplants as well," one of the captains said.

"Wouldn't do any good," Memnon asserted. "Most of 'em are already mushkenu, so they'd only lose a handful of slaves."

Gleb felt that was important and he worked it over as he served the coffee. Transplants were a violation of the Meleke Corporation's charter. They owned the rights to *native* wardu genomes but there had been infamous cases in the empire's deep dark past where Meleke had been selling genomes that weren't native to the buyer's planet. Those contraband genomes were based on non-extinct species from outside the empire.

Selling extinct genomes was fine. Indeed, Meleke spent enormous sums to fund expeditions searching for worlds with extinct species. Gleb's own species had come from just such a world. Humans may have spent thousands of years as a slave species but at least they existed again.

He finished setting out the mugs of coffee and moved back to stand by the trolley but Memnon waved him out.

So did they have knowledge of lords using transplant wardu? Such information would give them massive leverage, not only over the lords but over the Meleke Corporation as well.

Gleb shook his head as he left the room. Using that information just once would collapse the entire scheme. There was more to this. Memnon and his staff clearly didn't care if he'd heard them talking, or were they just careless around Humans?

Did they just look right through them like most lords would do with their wardu?

One thing seemed fairly certain: Memnon was no Sandrak. He was careless enough to let his captains know a secret that had the potential to wreck a major part of the HQE's economy. He frowned. Was he reading too much into one comment? Perhaps they had just been referring to some isolated incident...

He had reached the lowest deck and, sure enough, the more crowded accommodations here were reserved for the Human crewmen. The scent of stale sweat and poorly washed suits gave him a feeling of home. Not a particularly well-kept home, but at least he was among his own kind.

A Quailu warrant officer was in the common area shouting at the Humans. One Human was standing next to him, eyes cast down to his feet, shoulders slumped.

"Sickness," the warrant shouted, "is not a valid excuse for being late to your shift! The enemy won't wait on us while we drag our sorry asses to our duty stations!" He pulled out his sidearm, putting it to the head of the Human beside him and squeezed the trigger.

There was almost no reaction, physically or emotionally, as the man fell to the deck.

So, Gleb thought, watching the warrant officer leave through the aft portal, *the Humans on these ships must be mushkenu. That warrant would catch seven kinds of hell if he'd killed Memnon's property.*

77

How is that even remotley legal? He shouldn't be able to purchase wardu Humans, much less arrange for mushkenu...

He could see many different types of suit on the sad group of Humans. There were engineering techs, ordnance techs, aircraft handlers, fitters... All the kinds of jobs you couldn't get away with assigning wardu to.

They'd be laughed out of the empire if they let slaves serve on house warships.

Gleb's suit bore the dark blue bands of a comms-system tech, which he hoped would get him access to a quiet corner of the ship where he could tap into the database and clone a copy.

But he was starting to think he was on the wrong ship. He should try to find a way of getting aboard Sandrak's flagship. He had a wide range of options, thanks mostly to Noa's ingenuity, but the simplest would likely be best. He could probably find a way to walk onto a shuttle or courier vessel. He just needed to find one headed in the right direction.

He was here to learn more about Memnon and what his goals were but he had a feeling that the real key to the enterprise wasn't here. Sandrak would never trust his second son with anything that might compromise his plans.

Gleb had actually suggested kidnapping Memnon and conducting a thorough interrogation but Eth had shot it down before Mishak had time to even consider it.

"What's the sense in finding out what Memnon is up to if we're taking him out of circulation?" he'd asked, and Mishak had grunted in surprised agreement.

"We'd be back to square one," their lord admitted.

"Knowing what your enemy is up to," Eth added, "is far more useful than knowing what he *might* have done if you hadn't slit his throat and dumped him in the ship's composter."

Gleb approached the dejected Humans, nodding a greeting to another crewman in dark blue. The fellow's face was a mass of bruises. "Just transferred over from the *Bilbao*," he told the man. "Any unclaimed bunks?"

"Yeah," the man answered dryly. "A bunk just opened up, or didn't you notice?" He peered more closely at Gleb. "Transfer?"

"Yeah, for… um… reasons…" He laced his voice with vague reluctance and the other man let it go, though Gleb could clearly sense his curiosity.

"Fair enough," the crewman conceded. "Might as well take that bunk," he pointed to one of the sleeping platforms recessed into the bulkhead. "And you can join us on the middle watch. We're understaffed during the dark hours."

Gleb couldn't help but notice two crewmen getting into their bunks as the comms-tech talked. One man and one woman, each simply stepped out of their armor and climbed into their beds, nude. Neither seemed to notice the other.

There was no reason for the lack of privacy. *Or was there?* He felt a surge of anger. Even the lowest Quailu crewman had his own cubicle. This must have been just one more way of putting the Humans in their place. That was probably why they had no under-armor suits. They were cheap enough, and that would underscore how insignificant the Humans were.

"Name's Gleb," he offered. He was surprised at the anger he'd just triggered in the other man.

"Did I ask for your name?" the man snarled. He hit Gleb on the side of the head hard enough to make him think he could see the stars outside the ship. "Just be on time tonight!" He walked away.

Gleb staggered over to the bunk and grabbed the rail. He closed his eyes and tried to settle his reeling senses. The urge to vomit creeped up his throat but he forced it away.

It frightened him. He'd taken a few blows to the head before but that asshole had a punch like a drop-hammer.

He stepped out of his armor and pulled himself into the bunk before anyone could notice his under-armor suit. He wormed his way out of the clean garment, stuffing it under the lumpy mattress that smelled strongly of its previous owner's sweat.

Gleb lay there, staring up at the ceiling, only a few hand's breadths from his face. He'd be safe enough here until the middle watch and he'd be able to concentrate on what he'd seen so far without fear of stumbling into a Quailu and having his head blown off.

Sandrak clearly had leverage over the lords who'd been taking his side against Mishak and it had to be more than just the fear of his displeasure. Sure, Mishak's father was powerful, but there were always limits to the application of raw power.

His allies had to know that, if they stood up to him, they could count on support from the HQE. The vast majority of noble houses were nervous of Sandrak's pre-eminence and many of them had lost systems of their own to the powerful elector.

Perhaps it had something to do with the Meleke Corporation, though he couldn't see how such a thing would work. A threat had to be executable or it was no threat at all. If Sandrak had dirt on illegal genome use against his compatriots, a threat against one was simultaneously a threat against all.

It lacked the ability to apply targeted pressure. It had worked for Mishak against the Chironians because they represented an isolated incident. *Wasn't it?*

That the Meleke Corporation also faced peril was neither here nor there, as Mishak had since made clear his intention to liberate the entire mushkenu population of Kish.

Get into the database tonight, he told himself, *and then keep an eye out for a chance to get close to Sandrak.*

80

He set an alarm on the panel above his face, though he doubted he'd actually sleep, having just snuck aboard an enemy cruiser and served coffee to his master's latest arch-enemy. He woke to the loud warbling of the alarm and nearly hit his head on the ceiling.

"Suit up," Gleb's newest co-worker said, standing just outside his bunk. "You *really* don't want to be late."

Gleb slid his legs over the edge and hopped down, an undignified maneuver when nude, regardless of gender. He stepped into the foot-pads of his armor and pushed his heels back to activate it.

He saw that the other tech was staring past him and he turned to follow his gaze as his suit closed up. A blanket was pushed up in a hump and it was moving rhythmically, small gasps coming from beneath the tattered fabric.

The force of their feelings hit Gleb before he could think to block it; the desperate desire to block out their dull existence, even if only for a few moments. It was empty, soulless, and Gleb was more shocked by it than he had been by the casual execution, a few hours earlier.

And he was no stranger to casual mattress maneuvers.

He shuddered. "I thought we were in a rush to report for duty?" he demanded.

The other man snorted. "They have you chem-laced or something?" he asked. He started for the exit hatch. "That how they punish Humans on the *Bilbao*? Take away your ability to get a rise?"

"I just don't want a bullet in the head on my first day." Gleb didn't care for what he could feel in the man's mind.

They passed through an unnaturally quiet ship. Most of the crew would be sleeping and the few who weren't were either on their way to start a shift or waiting for someone to come relieve them.

The communications suite was just aft of the bridge. The feeds from all external sensors fed through this room before linking to the bridge workstations.

The data core was also here, which was why Gleb had shown up wearing blue stripes. He nodded to the man who was standing at a data interface holo.

"Show the new guy how things work in here, Mel," Gleb's erstwhile guide ordered, though he wore no rank that Gleb could see. "I'll be aft, checking on the backup systems."

"What he means," Mel explained after the portal had closed again, leaving them alone, "is he'll be aft, backing Siri up against a bulkhead."

"During his duty shift?"

Mel grimaced. "What universe did you just drop out of? Duty shifts are the easiest time for him to get someone into his clutches. All he has to do is move our duty stations around. The aft section was already understaffed and, yet, he puts you in here with me?"

"How's he doing that?" Gleb asked before considering how much he might be putting his own ignorance on display but he pushed on anyway because he was far more comfortable with the way Mel's mind felt. "I see no rank on his suit."

"Just like on any ship," Mel said, staring at Gleb thoughtfully for a few seconds. "You know how it is; shit always seems to stay at the top of the composter. Davu is just another officer's pet.

"Look," he continued, "I don't know how things worked on your last ship, but stay out of his way, right? Malik got in his way and now he's dead. Late for duty, my ass."

"Shit!" Gleb exclaimed. "You mean that guy who got shot a few hours ago? I saw that happen."

Mel nodded. "Malik and Siri liked each other, well enough to not mind sharing a single bunk from time to time. Davu took an interest in her. Malik caught him shoving her up onto a data table in aft comms. He'd already shut off her armor but Malik arrived just in time to go berserk and put a stop to it.

Mel shrugged sadly. "Gave the bastard a well-deserved beating, which was a mistake, of course."

"I'll say," Gleb agreed mildly. "He should have killed him and shoved his corpse out an airlock."

Mel nodded thoughtfully. "It's probably not what I *would* have done but, now, having thought it through…" He looked up at Gleb, "Definitely what I *will* do if I ever find myself in that kind of situation.

"In the meantime, you have to give him a tenth of your ration credit every day."

"My rations?" Gleb burst out before remembering he was supposed to be used to this fleet and its ways.

"Nice try," Mel chuckled, "but you're not convincing me and you certainly won't be fooling Davu with that act. There's not a ship in the fleet that doesn't reward their pet Humans with unofficial perks."

"Worth a try." Gleb pointed to the back of the compartment. "I'll take that back station, if you aren't using it for anything."

"Help yourself," Mel declared grandly. "All of the starboard half shall be your dominion! May the cheevers cower in fear as they climb through your storage banks and electrocute their furry little asses on the power-scrubbers!"

Gleb chuckled as he opened up an interface, then stifled a mild curse. The systems on this ship were standard, fresh-out-of-graving-dock installs. It was the case on most ships but Gleb was accustomed to Noa's custom creations. Most of the error codes he saw on his screen were unheard of in Eth's and Mishak's forces.

The companies that programmed the systems would be upset at that but it was highly unlikely that any of their representatives would ever set foot on those ships again. Looking at the workload piled up in his terminal, Gleb wished it were the case on this ship as well.

He needed time to pull out a data extract but he was going to have his hands full fixing errors in the data-stream.

He was no Noa, but he knew enough coding to consider fixing a few bugs. *No, screw that. I don't want to leave this ship working better than I found it.* He considered adding in a few bugs of his own, but he didn't have the skill to avoid getting caught and he just didn't have time.

Plus, he was fairly certain they'd make Mel pay for any mischief in the comms suite and Mel seemed like a decent guy.

Why the hells were these Humans on Memnon's ships?

He opened up a link to the data logs and inserted a coding anomaly that Noa had prepared for him.

"The trick," Noa had explained in a muffled voice, his head buried inside a generator housing, "is to fool the system into thinking it's picked up a virus. It'll trigger a dump into a series of separate, offline storage banks. If you're sitting in the comms suite at the time, you'll be able to skim a copy as it flows through the room."

Gleb had a pretty good cover, seeing as it put him exactly where he needed to be in order to get the data, but he'd have to wait until the end of his shift before he could review it.

"Worst coding I've ever seen," he grumbled, looking up when he felt Mel's surprise. "Or at least it feels that way. So much tracing to do."

"Pace yourself," Mel advised. "We only need to meet an eighty-percent clean rating. What kind of ship did you come from if you think you need to catch it all?"

Gleb was saved from answering by an alarm chime. "Hells!" Mel exclaimed. "Something nasty got loose in the system.

Godsdamned blockers never work. We get one of these at least twice a week. Help me lock it down!"

"Sure, Mel," Gleb said, bringing up a screen to see how much of the ship's database he was downloading. "I'm on it!" He could see that he was going to be pulling far more data than his suit's system could hold so he cut out anything older than two months.

He glanced up at the hatch, a look of distaste on his face. He shut off the progress screen and started shutting down the primary keys that connected the various data banks.

The hatch slid open and Davu stormed in. "What the devils?"

"Low-level virus," Mel said, eyes still on his work. "We're cutting the keys right now."

Gleb could feel Davu's lack of comprehension. How had this idiot ended up in comms? He sighed. *Officer's pet.* He could also feel Davu's desire to leave this in their hands and resume his trip to the backup bank where Siri worked.

He was giving serious thought to following Davu and killing him but he couldn't afford to indulge in emotions, not when he'd come here for a purpose.

Still…

He reached out, feeling Davu's form but, instead of looking for something like his cranial artery, he went lower, almost grinning at what he found in his kidneys. There was a moderately large chunk of calcium oxalate in there, not quite ready to cause mischief but if Gleb was to give it a little nudge…

Davu shivered. "You don't have to keep it so cold in here," he complained. He grabbed Mel's coffee mug and drained it. "I'll be at the backup if you need me."

"Probably the first time," Mel said after the hatch closed, "that I wished he'd stick around longer."

"You mean... Siri?" Gleb asked. "I find the universe tends to balance itself in most things. Davu's built up a lot of bad kismet. He'll be paying it off with interest, I think."

"Why would you thi..." Mel jumped at the sound of a blood-curdling scream from out in the corridor. "What the hells?"

Gleb smiled, knowing Siri was safe for the immediate future. "If I had to guess, I'd say that Manu has just called in his marker on Davu. Sounded like Davu, anyway."

"You reckon the god of fate is out there torturing him right now?" Mel grinned broadly.

"Metaphorically, at least," Gleb said, returning the grin. He opened a security holo and moved it over to hover between him and Mel.

It showed Davu, doubled up on the decking with both hands grasping his groin. He was breathing rapidly.

Gleb was a little surprised it had moved down so quickly. He'd figured it would start with back pain, but who could tell when you moved the stone on purpose?

"Should we go out there?" Mel asked.

"I don't think laughing at him in person would be any better for him than what we're doing now," Gleb countered. "Besides, I just got this seat nice and warm. If we go out there, all that ass-heat will be lost."

"That's a very good point." Mel nodded solemnly. "You gotta conserve ass-heat. It's the only heat that gives so much back to you."

His eyebrows lowered in the middle, just a tiny fraction but enough to confirm the speculative feeling that Gleb was getting from him.

"Pretty weird timing, wasn't it," Gleb said, trying to stay ahead of the curve. "I say he's got some payback coming and then BAM, down he goes like a sack of turds." He suddenly remembered Eth doing

86

the same thing when Gleb had begun to suspect him of having unusual abilities.

It hadn't worked for very long and now Gleb, exposed to his leader's expanded *understanding* of the universe, found himself wondering how long *he* could keep from being exposed.

He had to ease up on using his abilities and he certainly should refrain from the urge to take credit for such acts. His speech about kismet and Manu, the god of kismet, served nothing but his own ego.

Still, the holo of Davu writhing on the deck was just too satisfying. He knew he wouldn't have done anything different if he had the chance.

Except maybe keeping his mouth shut.

"I'm linking Siri's station to this feed," Mel said. "She's probably back there dreading the moment when her hatch opens. This should give her a little relief, for this shift at least."

Gleb could feel Mel's affection for her. "Malik is tormenting her." He said without any doubt. "And you'd like to rid her of him."

Mel shook his head ruefully. He finished sending the link so Siri could watch her tormenter's agony. "Pretty transparent, aren't I? Sadly, it takes more than wishes."

"It also takes a willingness to get murdered by an officer's pet, apparently." Gleb reopened his progress screen to see he'd be able to get a complete set of data. "What do you think's wrong with the bastard? Genital parasites, maybe?"

"We can only hope," Mel said. "On a less satisfying note, it looks like we've got that viral code isolated to a maintenance data subbank. The older backup is clean and it hasn't been written to since the virus showed up, so I'm gonna go ahead and kill the original and replace it with the older version."

"Well, I suppose we can spend more time watching Davu now." Gleb shut down the link to his suit and erased the link trace. "Maybe he's just into interpretive dance?"

"Oh! Maybe you're onto something there," Mel chuckled. "Very artistic, brilliant nuance from old Davu! I really think he's captured the emotions, the sheer pathos of getting a really solid kick in the balls."

"Believable and utterly gratifying," Gleb added. "I'd recommend this performance to anyone, though I'd love to see him tackle a really difficult subject matter. Something like 'asphyxiating in space' would really be a fitting challenge for a performer of his caliber."

"Perhaps with the right producer we could get a show like that up and running." Mel's tone was suddenly darker and Gleb could feel how much the man would like to see Davu gone.

He risked another link and used it to project a holo linked to his suit's data core. Mel was far too interested in Davu's predicament to notice what his co-worker was doing.

"Look at that!" Mel exulted. A Quailu was stepping around the writhing Human and continuing on as if there wasn't a crewman in agony in the middle of the corridor.

"Everybody's an art critic," Gleb said, trying to make sense of the data. One folder was named 'Leverage'. *Let's start with that.* He opened it to find dozens of sub-folders, each with a system name and each filled with similar economic data-points.

He created a table and used it to pull up the data from each folder. It showed a long list of expenditures and revenues. He filtered out any data that didn't relate to the Meleke Corporation.

Each one showed an extinct-species surcharge for their wardu purchases. There were other commonalities, but this seemed the most promising.

Many worlds in the HQE had never developed sentient life but still had perfectly habitable biospheres. In such a case, the ruling lord could contract with the Meleke Corporation to take over the rights to a suitable, extinct species for use as wardu.

The corporation maintained a host of explorers who conducted deep expeditions outside of HQE space. There was no shortage of planets where a species rose to pre-eminence and then managed to destroy their world's ability to support them but they had to be found and their genes catalogued for sale.

What if they'd gotten lazy? Could the lords in this file be vulnerable because their wardu populations weren't extinct? Gleb looked up in response to a chuckle from Mel. The holo showed Davu on his feet, one hand against the bulkhead, trying to make his way in the direction of sick-bay.

Could pressure be applied individually if an 'outed' lord was willing to expose the Meleke Corporation's role? They'd almost certainly claim innocence and they'd be believable. Gleb certainly would have believed them. *Who the hells would choose a non-extinct species when there were so many extinct ones to choose from?* He frowned.

Weren't there?

A Useful Idiot
The Mulge, *Eridu System*

"Normalization complete," the helmsman announced.

"No unexpected activity," the tactical officer advised. "We are clear to begin falling in to the primary planet."

Ilgi could feel the eagerness from his bridge crew and he fed it right back to them. *Finally let off the leash!* He gave a silent prayer to the gods, thanking them for bringing Memnon to their tiny holdings.

Ilgi's *illustrious* father had been content to sit on his two-world fief, despite all the churning conflict infesting the empire. Ilgi had scorned the old man in secret and, when Memnon had come suggesting expansion, openly for all to hear.

As a third son in a two-planet fief, he stood to inherit nothing. He'd be a penniless awilu, unless the family grabbed whatever they could while the grabbing was good.

After an hour closeted with Sandrak's new heir, the old man had surprised his entire court by announcing he would press a claim against Eridu. It had caused a stir. The old fool had been musing with the idea of letting the claim lapse last year so he could save the handful of credits it cost to keep it registered.

And now he was sending Ilgi to Eridu.

And this would just be the start! Memnon had favored Ilgi with a chat before the empire's richest heir had departed for Throne-World. He'd hinted at a string of small holdings that would, if taken quickly, put their family on the voting roll for the next emperor.

Memnon had said nothing explicitly, but he'd hinted at the possibility of assassination. Nothing too overt, but the idea of moving Ilgi up the ladder was clearly on the wealthy visitor's mind. It was incredible, the young noble had said, how many unexpected young awilu were rising to the rank of elector in these tumultuous times.

"Engage the pitch drives," Ilgi commanded. "Bring the fleet into attack range."

An elector! Ilgi thought. *A prince of the empire, and it starts here.* His father had turned him loose with a small fleet. He had orders to take Eridu with the understanding that Ilgi would become its new lord.

But he'd said nothing about taking any *other* systems! Once they were done here, he planned to leave a token holding force, conscript the local forces and use them to help take the *next* world in his grand scheme.

Fallow and graze, he thought. Repeat the process enough times and he'd be on his way to greatness. He had an older brother and sister to deal with but he'd find a way to get rid of them.

The crew, of course, didn't know exactly what he was thinking but they could feel his aggressive optimism and they were amped up for the fight ahead, which fed back into Ilgi's wild optimism. The loop was interrupted abruptly when an intrusion alarm sounded and everyone jumped in surprise and their helmets flowed shut with a series of loud clacks.

His dreams of glory stepped politely aside, making room for the fear that now assaulted him, amplified, of course, by his relatively green crew. "How could there be intruders out here?" he demanded.

The tactical officer was glaring down at his displays. "We saw no evidence of ships in the area," he insisted. "No vessels approaching…"

Every head on the bridge turned to a hole that flowed open on the starboard side of the bridge. Only one of the crew thought to pull out a sidearm and she had it halfway raised when she simply froze.

Ilgi growled in anger, broken from his fear-trance by the sight of someone coming up with a good idea and stopping in mid-implementation. He'd show the intruders what happened when they messed with the wrong ship! He reached for his sidearm…

Anger decided dreams of glory had been wise to leave and quickly followed suit, replaced again by fear. His hand should have been grasping the hilt of his ceremonial firearm, by now, but it hadn't moved. He tried again, alarm growing as he realized that none of his muscles were answering to commands.

The bridge lighting levels dropped by half and began to flash slowly in an erratic pattern. Ilgi felt the lights nudging at his fear and he could feel the rest of the bridge crew, their fright ebbing and flowing with the light.

They were all frozen in place, most of them looking, like Ilgi, at the opening in the hull and their imaginations were running wild. Whatever came through that opening couldn't be good.

Footsteps sounded on deck plates, proving that the atmosphere hadn't been vented during the breach.

Ilgi twitched in time to the footsteps, his rapid breathing beginning to fog the lower edges of his visor. A bipedal creature encased in standard, armored EVA gear strode slowly onto the bridge. The armor was adjusted for a species with a relatively flat face and the intruder stopped for a moment while more of its kind flowed around him to disarm the crew.

It had a light gray skull painted on the face plates.

Humans? Ilgi thought with an involuntary shudder. He'd heard the stories. Mishak's pirates. They'd supposedly savaged Memnon's fleet at Sippar and nobody had seen the attack coming, nor could they find where the Human ships had been concealed. They'd smashed five ships as a friendly warning.

And now they were taking an interest in Ilgi.

The Human with the skull on his helmet began moving again, slowly, head turning from side to side as he passed between Ilgi's crewmen. He passed out of sight to his left.

Ilgi's breathing slowed a little and his suit's ventilator started to catch up with the moisture on his internal-display visor. He didn't know how they were doing this or what they wanted but…

He took a sharp intake of breath on reflex as he suddenly felt the Human's mind on his right. The shallow, rapid fear-breathing returned in full force as he felt the alien's attention focused on him.

It was as if the creature had just materialized next to him, staring at him. Ilgi had felt absolutely nothing from him and then there was sudden awareness of a cold mind, stark and disciplined, malevolently powerful.

He let out a strangled sound, not quite a yelp, as strong hands grasped his arms and began dragging him toward the hole. His skin darkened in shame as his suit's moisture reclamation system began filtering a fresh flow of liquid.

He wanted to scream as he passed through the makeshift portal but he had no voluntary muscle control. They pushed him up against a bulkhead and restraints snaked out from the nanite panel to hold him.

The Humans flowed back into their craft and the hole closed behind the last one, the one with the skull. The hum of pitch-drives told him they were underway and he felt a stab of hope.

Surely, they'd be detected as soon as they move away from the hull! Ilgi thought.

"That's far enough." Ilgi heard the voice over his helmet's speakers. They moderated their individual volumes to replicate the direction from which the sound came. It was the skull-suited one, though that was hardly a surprise. Ilgi had formed the very definite opinion that he was the one in charge.

But why let Ilgi listen in on their channel? He felt a prickle of fear that they might not be planning on letting him survive whatever they had planned.

And why were they staying so close? Did they not care if they were detected? Were they using him as a hostage to prevent the fleet firing?

The skull melted away as the Human helmet opened.

And Ilgi wished it hadn't.

He'd realized, staring into that flat face, that he was no longer feeling anything from him. He could sense the other Human crew but there was nothing from this one. It was like staring at a corpse or a Zeartekka.

It was probably just the unsettling silence from his captor's mind but Ilgi couldn't shake the feeling that the Human was somehow sensing *his* thoughts. That was nonsense, of course, because no other species in the empire or even beyond its fringes had ever been known to have that ability.

It was an incredibly uncomfortable feeling and, as the silence stretched out, he could take it no longer.

"What do you think you're doing?" he demanded, trying to sound fierce but fairly certain that fierce Quailu didn't speak in hoarse squeaks.

No response.

"We're still sitting in the middle of my fleet," he warned, pleased to hear his voice sounding a little steadier now. "They'll come for me and, when they do, you'll be begging me for death!"

The alien's mouth curled up at the corners, making Ilgi think the Human was about to bite him, but then he felt amusement from his captor. *So his control has limits,* Ilgi thought, but then he shuddered again. *Or is he deliberately showing me his amusement?*

Either way, the threat of capture clearly held no fear for the Human. Were Ilgi's officers on the take? Had the captains accepted bribes to let this creature seize him from his own vessel?

"By now," the Human said calmly but startling Ilgi out of a year's lifespan, "you've gotten around to wondering whether I've suborned your senior officers to let me nab you like this."

Ilgi wished they could go back to the silent treatment. How the devils did the vile creature know?

"Please understand…" The Human raised a warning hand. "I'm not mentioning this because I want to put your suspicions to rest. I mention it because I'm fairly certain that I'm right and it's vitally important for *you* to understand that I can think rings around you."

The flat-faced creature tapped the side of his head. "I have the incongruous good fortune to have been grown as a combat slave, a *leader* of combat slaves, to be more precise. It gives my brain a *good turn of hoof,* as you Quailu are fond of saying."

"How wonderful for you," Ilgi retorted, angry that he couldn't think of anything better.

"It can be useful," the Human acknowledged. "For example, you're almost certainly not happy with your rejoinder. Not a very elegant riposte, as I'm sure you know. It could apply to my statement, I suppose, but it works equally well for news of a betrothal or the announcement of a naming day celebration…

"You might have tried any combination of the words *hoof* and *head*. I *did* leave that lying in your path, you know."

Ilgi had to fight the absurd desire to come up with something witty, especially now that the dratted creature had neutralized a particularly good line of possibilities by mentioning the same two words he'd been feverishly working on combining. His mind was spinning.

He bumped his head against the bulkhead when the Human suddenly moved in close, eyes only a hand's-breadth from his.

"Why are you here?" his captor demanded.

"Why am I here?"

"Hey!" An admonitory finger appeared between their faces. "No jumping the queue; I asked you first!"

"We're taking this system!" Ilgi was completely bewildered. "I'd have thought your nimble brain would have discerned such an obvious fact!" It felt better, getting a decent insult in. *When I'm an elector, I'll track this creature down and...*

"Perhaps I give you too much credit," the Human suggested. "Let me be explicit so your next answer isn't something along the lines of 'because you dragged me here and stuck me to a wall'.

"Why are you suddenly intent on taking systems? Why draw the ire of the powerful houses friendly to your victims? You can't hope to fight them off when they come."

"I can if I'm stronger than them by the time they mobilize," Ilgi blurted, wanting to show this Human that he wasn't a complete fool.

"Still..." The Human paused for a moment, gazing down at the sigil on Ilgi's chest. "... There aren't many systems you can take on in this sector..." He looked back to Ilgi's face. "You think you can turn yourself into an elector and claim imperial privilege?"

Ilgi's mouth gaped open, though he was unaware of it. *How had the Human ferreted that out so quickly? Not that it mattered, of course, because...*

"How much time have you spent researching the electoral system? I ask because it seems as though you've heard someone mention imperial privilege once but never bothered with the finer details.

"For example," he continued, "a claim to elector rank must show evidence that your holdings are in good economic and civil order.

96

You would need the military and civil authorities on each world to swear allegiance, much like they did at Dur, when my own lord seized his traitorous uncle's holdings."

The Human moved his head from side to side for some reason. "I doubt you'll find things so easy. The locals will hold out, go into hiding. They have to know they can count on the very interference you hope to forestall by becoming an elector."

That strange head movement again. "Your plan... It defeats *itself*! Someone's been whispering sweet nonsense in your ear." He leaned back to give Ilgi some breathing space.

"I'll ask you something more specific. Why did that *someone* send you out here and how did he induce your father to ignore the backlash that would almost certainly cost him one of his more disposable sons?"

Ilgi was appalled. If it seemed so clear to him now, why had he not come to the same conclusions without having to be abducted and subjected to the scorn of a former wardu?

"What leverage does he have over your father?" his captor demanded.

Ilgi wanted nothing more than to turn his fleet around and ask his father the same question.

The Human sighed. "Take us back in," he called over his shoulder. "This one knows nothing of use." He turned away from Ilgi. "Open a portal back to the home universe."

The Human facing him was also unreadable. "A... portal... Yes. Very well, sir." He turned and stalked away with a purposeful stride. "All hands!" he shouted, "Secure all gear and stand by for transdimensional maneuvering! Bring the singularity back online!"

Trans-dimensional maneuvering? Ilgi shivered in horror. *What kind of technology does Mishak have at his disposal?*

"All hands, activate phase-shift shielding," the leader commanded as his skull-faced helmet flowed back into place. "Harlan, that means you as well. If I find you frozen in place, I'll have you dragged aboard this one's ship and leave you with him!"

The fool has no concept of security, Ilgi marveled. *He's given too many hints. So the paralysis was some kind of by-product of the trans-dimensional shift?*

He didn't know if he'd be able to do much with that information, but it would at least save him from soiling his armor if it happened again. The best news, of course, was that they were returning Ilgi to the *Mulge*.

He could feel the paralysis come over him again, but this time he knew it was just a by-product of trans-dimensional travel and not some malevolent whim of the gods.

"We're home again." The other Human stuck his head around the corner. "Hard against the *Mulge's* bow."

A hole was opening in the outer hull, just where Ilgi had been dragged into this ship.

"Give me a hand." Skull-face grabbed Ilgi's wrists as the restraints retracted. The other one grabbed his feet.

Together, they hauled him through the portal and back onto his own bridge. The crew were still there, though he didn't know if they'd been frozen the whole time or if they'd been able to move while he was gone.

They dumped him in a heap in the middle of the central space where the holo-screens were projected. He was face down, knees pulled up and his posterior pointed at the ceiling.

Not at all consistent with the dignity of an awilu but, then, they'd probably spared his life.

The two Humans left and the portal closed again. In a few heartbeats, the paralysis wore off and he scrambled to his feet, trying to pretend he hadn't been presenting his rump as if to entice any interested parties.

"What keeps freezing us?" a plaintive voice asked from behind him.

"Tactical, report!" Ilgi demanded.

"No trace, sire. No indication whatsoever of any ships but our own."

"And you won't find any," Ilgi insisted grimly, pleased at least to know more than his crew. "They're no longer in the same universe as us."

"No longer in the same..." The tactical officer trailed off.

"Their drive involves a singularity," he told them. "Beyond that, I can't tell you much, but one of the side effects is the paralysis. They employ phase-shift shielding to avoid it."

The officers all turned to the chief engineer, who was mulling it over. "It might explain how they managed such a devastating strike against Memnon's fleet at Sippar," he allowed grudgingly, "but there's a hells of a lot of science needed to back up those vague concepts."

"What more do you need?" Ilgi demanded. "There was nothing near us and then, out of nowhere, there's a ship burrowing through our hull and we can't move a muscle. What alternate theories do *you* have that explain this?"

"I have none, sire."

"Nor do I," Ilgi admitted generously. "So let's set a course for home and bring the path-drives online."

"Home, sire?" the tactical officer asked. "This system is ripe for conquest..."

"But Mishak's forces have technology that we can't hope to match and they're firmly opposed to this venture!" Ilgi thought it wiser not to explain that he'd seen the end of this course of action and it almost certainly led to his own death.

He wasn't about to tell his crew that he'd probably been sent out here to get himself killed and them along with him.

What he wanted to do was go home, shove his pistol into his father's face and demand to know what leverage Memnon had applied. He wanted to know why he'd been chosen to die fighting for some insignificant back-galaxy dust-hole, aside, of course, from the fact that he'd been stupid enough to fall for it in the first place.

Human Intel
Hab-Ring, Kurnugia 2

Jay stepped off the orbital shuttle, his outrage not entirely feigned. The price quoted at the orbital station had been thirty-eight thousand credits – an already extortionate sum – but the 'customs clearance' fee had been an extra fifteen thousand.

They don't announce that, of course, until they reach the hab-ring. From there, it's either pay the fee or pay *twenty* thousand to return to orbit. The third option was to make a sudden descent to the lava-fields, five kilometers below the massive hab-ring circling the planet's equator.

He shook off the anger and took in his surroundings. He had to admit...

This made sense.

He'd accumulated a long list of minor infractions while aboard the *Mouse*. He'd set up a gambling-ring, a small black-market in 'lost' gear and he'd set up an external network to sell reactant within the empire's much larger black-market.

Okay, he thought with an unconscious shrug, *that last one was pretty major*. But he'd been grown for a certain type of life and serving aboard a cruiser was just too dull.

There *were* others who had trouble adjusting to fleet life but he knew he was feeling it more than most. The urge to go 'on the hunt' was just too strong in him.

When they'd hauled him in front of Eth, he'd been certain the commander would hand down a harsh sentence. He didn't expect the meeting to turn into a recruiting session.

He took a deep breath and joined the flow of pedestrian traffic, letting it show him the pulse of the place.

"Kurnugia is a nexus of criminal activity," Eth had said, startling Jay who'd been expecting the worst. "Few places generate useful intel like a criminal hotspot. I need someone to settle in there, to be our eyes and ears on the *hab*." He'd stabbed a finger at Jay's chest.

"You seem like someone who can pull that off. You were setting up a minor criminal enterprise right under my own nose. If I turn you loose on Kurnugia, you'd be able to… 'fit in'."

There'd been no need to elaborate. 'Fit in', meant looking like he belonged. He knew it meant more than just showing up with funds and renting an apartment.

He needed a local back-story. He needed the criminals of Kurnugia to remember his arrival, remember how he started his hard-scrabble climb from the bottom of the heap. That was what it would take to be effective here.

He slipped sideways through the flow of pedestrians and made his way through the progressively slower sides of the slidewalk until he'd reached the stationary zone. He gazed at the plaz-shielded front of a weapons-vendor.

The reflection showed the Enibulan who'd been tailing him since he'd left the shuttle docks and he forced himself not to show the grin that he felt.

He'd noticed an arched tunnel, twenty meters up the street. A perfect spot for the Enibulan to *educate* Jay on the perils of ignoring the sub-syndicate that ruled this small region of the city.

Jay turned and strolled toward the tunnel, gawking around like a typical new-arrival. *Should I let him beat me up or start out a little stronger?* He mused.

Either way, the process had begun.

Covering
The Deathstalker, *Henx System*

Gleb stood in the common area, eating his main meal for the day. The Humans were allowed to get their food from the mess hall but were forbidden to sit and eat there.

A heavy hand fell on his shoulder, spinning him around, nearly spilling his food from the tray.

"Where are my food credits?" Davu demanded, his tone jumping sharply upwards at the end.

Gleb had been keeping a steady flow of small calcified fragments flowing from the man's kidneys. His diet, fuelled by extorted meal credits, was the satisfyingly-ironic cause of his current distress.

"Oh, that," Gleb muttered around a mouthful of something starchy. "I forgot."

"You forgot!" Davu mocked. "Well, now you're gonna learn what happens when you *forget*! What?" This last was to Mel who'd come to stand in front of Davu.

"It's my fault, Davu," Mel insisted. "I must have forgotten to tell him how things work here."

"This true?" Davu demanded of Gleb.

"What?" Gleb blurted, truly surprised at this turn of events. "No! He warned me I had to give you a cut!"

"I'd believe Mel before I ever believe a new guy like you," Davu insisted, "and the fact that you haven't been complying for the last three days tells me he's right."

He drove his fist at Gleb's face and Gleb had to remind himself not to duck. The impact hurt like the demons but didn't do enough damage to keep him from his next shift.

"That's for lying to me!" Davu shouted, barely hiding another wince.

"You'd all better get your heads out of your exit portals!" he yelled at the crowd of quiet Humans. "You've forgotten how lucky you are to be serving on this ship as free-borns! Those slave-borns on Mishak's ships don't get the same perks you do!"

He turned on Mel. "Suit," he ordered.

Mel deactivated his suit, stepping out from the footplates with a quick warning glance at Gleb.

Gleb understood. If he interfered in what was to come, he'd only make things worse for Mel. *Dammit, Mel! Why the hells are you doing this? You barely know me!*

They'd been getting along well enough in the comms suite but Gleb didn't think that would justify taking a beating for him.

And it was a hells of a beating. Davu may have been practically illiterate in terms of the comms systems, but he was an artist at the careful application of violence.

Gleb's fingernails were digging into his palms, drawing blood. If he knocked Davu out by pinching off his cranial artery for a brief instant, the bastard would take it out on Mel to assuage his own embarrassment. If he killed Davu outright, the Quailu officers would never believe he hadn't been killed by some or all of the Humans in the room.

All he could do was stand there and watch.

This was how people like Davu gained power over others. Even Gleb, who could kill the man with a thought, who'd been keeping him in agony for several days now to protect Siri, came to realize he should have just given him a cut of his ration credits.

Davu almost certainly knew Mel was lying but he'd rather punish someone else and leave it on Gleb's conscience.

And this was Davu's proof of how much better off they were on this ship than on one of Mishaks? The sad thing was that it worked. Gleb had felt no disbelief from the Humans at Davu's assertion.

There they all stood, feeling grateful that they had it so good.

It wasn't until the distracting feelings of the beating had ceased and subsided into a dull agony that Gleb finally registered what he'd heard. *Free-born?*

These people had all stepped out of their maturation chambers as mushkenu?

Where they'd come from was already a mystery but they'd been grown as free citizens? That small fact seemed enough to let these Humans, who were treated worse than slaves, place themselves above those like Gleb.

Gleb was proud of his hard-won Mushkenu status. He frowned. *Aren't I?* He had to admit that a part of him would rather burn the whole damn system to the ground.

He pushed the idea to the back of his mind and joined the others as they helped Mel back to his feet. He placed one of Mel's feet onto a footplate and stepped back to give the suit room to close up around the heavily bruised body.

He could have carried Mel to the comms suite – he'd still have to serve out his full shift, which was about to start – but the suit would do a much better job, practically doing the walking for him.

Davu stormed out, smacking a tray out of a woman's hands and sending her food flying all over the compartment. "Clean that mess up!" he snarled as he left the compartment.

"Dammit, Mel!" Gleb hissed at him. "Why the hells did you have to go and do that? It was my own damned fault for not handing over the credits, you silly, soft-headed bastard!" Shaking his head, Gleb put a gentle hand on the back of Mel's neck. "You'd better screw something big up so I can return the favor!" He grimaced as he felt a fresh wave of pain from the man who'd started to laugh but only aggravated his wounds. "It hurts, doesn't it?"

"Like buggery," Mel wheezed.

"C'mon. Let's get you up to the comms room. You can lie down behind the cryo-bank and rest while I handle the coding."

Nobody asked you to do that! He thought. The last thing he needed on an enemy ship he was trying to get off of was a friend, someone who'd be in trouble once Gleb was found missing.

But now he was stuck with one.

Family Chat
The Deathstalker, *Outer Henx System*

Even as a hologram, Sandrak was intimidating. He leaned forward, making Memnon take an involuntary step backwards. "Five ships?" he growled. "Your brother destroyed five of my ships and you scampered away like a frightened child?"

"It was a legal demonstration," Memnon protested, his face darkening, sweat stinking of shame. "I can't agree to a demonstration and then retaliate. The forms must be observed!"

"The forms must be observed," Sandrak mocked in a whining tone. "Do you even understand what the forms really are?"

Even though he knew he was giving the wrong answer, the obvious answer, Memnon was unable to stop himself. "They're the agreed rules for conduct between belligerent parties. They govern our interactions so we…"

"Shut your weed-hole!" Sandrak said calmly, which he somehow managed to make more menacing than a shout. "The forms are rules made by the powerful, people like me, to control the weak and spineless." He extended his neck forward toward Memnon, giving the clear impression that he'd meant the second group to include his new heir.

"When you act as though you're bound by those rules, you send a clear message to others. You're telling them you're not one of the powerful, not someone to be feared."

Memnon tried to hold his emotions in check but it was hard. Even though his father couldn't read them through a holo-interface, he still held his anger back. "So you would have attacked?" he asked sullenly.

"Of course!"

"Against ships you couldn't see? Ships that had to be so close that they could have boarded us? Those missiles closed so quickly our point defense systems didn't even get target locks!"

"Yes!"

"We've heard they have some kind of trans-dimensional capability now," Memnon insisted. "How do you propose to hit a ship that can just jump into another universe at will?"

"That's a pile of turds!" Sandrak scorned. "If your enemy tries to deceive you, I find that swift and brutal force evaporates that deception like a fart in a strong breeze!"

Dammit, does the old goat have an answer ready for everything? The worst of it was that Memnon couldn't say his father was wrong. Perhaps, if he'd gone on the immediate attack, he would have found those damned ships.

Sandrak was the lord of nineteen systems, after all, and you didn't reach a pinnacle like that without making a lot of smart decisions.

Repressing a sigh, he straightened his back and looked his father in the eye. "I'll adjust my responses regarding the forms."

"*There's* a big part of your problem," Sandrak lectured. "You talk of your responses. Why let others dictate the pace? Make them respond to *you* or I'll take those ships back and find someone who knows what to do with them.

"And get that gods-damned holo-crest fixed!" Without another word, Sandrak faded from sight.

Memnon blew out an explosive breath. Every time he thought he'd caught up, his father found a way to prove he was really ten steps behind.

Curious, he opened the call-reception menu and brought up the holo-crest that callers would see while waiting for him to step into the holo-camera's field of view. His fists clenched.

"Comms officer," he roared, "get in here with your team right now!"

He wanted to smash something but he didn't want the comms team to see evidence of a tantrum when they entered. He stewed in his anger as he watched his senior comms officer enter from the bridge hatch.

She sensed his rage and radiated the appropriate alarm at his state. Her petty officer and two ratings followed her in and they reacted with even more alarm, given the gap between them and their enraged commanding officer.

"Perhaps you could explain how this came to be?" Memnon inquired in silky tones, just the sort of silk used to strangle an awilu for high crimes. He gestured to the holo-crest.

He could feel the brief instant of amusement from them all that was quickly smothered with horror and that was to be expected. Who, after all, wouldn't find it somewhat amusing that his holo-crest identified him as *Melvin the Bastard*?

The horror, of course, was because they knew he'd felt the amusement and, given the fact that they were responsible for anything related to communications on the *Deathstalker*, they'd only be making their predicament worse by being amused. There was no way this little meeting was going to end well for them.

"Sire, I can't believe that any of my people would do something like this," the officer insisted. "It's inconceivable!"

"Is it really," he asked, mimicking his father's quiet tone of menace, which he felt he was carrying off reasonably well. He moved so the crest hung between them. "You think such a thing is impossible?"

"I know my people, sire, and none of them would ever be so foolish!"

"And yet," Memnon replied, his rage tempering to a cutting edge, "the evidence would seem to indicate a discrepancy with your views."

"But they would never…" She quailed at what she felt in her leader's mind. "There are Humans working in our division, sire…"

"Those half-wit apes?" he sneered. "If you want to find a scapegoat, lieutenant, then I suggest you come up with something a little more believable than some hairless arboreal."

"We've heard they can be pretty dangerous, sire…" The petty officer trailed off under the full weight of his anger.

"Who is responsible?" Memnon shouted, drawing a dagger from a sheath on his chest.

The lieutenant tore her eyes from the blade, knowing it would take a life before it returned to its sheath. She took a deep breath, standing straight. "I am responsible, sire. However it happened, it's ultimately my fault that it did."

Damn her for being noble! Memnon raised his blade and drove it down into the forehead of the petty officer who'd spoken up earlier, easily penetrating the thin band of bone that ran between the frontal and temporal plates.

He yanked the blade out as the crewman slumped to the deck. "This also is on your account, lieutenant," he said loudly, not from anger but because he wanted to be heard over the drumming of the dying crewman's feet on the decking.

There was a piquancy in the lieutenant's shock and it pleased him. He'd managed to set an example and, though many of the crew would soon forget it, *she*, at least, never would.

"Now," he said, feeling in control again. "Trace this abomination. How did it replace my sigil and how long has it been there?"

He was far more concerned about the second item than the first but he felt it was more important to show concern about the system's security. "Now!" he prompted them, waving at the holo to indicate they should work there in the ready room.

He certainly didn't want them pawing through the coding for this in front of the bridge crew. He'd be known as *Melvin the Bastard* throughout the ship in a matter of days.

One of the ratings opened the underlying code for the holo-crest. He scrolled through the rows, his consternation growing as he worked.

"What the hells is eating at you?" Memnon finally demanded.

A shudder of fear. "Sire, the code for this is widely dispersed, both in function and in its incursion."

"Pretend that I'm not a comms rating and say that again," Memnon suggested acidly.

The rating seemed to contract, as though he were trying to pull his head inside his body. "The code for this, sire... It seems to have arrived from a variety of sources, over the course of several days. It's also dispersed in separate subroutines.

"You'd never find it, unless you knew it was there," he added, gesturing fearfully up at the shimmering insult. "I don't know if it's even possible to trace it back to a source."

"Alright." Memnon surprised the tech with his calm response. He'd already killed someone for it and *who* was far less important to him than *when*. "When did this start replacing my original crest?"

"Three days ago, sire."

Memnon didn't move a muscle for several heartbeats. He stared at the terrified rating. *How many lords have I talked to in the last three days? Five? Six?*

And hadn't they looked amused at the start of those conversations? He knew that might be his imagination, but there was no doubting that they'd all seen that embarrassing name.

Forget it spreading on the ship, the bridge crew had all heard him called that name by his brother, anyway. Now it was going to spread throughout the entire empire.

"It would be easy enough to put together a list of who was on the bridge when you're brother misheard you," the officer suggested, probably prompted by Memnon's own feelings.

He waved it off. "No, by now, some of them have almost certainly told the story to their friends. The entire ship probably already knows. The lesson learned here is vigilance."

He stepped in closer to the three Quailu. "You will ensure that safeguards are put in place to prevent this from happening again. Is that clear?"

They all voiced their assent.

"Good! Now have that cleaned up," he pointed at the dead petty officer as he left the room.

A lesson well learned, he thought and he didn't mean about comms security. The rules regarding crewmen in dereliction of duty were clear in calling for a proper tribunal. He'd ignored the rules and simply acted in killing the PO. He'd set an example and, more importantly, showed his crew that he *was* one of those exalted Quailu of power for whom the rules had no shackles.

He might not yet have the title that came from ruling a system of his own, but he had power and that was infinitely better than being called *lord*.

Exit
The Deathstalker, Outer Henx System

"You're kidding me," Gleb insisted, laughing. "His ass?"

"Burnt a patch of hair off each cheek," Mel insisted. "Looked like one of those ground-apes from Sulis Prime!"

"He must have taken revenge for an 'accident' like that!"

"Well, yeah, but he never found out who was behind it, so he was just a miserable bastard to all of us for nearly a standard lunar... well... more of a miserable bastard." Mel grinned. "So it was more than worth it!"

He shrugged. "Mostly, he seems to just let it slide if it's some small bit of mischief. Like that shock he got from the door to our sleeping quarters two shifts ago. If he can ignore it, he usually will. Probably figures it's the price to pay for his other perks."

Gleb frowned. "Two shifts ago? Didn't hear about that one."

"Sure," Mel nodded conspiratorially. "I'm sure you didn't even 'notice' the crossed wiring when I saw you fiddling with the access panel a few minutes beforehand.

"And, of course, you didn't spend an hour chumming around with him before that just so he wouldn't suspect you..."

Gleb kept his emotions away from his face but this was disturbing. He'd hot-wired a door to shock Davu? He approved but he just wished he could remember doing it.

And what the hells was he doing hanging around with a treasonous piece of refuse like that?

More to the point, why did he have no memories from any of this?

"But you'd think..." Mel began but stopped when a chime caught his attention.

He'd set up a chime to go off every time the door to the comms backup suite opened. Every time, Gleb could feel the man's apprehension as he checked the holo-feed. Every time he could feel his relief at seeing it was just Siri who'd set off the warning.

This time the relief didn't come.

"It's him!" Mel's despair was palpable, even if Gleb *hadn't* been able to read feelings. Davu was there, on the holo feed, along with three of his cronies. Then, as Siri backed away from Davu, fetching up against a bulkhead, the despair gave way to something far more palatable, something that offered options.

Rage.

"Mel," Gleb said in urgent warning. "You'll both end up getting killed…" He watched his friend jump up, his mind a riot of anger and violence, and run out of the compartment.

"Dammit!" he whispered to himself. He was planning on leaving the *Deathstalker* in favor of sneaking aboard Sandrak's flagship. He'd managed to find several rendezvous points where Memnon could count on meeting with his father, if necessary.

He was going to wait for a few more days and then ride to Sandrak's vessel on the outside of a shuttle during an upcoming meeting. Since none of the ships in question were under Mishak's command, none of the Humans were anywhere to be found in any ship's database.

He'd be able to repeat his strategy of claiming to be a transfer and just start working a shift. Humans were nothing more than a pool of emergency labor to keep these vessels running. A pool that merited no records.

He'd have been able to fit in easily, if it wasn't for the fact that he was about to meddle where he really shouldn't. He didn't see how he had any choice, though, so he jumped up and ran for the exit.

Screw it! he thought. *Careful plans were never my strong suit!*

He skidded to a halt, just inside the hatch to the backup suite. Mel was on the floor, one of Davu's cronies stood over him with a suit-lock. Gleb's friend was completely immobilized. The rage was still there but, absent the promised options, despair was shouldering its way back to the forefront.

Siri was still up against the bulkhead with a large wrench in her hand, the handle's pointy end held out toward Davu. She shot a confused glance at Gleb, not knowing whether he was there to help her or simply join Davu and his minions.

"You again!" Davu sneered at Gleb. "If you promise to behave, you can watch from there!"

"Are you out of your fornicating mind?" Siri demanded. "You move one step closer and I'm gonna smash your head open!"

"And then," Davu replied, "Mel, here, is gonna suffer an 'accidental' but entirely fatal suit-overload. That what you want?"

The room was a riot of emotions. Gleb felt Davu's sickening anticipation for what he had planned, Mel's shame at being the leverage that would make it all possible and Siri's growing resignation.

"Fornication!" she cursed, a little too appropriately, tossing the wrench aside. She activated the shutdown for her suit.

Gleb was too busy to notice. He'd managed to locate the right spot in each of the four intruders and he willed their arteries to pinch shut, drawing all of the necessary heat from Davu for the difficult attempt.

Just doing this on one target was hard enough but four was damned hard and the movement of physical matter took more energy than one might expect. He only needed a few seconds to shut down their brains but he held on for a little longer this time.

He wanted to make sure it was permanent.

He finally let go to find Siri, naked but still in the foot-pads of her now-folded suit. She was staring at the four bodies on the floor in clear bewilderment and not a little relief.

He shrugged when she turned to him. "A sight like that could give *any* man a heart attack," he told her with a friendly grin. "Not that I'm complaining," he added significantly, "but I think you can go ahead and close up your suit now."

She twitched her heels as Gleb walked over to kick the suit-lock away from Mel's back.

Mel climbed back to his feet. "That was you," he insisted, "but what the hells *did* you just do?"

"I really don't have time to go into it, at the moment. The question we need to ask right now is whether you trust me."

Mel and Siri exchanged confused glances.

"Right, fair enough!" Gleb conceded. "I've only been here a few days. Maybe a better question is *do you want to survive this situation?*"

They both looked down at the bodies.

"They're dead?" Mel asked.

"They sure as hells aren't taking a nap."

"Yeah, well…" Mel shrugged at Siri. "Sure, living sounds like a better idea than getting shot."

"Right." Gleb grabbed the wrench from the floor and smashed the power couple for the data storage containment unit. With the magnetic fields collapsed, the data disappeared in milli-seconds. "Let's get moving." He tossed the wrench.

"Stay calm," he said on his way out the hatch. "The state you two are in, you'll draw Quailu like cheevers to fresh grain."

"Where are we going?" Siri asked, rushing to catch up.

"Mess hall for emergency rations," he said, glancing to make sure Mel was keeping up, "then main comms to blind the bridge."

He held out an arm to stop them. A Quailu came strolling out from a side corridor, browsing messages on his wrist-holo. He couldn't help but feel the heightened emotions from Mel and Siri and he looked up in alarm, one hand reaching for his pistol.

Gleb *twitched*. He couldn't think of any other description for it. It was if he'd suddenly jumped forward in time a few seconds. He was even a couple of steps closer to the Quailu, who now had his weapon pointed straight at him.

"What are you filthy apes up to?" the junior officer demanded. "I can feel the mischief coming off you like reactor leak!"

Gleb tried to reach out for the Qauilu's cranial artery but it wasn't working. He felt a momentary flare of panic. To experience the kind of abilities he had, only to lose them, was horrifying, even worse than going blind.

He crushed the emotion, seeing the reaction to his fear in the Quailu's eyes. He could feel the alien's contempt, his curiosity...

He could *feel* it!

Gleb reached out again. He killed him quickly, starving his brain of oxygen, and snatching the pistol from his hand as the Quailu started slumping to the deck. He shivered, having forgotten to use his victim's heat, rather than his own.

Is this connected to what I did earlier, sabotaging the door? he wondered. *I seem to be two people in one brain...*

And the *other* person in his mind didn't seem to have access to his extraordinary abilities.

He shook his head angrily. This wasn't the time to dig into it. He was stumbling around the ship like a rank amateur.

Detailed planning may not be his strong suit but he at least had to stop acting reflexively. He pushed the Quailu corpse over to sit with its back to the bulkhead, arms draped over its knees.

Fortunately, they were on the middle watch and the ship was quiet but there were still three more Quailu that ended up sitting on the decking in the same pose as the first. Fortunately, he'd managed to remain in control of his mind the entire time.

When they reached the mess hall, Gleb had to repeat the performance with a junior lieutenant who'd demanded to know why they thought they could just wander into the mess outside of meal-times. This time, Gleb left the unfortunate fellow in his seat, hands on his knees.

Mel started shoving ration packs and water into a large duffel. "What the hells did you pose them for?"

"They like to claim they aren't superstitious," Gleb replied, staring down at his latest victim, "but we've seen a major lord launch an ill-advised invasion against Sandrak based on the blatherings of an oracle."

Mel stared at him until Siri grabbed his shoulder and pulled him over to a meal supplement dispenser. "Who are you?" he demanded.

"Their empathic connection to each other gives them a healthy respect for the supernatural," Gleb continued as if Mel hadn't spoken. He nodded at the body sitting in front of a cooling coffee. "When they start finding crewmen dead with no explainable reason, all posed the same, it'll spook the hells out of them."

He turned and swept past them, ignoring the look they were giving each other. "That's gonna have to be enough food. We need to keep moving."

He led the way up to main-comms.

"Where the hells have you scum been?" a Quailu senior lieutenant demanded when they walked into main comms. "The bridge holos are riddled with glitch-haze. By the gods! I'll see to it that all three of you are…"

He slumped to the deck.

118

Gleb raised an eyebrow at Mel who was dragging the officer over to one of the workstation chairs. The other man took the Quailu's weapon and posed his hands on his knees.

"What?" Mel demanded, shoving the pistol into his belt next to two others he'd already taken.

Gleb held his hand out. "His pistol is a family heirloom," Gleb explained. "It should do nicely."

He took the weapon from Mel and put it back in the dead officer's hand. Putting the Quailu's finger on the trigger, he fired one shot at the storage containment for the main system.

The data scattered and the collator algorithms, a finely crafted network of sub-atomic spins, lost cohesion. Data from the sensor suite, collectors mounted on the hull, had nowhere to go. It just routed into this chamber and returned to relatively homogeneous energy.

The ship was now blind.

"Good luck figuring this out," Mel muttered as Gleb put the dead officer's hand, still holding the weapon, back on his lap.

"Hangar," Gleb said, leading the way back out into the corridor.

They posed a petty officer at the bottom of the main ramp and a security NCO at the entry to the hangar.

Gleb peered around the corner of the larger cargo door leading into the hangar. "Fornication!" he muttered. "Two Humans in there with a Quailu officer."

He hadn't minded killing Davu and his cronies but *they* had it coming. He didn't mind killing the Quailu because he figured their species, with a few exceptions, could do with a little thinning out. The Humans in the hangar were another matter.

He didn't want to kill them but they'd be executed for sure if they lived while their Quailu PO didn't. He stifled the urge to indulge in further useless curses.

"Mel," he whispered, "none of us are in the system, right? None of the Human crewmembers?"

"That's right."

"So they won't know who's missing when we're gone?"

"I doubt they'd bother trying to figure it out. We're disposable."

Gleb had an idea of how to escape without getting the two Humans in the hangar executed. It was a bit over the top but the idea amused him and he couldn't let it go. "When the Humans freeze, approach them from behind and tie their wrists behind their backs. Don't let them see you. Put them face-down on the deck and make absolutely no sound. Stay with them; don't come close to the officer. If he approaches, move away."

"Okay." Mel stared at him, plainly wanting to ask several questions. "Then what?"

Gleb grinned. "Then I use the superstitious tendencies that lurk just below the surface of every Quailu."

He checked again. The officer was standing at the hangar bay's main launch portal, staring out at the other ships while the two Humans were moving cargo to a staging pad. He concentrated on them first, freezing them in place.

Mel and Siri moved as quickly as they could though the rubber pads on the soles of their armored feet could only attenuate so much sound. It kept them to just under a jogging pace.

They reached their targets, securing their wrists with the ubiquitous cable-tie dispensers that any comms tech had on their suit. They pushed both prisoners down onto their faces and Gleb released them to concentrate on the Quailu, who was starting to turn at the noise made by the surprised and now-released Humans.

He'd been stopped halfway and couldn't see past the pallets that hid the Humans. Gleb swung wide to get behind him unseen. He skirted around a row of shuttles, coming out behind the Quailu, who was starting to shiver, partly from fear and partly from the loss of body-heat.

Gleb shifted into character.

He was Nergal in the flesh, the lord of the underworld, the god of war and misery. The kind of god who'd kill you as soon as look at you.

For Gleb, that last part wasn't so much of a stretch…

He wanted to kill this interfering Quailu, to rend his flesh from his bones for daring to get in his way. He let his mind explore the many ways he could destroy this puny creature in front of him.

And he didn't try to hide it from the immobile officer. The fear washed back over Gleb in shuddering waves.

And then it happened again. He was suddenly two paces closer to the officer and he could feel nothing from him.

Gleb had to improvise and quickly. He drew back a fist and smashed it against the rear of the officer's skull, just where the transitory lobe connected the two hemispheres. He wasn't sure whether the Quailu had survived the blow but he couldn't wait for his ability to re-surface.

He waved Mel and Siri over. "I don't suppose either of you are flight rated? Never mind," he whispered as they both shook their heads in surprised negation. "I actually had this part planned out. Get in that one." He waved them up the ramp of a shuttle and followed them in.

He ran to the pilot's seat and opened the formation menu, setting the shuttle next to them to follow mode, a useful bit of programming for when a pilot found himself too injured to fly on his own. He fired up the engines on their shuttle and the other one whined to life as well.

"Strap in, folks!" He took over manual control, not wanting any more interaction with the ship's systems than was absolutely necessary. He managed to wobble his way across the deck without incident until he was passing out through the main launch portal. The belly of the craft hit the lower lintel of the opening with a screech, the following shuttle doing the same.

Once outside, he parked them close to the hull of the *Deathstalker* before getting up and running back to his shuttle's main data terminal. He linked it up with his suit. "Initiate scout-ship," he said, activating the code that Noa had diffidently suggested might come in handy.

The three helmets snapped shut and his two friends started with alarm as the hull began melting.

"Get over here," he urged. "Get between the attachments for the drive mounts. Those are the only sections of floor you can count on right now."

They didn't need to be told twice. Having spent most of their time in the belly of a heavy cruiser, they weren't terribly comfortable with the idea of a melting shuttle.

"I'm turning these two shuttles into a fast scout-ship," he told them, mostly to distract them from their fear.

"So you have time to answer a few questions, then?" Mel asked, reaching out to grab a bundle of conduits that snaked their way down the outer shell of the pitch drive.

"We *do* have a few minutes," Gleb admitted.

"You're not one of us, are you?"

Gleb chuckled. "Well, I'm not a free-born, if that's what you mean."

"You're from one of Mishak's ships?" Siri asked in amazement. "Did you desert?"

"No, I volunteered for this."

"No," Mel countered. "There's no way they'd trust a Human so far from their control, not even for free-borns and we get far more latitude than you."

"Do you really?" Gleb looked at them, waited until he could feel the doubt creeping in. "You've never been aboard a Human ship. All you *know* is what sphincters like Davu tell you."

The two shuttles were merging. The hulls opened up to show the drive from the other vessel sliding toward them, pulled in by long tendrils of nanites that flowed to join the growing deck plating as the gap closed.

"A Human ship, you said?" Siri said. "You meant us to pick up on that, didn't you?"

The hull was mostly closed now and the fine-tuning was well underway, placing seats and terminals from the old shuttles in their new locations.

"I did," he replied simply, "and you *did*. So you can both count on employment when we get out of here because I like clever people and I can always find a use for good comms techs."

An icon began blinking in his HUD. "That should do for now," he told them, stepping away from the drive. "Keep your suits buttoned until we get a chance to run some checks. For now we'll just confirm the base calibration on our engines and then take our chances on a full acceleration run. I'd rather die trying to escape than die on my knees in that fornicating dung-hole of a cruiser!"

He stepped to the newly placed data terminal, now between the two drives. The diagnostic showed an acceptable level of field coordination between the two pitch-drives. Gleb sighed. It also showed what Noa considered to be an *acceptable* output level for the grav compensators.

He remembered the stories from early tests on the scout class. "Hope you two have strong stomachs," he warned. "It's gonna get pretty uncomfortable but you should survive, as long as you don't drown in your own vomit."

"Well," Siri said, moving over to the co-pilot seat and activating the restraints, "I suppose that passes for a reassuring chat where Gleb's from."

Gleb patted the patrol commander's seat, set between the pilot chairs but set back far enough to allow the pilots to squeeze past. "Sit here, Mel."

Gleb slid into the pilot's seat and activated the restraints. He looked back to ensure Mel was secured. "Deep breaths, stay calm," he advised, turning back to activate the nav panel. He selected Henx 12 as his primary destination. "This is gonna feel weird."

He activated the course and the small craft leapt away from the *Deathstalker*. He could see Siri's arms come up to protect herself from the expected collision as the other ships of the fleet came racing their way at horrific speed.

They darted around the ships, their bodies being pulled in several directions at once as the grav emitters struggled to keep up with the wild variations in acceleration. Then they were clear of the fleet and racing out toward the distant point of light that was Henx 12.

It was a gas giant, which was why Gleb had selected it. If they picked up a pursuit, they should be able to shake it off in the dense gasses or at least wait until their pursuers' patience ran out.

"Feels like my chest wants to get up and walk around while the rest of me wants to stay put," Mel complained.

"Yeah, we use more emitters in this kind of ship," Gleb explained. "Didn't really want to waste time scavenging the other shuttles for spare parts, though. We were in kind of a rush to get out of there."

"Not a problem," Mel replied, "just saying…"

"We're getting a hail from the fleet," Siri announced.

"That's fine," Gleb told her. "We'll be in the soup in another six minutes. We'll ignore them until we can't hear them." He pulled up a small holo of the sector and put it between himself and Siri. "Still no pursuit. I think we're clear."

"What's the plan?" Mel asked. "We hide in the gas for a while but what then?"

"We'll head to Henx Prime." Gleb nearly lost his lunch and had to take a moment to bring his rebellious stomach under control. "You guys will be too recognisable so I'll have to go on to the next phase alone."

Siri's frown was barely visible through her visor. "How are we any more recognisable than you?"

"You'd be broadcasting thoughts about your daring escape from the *Deathstalker*," he explained. "The minute one of you got near a Quailu, they'd sense that something wasn't right and they'd be on you like a patch of prime sweet-leaf."

"I still don't see how that makes you…"

"They can't read me," Gleb cut her off, "unless I let them. I can control what they get from my mind."

"This has to do with how you killed them on the *Deathstalker*," Mel said quietly, "and how you froze those guys in the hangar."

"What are you?" Siri asked hesitantly.

Gleb could feel their fear and their desire not to offend him but their curiosity was stronger. He approved of that but there was a time and place for everything. "I'm a Human," he told them. "There's an explanation for everything you've seen but I can't tell you just yet."

"Because you're going back in?" Mel suggested.

"That's right." Gleb turned to look at them. "I can't risk you guys getting pinched before I get back here to pick you up. I *will* tell you everything, but not until we're all back with the fleet. Mishak's fleet."

He paused, realizing how much he was taking for granted. "I'm assuming you'll both want to take service with the Prince-presumptive's forces, I suppose. But it would be a waste if you didn't. You guys have NCO written all over you."

Mel laughed at this. "Human NCO's, right! Next you'll be telling us we'll have our commissions within the year!"

Gleb almost told them there were already a lot of Humans with the prince's commission but he held back. Their disbelief would hardly melt in the face of even more outlandish claims.

If he told them he was a ship's captain, they'd be certain he was lying. He would come back to Henx Prime only to find they'd disappeared.

"I know it's hard to believe," he began slowly, "but that's how things work in the prince's house forces. There are a lot of our people with ratings. The two of you would probably start out as petty officer 3rd class, as long as you start learning how to code while you're waiting for me to come back."

"That's a contract violation!" Siri exclaimed. "If the shipyards find out, you'd be cut off!"

"We were cut off three lunars ago," Gleb admitted, "but who gives a wet fart about something like that? What kind of fool would contract a shipyard when there are so many enemy ships out there, just waiting to change hands?"

"They can disable your captured ships, along with all the others," Mel said dryly. "It's not like they don't have safeguards against this sort of thing."

"That was actually the last straw," Gleb told them. "One of our programmers, the best of them, actually, managed to kill off all the poison-pill algorithms. He'd already found most of them when he started developing the first scout-class but our lord asked him to make a concerted effort so he could get out from under the Shipbuilder's Guild's hoof.

"The Guild cut us off but it was already too late by then." Gleb grinned wolfishly. "They shot themselves in the haunch, if you ask me."

He went quiet long enough that Mel finally obliged. "OK, I'll ask you…"

"When our Guild contract was still in place, they were entitled to keep us out of their designs and coding but they also had the right to lay claim to any innovations we might have come up with and we've been *very* busy.

"The rules have done a good job of keeping unrest to a minimum. Nobody can build up a technical advantage, as long as they have their Guild *privileges…* "

Gleb looked back at the windows at Siri's startled yelp and even he recoiled in horror as the gas giant expanded in their view with a brutal speed. He looked down to reassure himself that the pre-set course included a safe insertion into the atmosphere, but it already showed as complete. He looked back up to see a blue haze outside.

The gravity envelope in the small craft had stabilized but he still felt as though he might like to throw up, just from the fear of their suddenly terrifying approach to the planet. He could feel the cold sweat on his back, though the suit wicked it away for recycling almost immediately.

"OK, so FYI," he said shakily, "high-speed, automated approaches to anything can scare the skin right off you."

"Yeah," Siri replied in a small voice. "Timely warning, there, fella."

"I don't know how you guys came up with this design," Mel said, "but I'd be surprised if you didn't accidentally kill a lot of test pilots in the process."

"Probably took a few years off Hendy's lifespan." Gleb started moving the ship back up to a level where they could see out of the haze. "Nobody died, though. Just a lot of gut-emptying fear and physical discomfort."

"Funny they didn't even try to come after us," Mel mused.

"They don't have anything fast enough to catch us," Gleb slowed their ascent giving Mel time to work out the tactical implications. "Remember, we combined two pitch-drives. When they're calibrated properly, they put out an incredibly strong gradient.

"They'd have to use their path-drives and, even if they micro-path to the right spot and catch us up, we can just run from them all over again. Even their missiles can't catch us because they rely on pitch technology to fall toward us."

They emerged from the denser levels of the atmosphere and Gleb breathed a sigh of relief. "They're already gone."

"Not surprised," Siri enlarged the image. "We were on a high-alert status because you never know when you might get jumped. No sense sitting around in the same place if you've just had someone scamper off with the coordinates for every one of your ships."

"We'd do the same," Gleb confirmed, "if anyone ever ran off, that is."

"You've never had deserters?" Mel laughed. "You've been taking the official line a little too seriously, don't you think?"

"Operational fleets can get pretty boring when you're not busy tossing missiles around," Gleb replied. "Gossip is one of the few distractions. If we had someone desert, I can't imagine it staying quiet for very long."

Mel's amused snort showed his opinion of that and Gleb decided to let it go. "Let's fall down-well to Henx Prime." He set the new course and velocity. "But let's go at a more leisurely pace. At three-quarters speed, we'll still get there damned fast but without the intestinal gymnastics."

He activated the new course and the haze was whipped away in a heartbeat. He got up. "I've got time for a nice long nap. I'm gonna go stretch out in the back."

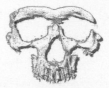

"The first batch is just around this corner, sire," the security officer said, his mind shivering with formless dread.

Memnon followed him into the side corridor where a holographic screen surrounded a Quailu who, at first glance, appeared to be sitting on the deck, leaned up against a bulkhead taking a nap. The holo-screen had a security warning scrolling across it and Memnon waved it away to get a better look.

"How did he die?"

"How do most folks die? Lack of oxygen to the brain." The security officer stared at the body. "The thing that unsettles me, though, is the scans don't show any underlying reason for that. No wounds, no congenital defects, no cardiac events. He's just a Quailu in the prime of his life…"

"A glitch in the shield matrix during a local stellar flare perhaps?" Memnon suggested.

"No signs of radiation, sire. Like I said, he was in perfect health and he just died."

"And how many more have you found?"

Another mental shudder. "There's three of them in the central corridor, one back near engineering, three Humans in the aft comms suite and an officer in main comms. All of them sitting like this, except for the lieutenant…"

"Who seems to have shot out the containment unit before shuffling off his mortal coil," Memnon cut in.

"It's as if someone or… something used them and then just took their souls…" The security officer trailed off under Memnon's scorn.

"There's always an explanation, lieutenant, no matter how incredible the evidence may seem, so let's go to the hangar and talk to our only live witness."

He let his scorn continue to radiate as they followed the ramp down to the flight operations deck. He didn't want this credulous fool reverting to his supernatural theories, so he made sure his own feelings were clearly known.

They entered the hangar bay to find the flight-deck duty officer sitting on a pallet of water condensers, rubbing at the back of his head and neck. The ship's surgeon was fussing over him with one of his trinkets but he moved aside as Memnon approached.

He checked in his stride for a heartbeat as he picked up the officer's emotions. Whatever had taken place down here, he'd been through a profoundly terrifying experience.

For the first time since he'd been paged by security, Memnon began to feel a trickle of fear himself. He almost didn't want to question the witness but he imagined how Sandrak would react to such a sentiment and forced himself to keep walking toward the injured officer.

"I'm told you met our unwelcome guest," he said. "Did you see his face?"

The officer let out a shuddering sigh and Memnon nearly recoiled from the emotions that came roiling out with the exhalation. "No, sire. I saw nothing. I felt him, though. He was less than an arm's reach behind me."

"And it never occurred to you to simply turn around and look?" Memnon demanded acidly.

"That's just it, sire! I wanted to, but I couldn't move a muscle!" He jumped up from the pallet at the feeling of scorn from his commanding officer. "No, sire. It wasn't from fear. I was simply frozen in place, which was certainly disconcerting, but I was stuck like that for a few moments before I ever felt him."

"Felt him?"

"That's right, sire. There was nothing at all and then, all of a sudden, I *felt* him, right behind me, full of menace, he was. He was powerful and he wanted to tear me to pieces. He wanted chaos, pain, destruction…"

"But who the devils *was* he?"

"He… he seemed to feel that he was…"

"Yes?"

"Nergal, sire."

Memnon had to force down a wave of fear. *Look at the facts!* he told himself as he stepped away from the flight-deck officer, seeking some distance from the turmoil in his mind.

He wasn't sure how to handle something like this but he could imagine what his pragmatic father would do. Whatever Memnon might or might not believe about this mess, he had to make his crew believe that he put his faith in a logical explanation, even if he didn't have one.

He watched the surgeon's mate, who'd finally gotten around to releasing the three Humans they'd found behind some pallets of supplies. He stepped over to them, ignoring their apprehension, and he bent down to pick up one of the cut restraints.

He left them rubbing their wrists and he walked back over to his two officers. "You feel that Nergal came here and showed you his mind?" he asked mildly.

"It's how it seemed, sire."

"And it doesn't seem the least odd," Memnon asked sarcastically, "that the lord of the underworld, the god of chaos and war, uses the same brand of prisoner restraints as half the empire's forces?"

Both junior officers stared at the restraint as though shocked that such a thing could exist in a rational universe. In truth, they were probably surprised to find such a mundane element in their otherwise supernatural narrative.

"Did neither of you find it disappointingly pedestrian that a god would need to borrow two of our shuttles?" he continued. "Perhaps he also uses public transit?"

Memnon wasn't entirely sure he was convincing them, but he was certainly starting to convince *himself*. "There are endless possible explanations for all of this," he insisted. "An odorless gas that causes temporary paralysis. Maybe it even causes death, if used improperly."

"But the officer in forward comms, sire?" the security officer asked. "He shot the containment unit. Blinded our sensors…"

"And why would a god need to blind our sensors? Couldn't he simply transit back to the underworld, rather than sneaking off with our shuttles?" Memnon waved his hand in a broad arc to dismiss the idea.

"Someone killed that officer and posed him to look like he did it. They blinded our sensors and then ran off in our shuttles.

"Mark my words, gentlemen. Some unremarkable explanation lies at the bottom of all this but I don't care enough to waste time and energy trying to figure it out. It's done and the cost is a few crewmen and a couple of shuttles. Whoever did this is long gone, so let's concentrate on our own tasks."

He turned and stalked out of the hangar before cracks could form in the aura of confidence he'd been projecting. He kept his mind as blank as possible until the hatch to his quarters slid shut.

He dropped into a chair and sighed at the ceiling.

What the hells happened on this ship?

Risk and Reward

Oracles
The Mouse, *Ataqlat system*

Eth opened his eyes and looked around the ready room. He let out a sharp breath, looking down at the floor.

"You can't force it," Scylla told him.

"Maybe I can't do it at all," he said, shrugging.

"I know you can," she stated flatly. "I can see into your mind, remember, and I can feel your readiness for this. Few of the minds on this ship are open to this level of transposition and most could never do it with a lifetime of preparation but you're ready. You just need to see that yourself."

He squinted at her, chin up. "Why are you always the same when you... transpose? You use the analogy of a finger being pulled out of two dimensional space and then reinserted elsewhere. Wouldn't some circle watching this notice you starting out small and then increasing in size as the finger is inserted?"

"It's an imperfect analogy," she admitted. "You can't expect every aspect to carry over completely to a higher order of complexity. That circle would see a line appear and then increase its *presence* as the two dimensional plane moves up to a wider part of the finger.

"Surely, you've noticed that my own presence has changed since you first saw me looking for scraps in Kwharaz?"

"Well, you're free of your conditioning, and you have an understanding of the universe that exceeds my own…"

"That understanding," she said with the slightest of interrogative tones, "that represents a change in the length of my line segment, if you will. Though it's still far from a perfect analogy."

"Yeah," Eth agreed. "Like, if you pull your finger back out, the line shrinks again."

"I could shrink," she countered. "If I lose faith in what I know, if I suffer from a blow to the head, I could revert to what I was or even less. The factors in our three-dimensional realm are far more complex than a collection of line segments, after all. The differences grow exponentially when you move to the fourth dimension.

"The changes you've seen in me are in the dimension that our biology leads us to view as *time*. We all change in this dimension but I see it as something that time doesn't quite explain."

"What's wrong with time?" Eth asked, feeling a hint of the same dread he'd known while visiting the Varangians, like tendrils of a late-morning mist.

"Time doesn't explain how I can see into your mind," she said. "If you come back to the fingers, for a moment," she suggested, sticking an index finger down through an imaginary two-dimensional space, "and add another finger…" She lowered the adjacent finger and then tapped her palm with the index finger of her other hand.

"What is this?" she asked rhetorically. "These fingers belong to the same hand; they're connected." She held the hand in place, giving Eth time to absorb what she was implying.

"You're saying you can see into my mind because we're two parts of the same lifeform? A lifeform that projects parts of itself into our three-dimensional realm as individual Humans?"

"Not all of your mind, apparently," Abdu whispered.

"That's right." She lowered her hands and leaned in. "If you're going to understand how that works, you need to let go of your biologically informed perception of time."

"But I believe you," he insisted. "Why am I still stuck?"

She blew out a sigh, head shaking slightly from side to side as her breath whistled out between her teeth like a pressure release valve. "Maybe I'm being unfair. Did I simply understand and believe or did I *see* it while among the Varangians before I was able to believe it?

"Maybe I need to make you see before you can truly believe…"

She grasped his shoulders, pressed her forehead to his and closed her eyes.

"Scylla, what…"

"Shut your noodle-hole," she urged patiently. "Don't fight this."

That's not alarming at all, he thought dryly.

Okay, maybe my 'head-side' manner can use a little work, she admitted.

Eth shivered. He could feel her – her thoughts, her way of thinking, her presence. She was in his mind. *What is this?*

This is me, she replied, her calm reaching across to his mind. *I'm reaching back through our connection in, for lack of a better description, four dimensional space.*

Her mind, experienced so intimately, was terrifying. It was almost like stepping through the portal on the Varangian ship. She'd had a gentle mind but it had been overlaid with terrible knowledge. It knew things that would give most of her fellow Humans nightmares and there were ragged tears in her mind where the Chironian conditioning had erased parts of her.

She'd retrieved most of what was lost, but the scars were still there, livid rifts in the flow of her thoughts.

It's a mess, she agreed. *Your own mind is quite soothing, like leaving a war-zone for a vacation on a nice passenger liner.*

Sorry, he thought, momentarily forgetting his fear, *I didn't mean to insult you. I just didn't expect our minds to suddenly join like this.*

You weren't thinking with malice, she replied, *and none of it was untrue. There's no need to apologize. There's no way to hide thoughts when we're linked like this.*

"Are you sure?" Abdu asked sweetly.

She gave no indication that she'd heard the extra voice.

Eth had never felt more powerless in his life, even when he'd been a wardu, but he was surprised to realize that he didn't mind at all. Scylla's mind, despite the scars, despite the terrible knowledge, flowed around his thoughts like a warm summer breeze.

That's nice! she thought. *I like this connection too!*

A Chat
The Dibbarra, *Ataqlat system*

Eth took the proffered cup of coffee from Mishak's hand, recognizing the honor with a Human nod of thanks that acknowledged both the coffee and his lord's ability to perceive the gesture, even though most Quailu couldn't. One of the things he appreciated most about his lord was his subtlety.

"Yeah, he's more subtle than most," Abdu admitted. *"Still didn't stop me from taking a bullet to the brain. A tradition that died with me..."*

Eth stifled a flare of annoyance.

He knew his lord would make a good emperor, as long as he could keep him alive long enough to take the throne.

"So..." Mishak dropped onto the low couch in the middle of his receiving room, waving Eth to sit in one of the chairs. The suite had been built aft of the bridge, just behind the comms suite, and it gave him the ability to conduct matters of state without having to tramp through the bridge to use Captain Rimush's boardroom. "... What have you learned?"

"Lord, I've learned that Ilgi knows nothing. He has no idea what motivated his father to send him out on that rump-humped errand. That couch beneath you has a better understanding of its purpose than he does."

"So we've risked exposing our stealth abilities for nothing," Mishak grumbled. "It's my fault. I really thought we could squeeze something from that idiot."

"I think we've managed to mask our stealth abilities," Eth said. "I might have given him the mistaken impression that we were shifting between alternate universes, rather than relying on something as mundane as carbon nano-tubule coatings."

"You always were a clever one…"

"Alternate universes?" Mishak stared at him in disbelief. "You can't possibly expect him to fall for that! It's a proven impossibility!"

Eth stifled a knowing smile and the feelings that would have accompanied it. "You did just say he was an idiot, lord," Eth countered mildly. "He seemed to buy it and, since it's such a massive whopper of a lie…"

"The whole empire will be buzzing about how deadly we are within a half-lunar," Mishak chuckled, a deep throaty rumble in his chest.

"In all fairness, lord, we *are* deadly." Eth drained his coffee and glanced at the carafe on the sideboard. Mishak waved his assent. "And I'm much happier if the rest of the empire thinks it's for some other tech than what we're *actually* using."

He poured another cup, then stepped over to refill Mishak's with an ease borne of many such discussions. "So we got no information from him but we managed to disseminate some favorable rumors, at least."

Mishak stared into the dark liquid. "I need to know what my father is up to. Waiting until he reveals his ultimate goal is not a viable option. By the time that happens, it will already be too late to do anything about it."

"The sheer number of electors involved could indicate an attempt to keep you from the imperial throne," Eth suggested.

"It could, but what does he gain? He doesn't want that throne. It has little real power, only influence and prestige. He wants to declare himself king of his own territories. That way, he gets to keep his raw power and still sit a throne. Keeping me from becoming the emperor seems irrelevant to his goals."

"His goal would be much easier to accomplish if the crown couple aren't able to interfere directly in his affairs," Eth said.

"Keeping you busy elsewhere in the empire makes his work easier and it makes the citizens question the empire's ability to keep the peace."

Mishak grunted. "It makes them more likely to accept a strong polarizing force within the empire."

"Like a king," Eth said simply.

"But how is he doing it?" Mishak asked as though Eth hadn't spoken. "So many awilu are launching attacks that make little or no sense. They must know they'll face backlash, so what is Sandrak using against them for leverage?"

He looked up at Eth. "Your man, Gleb – when do you expect to hear from him?"

"He sent a coded message just before I came to see you. He thinks it may have to do with extinct species. He found a list of awilu who contract to Meleke for extinct genomes. The empire doesn't regulate extinction registrations because they'd have to fund their own expeditions. Meleke has never allowed imperial interference in their long-range groups. If those species aren't really extinct..."

"Then their economies are sitting on an illegal foundation?" Mishak set his mug down. "How can my father use something like this? A threat to expose any single lord with such information is, by its nature, a threat to destroy the Meleke Corporation as well."

"What I'd like to know," Eth added, "is how he *gets* this information in the first place." He made a dismissive gesture. "Those who use extinct species as their wardu labor force are a matter of public record but the list Gleb sent us is very specific. Some he singles out for pressure and others aren't even on the list.

He shrugged apologetically. "No offense intended, Lord, but, if someone had information that could do them serious harm, your father..."

"Is the last person in the universe you should entrust it to," Mishak finished for him. "So that means he has some kind of leverage

over the folks at Meleke. Send me the list and I'll look through it…"
He tilted his head suddenly. "Are *we* on that list?"

"No, lord."

"I suppose we shouldn't be," Mishak said, sitting back on his couch. "Your lot went extinct tens of millennia ago."

"How *did* we go extinct?" Eth, not alone among his kind, had always wondered but there was almost no public data available on the subject. The Meleke Corporation kept close controls on any data. If it could be sold, they kept it under lock and encryption-key.

"Who knows?" Mishak rumbled as airily as any Quailu could. "Probably killed yourselves off fighting over resources or some gaudy trinket with religious significance. That's what usually happens."

"Bet he knows something," Abdu growled. *"I liked him but, at the end of the day, he's still a Quailu!"*

Eth's gaze drifted slightly as he considered this. "Or Meleke released some kind of non-persistent nerve agent in the atmosphere?" he suggested darkly.

Mishak looked at Eth for a moment, his surprise clear to the Human, though he didn't know it. "You don't really think they'd do something like that, do you? Even for an evil corporation like them, it's too much to even consider!"

"Perhaps, lord. Perhaps."

"Look, all we know is that your kind had developed a basic sort of civilization, fairly low-tech, and then you'd all managed to snuff it."

Eth nodded. "And then along comes Meleke with their sniffers and their reconstruction algorithms and Humans become available for license as a wardu labor force and that's all assuming that we really are extinct."

He shrugged, a small compliment for his lord. "Given what we've learned so far and, given where I stand in the empire, can you blame me for my suspicions?"

"I suppose not," Mishak conceded, "but where *do* you see your standing in the empire? You're mushkenu, no longer a slave, and you hold my commission as well as a substantial rank in my house forces."

He leaned forward aggressively. "And that's a rank given by one of the foremost electors in the HQE, not to mention, gods willing, the future emperor!"

"But what are we?" Eth demanded.

"What are you? You're Humans."

"But what does that mean?" Eth pointed at Mishak. "Your parents lay together and you were born ten months later. I was grown in a chamber. I have no parents, no ancestors. Even the *freeborn* Humans on Memnon's ships came from chambers and I'd be surprised if he didn't have some sort of agreement with Meleke to make sure they don't reproduce."

"*Does Scylla have a steriplant?*" Abdu mused. "She *wants to play house…*"

"If it's reproductive rights that you're concerned about…" He stopped as Eth shook his head angrily.

"No, Lord… Well, not entirely." He frowned, not sure how to phrase it, even to himself. He hadn't planned on unleashing this outburst but Abdu seemed adept at pushing buttons.

"To make you exist, your parents made a choice, a free choice. To make me exist, *you* paid a licensing fee to the Meleke Corporation. All Humans exist as a result of a licensing fee."

He shrugged. "Are we a species or are we still just a commodity?"

"Hmmm…" Mishak set his mug down. "Now I see what's been eating at you lately."

"Lord?"

"I've been picking up on some subtle physical cues," the Quailu said, not without a touch of pride, "and whatever the Varangians did to

141

you seems to have worn off a little as well. I get the occasional hint of a feeling."

Though his students in the *Understanding* took care to keep their feelings readable to the Quailu, Eth had to take a more gradual approach, easing back from the total blankness that his lord had already noticed. He hadn't realized that he was letting some of his discontent seep through.

"Are you saying you've developed a better understanding of physical cues because of my… injury?"

Mishak leaned away slightly. "Ah, well…" he temporized. "I have paid closer attention since your visit with the Varangians," he said, telling part of the truth in the manner of an empathic individual who's trying to hide the other part.

Eth suddenly felt a mix of fondness and guilt in his lord. He found himself thinking of a Human, one he knew but couldn't quite identify. It had to be coming from Mishak. A Human female…

He decided to steer away from that. "Even if the current group of mushkenu Humans decide to exercise our reproductive rights," he mused, "at what point do we stop being an anomaly and start being an actual species?"

"Given your species' reproductive statistics," Mishak said with a grin, "it would be pretty damned quick! Have patience. Things are changing."

"Change happens damned slowly," Eth grumbled.

"That's why it's not called chaos!" Mishak retorted. "And from the Quailu perspective, it's happening with terrifying speed. Remember how Abdu died on Chiron? He shielded some lowly Quailu office minion from getting shot by local security troops. Gave his life for someone of little importance simply because of his species."

"Yeah," Abdu drawled, *"might have heard something about that!"*

Mishak pointed a finger at Eth. "How many Quailu have *you* killed since then? Bau told me how you threw her crew off that scout-ship." He held up a hand. "Don't concern yourself. She explained how it was necessary to get her to a more-or-less *safe* landing.

"The point is, the various native species of the empire, in just a few months of conflict, have gone from a point where they were sacrificing themselves in order to save Quailu lives to one where they're actively killing them. It's not just Humans, either. The HQE can never go back to the way it was.

"Those who fought for their lords aren't going to meekly lay down their weapons and go back to their old ways." Mishak drained his cup and set it down. "You want change and, though it seems slow to you, it seems terrifyingly fast to the Quailu, at least to those of us who've bothered to give any thought to where all this is leading."

Eth bristled. "They're afraid they'll have to be polite to us savages?"

"They're afraid," Mishak countered gently, "that they'll end up going from positions of power to complete irrelevancy. We've already met a delegate from the Zeartekka Hive. They want their queen to rule the Zearta system for real. Not even a token Quailu lord or governor."

Eth frowned. That, in itself, wasn't terribly surprising. The Zeartekka were, by far, the most unusual species in the HQE. Their loyalty to their queen was absolute and always would be.

It wasn't just a question of sworn loyalty and tradition for them. They might have different fathers but the queen was, quite literally, their mother. She would always have first claim on their allegiance.

He tried, but he couldn't imagine having a mother. He couldn't begin to understand the concept of having his own parents.

Eth had the feeling that an iceberg lurked beneath the Zeartekka delegation. "Who else has petitioned you?" As the presumed heirs to the throne, Mishak and Tashmitum would be a logical target for lobbyists.

"An endless stream of them," Mishak sat back with a sigh. "Some want native seats on planetary councils, some want full proportional representation. It goes all the way up to those who want out of the HQE altogether."

"Lord! The empire won't survive if we start letting systems secede!"

"I fear Tashmitum and I may be the last royal couple to rule the HQE. Not a very distinguished epitaph but, there it is and the longer we take in uncovering my father's schemes the greater the changes to the empire. Your fellow had better work quickly!"

"If anyone can do this, it's Gleb," Eth assured him. "He can only move so quickly, though, when he's waiting for chance to look his way. That's how he got that list from Melvin the Bastard."

Mishak chuckled. "Did he learn where *Melvin* got those Humans he has on his ships?"

"Not exactly. He did learn that the Humans on Memnon's ship are considered free-born but they're also all indentured in order to cover the cost of their emancipation."

"That may actually be legal," Mishak mused, "though it's murky enough to tie me and the Meleke Corporation up in the courts for decades. Technically, I'm the only legally licensed user of the Human genome, but it's specifically for wardu use. If there are free Humans like yourself…" He grinned, or at least moved his facial features in a very Quailu parody of a Human grin. "So they see the value in using Humans on their ships?"

"They're no more useful on that ship than any Quailu. They just fill the bottom end of the labor pool."

"That's because Melvin's not the great visionary that I am," Mishak said dryly. It was something he never used to do, employing sarcasm with a non-Quailu, because it was so hard for them to know when he was being serious.

But Eth seemed to pick up on it and Mishak assumed the Human was just better than most at picking up on the miniscule body language of the ruling species.

"Perhaps, lord, he doesn't have your extensive background at ripping off your neighbors?" Eth suggested lightly.

Mishak threw back his head and rumbled with laughter. "Gods, I needed a good laugh!" He chuckled. "A little impertinence goes a long way," he said, suddenly leaning toward Eth. "A *little*!"

Eth held up his left hand, thumb and forefinger close together. "A *little*, lord," he agreed.

"Here I am," Mishak said, "lamenting my stressful existence while Gleb is on my father's ship, surrounded by potential enemies. I can't imagine how he keeps it together."

"You'd be surprised, lord." Eth tilted his head, frowning. "Not to take away from the difficulty of what he's doing, but he's a Human on a ship where the Quailu look right through Humans as if they don't exist."

"That's a bit strong, isn't it?"

"Not really, lord. With respect, you can't know what it's like. You grew up at court. The princess royal was a childhood friend. People *always* see you. I know you possess the imagination to work most of it out, intellectually, but you'd have to actually *live* it to know that staying hidden on your father's ship is the *easy* part."

"If that's the easy part, what's the hard part?"

"Not killing the other Humans. Gleb says it was bad on Memnon's ship. The folks he's hiding among were grown recently and just crammed aboard the ships. They're trying to figure out what it means to be Human with no real frame of reference, no pre-existing society or traditions to guide them.

"Some have turned out alright but there are more than enough of them who see ways to exploit their crewmates and they're acting without any restraint – coercion, theft, rape and murder, just for starters."

"That's unconscionable!" Mishak exploded. "The officers are supposed to be responsible for everything that happens on their ship. There's no excuse for allowing any abuse to take place!"

"They can't know everything," Eth countered. "There are endless little moments where pressure can be brought to bear without anyone knowing about it.

"You'd probably be surprised at how close I came to knuckling under to a petty officer third class when we first reported aboard the *Dibbarra*. He came storming up the boarding ramp of our shuttle, shouting insults, and tried to lay hands on me."

"What?" Mishak's head reared back in surprise. "But you were a warrant officer! You outranked him by a wide margin…"

Eth offered a wry grin. "It's one thing to know that sitting here, but *being* there, caught up in the adrenaline and uncertainty with a Quailu coming at me as though he had every *right* to do so and only days after Ab sacrificed himself for some nobody simply because he was a Quailu…

"I had to force myself to twist that petty officer's arm half out of its socket."

"That was funny!"

"You did that? How is it that I've never heard of this till now?"

"Lord, if I'd come to you every time someone on your ship was behaving like an asshole, you'd have concluded that it was a mistake to write out a warrant for me. If we couldn't prove we were capable of looking after ourselves, we might have ended up like the Humans on Memnon's ship."

He held up his hand again to forestall his lord's protest. "I know you would never have ordered such a thing but it would have happened naturally from the constant pressure we got from the rest of the crew, and you would have been disappointed that we allowed it."

Mishak was quiet for a moment, looking down at the empty mug. "And now Gleb is living that alternate reality – the one where you never roughed up a petty officer…"

"Or punched that engineering PO in the gut, just before you walked in," Eth added casually, though he was particularly proud of that encounter.

Mishak stared at him. "The one who was covered in his own vomit? You did that?" He laughed again. "By the gods! What have I turned loose upon our Holy Quailu Empire?"

"Change, lord, but, to be fair, your father had some large changes in mind already. A powerful king within the empire? Folks will forget all about the antsy subject-races if he's rampaging about your throne room implying threats and making demands."

"The ancient, hereditary kings *were* allowed to bring armed entourages to throne room," Mishak said darkly. "You can wager your life my father will insist on that particular honor. I need to find a way to stop this."

"I could send a small scouting force to Heiropolis," Eth offered.

"Heiropolis…" Mishak leaned back, staring up at the conduits and cables that lay exposed in most military vessels' ceilings. "My father-in-law's old scheme…"

Tir Uttur, the four hundred twenty-ninth emperor of the Uttur restoration and Tashmitum's father, had convinced Mishak's uncle to turn on Sandrak and seize Heiropolis. Mishak, who'd gone on to seize his renegade uncle's holdings, had foiled the plan.

That had made Mishak an elector, one of twenty-eight nobles with eight or more systems in their fief. It gave him the right to vote on who would succeed the emperor after his death. It had also made him a fit candidate for Tashmitum's hand.

And now, he was thinking about taking that same system from his father. "That didn't work out very well for Uktannu, if you recall."

"It does involve risk," Eth said, "and we have no *cassus belli* for that kind of attack. It would doubtless cost you succession votes from some of the more… pacifist nobles."

"I'm not worried about a CB for an attack," Mishak still stared up at the ceiling. "They tend to decay pretty quickly. You want something fresh if you plan an attack and I'm reasonably sure we can egg my brother into providing us with justification, if we decide to attack."

He looked back down at Eth. "You know my uncle consulted his oracle before that attack? He was told his plan would bring down a noble house!"

"Oracles are slippery bastards," Eth said lightly. "Though your uncle *did* bring down a great house, just not the one he was expecting."

"What about your old pal, Sulak?" Mishak needled.

"Oh, he's slippery too, lord. He's just honest about it!"

"Well," Mishak stood to signal that the interview was at an end. "I'll ask my wife if she can spare him for a few days."

Eth stood as well. "Spare him, lord?"

"He's spent a lot of time on Heiropolis. Knows the people. If you're going to scout the place, he might be of use."

Eth grinned. "At the very least, he can lend us an air of respectability if we get nabbed."

Mishak shuddered.

For an oracle, Sulak was a remarkable slob.

Eth left his lord's quarters, turning for the main shuttle-bay. He nearly bumped into Fleet-Captain Rimush as he turned a corner and made a polite apology to the senior officer.

Rimush accepted the pleasantry and they went on their respective ways. Eth frowned to himself, resisting looking back over his shoulder at the other officer. He shook his head. *Too much on my mind,* he thought. *No need to look for trouble where it probably doesn't exist.*

"Thought I taught you better than that, boy!"

Marching Orders
Hab-Ring, Kurnugia 2

Apsu stepped from his shuttle, flanked by six of his best security operators. He had good reason for a strong presence. Kurnugia was a treaty world. Somehow no one had managed to snap it up over the millennia and a series of agreements among powerful lords had gradually nudged the world into a permanent off-limits status.

The empire, nominally in charge, fearing the backlash that would have come from inserting a governor of their own not to mention the cost of maintaining a security force, acted as though the place wasn't even on the charts. The only time you saw a Varangian here, it was because they had personal business.

Naturally, the world was ruled by a coalition of criminal syndicates.

It was, Apsu reflected, a shame that the place was so unruly. It had a brutal beauty to it. The vast majority of Kurnugia's surface was covered in volcanoes, flowing lava or cooling lava. A ring circled the planet five kilometers above the surface and it was held in place with thousands of pitch-drives.

So many pitch-drives that Apsu made a tidy profit shipping replacement units to keep the gigantic ring of gleaming blue towers, filthy slums and smoke belching industries from thundering into the surface. Even considering that he lost nearly five percent of the ships sent here, he still made more than enough credits to justify the business.

They found the bar easily enough. He simmered with anger, walking in under a holo-sign that showed an endless succession of startlingly illegal sex acts. It figured that a bar like this would be chosen for the rendezvous – the humiliation was part of the package.

And yet, he couldn't simply stand inside the doors radiating his disgust. He had to avoid sticking out. He led the way up the stairs to the catwalk level, assuming – correctly – that it would at least conceal his group from the main crowd below. The thumping beat from the bar's sound system changed the cadence of his stride, irritating him even more than the insistent pounding of the alien rhythm itself.

They settled at an empty table, ordering ales from a server. Apsu scanned the place, looking for their contact, but there were almost no other Quailu in the bar. The clientele were mostly a mix of the empire's native races and they'd watched his arrival with interest.

A group of seven young Nippurian natives, dressed in expensive tunics, sat at a nearby booth, cold eyes on Apsu like a hive of Zeartekka. A game of *loser* lay half-dealt on their table amongst innumerable cups of tea and assorted pistols.

Low-level syndicate muscle.

He turned from them in lordly disdain, just in time to notice that his order of ales had somehow changed. The server was setting out drinks with light paper streamers attached to the rims of the glasses. An endothermic reaction in the drink itself was releasing carbon dioxide, blowing the streamers straight up in the most ridiculous fashion imaginable.

He couldn't hear the Nippurians laughing but he could *feel* their derision. He shoved the offending beverage into the center of the table just as the crowd roared and, for a brief moment, he thought they were approving of his action.

Then he felt the amazement of his guards and, following their gaze, saw that he wasn't the only high-ranking Quailu in the bar. A pair of Quailu, one male and one female, were mounting the steps to the central stage on the main floor.

Apsu wanted to shout a warning, let them know the kind of establishment they'd wandered into but the roar of the crowd made that impossible. The richly dressed couple, her hand resting lightly on his in courtly fashion, bowed before the crowd as if they were greeting some dignitary in the emperor's throne room.

Except the dignitary, in this case, turned out to be a Chironian. The hulking, brutal creature sketched an ironic bow, grabbing his tunic and ripping it away as he straightened.

And then Apsu understood what he was seeing. He looked away, face purpling with rage, as the two Quailu offered the mating position to the Chironian.

The crowd shouted their choice, arguing over who would be the Chironian's *partner* and Apsu strained to shut it all out. He realized he was squeezing his eyes shut and he forced them open to find one of the Nippurians staring at him while his fellows were shouting toward the stage.

The Nippurian snatched up a knife from his table as the sound of ripping fabric wound its way up from below. He approached Apsu's party and there was a deafening cheer just as the young criminal drove the knife down into the memory-wood table and walked away, his crew getting up to follow him.

Apsu looked away from the Nippurians to his own guards, spitting with rage that they were still staring at the spectacle below. A dangerous criminal had just come close enough to slit their lord's throat and none of them had even noticed!

Then he noticed the tiny holo projecting up from the knife's hilt. *Menchuru 15 6 63.* As soon as he'd had time to read it, there came a crackle of electricity and the holo faded, replaced by tendrils of smoke.

He slammed his palm flat on the table, getting no response, and so he did it again, this time hard enough to hurt. They looked at him, their demeanor shifting from mildly interested disgust to shame as they saw the knife he was now pointing at.

The Nippurian passed a table with a single occupant near the back of the mezzanine on his way to the fire exit. He dropped a small holo-chip on the table, scooping up the credit chip that lay next to the occupant's ale.

Jay took a drink, set his glass down and touched the chip to activate the holo-projection. He noted the address before crushing the chip with the heavy ale-glass.

It was too noisy to speak so Apsu simply got up and headed for the stairs, forgetting, until he reached the bottom, that the only way out led past the stage. He kept his eyes straight forward, though they still showed the Chironian who was beckoning to him as he passed.

The crowd hooted with laughter at the Chironian's apparent offer but there was nothing Apsu could do about it but press on for the exit, yearning for the relative sanity of the crime-infested streets.

He burst out onto the slidewalk like a drowning victim breaking the surface. "I was told," he began in a quiet rage, "that you were our best protective operators and, yet, some low-level thug could have easily slit my throat just now and you probably would have thought my blood was just someone splashing their drink on you!"

He stood there, the slidewalk slowly taking them away from the bar as he fed his anger with their own shame. "If any of you wish to keep your positions, I'd recommend keeping your heads out of your cloacas until we're back aboard the ship. Let's just get to the meeting and get this over with!"

"The meeting…" the guard began before realizing that keeping his mouth shut was probably the best strategy, at the moment. He must have also realized that stopping at that point was even worse. "…It wasn't at the bar, Lord?"

"In a bar with two Quailu getting buggered witless for entertainment?" he demanded. "Did you not notice how loud it was in there?"

He looked around and spotted a transit station. "We need to get to that station," he said, pointing at the large holo-sign. "Our meeting is in the Menchuru district, block fifteen."

He could tell they wanted to ask how he suddenly knew this but he could also feel that they suspected the information had been imparted to Apsu while they were displaying their incompetence. It would have almost made him laugh, if he hadn't been dragged here in the first place.

So what is the message inherent in summoning me here? he wondered. The summons was message enough, as far as Apsu was concerned. He'd bridled at such a peremptory demand from a relative nobody to an elector like himself.

A large ground-car sidled up, the driver hopping out to beckon them inside but Apsu pushed on and one of his operators shoved the driver back into his own vehicle. The driver barked an order to someone out of sight, admonishing them to hold their fire.

Every fool knew there was no hire-car industry on Kurnugia. There was, however, a thriving kidnapping and ransom industry that did a fairly decent impression of a hire-car industry.

One of Apsu's guards at the rear of the procession casually tossed a frag grenade into the vehicle, killing the would-be kidnappers with a sharp blast of noise and fragments. Nobody would think to challenge straight-up murder on this world, much less the killing of a few dim-witted ransom-jockeys.

They'd landed in one of the most up-scale regions of the ring, which only meant the criminals here were more presentable and they kept their trade off the slidewalks. The drug-pushers wore expensive clothing and their shops displayed an astounding array of products. The sex-sellers also had lavish shopfronts and menus catering to at least seven gender-configurations.

But nobody was shoving their business in Apsu's face as he made his way to the public transit system. This, undoubtedly, was part of the reason for meeting here. A prince of the realm taking public transit like a mushkenu was unthinkable anywhere else but, here on Kurnugia, it was the only method of travel that received any policing.

If you got into a local ground-car, then you were a fool who deserved to get kidnapped. If you brought your *own* ground-car, you were an even bigger fool for broadcasting how much ransom you could afford.

If you came with a modest security detail, you were proclaiming yourself as someone who was just enough trouble to not be worth molesting. That, at least, was what the guide-page for this world had said when Apsu's staff had looked into it.

Three generations of transporting pitch drives to this world and this was the first time a member of Apsu's family had set foot on this living hell. He hurried past a pair of Zeartekka who were dismembering a Quailu corpse.

Crime was less prevalent in this region but it still existed. He didn't know who might have killed the Quailu but he had no doubt the poor fellow would end up in a Zeartekka broth-shop before day's end.

He stepped off the slidewalk onto a train platform, his guards shoving people out of his way so he'd be one of the first to board. It was probably not a good idea to cause such a stir. The crowd waiting for the train were now ignoring the fornicating couple at the far end and turned to see who the apparently important new arrival was.

Apsu could feel their curiosity, their avarice and he was relieved when the train finally hissed its way into the station. It slid to a halt with a rattle of loose magnets that did little to improve his opinion of public transport. Nonetheless, he stepped aboard the last car, wrinkling his nose at the smell of sweat, and sat at the back with his guards between him and the peasants.

A Durian hopped through the door just as it screeched shut, leading a short bipedal creature by a rope around its neck. The Durian took a quick look at the guards, darting curiosity Apsu's way, and then turned to move forward, calling out his sales-pitch for fresh meat.

From the captive creature, Apsu could feel an abject sadness, tinged with terror and the terror spiked as a buyer was found. The Durian slapped two tourni-clips on one of the creature's five remaining arms and sliced off the arm with one swipe of a nanite-edged blade between the clips.

The buyer took a bite, grinning at the poor creature as he chewed and Apsu was relieved when the poor creature passed out from shock. The Durian kicked it once but, when that didn't revive his victim, gave up, hoisted him over his shoulder and resumed his sing-song call.

It wasn't compassion, of course. The vendor didn't want to bruise the product. Apsu shuddered as the vicious butcher passed through the doors into the next car, fervently glad that he'd been born above such barbarity.

The train pulled into the next platform and the doors opened on the opposite side from the one they'd all entered. The problem, from Apsu's perspective, was that there was one door at each end and the exit he needed was now at the far end of the car.

"Wait," he snapped, not wanting another spectacle drawing attention to his ransom potential. He was more than content to let the unruly mass of mushkenu disembark ahead of him. He edged forward just behind the crowd because he was unsure of how the train operated.

Will it just move on as soon as all the doors are allowed to close? he wondered. He had no wish to spend any more time than necessary on this damned train.

There was a scream followed by an ironic cheer just as he reached the door. As his small group moved along with the flow, he saw the Durian butcher lying on his back, a look of indignation on his face, though his eyes were already glazing over.

The smaller biped was sitting on his chest, the tourni-clip still on his stump, and the blood on his face left little doubt about the reason for the Durian's ravaged neck. He was chewing on something, windpipe and gristle no doubt, while his remaining arms patted down his erstwhile captor's pockets.

He pulled out the nanite knife with a chitter of triumph and set to work digging out the Durian's credit-chip implant.

"Looks like something the Durian ate disagreed with him," one of Apsu's guards muttered, startling the others into laughter.

They left the platform and moved out to the far side of the ring from where they'd landed. The address turned out to be a residential tower on the very edge of the planet-spanning ring and they took the elevator up to the sixty-third floor.

There was no entrance hall. The residence was the entire floor – two floors if the ramp by the elevator was any indication. To the left, a female Quailu lay on a low couch, watching as two naked Humans battered at each other with antique Quailu war-hammers. Three other Humans lay in a red-smeared heap on the bloody marble floor.

That explained the stink of blood.

An imposing guard in a combat EVA suit and carrying a heavy assault weapon nodded toward a group of eight more guards, one of whom stuck out an arm to indicate a figure at the balcony. Apsu moved toward the figure, flinching at the sense of pain that followed a grotesque crunching sound.

He glanced over to see one of the Humans on the floor, her thigh bent in the middle at an impossible angle where a hammer had smashed the bone. Her opponent, war-hammer poised for a killing blow, looked to the Quailu for confirmation.

"Slowly," she laughed. "We paid good money for her, after all.

The victor's mind shivered with disgust but that, also, was what the Quailu on the couch was paying for. He set about the systematic destruction of his opponent's body and Apsu picked up his pace, even though the place wasn't nearly big enough to escape the agony of the dying Human.

He wasn't terribly surprised, given her reputation, to find Mot here – even less so than he was to receive a summons from her brother. He stopped a few feet from the balcony, waiting for Memnon to turn and show the proper acknowledgement due to an elector.

The agony-laced silence dragged out, punctuated only by the gut-wrenching impacts of the war-hammer crushing flesh and breaking bones.

The longer this goes on, Apsu realized, *the more foolish I'm looking*. He gave up and moved to stand next to Memnon at the balcony, looking out at the view, which, he had to admit, was incredible.

They were on the night side but, rather than the usual blackness of a habitable world, Kurnugian night was a dramatic tracery of black crust and brilliant lava, fading to a light orange haze toward the horizon.

Apsu forced himself to focus on the scenery, rather than the butchery behind him. *The longer this drags out,* he consoled himself, *the bigger the apology he'll owe for his rudeness to an elector. The forms must be...*

"You call this coming alone?" Memnon snapped, startling Apsu into looking at him.

Apsu eased his mind with a supreme effort. "For this world, yes, I call this coming alone. Do you have any idea how many corpses I saw on the way here?"

"I don't," Memnon admitted, "nor do I care. We have a hangar two floors up from here."

A hangar you couldn't let me use? Apsu strangled the petulant thought. Any fool could recognize an exercise in humility.

"There is significant unrest," Memnon stated flatly, "at the Noori system."

"Is there?" Apsu wasn't really asking.

"No, not really. Nonetheless, there is significant... unrest."

Apsu mulled it over for a moment. "I suppose there is also... unrest in Basrillah and Andaluria?" he asked mildly.

Memnon grunted. "You find the heart of the matter, then. Yes, those two systems are also in need of pacification."

It was Memnon's apparent surprise that unleashed Apsu's anger. Of course the three systems were connected. If Sandrak wanted Noori, then of course he wanted Basrillah and Andaluria. Any one of those systems was insignificant to such a powerful lord but together the three would open a new corridor connecting the two halves of his holdings.

After the harrowing journey through Kurnugia's crime-ridden streets, after the lack of respect, after seeing that this young pup thought Apsu too dim to comprehend such an easy connection, he was in no mood to comply. "Then I suppose you'd better move in," he suggested dryly, "and restore order."

He turned at the sound of a scuffle behind him. His guards were facing an unequal foe. Wearing only lightly armored EVA suits, they were facing Memnon's heavily armored goons and the numbers didn't favor them either. One of his lightly armored guards was on his posterior, a hand held ineffectually to the side of his closed helmet.

"Stand down," he ordered. There was nothing to gain from this unequal show of force and much to lose.

Memnon's troops moved in, taking away the guards' weapons and slapping restraint units on their suits. Before Apsu could even protest, all six were forced to the balcony and tipped over the railing.

He watched in mute shock as they tumbled down out of sight. This side of the building faced out to the planet and the building was on the very edge of the ring, so there was nothing to break the guards' fall but lava.

"I said to come alone," Memnon reminded him casually. "Now, let me make this very clear. You will take those three systems to restore order and you will hand them over to me because you're much too busy with your own worlds and, after all, you only did it out of concern for the poor citizens who were in danger.

"And if you refuse," he added, stepping closer, "then you will find out how it feels to have the citizens of *your* worlds in danger! You'll also find your economy in tatters because we know the wardu population on Kells is illegal."

He knows our slave species isn't actually extinct? Apsu, by no means an idiot, suddenly understood. "That's why others have been fighting for you, isn't it? They all have wardu on at least one of their worlds and you've managed to find the ones that aren't really legal for sale!"

"Of course." Memnon actually looked bored, not at all alarmed at this unmasking of his leverage.

"Then this must affect a major part of the imperial economy. Revealing this information would result in backlash against Meleke as well. The full story would come out and your hold would be at an end."

"And we'd unleash chaos on the HQE," Memnon added.

"Then I don't understand how you're able to use this," Apsu said, voice rising. "Why are the other lords falling into line over a threat you can't make good on?"

"Can't make good on?" Memnon asked, radiating amusement. "Well, of course we can make good on it." He turned to lean back against the railing, idly watching the fighting Humans. This time, a young female was facing off against the victor but with a light sword instead of a heavy war-hammer.

"What you're failing to understand, Apsu, is that chaos would serve us almost as well as compliance."

Is it really that simple? Apsu wondered. Was Sandrak willing to plunge the empire into chaos? He owned far more of it than any other lord, but did that mean he was best positioned to survive the fallout, or did it mean that he had the most to lose?

The female with the sword had managed to drop under a wild hammer swing and she rolled in, quick as lightning, to sever the tendon in the male's heel.

The hammer fell to the floor, followed quickly by the body of the one who'd wielded it. His hand darted out for the hammer's shaft but it was severed by a tightly controlled sword stroke that stopped a finger's-breadth from the blood-slick marble.

She stood over him, her sword now above his throat, and looked up to Mot.

"This one fought well," Mot said. "I want a talisman to remember his prowess but make it quick – one stroke."

The sword flashed and Apsu turned away from the screaming human who was vainly trying to staunch the rush of blood from his center with his only remaining hand. "Disgusting!" he muttered.

"But educational," Memnon said.

"What can that possibly teach you," Apsu retorted bitterly.

Memnon grasped the elector's shoulder and forced him to look back into the room. The young woman was bearing the grisly trophy to Mot, her body streaked with blood.

"Strip away all of our advantages of rank and privilege and what do you get?" he asked rhetorically. He pointed at the bloody spectacle.

"That."

"Preposterous!"

"Oh really?" Memnon turned his gaze to face him. "Perhaps a demonstration? I admit I haven't had much reason to love that word recently, but I find it has its uses.

"I'll give you two options. The first is that you will leave now, collect your forces and proceed directly to Noori."

"And the second option?"

That face loomed closer. "You will wait here and *I* will leave to collect my forces. I won't be going to Noori, though."

It felt as though the blood in Apsu's veins had suddenly been replaced with ice-water.

"What *principled* choice will you make, Apsu?" Memnon sneered. "When faced with the destruction of your progeny, what atrocities will you commit for me?"

Apsu's shoulders sagged. He watched as Mot took the sword from the young woman and sliced her head off. She turned away in disinterest even before the woman's head hit the floor.

Parting
Ashurapol, Henx Prime

Gleb finished slipping the new power-cell into his suit and closed the access port. It was an after-market part from the bustling hub of commerce a few dozen blocks below their apartment.

His two new friends had been amazed at the spaciousness of their new housing arrangements. They still had to share a common shower in the center of the building's floor with roughly twenty aliens of various species, but the rooms were beyond their experience.

They'd been shocked to realize they weren't going to be sharing the apartment with anyone else. It had taken a full night of sleeping in their own rooms to finally accept that they had all that space to themselves, though Siri had dragged her cot into Mel's room on the second night.

It can be terrifyingly lonely, sleeping by yourself in a room when you've only ever slept in a dormitory-style setting your entire life. To Mel and Siri, this was luxury on a staggering scale.

They were in Ashurapol, for the love of the gods. One of the worst cities Gleb had ever seen.

Ashurapol was in the midst of a desert in what was, for the most part, a desert world but the city was always damp with the breath, sweat and evaporation of eighty million live bodies. The air was heavy with the moisture and stink of a hundred alien races. The scents of myriad spices assaulted and comforted.

It was a major hub for, of all things on a desert world, fresh produce. Most of the city was a giant collection system, channeling the breeze into condensers that sent the water for sale to citizens or for use in the hydroponics systems.

That was why Gleb was in such a hurry. Sandrak's fleet was here and they were stopping to replenish their stores with fresh produce.

"Wait for me here," he told Mel and Siri. "I'll come back for you. In the meantime…" He nodded meaningfully at the second-hand holo-emitter in the middle of the common room. "Keep practicing your coding skills. When we get back to the fleet, you'll be assessed on experience and ability. A little hard work now could mean the difference of a whole rank-grade when you sign on."

"I don't doubt the skills you've been pushing us to practice are useful," Siri told him, "but I'm still not sure I buy that we can be petty officers in *any* Quailu house force. It's unheard of!"

Gleb closed the tabs on his second-hand under-armor suit. Having left his own under a mattress on the *Deathstalker* he'd had a hard time finding a replacement. He'd ended up settling for an old Varangian suit that more or less fit him but it hadn't been cheap.

He didn't want to run the risk of showing up on Sandrak's ship only to find that the Humans aboard that vessel – hoping, as he was, that there *were* Humans on the ship – had under-armor suits. Nothing makes you stand out like being naked among a crowd that wasn't.

He stepped into the footplates and pushed his heels in to close the suit up. "It used to be unheard of, Siri, but there are quite a lot of our kind with rank now." He grinned. "And I have a bit of pull with the new captain of a Scorpion-series fast-attack scouting corvette. I'll put in a good word for you both."

"Hobnobbing with officers, are you?" Mel asked, half joking, half curious. "On a proper-name basis with the Quailu running that ship?"

"Just practice your coding!" Gleb jabbed a finger at the holo-emitter. "I've got a runabout waiting, so I'll see you when I see you and, don't blow all the credits I'm leaving you on fancy crap!"

He stepped out the open window onto a narrow ledge that overlooked a twenty-story drop to where a public square hid an even longer drop.

A runabout hovered a hand's-breadth from the ledge and Gleb vaulted over the gunwale, sliding into a bench seat that ran around the open-topped passenger compartment. "Orbital consignment yard," he said, forcing himself to sound casual.

It wouldn't do for the driver to be able to recall an overly excited person yelling about going to the consignment yard. He didn't expect any inquiries regarding his movements but there was no sense in increasing the risk factor.

Orbital consignment was near the summit of the city. It had once, according to some of the older locals, been at the very summit but the city had grown up around it, leaving the yard in the middle of a deep canyon. Controlling the orbital traffic in and out of the yard was a bit of a nightmare but there were no plans to change it.

Governments. Gleb shook his head in resignation. *They take taxes and then blow it on shiny issues that win votes.* The sad thing was the government here couldn't seem to grasp that a more efficient yard, one that could handle traffic more effectively, would generate even more tax revenue.

He could see two shuttles with Sandrak's crest emblazoned on their rooftops and he told the driver to put him down near the two craft.

After much clever thought on ways to insert himself into Sandrak's ship, he'd given up on all of it and elected to walk right onto it. He paid his driver and hopped over the gunwale.

Without a moment's hesitation, he started walking toward the two shuttles. *Look lost and you sure as hells deserve to get caught!* He was fifteen paces away from the craft when one of the Quailu pilots, who'd been watching the pallet-lifters, noticed him.

Just before the pilot could demand an explanation, Gleb cut him off with a question of his own to get control of the decision cycle. He gave the pilot a polite nod of respect. "Sir, they told you I was coming back up on your shuttle, didn't they?"

"N... no," the pilot stammered, mildly befuddled.

"Well, no matter," Gleb continued cheerfully. "They might have meant the other shuttle, over there." He nodded toward the second shuttle. "Either way, the reaction assessment came back clean. Nothing in this load is toxic to Humans."

Now, the pilot was amused and, more importantly, feeling superior to this insignificant native. "So they sent you down here to see if the produce from this world will kill you? Whose soup did *you* piss in?"

"Wish I knew!" Gleb moved closer. "I'm just glad to be alive! You know there was this one time when we all had to eat a..."

"Wait inside the shuttle!" the pilot snapped pettishly.

"Very good, sir!" Gleb bobbed his head and scuttled inside the shuttle, hiding his amusement.

Sometimes it was very helpful to be so insignificant.

Taking a Peek
Heiropolis System

"Normalization complete," Hendy announced. "Judging by the terrible visibility, I'd say we're right on target, as if anyone's surprised…"

"Very good," Oliv replied. "Secure the path-drive. Outside temperature?"

"One fifty-eight above absolute," Meesh answered her over the intercom link to engineering. "Opening the interchange valves."

Eth was impressed but he kept it to himself. He didn't want to interfere in Oliv's command of the ship and, though a compliment regarding Hendy's navigation wasn't exactly interfering, it would almost seem pompous. Still, they'd dropped into this gas giant at nearly the perfect altitude for charging the cryo-banks.

"Nice flying, Hendy," Oliv said, earning a grin.

Eth supressed the urge to fidget. He much preferred being in command of a vessel to being a mere passenger.

"How fast do we want to get to target?" Hendy asked.

"No rush this time," she told him. "Let's go for a max time-on-target."

"As long as the new shunts on the cryo-banks can hold out, I'd say half pitch for three drives will give us three quarters of a day on target," Meesh suggested.

Oliv frowned. "You worried about the new shunts, Meesh?"

"Not exactly worried," he said. "It's just that this is the first test we're doing where they can get us shot at, if they fail."

"Noted." She gave it a moment's thought. "We'll go in at half pitch, all three drives."

"Laying in a course," Hendy said. "We've got a few planets in conjunction right now, so I'll have to divert from the least-time path but not by much. Should only cost us... an hour or two. Just say the word and I'll pretend to fiddle with some buttons and then activate the course."

Oliv laughed. "Are you telling me half the stuff you do is just for show?"

"Hey, you gotta make it look good when the boss is watching you all the time!"

"Yeah," Oliv replied before Eth could say anything from a boss' perspective, "I'm just such a hard-ass!"

"I'm not even touching that one," Hendy retorted, then turned red. "Your comment, I mean, not your, um... Meesh! You got those cryo-banks charged up yet? We're all waiting on you up here!"

"Almost there," Meesh replied, "but you got more than enough time to finish whatever you were saying to the captain."

As far as Eth knew, none of his people had gotten their steri-plants removed since earning their release from wardu status. Nonetheless, even without the possibility of procreation, their attitudes toward sex had started to change.

Romantic attachment had always been a thing but it had tended not to be a big deal. Embarrassment about any sexual topic had pretty much been non-existent but, now, as mushkenu citizens, they were starting to change how they viewed sex. This wasn't the first time he'd seen one of his fellow Humans get embarrassed.

"A little smug," Abdu chided, *"given how you reacted to Scylla's proposition..."*

Quiet, old man.

"Fine," Meesh grumbled. "If you're not going to keep stammering, the cryo-banks are charged. I'm closing the valves. We're ready to bring the emission management system online."

"Thank-you!" Hendy said with exaggerated relief. "Can we go get shot at now?"

"Always in such a rush!" Oliv rolled her eyes. "Let's take a look around first, *then* get shot at. Bring the EM system online."

"Aye, ma'am," Meesh replied. "EM system is operational."

"Very well." Oliv stepped up to her command holo. "Hendy, bring us up. Time to see what they've done with the place since we were here last. Computer, set holo to tactical; focus on Heiropolis and surrounding orbits."

The holo remained blank, having no data to project, but, as they began to leave the denser layers of the gas giant's atmosphere, fuzzy data points began to form.

One of the advantages of the carbon nano-tubule coating on the hull was the massive signal gain. The entire nanite hull, configured as a series of meta-materials – materials that, because of their orientation, performed functions that the material alone never could – did double-duty as a sensor array.

The nano-tubules gave stealth by refusing to let most of the electromagnetic energy bounce off the hull. Light and most other energy waves simply bounced down between the microscopic filaments and never came back out.

Not only did this make the ship stealthier, it also meant that her surface collected a massively increased amount of data.

"Have I missed anything?" Father Sulak strolled in with a mug of coffee in his hand.

"Not yet," Eth told him, looking pointedly at the mug until the Quailu oracle noticed and handed it over. He took a drink, sighing with satisfaction as he handed it back. "Just starting to get data now, but it doesn't look to be heavily defended."

"Something doesn't smell right," Sulak muttered.

"No offense, Father, but coming from you…"

Sulak chuckled.

"Do you belong to some obscure order that takes exception to bathing?"

"Not the *whole* order," Sulak replied. "Cleanliness, after all, is close to godliness…"

"In a Zeartekka dictionary, maybe," Oliv needled Sulak with a fond smile.

"Oh! I might use that." Sulak gave her an elaborate bow before turning back to Eth. "It was my mentor, if you must know."

Eth frowned. "Your mentor?"

"Famously filthy!" Sulak said proudly. "He always maintained that his clientele took him more seriously after he stopped bathing. They seemed to feel he was too busy communing with the gods to waste time on such trivial matters as personal hygiene."

Eth gaped at him. "It's just marketing?"

"That's a pretty bald way of stating it but, yes, I suppose you could call it that." Sulak finished his coffee. "Anyway, it worked. When he retired, he bought his own moon in the Arbella system."

"His own moon?"

"That's right. Seven eighths standard gravity and fully habitable."

"I want a moon too," Hendy said innocently.

"Maybe the father's mentor needs a personal pilot," Eth suggested. "In the meantime, drop us in closer, if you please, lieutenant."

"Aye, sir," Oliv replied. Hendy, take us in at one half max velocity."

The display remained the same but the magnification indicator began scrolling down at an alarmingly fast speed and the resolution of the images began to firm up. What had been fuzzy clouds with ship number estimates soon became individual vessels. Those vessels then started resolving themselves into passenger ships, freighters, cruisers, frigates and shuttles.

"Reading just one cruiser and four frigates," the sensor officer advised. "Everything else is just civilian traffic."

"Everything?" Oliv enlarged a section of the display in a new projection. "What are these orange coded entries?"

"Those appear to be…" The sensor officer bent to his panel and keyed in a flurry of commands. "… Shuttles, possibly military. Looks like two of them moving away from the warships."

"But not heading for Heiropolis," Oliv said meditatively, "and I doubt they're practicing orbital insertion, so what's on the other side of the planet? They're going there for a reason."

"Is there a minefield?" Eth asked.

"Standard configuration, sir," the sensor officer confirmed. "Big gap left on this side for regular traffic."

"So," Eth mused, "whatever's in there…"

"Ain't gonna be spotted till you're right on top of them with your back to the minefield," Oliv finished for him.

Eth stared moodily at the display. *Pure waste of our time, coming here.* He'd hoped to find some way of seizing this system so they could slice Sandrak's holdings in two. It might not put a stop to his schemes but it would certainly put a crimp in them.

And it would win Mishak succession votes among electors who were nervous of Sandrak's power.

Even a minor action here could reflect well on our lord, he thought, a grin stealing across his features. *If we can contrive to make them look foolish, others will assume, correctly, that it was done by our forces.*

"*I like where your head's at, boy!*" Abdu's voice said approvingly.

"Have you ever had a day where everything was going badly," Eth asked, "and you just say 'screw it, let's have a bit of fun while we're here'?"

"Oh gods save us," Oliv muttered, not quite under her breath.

"Where is your sense of adventure?" he asked her, eyes shining with mischief. "This is a perfect time to try out the external portal cover."

Olive's eyebrows made a decent attempt at touching the bridge of her nose. "You're thinking of taking out the *Foot up Your Ass?* We didn't even bring along a crew for her. She's just there to hide the docking portal."

"The portal cover's also there to hide the portal," he countered, "and you can spare me a pilot and Meesh for a couple of hours."

"Meesh?"

"What I have in mind," he said obscurely, "is actually one of his specialties." He shrugged. "He's leaving this ship for the *Stiletto* soon, anyway, so it's time his second got a chance to run the engineering crew in a hostile action; see how he performs."

It had all started out so well.

Perhaps 'well' was an overstatement. As the captain of the only cruiser in the small squadron at the entry corridor, Hillalum was in nominal command, but he was still a sacrificial goat tied to a stake.

His father had always noticed his cognitive abilities and wanted him to become an oracle. Perhaps he would have seen this coming?

His plan was to withdraw at the first sign of hostiles. He'd pull his cruiser... and the frigates, he supposed... to spinward, where the main fleet would be approaching to pounce on the unwary enemy. Given the current position of the Heiropolitan moons, spinward offered the least interference in his ships' pitch fields, so it didn't even bear asking the commander of the main fleet about it.

He expected to escape with the loss of some frigates but he'd be alive to tell about it and, more importantly, he'd have an 'independent command' mark in his record to burnish his future career.

He'd been offered a turd sandwich but he'd at least turned it into a… turd platter?

And then the terror began.

He was trapped inside his own body. He'd always assumed he'd feel that way in his later years, corpulent and riddled with parasites, but not now, not in his prime. One moment, he'd been watching a polarized news feed, letting his crew think he was going over performance reviews and, the next, he was on the decking, half conscious and blinded.

He could feel a presence unlike any he'd ever felt before. It seemed to be the reason for his incapacitation and it frightened him.

He felt feet striking the decking, moving quickly around him, though he knew they weren't his people. He dimly perceived an alarm tone and urgent inquiries over his helmet. *When did that close up?*

Unbidden and quite unwelcome, the stories from Memnon's flagship suddenly intruded on his thoughts – crewmen found inexplicably dead in poses of apparent relaxation… One survivor claimed he'd been accosted by Nergal himself.

In his semi-conscious state, Hillalum couldn't be certain, but he was reasonably sure he was hyperventilating.

Then, when he was on the verge of slipping into unconsciousness, he felt the presence fade and his mind began the struggle back to full faculty. He sat up, looking at a set of gouges cut into the decking near where his head had lain.

It was a wedge-shaped cuneiform inscription and he shuddered with renewed fear.

"Nergal," he breathed in horrified wonderment.

What else could explain all of this but intervention by the gods themselves?

"Sir!" the tactical officer shouted, startling Hillalum both with the volume of his voice and the fear in his mind. "We're locked onto our frigates!"

"What?" Hillalum grabbed the back of a control station and pulled himself up to glare at the officer. "Don't just tell me about it," he snarled. "Disengage the targeting links immediately before they..."

"Incoming hail from our frigates," the comms officer announced.

"I can't, sir," the tactical officer insisted. "We're locked out of... We're firing on them!" he nearly screamed in his panic.

Hillalum spun to the tactical holo, staring in horror as missiles from his own ship streaked toward his subordinates.

The four frigates were turning to face him...

Sargon turned to his communications officer. "Say that again," he ordered.

"Sire, the frigates in our decoy fleet are demanding to know why the *Hizmaal* has opened fire on them."

"Hillalum!" Sargon trembled with rage. He'd hoped the fool would get himself killed and he'd accept the loss of a cruiser to do it but he never dreamed Hillalum would be so incompetent as to shoot at his *own* side. "What the demons is that idiot playing at?"

"No response from the *Hizmaal*, sire."

Damn it! There goes a perfectly arranged ambush! "Probably lose those frigates before we get there," he ground out, "but the attempt has to be made. Helm! All ahead full. Looks like we have an enemy to kill after all!"

The fleet, seven cruisers, not including Sargon's own heavy cruiser, and twenty-eight frigates, began accelerating toward whatever the hells was going on with the decoy group.

He could feel the confusion from his crew and knew he had to stamp it out. "Hillalum must stop or *be* stopped," he growled. "I want everyone ready. We must be prepared to do whatever is necessary to save our frigates from his folly."

"We have a signal from the *Hizmaal*, sire." The communications officer activated an icon for his general.

Sargon opened the call and a hazy image of Hillalum appeared, hands held out in supplication.

"None of this is our doing!" he insisted.

"The missiles are coming from your ship!" Sargon shouted. "Cease fire immediately and send the self-destruct to any missiles that…"

"We can't!" Hillalum wailed desperately. "We're locked out!" He wrung his hands at Sargon, voice dropping nearly to a whisper. "It was Nergal! He was here!"

Sargon supressed a shudder of fear and fought to ignore the rising hairs on his neck. He couldn't allow this to infect his own people. The rumors were already having a bad enough effect. He swiped angrily at the holo, swatting Hillalum's image out of existence.

"Destroy the *Hizmaal!*" he roared. "Wipe those traitors out of my universe!"

He was gratified by the renewed energy he felt from his bridge crew. He could feel their anger at the fools who'd fire on their own side. He didn't know what was behind the insane rumors but he'd damned sure…

A series of distant explosions preceded a wild lurch, the decking beneath his feet suddenly shifting hard to port. Sargon threw out his arms, teetering ludicrously on one foot for several seconds while he fought to regain his balance.

"Mines!" tactical called out.

"I'd guessed that for myself!" Sargon snapped, his already bad mood causing him to lash out, even though he knew it to be counter-productive. "What the devils are mines doing here? Are they strays from our own minefield?"

"Unknown, sire, but, if they are, then there can't be very many. The minefield appears to be intact."

Another dull crumping noise from beneath gave the lie to his assessment. A power-coupler above the bridge blew out with a demonic squelching sound and the main holo flickered and died. The smell of ozone permeated the air, rank in Sargon's nostrils.

"Let's assume there are more of the damned things," he said, forcing himself to calm down. "What's the status of the rest of our forces?"

Did that idiot Hillalum somehow lay a minefield to trip us up?

"Fleet reporting seventy percent combat-effective," the tactical officer advised. "Three other cruisers with heavy damage and five frigates knocked out of action. All damaged ships will be able to effect repairs but not in the near future."

"Back everyone off!" Sargon ordered. He'd finally overcome his rage and the cold hard facts were staring him in the face. He was down to seventy percent combat-effective, not even counting the probable loss of his entire decoy force, and he still hadn't seen the enemy.

Clearly, whoever they were, they wanted him to press on into their minefield and lose more ships. And how the devils did they lay a minefield right under his nose without him noticing?" He shuddered.

If he survived the day, Sandrak would ask him the very same question.

Eth and Meesh jogged onto the bridge. "What's the enemy status, Captain?"

"Looks like they came to their senses," Oliv said, nodding at the main holo. "They're pulling back from your minefield but their sacrificial goats are still beating the shit out of each other!"

"The ways of Nergal are ineffable," Meesh said solemnly.

Father Sulak grunted. "Well, there's no effing way they'll figure *this* out any time soon."

"If they're not going to play," Eth said, "then we'll leave them our toys and go home. Captain, I'll trouble you to deploy a coated drone programmed for SSD broadcast."

"Already spooled up," she replied. "Sending it now."

The drone, coated with the same carbon nano-tubules that rendered their ships almost entirely undetectable, would send out a search or self-destruct command to the similarly coated missiles in Heiropolitan orbit. It was the best way of sending the signal without the risk of giving away their ship's position.

The remaining missiles received the signal and, of the seven left, four were able to identify military targets. They activated their MA fields and streaked out toward their prey, hammering into two frigates and two cruisers at velocities that would make light blush.

The last three weapons decided they weren't going to be finding a target any time soon and so they maneuvered close to each other and group-detonated their warheads. Their radiant energy had little effect on the one weapon that had failed its detonation sequence but the vaporized osmium packed around the warheads did an excellent job of erasing the failed weapon from existence.

There would be no evidence of Lady Bau's gift for the enemy to analyse.

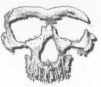

"The *Anuksha's* dead in the black," tactical announced, squinting up at the low resolution emergency holo. "*Sirabai* is crippled and those two frigates are little more than debris traces now."

"Signal the fleet," Sargon ordered. "All stop! Launch shuttles to sweep for mines. All call-signs to remain at full alert!" The last attack was different. The weapons had seemed to do more damage and now Sargon was down to less than half the force he'd arrived with. Two of his decoy frigates had been crippled and Hillalum's cruiser was nearly a hulk as well.

And he still hadn't seen the damned enemy!

Meesh shook his head in amazement. "At this point, we could probably finish them off and send our lord the good news that he's the proud new owner of a key system!"

Eth sighed, his good mood evaporating. "Y'know, I always felt, in the back of my mind, that this whole idea was half-assed. Taking Heiropolis sounds good on a planning board but then what do you do?"

Meesh shrugged.

"Then you die trying to hold onto it?" Oliv asked.

"She was always a smart one!" Abdu said.

Eth nodded his agreement. He waved at the display. "Nine cruisers and thirty-two frigates in total, when you count their decoy force. We made them look like a pack of rump sniffing idiots with *one* ship. Do we really want to be sitting down there, waiting for Sandrak to come looking for revenge?"

"He doesn't have stealth," Meesh countered.

"And we can't use it for garrison duty," Eth replied. "If you take a highly secretive stealth-platform and keep it in orbit, folks will figure out what it is pretty damned fast."

"And Sandrak does have stealth capabilities, I suppose," Meesh muttered. "Any old freighter can show up, packed to the gunwales with warheads and blast herself to fragments."

"So what the hells are you moping about?" Oliv demanded. "Sir," she added hastily, causing Eth to chuckle. "We've shown this world to be a running sore on the ass of whoever holds it. Sandrak can't let us take it or the entire HQE would be laughing at him. Let's leave it, for now, and come back when he's got more ships for us to destroy!"

"Either way, he's getting laughed at," Eth mused. "Let's hope our lord endorses this when we get back to the main fleet." That was the real reason for his unease. He'd been sent out here to investigate the possibility of an attack, not to enrage one of the most powerful nobles in the empire.

It wasn't a conversation he was looking forward to.

"That's enough damage for one day," he declared. "Captain, please take us back to the rendezvous point as soon as you can clear the heat out of the sinks."

"Bring us about," Oliv ordered. "We'll go to the opposite side of the gas giant, this time. Three quarters pitch."

Eth moved to the back of the bridge as Meesh went below to check on engineering. *Why the hells do I jump into these situations without giving enough thought to Mishak's likely response?* His lord was, by Quailu standards, downright intrepid but it seemed as though Eth was pushing his luck even more than when he'd intervened to save the Lady Bau.

That had worked out spectacularly well but, sooner or later, he was going to end up putting his neck on the block.

He just hoped that hadn't happened today.

"Might have…"

Shut up, old man!"

Anger Unleashed
Noori System

"Normalization complete," Hendy announced.

"We have contact with *Scimitar*, *Rapier* and *Cutlass*," the comms officer advised. "All ships report a successful normalization and they're charging their cryo-banks."

"Let's get started on that ourselves," Oliv ordered. "Secure the path-drive and start cooling the cryo-banks."

"Path-drive secure," Meesh replied from the engineering station. "Coolant is flowing."

Eth was glad he'd insisted on Meesh taking over the bridge engineering station. He'd practically dragged the young engineering warrant up here but it had to be done. Meesh's second had to gain experience in a real fight and Meesh needed to spend more time on a bridge. He'd be leaving to warm Gleb's seat on the *Stiletto* very soon and, if that went well enough...

Eth was going to need a new lieutenant to command the *Tulwar* when it was commissioned in a few weeks.

He was surprised to find that he didn't like having to expand his forces so quickly. More often than not, when one of his Humans showed proficiency at one job, they found themselves promoted into a new one. He was constantly looking for chances to rotate his leaders around, giving them a smattering of new experience before moving them up.

His people, like the species itself, were in a constant sink-or-swim situation and it felt far too much like flirting with disaster. Flirting might work in the short term but, as time wore on, you ran an increasing chance of getting to first base.

He'd nearly wound up in bed with disaster after the *reconnaissance* at Heiropolis.

He'd made full use of his ability when reporting to Mishak. Ordinarily, he would stay out of his lord's mind but he'd just made a fool of an incredibly powerful awilu and, though it couldn't be traced back to Mishak, Sandrak would still know. His actions would not be without consequence.

"We were considering a full assault and seizure anyway, Lord," he'd said, feeling Mishak's uncertainty and anger. "When I realized what a liability that system really is, I figured we could show that to the rest of the empire and leave less of a fingerprint in the process; make it harder for your father to justify a direct retaliatory move."

Mishak had sighed. "I would have sanctioned it," he'd replied, stressing the 'would'. "You could have come back with the suggestion."

Not quite a slap on the wrist, but it had shown Eth that his lord gave occasional thought to the degree of freedom he allowed his Humans. *Would he feel the same about a Quailu officer?* He shook his head, waving off Oliv's enquiring glance in response to the gesture.

No Quailu officer would operate under anything resembling the independence of Eth's forces. He supposed it was an outgrowth of his economic raiding days. There had been a need for Mishak to profess ignorance of what his 'renegade' combat slaves had been up to.

Somehow, that had carried over to their present relationship. So far, it had worked out, but he knew he had to avoid pushing the limits too much and a part of that was realizing just how much freedom, ironically, he and his fellow former-slaves now enjoyed.

That freedom accentuated the misgivings he felt from his lord. It made Eth even more eager to get back out into the black, away from his lord's court. Arriving in the Noori System was a welcome respite, even if Mishak would be following hard on Eth's heels with the main force.

"Closing the interlock valves," Meesh announced in a less-than-thrilled voice. "We are fully charged and ready for stealth."

Eth glanced over. Meesh, despite the tone of his voice, was working on five different holos at once. He might be missing his engine room but at least he wasn't letting that distract him from his job on the bridge. If anything, he was more focused than usual – probably an attempt to compensate.

It might help him when Eth forced him to accept a commission and take command of the *Tulwar*. He smiled, remembering when he'd been promoted by Mishak, who'd just promoted *himself* to elector status, and been given the cruiser he'd captured. Getting your own ship was a pretty effective way to help you get over the 'good old days'.

"All three sister ships report ready for operations," Comms said.

"Very well," Eth replied. "Send the launch order and go to comms blackout. Captain, I'd be obliged if you'd take us in."

"Aye, commander. Bring the emission management systems online."

Meesh slid one of his screens to the center of his workspace, frowning at it for a second until an icon turned green. "EM systems are online, Captain. We are ready for stealth operations."

"Thank-you, engineering," Oliv replied. "Hendy, take us to our assigned position, three-quarters pitch."

"Taking us in at three-quarters," Hendy confirmed.

The central holo suddenly populated with the initial data but it firmed up quickly. At three-quarters pitch, they were out of the dense gas of the local giant almost before Hendy had finished confirming his orders.

The ship, as previously decided, was turned sideways to maximize how much of the hull was capturing light from their target zone around Noori Prime. Given the local star's current position, they were actually giving the EM system a break, running nose-on to the star and flank-on to the planet.

When the pitch drives could shape their field of effect in any desired direction, the actual orientation of the hull had no effect on their direction of travel. They'd only been traveling bow-on out of habit.

"Looks like a lot of ships," Oliv commented quietly.

"Not so many that we can't make them regret coming here," Eth said calmly. "Send the sector-assignments to our sister ships, narrow-beam only."

"Do you think it'll come to a fight?"

Eth nodded, eyes still on the display. "Taking this system is the first step to making a new link between the two halves of Sandrak's holdings. He's been shown how vulnerable he is at Heiropolis, so he's not just stirring up trouble here. He's sent these fellows for a critical purpose. They won't be backing down."

She sucked at something stuck in her teeth. "I suppose there won't be any time to seize ships from the enemy, this time."

"Definitely not!" He took a deep breath. "This is going to be a straight-up fur-ball! Our lord may be hoping to play the diplomat in this confrontation but there's not much use for the velvet glove today. It's all about the iron fist. He'll take off the gloves; just you wait and see."

"Halfway there," Hendy said.

Eth glanced up at the voice pickups on the ceiling. "*Foot up Your Ass*, what's your status?"

"Strapped in and spooled up, Commander," Chief Warrant Carol replied.

She was one of the few who'd resisted a transfer and commission, and Eth was glad she had. With all the turmoil in his ranks, it was a comfort having her in charge of the scouting program.

Still, he was considering rolling the new scorpion-class corvettes into that program and he'd be needing a full lieutenant running the training program at the very least. It was far more likely that he'd have to find a way to move her up to lieutenant commander as fast as was decently possible.

She had the drive and force of personality to accomplish whatever task she took on. With the influx of Bau's new weapons, she'd corralled Noa into a re-design of the small scout-ships. They were slightly longer now and widened to accommodate twenty of the new missiles. A further twenty warheads were racked in the cramped walkway between the missile banks – a tribute to Meesh's minefield adventures in the Battle of Arbella.

All the warheads were coated with the same carbon nano-tubules that made the Human ships so hard to detect.

And Eth had no doubt they'd be using every weapon at their disposal today because this was shaping up to be a desperate fight.

"No defenders visible," tactical said. "Massive debris field consistent with an overwhelming victory for the aggressors. Planetary surface appears to be intact. No evidence of ground operations so far."

"So we're too late for Noori's defenders," Eth said, a cold feeling coming across him. "We stop them here. Cut their momentum while there are still two systems between them and their goal. We've exposed the weakness of Heiropolis; we will *not* be responsible for letting them end that weakness."

Hendy raised a hand to the throttle controls. "Approaching target area now. Reversing pitch. Bringing her about to put our dorsal surface toward the enemy."

"Tactical, stand by to launch weapons." Oliv turned to the velocity indicator and watched it drop down to zero. "Deploy missiles."

"Deploy missiles, aye, Captain."

"*Foot up Your Ass,* you have the green light. Deploy your weapons and get back ASAP."

"We'll be back before you know it," Carol's voice crackled from the ceiling. "Hull secure. We're separating."

Oliv brought up an enlargement of the exterior view of the ship. The *Foot up Your Ass* was invisible but for a section of the hull where they'd programmed a permanent docking collar. The one Achilles heel of the stealth coating was entry and exit points. Rather than coat them every time, the Humans had elected to create coated hatch covers that would rotate over the uncoated sections.

The disembodied hatch slid out of sight. "They're on their own," Oliv said quietly.

"And, yet, they're in far less danger than our enemy," Eth said.

With four scorpions and the scouts that each carried, they were able to box in the enemy formation, at least one ship on each side of a very large cube. It would take very little time to deploy an all-around crossfire – one that could destroy the whole enemy fleet in a matter of heartbeats.

"Missiles should be in place by now," the weapons officer said.

One of the problems posed by a stealthy missile became apparent when using them in this kind of standby mode. If you wanted them to move to dispersed locations in order to avoid their impact direction giving your position away, you had to trust that they'd reached their pre-programmed loitering assignments.

"Captain, I'd appreciate if you could initiate the signal-pair now."

""Aye, commander." Oliv nodded to the communications officer.

A space in front of Eth began to shimmer and then settled back almost to normalcy. He had to wait for several seconds until Mishak stepped into view.

"What are we looking at, commander?" the young noble asked.

Eth dragged a copy of his own tactical holo and tossed it into Mishak's projection. "Sixty-three cruisers, one hundred twenty-two frigates and one super-heavy cruiser. I'm pretty sure we have at least two electors sitting here and they've already wiped out the local defenses. Looks like they'll be conducting a few hours of repair work before moving on to the next phase."

"It would seem my father is serious about negating the bottleneck at Heiropolis, though the timing might indicate that he'd decided on this before our raid at Heiropolis," Mishak said mildly. "He's not an easy one to keep ahead of." He let out an exaggerated sigh.

"I'm not looking forward to his annual Solstice Address this year!" He leaned toward Eth. "You have his forces bracketed?"

"Our side is deployed, the other ships should be done and their shuttles docked by the time you drop out of path, lord."

Eth's holographic lord seemed to think for a moment, staring down at the deck. He finally looked up. "We'll launch into path right now. We'll reconnect when we arrive."

With a gesture, Mishak disappeared.

"Normalization complete," the helm reported.

"Initiate the signal pair," Fleet Captain Rimush ordered. "Fleet status?"

"All call-signs present and in formation," the tactical officer confirmed.

"We're being hailed," comms announced.

"Answer the hail and have them stand by."

It was usually best to establish the pecking order first and whoever was in charge of the hostile forces probably had something suitably dominant to say. Best to open the channel right away but make him wait. Mishak nearly laughed when he realized it was one of his father's favorite tactics.

Eth shimmered back into view and he gave a rotating hand gesture, silently assuring that all of the weapons were placed and the ships had recovered their scouts. The ships had *probably* recovered their scouts, that is. Given the need for stealth, they were relying on each other to get their jobs done, rather than blanket the area with signals.

"Open the channel and project it here." Mishak gestured to Eth's right.

A richly armored Quailu appeared in front of him. He was looking to his own left but turned when he heard the channel-opening chime. He got his mouth halfway open before Mishak spoke.

"Apsu? What in three levels of torment are you doing here?" he demanded angrily, leaning forward ever so slightly, the very picture of controlled anger. "You'd better have a damned good reason!"

Apsu seemed on the verge of taking a step back but then he steeled himself. "I might ask the same of you!" he replied stridently.

Mishak drew himself up, rearing his head back slightly to accentuate his ironic surprise. "That's your response?" he demanded quickly before Apsu could think of anything else to say. "You're just going to repeat everything I say, are you?" He chopped his hand across his front, indicating irrevocable action.

"It's a bad business, Apsu," he said darkly. "Thousands killed, Noorian sovereignty infringed and no *cassus belli* registered at Throne-World…" He trailed off, deliberately leaving Apsu an opening after placing him firmly on the defensive.

"It may be a bad business," Apsu conceded, "but it is no business of yours!"

"I disagree," Mishak countered. "We have always been a friend to the Noorians and, as a prince of the empire, do I not have a duty to protect those who cannot protect themselves? It would seem, noble *cousin*, that you've forgotten that duty."

"And it would seem," Apsu said dryly, "that you've missed your true calling. I'm sure you would have made a passable priest, given how much you love sermons."

"Then let's talk plainly," Mishak said reasonably, bowing politely as Tashmitum arrived on the bridge. He held out his left elbow and she linked arms with him. "We know why you've come here. You're trying to give my father a second link between the two halves of his... holdings."

Mishak had nearly said *kingdom* but he didn't want to be the one to start normalizing the concept. "We know you're doing this because my father knows everything that the Meleke Corporation knows about your slave populations. He can destroy you on a whim."

He was almost certain he'd noticed a few micro-gestures of alarm but it was still hard to be certain. He wished he still had Oliv around but then immediately felt guilty for his wife, who was standing next to him, sensing that guilt. He'd just have to muddle through without Oliv's help, which was also a good way to stop thinking about her.

Whatever had passed across Apsu's features, it was gone now. "So you know why I'm here," he scoffed. "That changes nothing."

"It changes the equations behind the leverage my father holds. I also possess the same information and I'll use it to stop you."

"And destroy half the economies of the empire?" Apsu laughed in Mishak's face, long enough to make the insult plain. "Your father needs no votes, young Mishak, but you do! There's no way you'd do it

189

and it's not just about votes. You're a decent fellow and a good leader but you don't have your father's ruthless streak.

"If I defy your father, I'll face horrifying retribution!" Apsu said, emphasising each word separately. "So, instead, I'll defy you."

Mishak's fists clenched. He could feel the anger on the bridge, the indignation from Tashmitum and it fed his own. He saw this for what it was – Sandrak was laughing at him. He might be using Apsu as a proxy but it was Sandrak.

It was always Sandrak.

No more! "Do you want to see what happens when you defy me?" he asked Apsu. "I will show you. In fact…" He glanced at Eth to make sure he was still listening. "… I'll even do you the courtesy of leaving you alive so you can fully appreciate what you've brought down on your head today."

And now the nonsensical orders would begin. He was angrier than he'd ever been in his entire life but he still remembered the need to provide a plausible explanation for what was about to happen.

"Confirm status of the signal-pair," he ordered.

"Signal-pair is active on our end, lord."

"Very well. Queue burst-message to read 'Destroy all hostile ships minus flagship of Lord Apsu. Deploy link-drone and execute evolution from current location. Launch weapons through burst-portals only."

The link-drone comment was intended to cover the use of a message drone from the *Scorpion*. It would be used to issue targeting orders to the cloud of stealthy missiles that waited in the darkness.

"Message queued and ready to send lord."

"Send it now."

Mishak looked up at the lights, which had dimmed considerably. Whoever had thought of that, it was a nice touch, giving the impression that the *Dibbarra* was suddenly expending a massive amount of energy.

"We managed to get a confirmation this time," the comms officer said, sounding mildly surprised. He looked up at Mishak. "That automated response from their *side* really makes a difference."

Apsu watched Mishak's piece of theater with growing alarm. Memnon had lost ships to this young awilu and there was still no consensus as to how it had been done.

All the cryptic talk referencing 'their location', 'burst-portals' and 'their side' was starting to worry him. Ilgi had claimed they'd attacked his flagship through some kind of trans-dimensional portal and, while he was undoubtedly a fool, no other explanations had been offered.

The entire bridge had been listening and they'd heard all the same rumors that Apsu had. The fear was building, threatening to take control of his mind. "What the devils are you doing?" he demanded of Mishak, his voice far more skittish than he'd hoped.

The smile from the holographic Quailu sent shivers up his spine. "You will see for yourself in just a moment."

"We're picking up an encrypted signal!" the tactical officer yelled, already keyed up by the atmosphere of fear on the bridge.

"Another fleet?" Apsu demanded.

"No, lord. It's coming from within our own formation but..." He looked up at Apsu. "Lord, there's nothing there! The signal appears to be coming from no source!"

"How can..." Apsu trailed off, mouth hanging open in cold shock as the main tactical holo showed sudden chaos in his fleet.

191

Damage reports were flooding his display and then suddenly going gray as if the ships were no longer reporting.

"We're under attack!" The tactical officer seemed to think that screaming the blatantly obvious would help matters.

It didn't.

Apsu, already unsettled by Mishak and shocked by the sudden influx of battle damage reports, froze up. He was rooted to the spot on the deck, his breathing coming in shallow, rapid gasps and his face was cold with sweat.

His mind screamed at him as he watched his ships go dark, and they went quickly. The entire time between the start of the assault and its apparent end must have been only a few heartbeats but the shock held him as his tactical interface updated.

Every ship – every single ship – had been struck simultaneously and the weapons had done horrific damage. They seemed to explode with incredible force, vaporizing anything that got in their way. Most ships were left with very little structure to hold the fore and aft sections together.

A small part of the hull and underlying structure surrounding the impact managed to escape the highly directional blasts. They were little more than salvageable nanites and engines but only in the ships where the engineering sections weren't hit.

Most of the ships no longer had engines or, for that matter, engineering sections.

"I don't believe it!" the tactical officer blurted out, at least capable of speaking. "I think we have only three frigates left that can still answer to their helms! I can't even tell who fired at us!"

Three frigates. Apsu had come here with sixty-three cruisers and one-hundred-twenty-two frigates and now he had his own cruiser and three damaged but serviceable frigates.

The calls started coming in now. The fleet-wide channel was inundated with panicked voices screaming for help.

"The enemy are firing again," tactical said. "The ships in *this* universe have launched missiles," he elaborated.

Apsu noted the reference to multiverse-combat but didn't bother to correct it. He was already overloaded by the sudden savagery unleashed on his forces and had little inclination to spare for such foolishness. He frowned.

Is it truly foolishness? Perhaps that moron, Ilgi, was right after all. Maybe Mishak had gotten his hands on something that let his ships slip between universes.

He shook his head, trying to force it back to the immediate problem. "Countermeasures," he snapped.

"They're active, lord, but we're not the target."

"Then who…"

The screaming voices were disappearing from the fleet-wide feed. It was somehow more horrifying for Apsu to watch as the missiles slowly sought out each of his remaining ships. Even the crippled vessels were being annihilated, the crews killed and he was helpless to stop it.

It was, he admitted to himself, the same thing he'd done to the Noorian defenders. Now he was on the receiving end.

The last of the transmitted voices went silent, except for one.

"Do you yield?" Mishak demanded.

Yield? Apsu's mind rebelled but what sense was there in fighting when his massive fleet had been wiped out in the blink of an eye? He should surrender now and concentrate on getting back to his own throne-world to start rebuilding his forces.

It would mean crushing taxes, perhaps even an emergency annexation of several corporations, but he had to replace his losses.

And do what? Would they just end up destroyed? He couldn't begin to explain how Mishak had done this.

He realized that, even if he couldn't defend against Mishak, he would definitely need to defend himself against his neighbors. His defensive fleets were only ever intended to fight delaying actions while the main fleet was brought in.

Once news of this defeat got out, powerful neighboring lords would see the chance to seize a system or two and elevate themselves to elector status. They'd be more than willing to throw their fleets at him in order to enter the inner circle of power.

And he'd be out.

There was no choice. "I yield," he snapped.

Mishak turned to say something that the pick-ups didn't catch. He looked back. "Stand ready to receive a boarding party."

The party was led by an ensign, a deliberate slight to Apsu's status as an elector. "The ship is yours," Apsu declared stiffly, feeling the shame of his crew, the disdain of this young enemy officer.

"I know," he replied flippantly, waving two of his party toward the rear of the bridge. The ensign simply stood there, four more of the boarders at his back, saying nothing as his men left through the aft hatch that led to the main companionway.

Apsu fidgeted without noticing it. He glanced around helplessly, uncomfortable in the silence. Whatever new humiliation was in store, he wished they'd simply get on with it. "What do you intend to do with us?" he finally demanded.

The ensign looked at him for a long moment. "Well, firstly, I intend to tell you that you should remain silent unless directly addressed. The ship, after all, is mine, is it not?"

Apsu couldn't believe his ears! He was an elector, a prince of the realm! Victorious or not, this young buck had no right to address him in this fashion!

The ensign leaned forward. "You were directly addressed," he offered helpfully. "You may answer, if you wish."

It was finally too much and Apsu exploded. "You insolent little gnat!" he yelled. "Your conduct reflects poorly on your master and, rest assured, I shall see to it that the empire learns of your disgraceful treatment of an elector!"

"That would be a neat trick," the youngster said obscurely, his back to Apsu now. He picked up a mug from the communications station, gave its contents a sniff and then took a drink.

"Lord," the tactical officer called quietly from behind him.

"Not now," Apsu snapped, too busy wondering about the ensign's comment to bother with his bridge crew. *What did he mean by that? Why would it be any kind of trick, complaining about his behavior to an elector?*

He could feel a clear sense of consternation from his tactical officer but he steadfastly ignored it. Who cared about tactical considerations on a ship they no longer controlled, anyway?

The two members of the boarding party who'd gone running off aft reappeared, breathing heavily.

"All done?" the ensign inquired brightly. "Good!" he enthused in response to their affirmation. "Well…" He waved the mug in a vague gesture. "… My lord, you can have your ship back." He drained the mug and handed it to the befuddled communications officer.

"Have it back?" Apsu had assumed he'd be transferred to the Dibbarra as a prisoner, if he were to be left alive.

"Well, we certainly don't want it, do we?" the ensign replied. "Don't really need another cruiser and, frankly, there are too many of your lot aboard her. Best we just cut you loose, at this point. Come along, lads." This last was to his boarding party. "Galley staff are serving *billeche* tonight and we don't want to miss out!"

"Oh!" He stopped in the portal that joined his shuttle to Apsu's cruiser. "My lord bids me to tell you that you're welcome to follow us, though, if you'd rather not watch, he understands that as well. The important thing is that you can't remain here. Noori is now under his protection."

"Watch... Watch what?" Apsu demanded.

"He's sending out couriers to inform your neighbors that you no longer have your fleet. He's also letting each know that he's telling *all* of them. I suspect there's going to be a mad rush to snap up your holdings."

The ensign's focus drifted for a moment, as if he were searching his memory to see if he'd missed anything. He looked back at Apsu and offered a cheerful wave. "Happy paths, my lord!"

He passed through the opening and the portal flowed shut.

Things were far more desperate than Apsu could ever have imagined. There would be no time to rebuild his forces, not even time to consolidate his planetary defense detachments, not if all nine of his systems would be under attack at the same time! He needed to do something but what?

"What's the status of the enemy fleet?" he demanded, hoping to jump-start his mind.

"I was trying to tell you, lord," tactical replied. "We're blind. Those two boarders must have destroyed our comms suites. We don't even have backups. Our database is wiped as well."

"The database..." *They don't want us reviewing recordings of the attack!* Apsu forced himself to shelve that consideration for later. Right now, there was only one sensible course of action. "Lay in a path for Kells."

"Laying in a path for Kells," the helmsman confirmed.

Get home, he thought, *pilfer the entire treasury and evacuate the family.* He'd have to come to terms with his downfall when time

196

permitted but, if he acted quickly, he could come to terms with it from a position of comfort and not as a penniless *beggar émigré*.

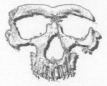

"I understand," Tashmitum told Mishak.

"I'm not sure you do," he countered. "I hadn't planned to take such extreme measures against Apsu. I let myself be goaded into it. My whole life, I've despised my father for his viciousness and, now, in my attempt to beat him, I'm *becoming* him."

"No," she said firmly. "You're afraid that you *might* be turning into him. You were ruthless, yes, but no awilu would have acted otherwise in your place, not if they wished to be taken seriously.

"Apsu laughed at the idea of your vengeance. Now the entire empire will shudder at the results. If you wish to join me on the throne, you can't deny the value of an example like this and you can't shrink from employing ruthlessness when it's needed."

"An emperor who fears his own power never rules for long," Mishak said, quoting one of Marduk's numerous lessons.

"The fact that you're conscious of your father's flaws only makes it *less* likely that you're going to become him," she insisted.

"But I didn't do it out of cold calculation," he countered. "I let anger force my hand. I let my father force my hand, even if it wasn't what he expected."

"Then we're very lucky it worked out for us," she admitted, stepping closer. "Next time," she continued, tapping the side of his head, "do your thinking with this." She lowered the hand and he hissed at the sudden, cupping pressure.

"Never let this take the lead."

They both looked toward the door of their quarters as a door chime sounded. "Enter," Tashmitum replied, stepping away from Mishak.

The hatch slid aside to reveal Fleet Captain Rimush. "Apsu's family have been retrieved from Kells," he said as he entered. "We'll hand them over to his care." He tilted his head, sensing Mishak's consternation but not understanding it.

"After hostiles arrive, of course," Mishak corrected.

"Indeed lord," Rimush replied, allowing a note of mild reproof at being *told how to chew grass*. "A large fleet of hostiles is already here."

Mishak sat up, opening a holo-display. He selected the tactical menu and saw that a fleet of roughly forty ships had arrived. It wasn't overwhelming force on the scale employed by Apsu at Noori but it would do against the small planetary defense detachment orbiting Kells.

"Gilbennu," Mishak said flatly.

"He might be of use to us," she suggested.

"I did tell him this opportunity existed," Mishak agreed, "but gratitude has a short half-life. He'll make himself into an elector today, but he'll emphasise his own efforts here over ours at Noori. The fact that he wouldn't have dared to try this if Apsu still had his huge battle fleet is something he'd rather forget about as soon as possible."

"So we should burnish our own role as much as possible," Tashmitum said. "This has all happened so quickly…"

"He wouldn't have had time to arrange for a Varangian presence to authenticate his claim," Mishak said. "You're suggesting that we stay?"

"Yes, long enough for the Varangians to come. Once they're here, no other lords would dare interfere."

"That takes care of Kells," Rimush said, "but Apsu had other systems…"

"And if one or more of them happen to be enough to grant a vote to the lord taking it," Tashmitum replied, "we can look at assisting them as well. No sense in fighting for every two-system minor lord who feels like rolling the dice."

"It's been a good day's work, I suppose," Mishak said. "Thanks to the data we took before frying Apsu's data-core, I know where my brother's still using the same hiding-place between atrocities."

"You're thinking of confronting him?"

"Soon, but only when we're ready."

Who Do We Have Here?
The Sar Ili, *pathing.*

Gleb picked up his pace, then he caught himself and slowed down again. No sense in acting different than the other Humans on this ship, especially now.

He'd gotten into the database on the *Sar Ili*, but he'd found little more than scraps. Sandrak was far more careful with information than Memnon. In the end, he'd resorted to bugging the elector's quarters and ready room.

What he'd learned had seemed so out of character for Sandrak that Gleb had suspected the bugs had been found and they were feeding him a false line. He'd come to see the sense of it, though, in the light of the Quailu's overall ambitions.

Now he just had to get off the ship and he'd need to reach the shuttle-bay before the ship dropped out of path. A courier was set to depart as soon as they restored normalcy and Gleb intended to be aboard.

He walked past the large, open cargo-doors of the bay and turned left into a corridor running just aft of the large hangar. He slipped in through a small door that opened onto the hangar just behind a stack of water-cubes.

Unfortunately, a junior petty officer was there, checking the levels in the cubes. He noticed Gleb and, oddly, seemed familiar with the Human.

"Not yet!" the Quailu hissed angrily. "I told you I need to talk to my superior. We can't just jump the chain of command, no matter how interesting your information is!"

"My information?" Gleb blurted. "What the hells…"

"Enough!" The Quailu drew his weapon. "It's much easier for me to just hand you over for…"

... Gleb was in agony. It felt like he'd been beaten for several hours. He winced at a fresh stab of pain in his abdomen and tried to put his hand over the area, only to find he couldn't move his arm.

He opened his eyes and looked around. The Quailu petty officer was gone. Come to think of it, so was the shuttle bay.

He was stretched out by his arms and legs, X fashion, in an interrogation cell.

"Oh!" he said simply, as if to say *fair enough, I feel as if I've been beaten because... I've been beaten.*

But how long had this been going on? It certainly felt like the beating hadn't been rushed and, yet, he couldn't remember any of it. *One advantage of these shifting personalities, I suppose. I don't have to put up with the worst of the pain.*

It must have been a standard Quailu interrogation; apply generous amounts of pain while repeating the questions, over and over. Their empathic senses could do a better job of sorting out the lies from the truth if you were busy trying to manage your agony.

Gleb frowned. *What did I... the other I ...tell them? What does he even know?* If the *other* Gleb knew what the original Gleb knew, the results of this interrogation might have disastrous consequences for the Humans.

His thoughts were interrupted by loud footsteps. At least two sets.

"So this is the culprit?" a deep voice asked, its owner moving to stand in front of Gleb.

Sandrak... Gleb made a conscious effort to still his thoughts. Even so, a shiver ran down his spine as he realized how bad this situation was. No harm done, though, as his surprise was an entirely normal thing, given the circumstances. Whatever *other Gleb* may have given up, he'd be damned if he gave them more than his fear.

"He doesn't seem like much," Sandrak observed. "He gave you what you needed?"

"Indeed, lord," another voice answered from behind. "These Humans have no control. Their minds are an open book, even without torture."

Gleb could sense the interrogator's disdain. It was the most beautiful thing he'd ever felt in his life. They'd taken away his under-armor suit before hanging him up in here but it was the lack of his abilities that *really* made him feel naked.

"We'll be dropping out at Ashurapol soon." Sandrak turned to leave. "Make sure you space him before we go into orbit. The Ashurapolitians get fussy about space-junk interfering with their weather satellites."

Gleb closed his mind, leaving only a thin veneer of fear for the two Quailu to pick up. He knew the interrogator's EVA armor wasn't going to fit him – the Quailu facial structure was far too different to adapt to a Human – but his weapon would work just fine.

The door hissed closed behind Sandrak. "Come on, you little turd," the interrogator said darkly. "Time to fly!" The restraints opened and Gleb tumbled to the decking.

All the bruises, cuts and cracked ribs that his mind had managed to put on the back burner suddenly forced their way to the forefront, screaming for attention. Gleb joined them, shrieking in agony.

The deep rumbling chuckle brought his focus back. He followed the sound, wormed his way into the Quailu's mind and went for the cranial artery.

His focus was a bit off and the victim let out a slurred exclamation, staggering back from Gleb and knocking over a tray of implements. Still, he went down and stayed there.

Gleb forced himself to stand and he wavered for a moment before risking his first, shaky step. He tottered over to the torturer and fell to his knees to pull out his pistol.

Get to the dormitory, grab a suit, he thought. The striate-gears in a suit would do wonders for his mobility and it would protect what seemed to be at least a couple of cracked ribs.

But how to get there?

He'd had enough trouble focusing on his tormentor's cranial artery, he didn't like his chances of transposing directly to the dorms.

A naked human staggering around the corridors would certainly attract attention. He winced, putting a hand to his ribs.

What if it looks like I'm supposed *to draw attention?* He looked down at the dead Quailu for a moment and then reached inside the neck-ring of the Quailu's suit. He pressed the retract button that was placed there so that casualty-aid techs could open the suits of unconscious patients.

The provost marshal on this ship had some strange ideas regarding the punishment of minor infractions…

He cursed, scrambling after the knife that had been sheathed on the torturer's chest. It was flowing away from Gleb as the armor's nanites carried it to a growing block at the feet. He pulled out the knife and set to work, cutting away the Quailu's underarmor suit.

He made a mess of it, shredding it without concern but not without reason. He made a few more cuts once it was free of the body, slicing it to make long, hanging strips.

He wrapped most of the suit around his head, making it into a crude parody of a jester's motley hat. He looked longingly at the pistol and knife, knowing they represented a false security.

His only chance, now, lay in folly, not force. With a sigh that morphed into a moan, he climbed back to his feet and shuffled to the door, leaving the weapons on the floor by their former owner.

He managed to get out of the provost section without incident but he ran into a lieutenant in the central corridor whose disgust slammed against him like a wave.

"What the hells is this?" he demanded of the nude Human.

Gleb sketched an elaborate but jerky bow. He had to play this to the hilt or else try killing everyone he met. He doubted he was in any condition to exert that level of mental control at the moment.

"Pardon, Sire, if my presence offends." He shook his motley headdress. "I pray my appearance makes amends?"

The officer, seeing just another Human, must have assumed he was seeing another of the humiliating punishment practices common on the *Sar Ili*. He pushed past, shoving Gleb against the wall.

Gleb hissed in pain, clutching his side. He took a moment, getting the pain back under control, and then he pushed himself away from the wall and set a course for the dorms.

There were another eight Quailu between him and the dorms and he managed to receive two kicks in the posterior and one slap to the side of his head. He was not terribly well-disposed toward the empire's master-race by the time he passed into the dorms to find a Quailu petty officer waving a pistol and screaming abuse at the dull-faced Humans.

The Quailu turned, wondering what the dull faces were suddenly so interested in and he roared in laughter. "What did they catch you for, rank stupidity?"

Gleb held up a hand toward the petty officer, savouring the moment. The hand wasn't necessary but he figured a little showmanship sometimes went a long way.

The Quailu slumped to the floor.

"Thank you universe," Gleb muttered. "I needed that." He stepped over the corpse and walked to the bunks where the suits stood packed in marked squares on the floor.

He chuckled at the looks the Humans were giving him. It sent a stab of pain through his chest, making him gasp. He stopped walking, struggling to control the urge to hunch up his left shoulder.

"You should see the other guy," he quipped darkly. He stepped into the closest suit-block and shifted his heels to activate it.

"Hey!" a person in one of the middle bunks protested. "That's mine you thieving piece of…"

He stopped, frozen by the look on Gleb's face.

"Listen up, you humps!" he growled. "I've been having a *really* bad day. If any of you even *thinks* of walking out that door in the next hour, you'll get a taste of what that PO just got."

He ignored their reaction. The suit had closed around his torso and, analysing his stats, applied pressure to his right flank, easing his ribs into alignment.

He gritted his teeth, cursing the sadistic moron who'd designed the suit's protocols. With his ribs now aligned and properly braced, an anaesthetic blasted through his skin.

He shuddered at the release from pain, blessing the sadistic moron, as he had many times during his life as a combat slave. *What a metaphor for the empire in general.*

The Real Gleb
Ashurapol, Henx Prime

"Mel!" Siri hissed angrily. "Come on! We're going to get caught!" She held the cargo netting on a pallet of square-melons as if it were the only thing keeping her on the planet.

"But look at the cipher on the side of the shuttle," he whispered back, as though the Quailu pilot could hear him from a hundred feet away. "It's from Sandrak's fleet!"

She gestured angrily. "If they see Humans, they'll assume we're deserters and they'd be right!" She let out a sigh of relief as he started back her way. *Finally, you reckless fool!*

They crossed the perimeter surface-road that surrounded the cargo yard and headed for the cover of a nearby coffee shop that also had an exit from its other side, leading to a slidewalk.

"If Gleb is up there," she told him, "then he'll come down and find us when he's ready. There's no need to risk getting captured."

"But what if that tracker you left in the apartment fails or gets found?" he countered. "We'd never know he was there and he'd have no way of knowing where we'd moved to."

"You can't plan for every possible contingency," she insisted, not for the first time. "Sometimes, you just have to accept a few risks. I'd just rather not run the risk of getting caught for no good reason. Don't you realize how stupid it would have been for us to simply walk right into their…

"Shit!"

"Into their what?" Mel looked up from the wrist-pad on his suit to find two Quailu, the only other people in the place, getting up from their tables, the sigil of two crossed encryption keys on a black background emblazoned on their shoulders.

They were looking intently at the two Humans.

206

"Ah," Mel said, sighing. "Context can be a real bitch sometimes. I was a lot happier with my first interpretation."

Siri couldn't help but chuckle, though it certainly didn't improve the demeanor of the two Quailu who came to stand in front of them.

"Who are you two and what the hells are you doing down here unattended?" the senior of the two officers demanded.

Siri reached out to rest a hand on Mel's shoulder, warning him to let her respond. She took a deep breath. *Bullshit meter to full.* "Who we are would seem rather obvious, wouldn't it? We're Humans in the service of your lord. As to what we're doing here, it should be equally obvious why you *wouldn't* know about it, if you gave it even the slightest bit of thought!"

The Quailu glanced quizzically at his companion but then pulled out his pistol. "You're just deserters!" he insisted, taking refuge in a more concrete line of thought. "We can take you back up to the flagship for execution or, if you prefer," he added with mock politeness, "I can just shoot you here and save us all the trouble. Which would you prefer?"

Before she could frame a response, there came a horrendous crash from the ceiling and the four of them, Humans and Quailu alike, raised their arms to shield themselves from falling debris. An armored shape hammered its way through the structure, thrusters firing, and came to a brutally abrupt halt, crouched on the now-cracked and bowed graphene floor.

"Nergal's ass-fungus!" the form exclaimed, placing his right hand against his torso.

The intruder stood, helmet retracting and Siri laughed aloud in her sudden relief at seeing Gleb.

"Don't answer that question," he ordered her briskly before turning to look up through the hole he'd just made in the building. He grinned, nodding toward the two open-mouthed Quailu. "That's an invigorating way to make an entrance! I'd highly recommend it."

The senior officer lowered his pistol. He stared at Gleb in shock and amazement. "Who the hells are you?"

"I'm their lawyer!"

"Their… lawyer?"

"Sure, why not?" Gleb took a step closer, almost causing them to back up. "Are you aware, Lieutenant, that their article of indenture would almost certainly be ruled illegal in any court in the HQE? They were made to sign in return for being grown in the first place and the law is very clear that you can't be indentured for something you already possess."

"Where the hells did you just come from?" Mel blurted.

"I was on a cargo shuttle coming down from the flagship. Seemed a better choice than the courier ship." Gleb waved vaguely back up through the hole. "I was monitoring all ship's personnel feeds and saw the two of you walking up to these two so I jumped through the hull."

"So, won't they come looking for you?" Siri asked. She turned as she heard what sounded like thunder from the cargo yard outside. Alarms started shrieking.

"Nope," Gleb shook his head. "The part of the hull I jumped through happened to contain the main bus so I think my disappearance will slip through the cracks. They'll be too busy recovering the pilot's remains to worry about me."

He was looking past the Humans to the door they'd come in through. "No fresh produce for a while, I think."

With a suddenness that startled her, he spun toward the Quailu officer who'd started raising his pistol again. He grasped the weapon, turning it in toward the officer's body. The grip and trigger rotated out of its owner's fingers as if they were coated with oil and Gleb drove his left shoulder into the Qauilu's chest, grunting with pain as he did. He stepped back, aiming the weapon at the other officer who'd started going for his own gun.

"It's all the same to me," Gleb said flatly.

The lieutenant was doubled over from the impact to his chest, trying desperately to hang onto the food he'd had for lunch.

Whatever the other Quailu saw in the Human's mind, it convinced him to surrender his own weapon. "When we get back to the ship," he snarled, "your kind will be finished! We'll shove them all out an airlock!"

Siri felt a cold chill. She didn't know any of Sandrak's Human crewmembers but she didn't want to be responsible for their deaths.

"May as well make it worthwhile," Gleb said with a note of resignation. He tossed the Quailu a credit chip. "Transfer your funds onto this or I'll blow your heads off!"

"And all this time," the lieutenant wheezed, now mostly standing erect, "I didn't think you were actually a lawyer. Turns out I was wrong!"

They both transferred their credits to the chip and tossed it back. "There's not near enough money on there to let you run forever!"

Gleb smiled and, though the two Quailu couldn't recognize the coldness of the expression, they both felt it from his mind and they shivered involuntarily. "I don't care a steaming pile for the credits," he told them. "They're just..." He darted a wink at Mel. "... context."

"Context?"

"That's right. Something to make life easier for your provost officers. A robbery gone wrong..." He pulled the trigger and the junior officer was thrown back in a welter of blood.

The senior threw up his hands, mouth moving silently and Siri wondered if Gleb could feel the other's mental scream. The trigger was pulled a second time and both of the enemy now lay dead on the floor.

Given his other abilities, it seemed possible.

She watched him walk over to one of the corpses and activate the officer's wrist holo. "What's the plan, Gleb?"

"The plan," he said, scrolling through holo-menus at an awkward angle, "is to get out of here before Sandrak's recovery and rescue teams blanket the area." He pressed a holographic button and an image of the planet came up.

"I was hoping there'd be a little more detail to that plan," she admitted.

He zoomed in on one of the orbital holding zones. "I thought I'd have a little more time to come up with something after I slipped away from the cargo yard but things got a little accelerated. I saw the two of you getting caught, so I improvised and now we need to *keep on* improvising."

"I was worried you wouldn't find us," Mel admitted. "We moved to another apartment, just in case..." He trailed off in embarrassment.

"In case I got caught and started talking?" Gleb asked, still staring at the ships in the display.

"Yeah," Siri said. "In case you got caught. I figured it would be best to move a few blocks away and leave a tracker in the old place so you could find us."

"Oh, yes!" Gleb exclaimed. "Just what I was in the mood for!" He enlarged the view to show a frigate off to the side of a fleet labeled with an icon of Sandrak's crest.

"The *Harpy of Irkalla*!" He grinned wolfishly. "Taken from the Lady Bau some four months ago. Sandrak's got her *en flute*; the Harpy, that is, not the lady. He's pulled all the weapons systems and he's using her as a prison ship. Crammed to the hull with folks he's seized and who might prove useful to him someday."

He looked up at Siri. "You made a smart call, moving to a new location. Coming here was a bit of a screw-up but I'd say the first outweighs the second."

"Especially since it was me who caused the screw-up," Mel admitted.

Gleb looked at him an eyebrow raised. "At least it was a decision. Better a bad decision than none at all. Taking ownership of your screw-ups is something I firmly approve of."

He nodded toward the back of the café. "Both of you need to head to the toilets and take ownership of any cleaning equipment and supplies you can find. They'll be crucial to getting us off Henx."

Siri led the way to the restroom. Her nose wrinkled at the smell of a room where dozens of different species, each with their own ideas on cleanliness, went to relieve themselves.

Though many washrooms kept their cleaning supplies stored in a closet, this was an automated café and the owners had left the supplies hanging from hooks on the wall in the mistakenly optimistic hope that they'd be used by the patrons.

"What the hells do you think this stuff has to do with getting out of here?" Mel asked.

"Beats me." She grabbed an entropy-neutral bucket which, by its smell, had probably not been recharged in years and snagged a bottle of emulsifying spray on her way back out. "He hasn't steered us wrong, so far."

They found Gleb by the door leading back out to the cargo yard. "There's a door back there," she told him, nodding over her shoulder. "

"No, we'll just go out this way," Gleb said with apparent unconcern. He nodded at the materials they'd collected. "Should be enough to convince them," he added cryptically before pushing out into the smell of carbon dust and burning hydraulics from the shuttle he'd come down in.

"Just stay quiet and follow my lead," he warned over his shoulder as he passed the wreckage. He angled in toward another shuttle with Sandrak's crest. A pilot was lounging against the side of the craft and he pushed away from the hull to confront the three Humans.

"What are you three doing down here?" he demanded, one hand moving toward the handle of his pistol.

"Shuttle taking us to the *Harpy* got redirected down here." Gleb waved toward the burning wreckage. "They told us to wait and that shuttle would drop us on the way back to the flagship."

"And why do you need to go to the *Harpy*?"

"Well, it's the uprising, see?" Gleb confided, happy to be spreading gossip.

"Uprising?"

"Yes, sir, almost managed to seize the ship from the provosts! After that, they put everyone into lockdown."

"So it's in lockdown," the pilot retorted, anger building. "Why does that have anything to do with the three of you?"

"Well, nobody's allowed out of their cabins. Food goes in but nobody can come out so, when a prisoner pounds on the door and tells a guard he needs to drop muffins, he's told to make the best of a bad situation."

The guard's anger was turning now to amusement. "So they're wallowing in their own filth?"

"Liquids and solids, sir!" Gleb said cheerfully. "That's where we come in. Come in literally, you might say, as we have to go into each cell."

A deep rumbling laugh burst from the pilot and he waved them up the rear ramp. It wasn't lost on Siri that the Quailu officer was far more willing to help them if it meant delivering them to a demeaning job. No doubt, that was exactly why Gleb had chosen his current story.

She noticed how the pilot winced away from her as she passed.

"Next time make sure that bucket is charged, you fool!"

"Yes, sir," she replied meekly. She scurried past him and buckled into a seat.

"Well, I'm not waiting around down here so you can stink up my shuttle," the pilot groused, brushing past between the Humans. "I'll take you up now and then come back down here to get the stink out."

He must have been serious about the smell because he left the back ramp open as they ascended, only closing it when the atmosphere began to thin appreciably. They approached the prison ship at almost full speed, slowing only at the last second, sidling up on her port flank and opening a portal between the two hulls.

Shuttles didn't generally land inside prison ships, as it left them exposed on all sides in the event of an uprising. Using hull-to-hull portals greatly reduced the directions from which any boarding attempt might come.

Gleb led the way through the opening, which sealed as soon as Siri and Mel had cleared it. They were alone in a cargo hold – not surprising, considering they weren't expected.

Siri turned to Gleb. "So... now what?"

"We make the rounds," Gleb told her as though it was the most natural thing to do. "The provosts guarding the ship will be a little surprised at our presence but we're only Humans. It's not out of the realm of possibility that someone might have sent us over here as sanitation laborers without bothering to tell them."

"So..." Mel frowned.

"Yeah, Mel. We're gonna take our cleaning gear and find out who's being held on this ship while we pretend to be cleaning. It might have escaped your notice, but my clever plan is to steal this frigate.

"There are currently only..." He made a show of looking around himself. "...three conspirators. Maybe we could pull it off, but

213

I'm no engineer and the two of you are comms techs, so I think we might want to find out if there are any valuable recruits on this ship before we *stir the nibblers' nest*."

"But why can't you just do your... mind-thing?" Siri asked.

"Too many witnesses. The ship is full of prisoners and I don't want them telling the rest of the HQE about a bunch of inexplicably dead provosts." He turned so he could face them both.

"Look, what I did on Memnon's ship represents a real danger, a danger to our species. If the Quailu find out I can kill them with a thought, they're likely to wipe us all out."

There was also the small matter of Gleb only being a part-time resident in his own skull...

"How long can you keep a secret like that?" Siri asked him dubiously. "Are we the only ones that know about it?"

"There are others who know," he answered cryptically, "and it's bound to come out sooner or later, but we prefer later. The longer we can keep this quiet, the harder it gets for them to get rid of us.

"For now, I need you both to get your heads into the right space. You're lowly Humans, glad, at least, that you're free-born but you're still subject to abuse. Siri, you're glad to be here, even as a cleaner, because it gets you away from some bastard like Davu and Mel's glad for the same reason because he likes you."

Siri supressed a smile at this. *Perhaps he can read people, after all.* While they had been waiting for Gleb's return, they'd studied the programming manuals, as he'd suggested.

But they'd also done other things...

The door opened and a provost petty officer stepped in with his pistol raised. He aimed it at the Humans.

Gleb raised his hands. "Cleaning detail," he said, his voice wavering slightly.

"Cleaning detail? Three comms techs?"

"We're... also a punishment detail," Gleb admitted, the wavering tone betraying his embarrassment, perhaps helping him to project the right emotions to the provost.

It must have worked because the Quailu snorted in amusement. "Fine, get to work but stay out of our way!" He holstered his weapon and left the hold.

Gleb called up a basic ship's menu. "First, let's see what they have listed in the prisoner manifest."

Siri, a comms specialist by trade, knew enough to understand that Gleb was changing the interface. "What exactly are you doing?"

"Well, I'm sure you know I can't just open up anything, except the most basic menus, without sounding an alarm on the bridge." He opened an upload window and held his wrist interface port up to it. "So I'm adding in an access portal designed by an old friend. It should let us go anywhere we want in the system without drawing attention."

He pulled his wrist back from the screen and closed the upload interface window. The entire holo flickered once, updating with a wide variety of new options. He brought up a list of prisoners. "At least half the *Harpy's* original crew has been either killed or transferred off but most of the engineering staff are still here.

"I was counting on that," he admitted. "You can't run a prison ship with just a handful of provosts. If a reactor went critical, they wouldn't know which wrench to hit it with. I'd bet we'll find half the staff down in the engine room right now, just running routine maintenance."

"You can pull up personnel locations on this class of frigate," Siri told him. "The Lady Bau must have just had this one grown before Sandrak seized it."

Gleb looked at her. "They teach you that as a comms tech?"

She shook her head. "You told us to learn programming while you were gone." She pointed at the display in front of his face. "The version number on the firmware has a date, if you know how to pick it out. This ship is only a few months old."

She frowned at the look on Gleb's face. "What?"

Gleb seemed to shake off whatever had brought the look of concern to his face. "Never mind. It's just one more reason to get in touch with the old crew, but it's my worry, not yours."

He gestured to the display. "Show me how to bring up personnel locations."

She reached out and opened a series of sub-menus. "It's in the engineering coding," she explained. "The ship has to track everyone aboard because it sends a suit-close command in the event of a hull breach or if we rig for combat." She smiled, giving a little shrug. "That was how I thought to look for it in the sample codes we were learning with."

"Clever!" Gleb grinned, nodding his approval.

She felt a surge of pride and she wasn't sure how to deal with it. She chose to focus on what she was doing. "Here we are, literally, as it turns out." She pointed at the new holo-image of the ship indicating the three forms that represented the Humans.

"Well done, future petty officer!" Gleb gave her a light punch on the shoulder.

She'd only ever known such a gesture as an attack but, given the context, she couldn't help but feel it was meant in a friendly, congratulatory way. "Engineering looks crowded," she said.

"It certainly does," Gleb agreed. "Twelve engineering crew and six provosts to watch over them. Typical linear provost thinking. They know there's a risk the engineers might cook up some mischief, so they put a heavy watch on them. Looks like a third of their total manpower is sitting down there staring at pipes."

"Waste of time," Mel said with a grin. "When engineers want to cook up mischief, they do it through holo-interfaces. It would just look

216

like they're doing regular engineering stuff until it's too late!" He noticed Gleb's raised eyebrow. "I wanted to be an engineering tech but they put me in comms."

Gleb nodded, a grin spreading across his face. "Ain't no way a provost is gonna know he's watching mischief brewing until it's too late to do anything about it!"

He closed the holo. "Right! Screw the cleaning routine! We'll go down to engineering and get them to help seize the ship!"

Siri put a restraining hand on his shoulder, turning him back. "What makes you think they'll help us?"

"Because they serve Lady Bau," he replied with a tone of unshakable confidence. "The Lady would never forgive them if they failed to assist us, especially when it would have brought this ship back to her."

They followed him out into the corridor. Siri couldn't help but think that there was a lot of missing context behind Gleb's statement. *Bau held a vote in the imperial succession. She was an electress, so why the hells would she care about whether some of her captured crewmen were willing to help a handful of Humans?*

Sure, she could get a ship back in the deal, but that would seem like a long shot to her. How would she even come to hear of this, anyway?

They walked straight up to the main entrance to engineering and stepped into the space between the inner and outer doors. The doors cycled and they stepped into the vast open space that housed the path drive.

"You're that cleaning detail?" a provost lieutenant asked them from a control room door.

"That's right, sir," Gleb confirmed. "Just a quick clean-up in here before we start on the prisoner cabins."

The officer waved them in and went back to his seat.

217

Gleb led them straight to a small group of five Quailu engineering crewmen and, as they approached, one of them glanced over and noticed them. Siri had no explanation for their response but she felt the thrill of a deepening mystery.

The crewman looked surprised, his stance altering slightly to elevate his head. It was an atavistic instinct that had allowed his distant ancestors to search for predators on the savannahs of his home-world. He turned back to the group, whispering urgently, and they all turned to look.

"Way to act casual, fellas," Gleb muttered under his breath. He looked around the space. "At least the provosts seem to have realized the futility of staring at the engineering prisoners for the entire shift. Probably all watching vids in the control rooms."

He walked up to the group and nodded affably.

A lieutenant wearing the stripes of a path-drive team-leader waved for his team to be silent. "You're Humans, aren't you?"

"That's right. Name's Gleb."

That touched off a flurry of surprised exclamations. Siri watched in fascination as they exchanged glances with each other. Some darted quick looks to the catwalk above but there were no provost guards up there. *Why is it such a big deal that we're Human and that he's Gleb?*

"You were there at the gas platform?" the lieutenant whispered. "You were one of the Humans who saved our lady?"

Now that's interesting! Siri thought, the hairs standing up on the back of her neck.

"It seemed like the right thing to do," Gleb said, as though rescuing powerful nobles was the sort of thing he might do on a whim.

The Quailu crewmen chuckled quietly. Their officer stepped in closer. "What are you doing here on the *Harpy?*"

"We noticed Sandrak is using her as a prison hulk and thought your lady might want her back," Gleb replied mildly. "Doubtless, you guys have already cooked up a scheme to do that, but we thought we'd drop in and see if you could use a little help."

Another deep rumbling chuckle. "So," the officer asked, "you're escaping from something or someone and our ship was convenient?"

"Also that," Gleb allowed cheerfully. "So what do you have in the works?"

The crewmen looked around them again, seeing no guards. "We're hoping to use the grav-plating to immobilize the guards. Came up with it a couple of weeks ago, but the damned provosts have two guards in the grav-control room 'round the clock. The old grav-gambit is one of the oldest tricks in the scroll."

"Mostly because it's one of the *best* tricks in the scroll!" Gleb said. "Don't worry about the guards. I'll get your boys in there. What else do we need to get things rolling? Clear a path up to the bridge?"

"We were planning to conn the ship from here, actually," the engineer said.

"Figures, seeing as you're engineers," Gleb said, arching an eyebrow.

"No," the officer countered. "Conning from engineering is a poor second-best but we have no way of grav-trapping *just* the provosts. We'd have to search the corridors one section at a time, restoring normal gravity as we went, until we found them all. The fleet would figure out something's up long before we ever reached the bridge!"

"What if I told you there was a way to locate them that didn't end up violating Lady Bau's software contract?" Gleb asked him. He turned to beckon Siri forward. "My friend, here, can show you how to use the emergency suit-close system to track everyone on board."

The Quailu officer leaned in. "Is this true?"

219

"Yes, sir." She nodded, unconsciously wasting the gesture. "The system tracks every suit on board because it has to confirm suit-close in the event of a hull breach. All you need to do is tie it to an output node and you can project the locations on a holo of the ship."

"Why does that sound so simple," the Quailu asked her, "now that you've explained it?"

She didn't know quite how to respond to that. This was the first time she'd said more than a couple of words at a time to a member of the ruling species and his question threw her, full, as it was, with self-deprecation.

"It sounds simple," Gleb said, coming to her rescue, "because it *is* simple. You've just never had much use for it, in the past. If you want to contact someone on the crew, the system just routes your conversation for you. Enemy boarders aren't tracked in the system because it doesn't give a pile of turds whether they suffocate…"

He paused, turning to the two Humans, eyebrows high.

"Shit!" Mel exclaimed. "If you could set your system to open the helmets of any hostile forces on your ship while you're rigged for combat…"

"Or find a way to corrupt the system on an enemy ship to kill off its crew…" Siri added.

"Now you're definitely getting outside the contract parameters," the lieutenant warned. "We can't get away with something like that."

Gleb held up a hand. "Yes, that would absolutely get you blacklisted, but *we* have no such restrictions, seeing as we've already been blacklisted."

He gave his two companions an appreciative nod. "I like where your heads are at, and we'll work on those ideas later but, for now, we concentrate on getting this ship back to its owner."

He looked back to the Quailu. "Who's your grav man?"

"Ramaat," the officer gestured to a warrant officer.

"Right, warrant, I need you to come up to the grav room with me. Siri will project a holo of the ship with enemy dispositions, centering it in the grav room to distract the guards inside."

He turned to her. "Do that just as we reach the door."

"Then…" He looked back to the Quailu crewmen. "I get inside, subdue the guards and Ramat will just grav-bomb the whole ship, except for engineering. After that, you can use the holo to restrict the enhanced gravity to the plates that happen to be holding the guards."

"Let's do it!" the Quailu officer said.

"Off we go, Ramat!" Gleb led him over to a lift platform and they rode up to the catwalk.

Siri got to work getting the holo ready and she gave Gleb a confirmatory nod when he looked down at them. *Now!* He mouthed at her and disappeared from view.

She activated the holo-display inside the gravity-control room.

She heard the door snap open but nothing seemed to happen for a moment. She heard a faint *'dammit, not again!'* followed by a cheerful *'Hey, fellas!'* as Gleb greeted the two guards. *'Are you aware that, in the event of a combat wound, your lord's blanket coverage may not pay for such items as restorative physiotherapy or extended convalescence?'*

'I… what?" said the first guard.

'Are you actually trying to sell us insurance?" another voice asked.

She heard the squeak of armored-suit sole-pads on the decking, a soft grunt and the unmistakable sounds of a sidearm scraping its way out of a holster. There was the sound of a blade slicing several times, deep into meat, and there were two heavy thumps followed by a desperate thumping of armored feet on the deck.

'It also won't cover death by edged weapons," he advised his victims, though it was too late to change their coverage now.

221

Insurance companies were notorious when it came to pre-existing conditions.

Siri snuck a glance at the engineering officer, who seemed to take the killing of two of his own kind with relative equanimity. It was hard to believe that, only a few days ago, it had been unthinkable that a Human would even look a Quailu in the eye and, yet, here she was helping Gleb kill two of them with the apparent approval of a Quailu officer.

"Ramat has an open path for us to the bridge," Gleb said from directly behind her, making her twitch with alarm at his unexpected presence. "I'll take Mel and Siri and we'll take care of whoever we find up there."

He led the way to the main entrance, stopping for a moment to casually shoot the provost officer in the main control room, where Ramat was unwilling to fiddle with the gravity because there were too many sensitive controls in there.

"How many Quailu have you killed?" she asked him as they waited for the engineering airlock to cycle.

"Dunno," he admitted. "If you count combat, then it's gotta be in the thousands. At the second battle of Arbella, Meesh and I were both tossing warheads from our scout-ships, kind of like mines but a little more up-close and personal.

"I know I put a couple of frigates down into the grav-well of that gas giant and probably a cruiser also. We'd set them to home in on the curvature of the pitch-effect from their drives. Take out even one pitch drive when a big ship like that is already dancing on the knife's edge and you pretty much guarantee them a one-way ticket to the after-pasture."

"It's just..." she frowned, shaking her head as she walked.

"It's hard to imagine killing a Quailu?" He was asking, but just barely. "I couldn't have imagined it, a few months ago, at least not seriously, but now?"

He came to a stop, turning to face Siri and Mel. "The thing is you're taught to revere them, to sacrifice your life for even the most worthless of their people." He looked over her shoulder, not really seeing whatever was there.

"And then, you see that the 'master race' can bleed. You see they can die and then, when they start dying by your *own* hand..."

He trailed off and then looked her straight in the eyes and she shuddered at what she saw there.

"The djinn is out of the lamp," he said softly, "and there's no way the Quailu can shove him back in. There's no way I'd let some salt-licking Quailu security hump tell me what's what, back on Kish."

"But the rules still exist," she countered.

"Rules!" he scorned, turning to resume his progress to the bridge. "A lot of rules are gonna have to change or the HQE will tear itself apart in short order!"

He glanced down at a provost rating who was gasping on the deck, every part of his body subjected to massive gravity. "You want to get a taste for how things are changing? Wait till we hand this ship over to the Lady Bau."

He looked back up at his companions, a hard expression on his face. "Just don't trust everything you see," he warned. He turned and started walking again. "In the HQE you're only useful until you're not."

Thinking Big

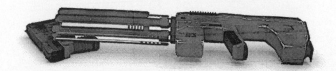

Plugging the Leak
Babilim Station, Babilim System

The horizon, even from orbital height, seemed almost flat.

Meesh stepped back from the glazed section of floor with a shiver. "You know, I've been this high in just an EVA suit – hells, I've been in some seriously fornicated crashes – but this is some unnerving shit, right here!"

"What's your problem?" Mila asked him.

"My problem," Meesh explained, "is that this damned structure isn't a ship. It has no engines to hold it up, just a flimsy elevator shaft."

"Well, this is the only way down to the station, so…"

"And why is it the only way?" Meesh demanded. "I'll tell you why…"

"Kind of figured you would…"

"Because they can charge us for access to the surface," he continued as if she hadn't inserted her sarcastic comment. "Ten to the fifth power more surface area than a standard planet and the only way down is on their elevators."

"Well, they're the only transit node in the entire region," Mila said, "so they can get away with any crazy rules they want to make up."

"Stupid would be a better way to describe it," Meesh grumbled. "S'why ninety-five percent of the surface is still just ruins. Nobody wants to invest in such a backward jurisdiction."

"Wouldn't mind seeing some of the ruins while we're down there," she said wistfully.

"You an amateur xeno-archeologist or something?" he asked, casting her a sideways glance.

"You sound surprised," she accused, looking around at the heavy rumbling sound that suddenly filled the passenger waiting-room.

"I dunno," he shrugged. "Just seems odd coming from someone in ops."

"You think only engineers could be interested in stuff like ancient civilisations that died out tens of millennia before the HQE came along?"

"I didn't say my surprise was based on any kind of logic," Meesh countered. "It's just a lame prejudice of mine against any non-engineering folk."

"You notice a weird feeling?" she asked, abandoning the previous line of conversation.

"Aside from feeling as though the place is on the verge of falling?"

"It feels like something is trying to get my attention."

He stared at her for a moment. "Something or some*one*?"

She shook her head slowly. "I don't know. It's like a ghost or something. It's creeping me out."

Meesh chewed on his lip, gazing around the room. "Nope. Not a thing, but I'm not as perceptive as you."

He looked over as a massive set of doors, big enough to slide an eight-story building through, began to rumble open. They moved along with the crowd as they headed for the narrow bridge that would lead through to the passenger lounge at the top of the elevator truck.

The bridge matched the overall design aesthetic of the ancients. Everything looked heavy, as though carved from stone. Even the bridge looked too heavy to hold its own weight and it was just as ornate. The heavy side-walls were a golden metal, richly decorated with relief carvings of faces, petroglyphs and angular border-lines.

Calling it metal, Meesh realized, *is a bit lazy*. When you looked at it, really looked at it, you could see into it. There were veins and whorls of thicker golden color running through an almost bronzish haze. The surface was smooth and reflective.

The railings were the thickness of Meesh's thigh and of a slightly more brassy internal coloring, complete with a greenish patina where hands rarely touched.

Everything up here looked like a temple – solid, ornate, heavy. Something that had no place balanced above a vertigo-inducing elevator column.

"Anyway," Meesh muttered quietly over his shoulder, "you'll be seeing plenty of ruins. This is an almost untouched sector. The official population below us is maybe a couple hundred at the most, which is why there are less than twenty passengers waiting up here with us. The place we're headed is off the books."

He looked behind her. "We stink or something?"

She looked back at the rest of the passengers. They were at least twenty feet behind them on the catwalk, bunched up between the railings but not getting any closer to the two Humans. "Huh!" She turned back to Meesh. "You know, I noticed they were staying clear of us in the lounge as well."

The huge doors began thundering shut even before they reached the passenger platform, suspended eight stories above the cargo deck. Meesh angled over to the railing on his right and stopped to look down into the gloom.

Three quarters of the cargo hold consisted of automated storage racking, though he doubted the robotic gantries had moved themselves in tens of thousands of years. The remaining quarter, apparently left clear of racking to accommodate large items, sufficed for shipments to this remote surface outpost.

Looking like tiny insects, the cargo handlers were locking down the grav-plating under the nine pallets of official supplies.

"Looks like smuggling is alive and well, despite the restrictions against shuttle traffic," Mila nodded at the forty-odd pallets that were being secured with physical netting. "They must bribe the staff to net their goods so it doesn't show on the grav-plate records."

"The grav-plates probably trigger a scan protocol," Meesh surmised. He took another look back at the rest of the passengers and snorted in amusement when he saw them standing, still twenty feet away. One of the Quailu raised a hand and drew his thumb down across his torso on a diagonal.

Meesh leaned close to Mila. "That guy just made the sign against Nergal! I think the false rumor we've been cultivating about ourselves is starting to take hold."

She started to turn her head to look but caught herself and looked at Meesh instead. "Unbelievable!" She shook her head. "I suppose the best lies are the unbelievable ones." She stepped back from the railing.

"We should keep moving, so those poor folk don't have to spend the whole ride cowering on the catwalk."

The elevator truck's lounge was an eye-opener. The waiting room out in the station was normally appointed, but much of the original furnishings were still in place on the elevator.

Perhaps because this elevator led to an out-of-the-way maintenance settlement, the old seating hadn't been removed. New

228

chairs had been chem-fused to the decking in front of long rows of seats designed to accommodate passengers twice the size of a Human.

It was decorated in the same style, a style that Meesh was coming to think of as *Sacred Ancient*. He didn't think it sounded quite right and, when he mentioned it to Mila, his misgivings were confirmed.

"I'd use a word more like hallowed or maybe monastic?" she suggested. "But I get what you're going for. The folks that built this place sure seemed to take themselves seriously."

They both threw out their hands for balance as the elevator began the drop back to the surface. The dampening fields locked the sensation down quickly enough but they were clearly designed for creatures that occupied more of the compartment's vertical space.

The other passengers were seated as far as possible from the two Humans, many of them pretending not to have any reason to look their way, even if it meant spending the entire descent looking to their left. Meesh chuckled. "Better to be feared than despised, I suppose."

Mila quirked her eyebrows at the odd statement but quickly turned her attention back to the rapidly approaching surface of the station. "Why bother to make mountains?" she asked.

Meesh turned to follow her gaze out the lounge windows. "That's no mountain," he said, getting up from his chair to stand beside her. "That's one of the thousands of abandoned cities that cover this place. The one they've refurbished as the trade-hub and capital is on the other side and they have about forty million people living in it. Forty million imperial citizens and they say the place is still like a ghost town.

"Place we're going is just outside this abandoned city, Commercial hub on one side and passenger port on the other but they don't use it. Nobody lives in that place."

She grinned at him. "Haunted?"

"Aren't these places always?" he said dryly.

"They must have to keep those lights on round the chrono," she said, nodding to the small dots of brightness in the distance. Might have been easier to build this nearer a star."

"Doesn't get any closer than this, or didn't you wonder what all those other planets were orbiting?" Meesh needled her.

Her eyes grew wide. "There's a star in there? How can they possibly contain a star in such a small construct?"

"This is an old system. They built around a white dwarf which let them build smaller and live on the outside. The star's gravity is enough to keep an atmosphere on the surface, not to mention the inhabitants. Thankfully, the ancient giants were accustomed to something close to Imperial Standard Gravity."

"Gods!" she breathed. "Can you imagine the kind of power they must be harvesting if they have a white dwarf contained inside that thing?"

"Or what they might have been forging with all that power," Meesh added reverently. "We plug the leak first and then we take a look around. Gleb will understand if we're a little late picking him up."

They both stepped back as nearby towers seemed to be racing up directly toward them but the heavy-boned, ornate structures proved to be at least a few hundred meters from the elevator. The elevator flowed past, slowing as the vehicle approached the end of the shaft.

They slid to a halt with another tug at their guts and the massive doors once again rumbled open. Meesh placed a hand on Mila's shoulder. "Let the locals off first. We'll draw less attention if we're not scaring their relatives on the arrival platform."

It took some time, but the other passengers eventually realized the Humans were waiting for them to leave first. It was like watching a hole blow out in the side of a hull.

The first few passengers started to move and the rest, triggered into motion, suddenly rushed for the catwalk. The usual disorderly gathering up of belongings was accomplished with a speed that astonished Meesh. Within a few seconds, the two Humans were alone and they moved toward the catwalk, at least fifty feet behind the closest local passenger.

They crossed the bridge, looking down to see that the cargo handlers weren't the only ones in the hold. A small crowd had come in the open doors to collect their illicit cargo. More were waiting outside with pallets and one of them was waving his credit chip over the forearm of a security operator.

Most of the passengers and those greeting them were already moving off the arrivals platform by the time Meesh and Mila stepped off the catwalk. One of the more richly dressed Quailu was still there, angrily accosting a large auto-cab.

"Open!" he shouted. "Open this instant or I'll have your license revoked!"

It seemed unlikely that he didn't see the 'reserved for Meeshkennu' holo-sign rotating above the roof. It was pretty clear that the cab was waiting for someone.

It seemed equally clear that the Quailu considered himself above such considerations.

"Guy's trying to jack our ride?" Mila said indignantly. She looked at Meesh and both stopped, grinning. "Nergal or just a couple of his minions?" she asked.

"Minions, I think," he replied laconically. "We don't want to overdo it. If Nergal starts popping up everywhere, folks will get suspicious. You unmask first and I'll follow your lead."

They both closed off their minds, Mila a little more quickly than Meesh. She'd take the lead because she was one of the most promising recruits in the *understanding*.

They both imagined the horrors of the underworld, a scene they'd all practiced for the sake of consistency. They adopted the attitude one might expect of Nergal's servants, released from the shadow-life of the dark, dismal underworld to wreak havoc upon the living. They focused their rage at the still-living upon the Quailu at the cab.

And they opened their minds.

The wealthy Quailu seemed to physically shrink under the sudden mental onslaught. He spun around, falling back against the cab, arms up to ward against his oppressors. He bumped his head against the vehicle's window as Mila leaned close, his eyes wide.

"We seek Meeshkennu," she snarled, baring her teeth, eyes flashing with barely controlled madness. She gestured to the holo-sign above the cab.

"He's trying to get into the cab," Meesh growled. "Clearly he's the one we seek! Get on with it!"

"It's not me!" the Quailu shrieked. "I don't know any Meeshkennu; I swear it before all the gods!"

"Liar!" Mila spat. "You would defile the gods over an auto-cab? Small wonder you've been given over to our keeping, Meeshkennu!"

His head shaking convulsively, the Quailu slid sideways against the vehicle. He made a break for it with a strangled yelp of adrenaline-soaked fear. His feet tangled and he went down in a heap of misfiring limbs.

Meesh took a step toward him and he scrambled away, coming back to his feet and racing off. "Running is a waste of time, Meeshkennu!" he shouted after the fleeing figure. "Now that we know your face, the scent of your soul, there is no way for you to hide!"

He turned away as their victim caught a foot on a railing and tumbled down the platform stairs. "That alone makes this trip worthwhile," he said mildly.

232

He stepped back to the cab. "I'm Meeshkennu," he told the vehicle cheerfully, holding out his hand so it could scan his implant.

The side slid open and the two Humans shared a glance. "Not nanite-based," he said, "and it's pretty big. Probably built by the same ancients that made the station."

They climbed aboard and the door slid shut. The seats inside, just like on the elevator, were twice the standard size. There were no smaller seats here, but someone had attached a step to help passengers climb up onto the original seats.

Meesh settled into the seat, his legs stretched out in front. "This must be what it feels like to be a child," he mused. "I imagine everything seems too large to a youngling."

Mila was on her knees, looking out a side window. "The grandeur of a place like this must take some getting used to," she said wistfully. "Hmm…" She turned back to Meesh. "We're already out of the settled zone, I think, but we're not slowing down at all."

Meesh joined her at the window. "So Eddu might win the pool, after all."

"He might share it," she corrected. "There were at least ten people saying this guy we're meeting is just killing whoever comes to buy his information and stealing their credits."

"Right," he conceded, "but he was the first to suggest it, so he's getting the biggest share of the pot." He gazed out calmly at the dark shadows that raced past the window for a few more moments and then sat back down.

"Let's hope there aren't too many of the bastards or we won't be able to freeze 'em all." He sighed. "I suppose we'd just have to start killing them instead. Start at the back of their group, so they don't notice what's happening until it's too late…"

"He might not be planning on killing us," she admonished. "Let's see what happens when we get there.

The cab dipped sharply and they could see what looked like a huge crater rim more than two kilometers away. The rim reared up to occlude the stars and they raced across to the far side, both Humans pressing their hands, uselessly, into the seat as they raced toward the sheer wall of integrated structures at a speed they couldn't even estimate.

A haze of light began to resolve itself into a collection of individual pinpoints. The points edged apart as they approached, now showing spills of yellow light on hard golden surfaces. The walls revealed their ornamentation and the inhabitants were suddenly noticeable as they moved about the landing pad ahead.

The auto-cab slid to a halt and they stepped out into a vast landing bay, where the cool air was dappled with the smells of decaying seals, oxidised metals and rarely-washed bodies. Nobody seemed to care about the two Humans.

"Doesn't seem like anybody here is expecting us," Meesh commented.

"Nor are they terribly upset at our presence," Mila said.

"Well, they're probably smugglers or unlicensed tech prospectors," he explained shrugging. "Probably both, really. The two professions are complementary, after all. They tend to be a pragmatic bunch, not so prone to supernatural rumors."

"Well, at least we aren't facing off against all these guys." Mel nodded at the forty-odd workers of various races. "If they knew a guy selling info about Humans, they'd sure as hells react to a couple of us suddenly showing up down here."

"An excellent point, Petty Officer Mila. Let's put that to the test."

"What did you have in mind, Master Warrant Officer Meesh?"

"We investigate by strolling around. If someone reacts with surprise or alarm, we have a chat with them." He tilted his head at her. "Unless you can suggest something better, that is."

"You want my honest opinion?"

"Of course."

"Sounds a little too indirect, seeing as most of these guys probably aren't in on the deal." She turned to a large Durian who had a flow-holo hovering in front of him, just under his line of sight. He was directing several workers to get some wrap on a pallet of jumbled parts.

"Hey," she called to him, "looking for Melchior."

The Durian looked up at her, taking a moment for her words to properly register, then he scanned around the space, nodding to a back corner. "That's him… the Ashurapolitan with the emergency suit-pack. Don't lend him any money, if you can help it."

She nodded her thanks before turning back to Meesh. "There, you see? We know he's an Ashurapolitan, he's bad with personal finances and, most importantly, he's over there, looking right at us…

"Shit! Come on!" She broke into a run just as Melchior did the same.

Their quarry grabbed a rack filled with metal levers and hauled it down behind himself to slow his pursuers, much to the dismay of a Chironian who'd been stacking more items on it. With an angry shout, he heaved one of the metal bars after the fleeing Ashurapolitan.

It struck him squarely between the shoulder blades and he stumbled straight into another rack filled with display units. The whole thing came crashing down on top of him and, when Mila pulled him out from beneath the pile, he was unconscious.

Meesh stood while she restrained Melchior's wrists behind his back. "Don't see anyone coming to his aid," he told her. "I think we have a low-level scam artist on our hands."

This would have been much easier if they could have just frozen Melchior on the spot but they'd come here to shut him up – if his information was true – not start more rumors. They'd just have to do things the old-fashioned way.

Unless, of course, his information proved to be a pile of random turds. If that were the case, they might even try to *encourage* him in his folly.

But first, they needed a place to talk. Meesh realized the offended Chironian who'd knocked Melchior down was now advancing on him, his features suffused with an anger that felt to be more a matter of form than fact. He would raise a fuss to avoid losing face with his comrades.

He slowed as Meesh put himself squarely in his path, one hand coming to rest on the grip of his pistol.

"I promise," he told the smuggler, "we'll give him a harder time than anything you have in mind." He forced a grin onto his face, lips peeled back from his teeth so the Chironian would recognize the expression. "We'll even throw in a little extra, just for your sake!"

The Chironian knew when he was being offered an escape and he took it like a good sport. You couldn't just wave a gun at his kind and expect them to back off. A gun and a little respect, however, often worked wonders.

"He's all yours, friend," the long-limbed smuggler conceded with a grin. "Just don't kill him. He owes me a lot of credits."

"Is there someplace quiet we can take him?" Mila asked.

The Chironian's head drew back slightly. "You two really aren't from here, are you? This is Babilim Station. Everything the ancients built is sound-proof. If you close a door, you're free to make all the noise you want." He gestured at a section of wall that flowed out at the second level to form a room with windows overlooking the cargo floor. "Use that."

With a nod of thanks, Meesh hauled Melchior over his shoulder, grateful that Ashurapolitans were, as a rule, skeletally thin. It was probably the only rule this idiot hadn't gotten around to breaking.

They walked up a set of stairs that the locals had modified by inserting carbon-crete steps up against each double-sized riser, giving the impression of a stair with steps of alternating bronze and black. They turned left at the second level and entered the room.

Meesh could feel Melchior's mind re-awakening. He dumped him roughly, but not roughly enough to cause harm. "Get that sheet of poly-film spread out," he told Mila.

She frowned at him for half a second and then her expression cleared. "I thought you brought it."

"Are you kidding me?" Meesh exclaimed. He could feel their captive clearly now. He was paying close attention. "Sure, there's probably no forensics facilities out here but that doesn't mean we get sloppy!" He felt hands close around his ankle.

"You don't need to do this!" the Ashurapolitan said urgently. "I don't actually know anything! I was just making up what seemed like a plausible story, so I could sell it to a few rubes. The Chironians stop at this station to trans-ship Humans from time to time, so I figured folks would believe a rumor if they heard it here." He let go when Meesh shook his leg.

"You just made something up?" Meesh turned an incredulous look at Mila. *Humans moving through here?*

"Swear to gods," the prisoner insisted. "Pure savannah-muffins!"

Meesh huffed out a breath, half laughing, shaking his head. "You silly half-wit! D'you have any idea how close you came to getting yourself killed?"

"I think the situation is pretty self-explanatory," Mila offered dryly.

Meesh looked down at the prisoner. "So what are you telling your *customers*?"

"Well, you're the first ones, as it turns out," Melchior admitted, his mind starting to recover from the adrenaline-addled terror of imminent death. "I was going to claim that you'd found one of the other hangar-craters on the far side and got the ancient ships working."

Meesh stared at him, not letting his face give anything away, but the idea of more centers like this one and of ancient ships..."

It was intriguing.

The uncomfortable silence grew and Melchior cleared his throat with a cough. "Then I'd tell them you'd managed to sneak some of the ships past the automated defenses, probably using an elevator."

"Automated defenses?"

"Yeah," he nodded earnestly. "Anyone who ignores the rules and tries to land on the surface finds out pretty quickly that the ancients gave this place some impressively dangerous defenses.

"Anything between orbit and two hundred feet above hard-deck gets fried to a crisp. Anyway, the story was gonna be all about how you were using the ancient ships' portal-generators to slip between universes."

It was a pretty lame theory. Still, Melchior clearly thought people would be fool enough to buy it, so he must have thought it was believable enough.

Meesh drove the smile from his face with a heavy sigh. "Shit!" he said, not quite under his breath.

Mila nodded at him. "It's too close for comfort."

"You stupid bastard!" Meesh glared down at Melchior. "You *made* that story up?"

The Ashurapolitan raised his bound hands. "I can change the story!" he begged, eyes wide again with fear. "I was just trying to make enough credits to get out of this hole. I had no idea..."

"Apparently," Meesh agreed. "Well, you can't change it now, not when you know how close you came with the first one!"

"We'll just have to make a mess," Mila concluded. "We don't have the sheeting with us."

"Yeah, *we* don't have it," Meesh needled her, his eyes rolling sarcastically.

"What the hells is that supposed to mean," she growled.

"You were the one who didn't bring the sheeting."

She threw out her hands. "Why am I supposed to be the one who brings it?"

"Because I'm in charge," he countered. "I don't carry the supplies; I tell someone else to do it."

"And you told me this when?"

Meesh opened his mouth but then closed it again. His left eye twitched. "It's just assumed!"

"I don't recall assuming it."

Time to climb down from our 'decision' to kill him. Meesh felt kind of bad, scaring the poor fellow, but his dumb story was too good to waste. "There's no way I'm going all the way back for sheeting," he said with an air of finality.

"We're gonna take our chances on the quality of local law enforcement?" Mila asked. "Witnesses can say all they like but, if there's no DNA found, there's no case. We're running a hells of a risk here."

Meesh pulled out his pistol. "You were the one who wanted to make sure we had time to look around after – see the sights, so to speak."

"Yeah," she said but in a way that disagreed. "Thing is, if we kill him, it lends credence to his story. Those guys out there have probably heard the whole thing from him already. If we show up and kill him…"

"It's true," Melchior nodded earnestly. "They know what I was planning to tell people. They laughed at me," he added indignantly. "Who's the fool now?"

Meesh looked down at him, tied up and waiting for death. For the life of him, he couldn't tell if he was making an ironic joke. "You told everyone out there?"

An eager nod.

"So, we can't rely on you to keep your mouth shut?"

He shrank back from the Human but then a gleam of hope sparkled in his eye. "You wanted to look around, right? I can serve as your guide. I can show you another transport crater, one of the craters that haven't been scavenged yet. There's thousands of them. You'd have seen one when you took the ships, but I know how to activate the systems, show you how they used to look in their glory days!"

"Glory days," Meesh mused. "That sounds like something worth seeing. How do we get there?"

Melchior looked around. "This is the control room. If we go out that door at the back, we'll be in a hall that takes us to a drop shaft."

Mila's hand came to rest on her pistol-grip. "Why don't I like the sound of that?"

"No, look, it's OK," Melchior insisted. "I'll go first to prove it's not some trap. It's the fastest way down to the hyperloop."

"Really?" Meesh raised an eyebrow. "We're back to the made-up stories again? A hyperloop that still works after tens of thousands of years and I suppose it still has vacuum?"

"It didn't when I found it, but I like to tinker. You gotta realize we're not really talking about tens of thousands of years with this stuff." He shrugged. "Sure, it's all really that old but the power-scrubbers tend to blow out after a century or so. After that, there's no wear and tear. The circuitry had no current in it, the parts weren't moving and these guys use some kind of alloy that's nearly impervious to oxidation."

Meesh looked up at Mila.

She took her hand from her weapon. "Couldn't hurt to take a look."

Meesh crouched to cut the bindings on the Ashurapolitan's hands. He gestured with the knife, waggling it in Melchior's face. "Don't screw with us or we go back to Plan A, got it?"

"You won't regret this!" The erstwhile victim scrambled to his feet and gestured to the rear door. "You two will be the only other two that know about this."

Even if Meesh couldn't feel his sincerity, he would have been able to read the sudden look of alarm on Melchior's face as he realized he was revealing another possible reason for killing him later.

"Tell you what," Meesh said, putting a friendly hand on his shoulder, "you do right by us and we'll return the favor. You said you wanted out of here, right?"

A wary nod.

"Maybe we help you out with that." He gestured. "Lead on."

They found the shaft at a junction of hallways.

"I'll go first," Melchior offered again.

And somehow get back out a few floors down while we drop to our deaths? Meesh wondered. "Can we all go at once?"

Melchior thought about it for a moment. "Probably," he finally conceded. "This would be quite a bottleneck if you could only send one passenger at a time."

"Hold hands," Meesh ordered.

They lined up on the threshold with Mila on one end and Meesh on the other. "Three, two, one, jump!" Meesh yelled and they hopped in together.

The walls were racing unnervingly up past the trio but they'd never have noticed if their eyes were closed.

"Why don't we feel the air rushing past us," Mila yelled unnecessarily.

"Don't really know," Melchior said a touch too loudly. "I think it has to do with the same system that stops us at the bottom. I think it selectively grabs us, somehow, along with the air."

"Are those other stops that I'm seeing?" Meesh asked, forcing himself to speak normally.

"Yes, but I haven't figured out how to stop there yet," Melchior said. "Maybe the ancients had implants that let them communicate with the systems. But I'd need to find a body to know for sure."

"No one's ever found an ancient's body?"

"Not that I know of but, then, I'm not briefed in on matters of state or high commerce. Might be one of the big defense contractors has something on ice?"

The bottom suddenly made itself apparent and it rushed up to them with such alarming speed that Meesh was tempted to use his limited telekinetic abilities on himself. He willed himself to trust the shaft's systems and, when his feet settled gently on the floor, he let out a breath he didn't even remember holding.

He stood there, trying to get his breathing back under control, and he stole a sideways glance, glad to see Mila was in the same condition. "Well, that was bracing," he said with more than a little understatement.

The other two both chuckled.

Melchior pointed to the left of the cavernous space they'd found themselves in. "Train's over that way."

He led them past rows of large seats and benches, following in the same direction as the massive arches that spanned the ornate, open space. An airlock was beyond the seating, attached to a large, transparent tube. Inside, a five-car train awaited passengers. It looked as though it had been stripped down to the basic framework and Meesh assumed it had been stripped by the prospectors for re-sale.

"You'll need your suits closed up," Melchior warned. "The tube is still able to hold vacuum but the train seals have mostly failed, so you have no atmo inside."

He approached to a spot where the footprints on the dusty floor became erratic and he jumped up in the air.

Meesh reached for his weapon as their guide waved his arms around in a bizarre fashion, still jumping. He grinned, letting go of the pistol as the large airlock doors suddenly whispered open for them.

The smuggler grinned over his shoulder. "Like being a kid again, eh?"

"I really wouldn't know," Meesh muttered quietly. They followed him into the airlock, closing up their suits.

Melchior pressed the control on his emergency suit and the nanites scrambled out of the housing, building a light flexible grid-work around his body and setting shield micro-gen tabs at strategic points along the framework. As the final tendrils of nanites stopped near his face, the entire thing came online, casting a hazy blue aura around him.

The airlock cycled and the inner door opened soundlessly. Meesh started forward but stopped in alarm, catching Mila by the arm. Melchior walked calmly into the open space, suspended, apparently, in mid-air. "Weird, no?"

"Thought the body had been torn out," Meesh said, taking a tentative step onto a floor that was invisible, though, now that he looked, he could see a light patina of dust and wear in the corners. "The bodywork is made of something with the same index of refraction as air!"

"They had good reason," Melchior told them. "There's some spectacular views along our route!"

It fit what they already knew about the smuggler that the voice pickups in his suit were so low quality. He was someone at the bottom of what passed for civilization out here. His barely functional emergency suit was emblematic of a life on the ragged edge of oblivion.

Here he was, calmly riding a train with no air in a suit with little in the way of long-term prospects. Meesh felt a surge of pity. *What sort of a life leads someone to this bleak existence?*

They all staggered aft as the train lurched into motion. Like the orbital elevators, this vehicle's acceleration management was tuned to a much larger species and the bulk of their mass would have been much higher than the current passengers.

The walls of the station slid past and they were in a tunnel, accelerating rapidly until their view was little more than a dark gray blur. Meesh was just about to offer a sarcastic opinion about the view when the tunnel ended and they found themselves in a massive open space.

Melchior chuckled. "Been through here a few times and it still startles the life out of me every time I get to this part."

"It's like being shot out of a rail-gun," Meesh agreed, his heart still racing. "The tube we're riding in seems to be made of the same stuff as the train body. I keep expecting us to start falling."

He looked down through the floor. Shafts of white light streaked up to bounce off convex reflectors, diffusing light throughout the chamber. "It's hard to find a frame of reference, but it looks like you could fit Kwharaz Station in here!"

"There's forests down there," Mila exclaimed.

"And up there," Melchior pointed to large platforms throughout the space. "I think some of them were for crop production but the birds brought up tree seeds in their digestive systems. It's all turned wild."

"There are still birds here?" Meesh asked. "Birds the ancients would have seen?"

The smuggler nodded soberly, eyes wide. "Yeah, you want to be careful out here. You can run into some seriously weird shit, if you're not paying attention!" He held out his arm, an angry red welt visible through the flickering blue haze of his suit.

"You see this scar?" he asked. "Some kind of flying insect, big enough jaws to take your head clean off! I was taking a leak by one of the rivers down there, and the damn thing came at me from behind!"

"Be glad it went for your arm, considering what you were doing when it showed up," Mila advised.

Melchior laughed. "True enough but, all the same, there are dangerous predators down there. I don't know what the ancients were thinking. It's all well and good to build a fully functional ecosystem but common sense should step in, at some point, and impose a few limits!"

"I very much doubt they intended it for use as a public toilet," Meesh said helpfully. "Perhaps it's a nature preserve. They probably brought all the genomes of their home-world with them, so they'd be less home-sick."

"Or this was their home-system," the smuggler suggested.

"Unlikely," Meesh said, still staring out at the nearly globe-shaped cavern. "Takes millions or even Billions of years to get through the red-giant phase. That's a long time to hang around waiting. They probably went out searching for white dwarfs to build around."

He suddenly turned to his two companions. "There are probably more of these stations! If they came here, who's to say they didn't set up stations anywhere else?"

"Gods!" Mila whispered. "They might still be out there!"

"Good luck finding them," Melchior muttered. "They only found this place by accident when a path-drive failed and stranded a freighter nearby."

"Yeah," Meesh admitted, "but they found it. If there are other stations like this one, don't you think these guys would have known about it? You ever manage to get a data interface working?"

Melchior shook his head. "No luck. The folks that run the place have managed to splice their own tech into some of the data feeds, like the elevator metrics, but that's about it. Most of the original computing tech was pretty heavily scavenged before the capital city even started organizing. Nobody's even bothered in thousands of years."

"What about where we're headed?" Mila asked. "The systems must be intact, if it's so remote. Might be worth a try?"

"I suppose." The smuggler sounded dubious. "But you'd still need to know their language and nobody's ever been able to crack it."

"Yeah but it's not an impossibility," Meesh insisted. "This could... Hells!" He threw his arms up in front of his face as the far wall of the gigantic cavern slammed toward them, the view suddenly darkening, once again, to a dark gray.

He lowered his hands, breath coming in short gasps. "This place is very unsettling." He fought to bring his body back under control.

"You remember that weird feeling I mentioned up on the elevator station?" Mila asked. Her icon on his HUD indicated the conversation was only between the two of them. "It came back when we reached that cavern and it's stronger."

Meesh reached out with his mind but he still felt nothing. "What are you picking up?"

"It's... detached, dispassionate, but it's definitely communication."

"And you're not just reading me?"

"No, it's the same as what I felt in that orbital station or, at least, it's continuous. It's like thought without emotion."

"What kind of thought?"

"Feels like an inquiry."

Both were distracted as they burst out into a new cavern. Its size was just as awe-inspiring as the last one but the bottom was missing and their visor shielding adjusted to filter out the increased light.

"Gods!" Meesh whispered and it almost sounded like a prayer, for once. He stared down through the clear floor. "That's the star, isn't it?"

Through the space where the cavern floor should have been, they could see the white dwarf. Though 'dwarf' led one to expect less illumination, the heart of Babilim Station shone with a pale brilliance that sent shivers of supernatural fear down Meesh's spine. Like everything on this station, the star was old beyond belief, so stable that a trillion years represented nothing more than the blink of an eye.

This was the eventual future of all life in the universe. A day would come when all the stars had settled down to this state.

And then the white dwarfs would start blinking out, turning into black dwarfs.

But that day, Meesh knew, would be more than ten to the power of thirty standard years away, at the very least. "So we've got some time," he muttered.

"What's that?" Melchior asked.

Meesh looked to the corner of his HUD, seeing the two-way conversation had shut down automatically from lack of traffic. He was glad he hadn't said anything of any importance in his distracted state.

"Do you think the floor just collapsed?" Mila asked.

"Maybe," Meesh allowed, "but I seriously doubt it. Whoever built this thing went to a lot of trouble and I imagine a big part of their reasoning was the longevity of white dwarf stars." He gestured at the star, brilliant shards of light stabbing out from its outer surface. "This is prime real estate. You build here, you build to last."

He forced himself to look up and his suspicions were confirmed. "Look up there," he pointed. "See how dark the upper surfaces are? Designed to absorb the radiation. This chamber was built with energy collection in mind."

"You know what I don't get?" Mila asked. "Melchior says he's the only one to come out this way." She cocked her head quizzically. "Why is that? Why haven't the folks holding the nominal claim on this station bothered to come out from their city and see what they can learn?"

They all flinched when the train hurtled back into a tiny hole on the far side.

Melchior tilted his head forward, peering at her from under his heavy brow-ridges. "Really? Are you talking about the same Quailu that run the HQE? The biggest, baddest mechiros ever to stride amongst the stars? Those Quailu?

"You think they want to come out here and face their own relative insignificance?" He almost looked as though he was going to spit on the floor but must have realized it wouldn't make it through his suit's shielding. "No, they sit in their city, collect trade-duties and pretend the rest of the place doesn't exist."

"Kind of stupid," she said mildly.

"Yeah," Melchior agreed, "but when you're the toughest guys around, you can afford to be stupid."

"Until you're no longer the toughest guys around," Meesh said.

The smuggler shrugged then nodded forward. "There's an untouched crater up ahead. That's what you wanted to see, right?"

Meesh nodded but twitched in a very un-heroic fashion as they burst out into the next open space. "That must take a lot of getting used to," he said, trying to pretend Mila wasn't laughing at him.

"You can see the cargo handling armatures," Melchior said with a nod downward. "The guys back where you found me had already removed most of the heavy gear in that crater but everything's still intact here. You can even see how they work. When I powered this place up, the gantries started working as if they hadn't spent the last couple hundred thousand years sitting idle."

"So everything just stopped one day, huh?" Mila leaned over to bring her eyes a few inches closer to a view that must have been several kilometers away. "There must be stalled cargo containers all over the place!"

"I bet the food's gone bad by now," Meesh joked, "but I'd love to spend some time getting into those *cans* and see what surprises they left for us." *This could be a useful place, if we ever need somewhere to hide.*

"Yeah." Mila rolled her eyes. "Like automated killer droid-swarms or bio-weapons with dodgy containment units..." She gave him a light punch in the shoulder. "This is why you needed an ops NCO along, someone to keep the engineer from running off looking for new toys!"

"Lots of ships still docked out there," he said, pretending not to have heard her. "So they used to fly freight in, rather than just using the elevators." He caught the queer look on Melchior's face and realized, a little late, that the Humans were supposed to have stolen ships from this station, at least according to the smuggler's accidentally correct narrative.

He sighed. "Listen, if you haven't sorted out by now that your story is way off the path, then you're not half as smart as I'd figured you to be."

He squared off to face the Ashurapolitan. "Why would we want you as a tour-guide, if we'd already been here shopping for stolen ships and, come to think of it, why say we somehow managed to launch them past the station's defense grid, if we had access to trans-dimensional portals in the first place?"

He felt the flare of alarm from their guide, mirrored by his features. Melchior must have taken the statement as a prelude to his execution.

Meesh waved, an impatient gesture. "We're not going to hurt you. In fact, we might have work for you."

"Work?" The alarm was fading but mild apprehension began taking its place.

"Sure." Meesh nodded out to the busy hive of commerce beneath them. "You know how to get all this up and running and we might have use for that kind of expertise, someday.

"Let's have a quick look around while we're out here, then go back. Not a word to your buddies back at your salvage operation. We just climb back into that auto-cab and fly straight to the elevator."

"We?"

"You wanted off this place, right?"

"Well, yeah…" The hope was rising but a sudden impediment knocked it over. Melchior wrung his hands.

Meesh chuckled. "The cab left already, right?"

A weak nod.

"Well, that settles the pool, doesn't it?" Mila asked, an edge in her voice. Betting on your own death was easy enough when you were still sitting in the wardroom. Hearing the plan from the would-be killer was a different matter entirely.

"Don't want to tell you how to run your business," Meesh said, "but, if you want to be an informant, you need repeat business." He shrugged as if to say it was no difference to the Humans personally. "A dead customer is unlikely to become a repeat customer."

"So…" Melchior darted his gaze between the two Humans. "… you're still not going to kill me?"

"Hey, a lot of folks were talking about killing," Meesh said airily.

"Including us," Mila admitted with a grin.

"Yeah," Meesh conceded vaguely, "I might have hinted at it…"

"You were talking about spreading polymer film so there'd be no DNA evidence," Melchior reminded him.

"Hey, if you're coming with us, you gotta learn to take a joke." Meesh leaned back as the train slid to a halt. They moved through the airlock and into the fresher air of the cargo crater.

"We'll take you with us but you need to stay on our ship for a while. You're about to learn the *real* reason why we're able to board ships undetected…"

"What about the *understanding*?" Mila had switched back to a two-person link. "He's bound to find out, if he's coming back to the *Stiletto* with us."

"Neither can be kept secret indefinitely," he answered on the link, "and this guy can be useful."

"Are you two talking about killing me again?" Melchior broke in on the open link. "I can see your lips moving inside your helmets. I only ask 'cause my personal physician told me not to let any projectiles go through my body."

He held out his hands in a 'what can you do' gesture. "It's an allergy, y'see. I get it from my father's side of the family…"

"Hey, would you look at that!" Meesh exclaimed, returning to the open channel. "He's learning to take a joke… and to make some of his own!"

"Yeah, that's great," the smuggler said. "Do I need to take precautions for my allergy or what?"

Meesh shook his head, still smiling. "Nah, you're still good. We were just having a private moment."

"Oh!" The Ashurapolitan leaned back slightly. "You mean you two are…"

"Hah!" Meesh laughed. "She wishes!"

"Wishes she didn't just get that mental picture," Mila corrected.

The trip back was uneventful, except for the need to play hardball while waiting for a new auto-cab to come collect them from the tech prospector camp where they'd found Melchior. There was an almost touching reluctance to see him leave, though it was entirely due to the amount of credits he seemed to owe them.

Hands had been resting on pistol-grips, when the cab finally arrived, and Meesh had tossed a credit chip over the prospectors' heads as a last resort. "That should more than cover it!" he'd shouted as he shoved Melchior into the vehicle.

The shuttle waiting for them at the top of the orbital elevator was decidedly pedestrian and Meesh had ignored their new friend's disappointment as they disengaged from the station and got underway for the nearest planet, a fried-out husk that had somehow managed to survive the local star's red giant phase.

"I get it now," Melchior announced.

"What do you get?" Meesh double-checked the nav settings.

"How you manage to get your ships so close to an enemy without them spotting you. You fly around in turd-buckets like this. Who the hells would even notice you, right?"

"You know, we started out not far from that concept," Meesh replied. "Small ships, not much bigger than this shuttle. Small cross-section to enemy scanners. We'd sneak up their baffles, hiding in their engine discharge."

"And then you found a way to make your ships look exactly like a shuttle?" Melchior asked, half joking, half exasperated. "I mean, I'm glad to get off that station but, if I'm gonna spend much time on this thing, I'll…"

His mouth had opened for his next word and it just stayed that way. Ahead of him, a large door was swinging open on the *Stiletto's* port hangar bay. The door wasn't required for any structural purpose but the ship needed something to hold a coating of carbon nano-tubules in front of the large opening in the hull.

Melchior must have thought he was right, after all, because it looked as though a portal had just been opened in space. Through it, he could see a ship's hangar bay with Human crewmen hurrying about their business.

"Welcome aboard the *Stiletto*," Meesh said proudly. "Fast attack corvette. You'll get your own cabin, three squares a day and a job, so you don't get too bored."

"And a proper EVA suit," Mila added, looking pointedly at Melchior's emergency suit-pack, "because, that thing's so sad it would make our whole *ship* look bad by association." She held out her hand, palm up.

"Nobody on our crew wears sub-standard junk like that."

Melchior looked down at the only protection he'd had for gods-only-knew how long. He took a deep breath and pulled it off his chest, handing it over.

She took it and set it on the console. "The under-armor suits in your cabin should be able to adjust for your body. We can get a proper suit calibrated for you by the quartermaster later today."

Meesh could feel the first stirrings of real hope from their new crewman. Something his crew took for granted, like an EVA combat suit, could mean a lot to someone who'd spent most of his life on the ragged edge of ruin. Melchior was trying to bring his old attitude, his only real armor, back online but the hope was having none of it.

The Human had to force his attention back to the controls before he got carried away by the moment.

And... we Bau...
Enbilulu System

Gleb grinned across the shuttle at Mel and Siri. He'd said little about what awaited them at Bau's court. It was partly because he didn't want to over-promise on their welcome but he also knew how hard it was for them to adjust to their new reality as free Humans, truly free Humans.

Belief came hard for them. If he told them that a Human was holding the rank of Commander, that he himself was a commissioned officer in the Prince-Presumptive's house forces...

They'll just have to see for themselves, he thought, realizing that, even now, they probably harboured doubts about where they were really headed in the small shuttle that bucked its way down through Enbilulu's atmosphere. "Nervous?" he asked.

"Nah," Siri answered gamely. "Just meeting an elector, right? We do that all the time."

The doubt was definitely there. Gleb could feel it, lurking beneath her calm façade. Both of his rescued Humans were half expecting this to prove an elaborate misunderstanding or ruse.

"She actually prefers the term 'electress'," he told them, "but she won't hold it against you, if you don't use it. And she's not just any electress. She controls nearly thirty percent of the HQE's food output. She may not have as many systems as Sandrak, but she's still one of the most powerful Awilu alive!"

"And you saved her life?" Mel asked, disbelief plain on his face and in his mind.

"They brought their dinky little scout-ship alongside her cruiser and took her off," the Quailu engineering lieutenant explained. "Otherwise, she would have gone down into the gas giant. Her ship had been rammed by the enemy and it was on its way to the after-pasture!"

"And then her own bridge crew tried to finish the job," Gleb added.

The engineer nodded. "They crowded onto the scout-ship as well but it was too much weight. They couldn't climb back out, so the Humans started throwing them overboard!"

"Throwing..." Mel faltered for a moment. "Throwing them... into the gas giant?"

"That's right," the Quailu affirmed. "Those fools had sworn a holy oath to our lady! They owed her their service and, yet, they were crowded onto that little ship, knowing they were trading her life for a few more seconds of their own!"

Gleb heard an increase in the engine's whine and his hands suddenly pressed down a little harder on his lap. A trio of closely timed thumps announced they'd landed and he released his restraints, standing as the ramp opened.

"Stay close," he advised the two Humans, "and follow my lead." He descended the ramp alongside the engineer, the most senior Quailu officer left aboard the *Harpy*.

They crossed the landing pad to a massive set of doors that could have easily accommodated the shuttle and, he suspected, one of the new *Scorpion* class corvettes. She probably used those doors to arrive at court by orbital shuttle.

It put Mishak's throne room on Kish to shame but he'd only been a one-system minor lord back then.

The large doors, elaborately formed frameworks of carbon-matrix holding amber-colored glass panels, slid out of the way and they passed a phalanx of guards to enter Bau's throne room, their names announced by the court herald.

They walked along a central bridge that ran from the south end of the throne-room to the north, where Bau's raised platform stood. It was only a two-hundred-meter walk, not a patch on the imperial palace, but it was impressive, all the same.

Especially when you counted in the roaring applause.

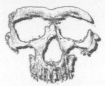

Siri didn't quite know what to make of this. She'd been willing to consider believing what Gleb had been telling her but this thunderous welcome of a Human to a powerful Quailu court was overwhelming.

Belief in a thing is sometimes poor preparation for seeing the proof, and the proof threatened to deafen her. Courtier barges drifted past them, filled with cheering Quailu, all straining to see the Human who'd saved their lady, the Humans who'd brought back a lost ship.

She still half suspected the guns to come out and the point of the whole cruel joke to be unveiled but they kept walking and stepped up to a large circle in the tiled floor, ten meters away from a stately female Quailu sitting on a carved wooden throne.

Somehow, her brain managed to register that Gleb was offering a half-bow from the waist, one hand over his heart. It was the standard form of respectful greeting when a mushkenu greeted an awilu, though she'd never really expected to do such a thing.

She'd been grown to be a mushkenu but she'd never have dreamed, in the squalid conditions on the *Deathstalker*, that she'd need to use such knowledge. It was a massive step to adjust to, in so short a time.

She realized, just in time, that she was in danger of accidentally showing disrespect to one of the most powerful nobles in the empire and she bent, hand to heart, ears red.

"Gleb of Kish!" the Quailu lady said warmly and Siri, released by the words of greeting, straightened to see, with shock, that the noble was on her feet, approaching Gleb.

"I thank the gods," she said, placing her hands on his shoulders, "that they chose to make us allies, rather than enemies!"

Siri was dimly aware of a small cloud of drones and realized they were probably holo-filming the encounter. Gleb's role in the local pantheon of heroes was about to get a new chapter and she felt a sudden shock of realisation.

She and Mel were now joining that pantheon!

Mel leaned close enough to whisper in her ear. "You're seeing all this too, right?"

She smiled, somehow reassured by his disbelief.

Bau gestured to the group by the dais and a creature with long limbs and wicked-looking teeth stepped forward.

"For only the second time in more than seven thousand years," Bau said formally, "and in recognition of services rendered repeatedly to our noble person and to the people of our holdings, a person of non Enibulan origin is hereby invested as a Knight of Enibulu!"

The creature, evidently a native citizen of Bau's home-world, stepped forward and draped a sash and star around Gleb's neck.

A knight? Siri had only heard the word once before during her short existence but it had sounded like a big deal. Some sort of honor used to distinguish members of the non-slave classes from the rest of the horde.

"Thank you, Lady Bau," Gleb said, sounding a little shocked. Siri was pleased to see this evidence that he wasn't completely unflappable.

"I am deeply grateful and I'm aware of the great honor accorded to me by your royal person as well as by my Enibulan brothers," he added, exchanging bows with the creature who'd draped the sash on him.

"I understand that time waits for no one," Bau said. "I will save you the trouble of trying to politely point that out to an electress by offering to convey you back to orbit in my own shuttle."

"You're coming up with us, your grace?"

Bau turned to the side, gesturing to a door behind the dais. "I wouldn't miss the ceremony for worlds," she said, "even though it's so quick and simple. It's long deserved and I wouldn't mind a look at her, before she has to leave."

Ceremony? Siri wondered. *What new surprises are waiting in orbit?* She caught Mel's questioning glance and shrugged.

"Time may wait for no one," Gleb answered, "but I'm sure even time could use a short break, now and then."

The door opened on a short corridor that led them onto an ornately appointed shuttle. Unlike most shuttles, this one had a raised passenger compartment surrounded by transparent armor plating that gave a view all around the occupants. A couple of officers were already waiting there.

Bau looked at Siri and Mel. "Are you crewmates of Gleb's?"

The walls of the palace's landing bay flowed past them and they glided silently out into the dark night of Enibulu.

Siri's eyes grew wide as saucers. Being two meters away from a reclining princess of the empire was nerve-wracking enough but now she was expected to make small talk. *Am I on somebody's crew?*

"They're new recruits," Gleb said. "They're already proving very useful. Siri, here," he added, indicating her with a wave of his hand, "was able to help your engineers find the enemy guards without having to go deck by deck."

"Really?" Bau turned back to her. "How did you manage that?"

Siri gulped. "Well, your grace, I used the system that tracks EVA suits. It just needed a link to the holographic interface, so we could display the data." *Gods!* She thought. *I'm talking to an electress! I just managed to say a complete sentence without making a fool of myself!*

"Very clever!" Bau said. "Gleb is very lucky to have you!"

Gleb is lucky? Siri wondered. *Does she think he and I are...?*

"You know," Bau continued, "we really must expand on our exchange program. More officers and ratings, especially now that we're exchanging so much technology. I shall have to suggest it to my royal cousin when next we speak. Ah!" she exclaimed. "We're slowing. Are we there already?" She peered out the windows.

What are we doing? Siri wondered. *There's nothing but empty...* Her mouth hung open, a shiver running up her spine. Directly ahead, where there had been nothing but blackness, a hangar bay was somehow sliding into view.

She could see crewmen moving around inside the strange window on what almost appeared to be another universe. As they passed through the strange portal, it became clear that they were inside a ship's hangar, even though there had been no ship to see from the outside.

Two rows of crewmembers were lined up along the far side of the hangar and she leaned forward, realizing that they were all Humans.

"The *Stiletto*," Gleb said softly, almost reverently. "Fast attack, Scorpion-class corvette." He looked at Mel and Siri, eyes shining. "Her hull's covered in carbon nano-tubules. She's like a sponge for most of the EM spectrum. That's why you can't see much from the outside."

They have invisible ships? Siri marveled. *And they trust Humans to serve on them?* For her, that was even more astounding.

Such a technology had to be highly secretive. Noone aboard the *Deathstalker* even seemed aware such a thing existed.

The shuttle turned to face back out the entry portal and settled on the deck. Bau gestured to the descending ramp. "It's your moment, after all," she said.

Siri stood to follow Gleb, wondering why they were making such a big deal of his return. Bau moved to stand beside her and, when Siri looked her way, offered a friendly nod, something she'd never seen a Quailu do before. As far as she knew, the ruling species left physical gestures to the less evolved.

If not for the nod, though, she'd be horrified at the idea of walking off a shuttle beside such an eminent awilu. Instead, she was merely terrified. Mel moved to follow behind them.

They stopped when Gleb stopped, ten meters from the assembled crewmen, and a Human wearing the rank insignia of a master warrant officer stepped forward.

Siri felt immediate alarm. Things had been going so well and now they were confronted by a Human masquerading as a warrant officer! There was no way Lady Bau could overlook something like this!

But no angry words came, no recriminations.

"Computer," the imposter said loudly and clearly, "recognize voiceprint of Meeshkennu, master warrant officer."

"*Voiceprint recognized,*" the computer replied. "*Meeshkennu, master warrant officer, currently commanding the* Stiletto."

"Lieutenant Glebkennu of Kish," Meeshkennu said formally. "I am ready to be relieved."

"In accordance with orders issued by our lord, Mishakwilu, Prince of the Empire, I hereby take command of the *Stiletto*. Computer, recognize voiceprint of Glebkennu, lieutenant, officer commanding."

"*Voiceprint recognized. Welcome aboard, Captain.*"

A Human as captain? Siri thought her experiences up to now had been unbelievable but this made the rest seem tame. *Gleb? Gleb commands a ship in Mishak's house forces?*

Gleb nodded to Meeshkennu. "You are relieved."

"Oh," The other Human grinned. "You have no idea! Congratulations!" He turned and bowed to Bau. "My Lady! It's good to see you again! I was hoping you'd find time to take a tour?" he added hopefully.

"Of course," she replied. "and I brought one of my weapons designers with me. I wonder if you might be able to walk us through the modifications your people have been making to our missiles."

"Have there been new developments while I was away?" Gleb asked them.

"You could say that," Meesh answered, gesturing to a large hatch. "I have a missile opened up in the engineering bay. If you'd like to come along, I can walk you through the changes."

Siri and Mel, not knowing what else to do on this strange ship, followed the group. They filed into engineering behind the rest and tried their best to stay out of notice.

"The mass attenuation field is a brilliant piece of engineering," Meesh began, looking mostly at the weapons expert who seemed to be taking it as a personal compliment, "but we noticed," Meesh continued, "that damage from the missile body itself rivaled what the warhead was doing to the enemy ships.

"At those velocities, even a little mass made a hells of a mess, so we tried putting osmium inserts in the casing to increase the damage. That worked amazingly well. Even if the warhead proved a dud, your original design still proved a potent kinetic weapon." He grinned. "And, when you add in all that extra mass…"

Meesh turned his gaze to include the rest of the group. "That's when Noa and I started talking about the idea of reversing the field on your MA units."

"Reversing?" the designer said, stepping forward.

"The science was simple enough, Doctor, after you'd blazed the original path for us. We just had to tinker a bit with one of your generators. Turning mass attenuation into mass augmentation was easier than we'd expected."

The designer stared at the weapon on the table. "What effect does it have on impact?"

"The first time?" Meesh shrugged. "Not at all what we were hoping for because the field was cast too far out from the weapon. It ended up increasing the mass of the target's hull just before contact."

He pointed to the thick metal casing inside the outer shell. "We had to adjust the MA generator to project its augmentation field inside the outer boundaries of this osmium casing, with the power lines just inside the nose, otherwise the field would remain active for too long."

"I can see *how* you've done this," the designer said, "but what escapes me is *why*. The weapons we sent you are more than enough to destroy even a capital ship. Why the need for more power?"

"Because we rarely face a single ship, Doc," Meesh replied. "The boost in initial penetration we get from mass augmentation usually leaves a lot more of the weapon intact by the time it reaches the far side of the target. That means decent-sized chunks of osmium travelling through a tight formation at nearly relativistic velocity."

"Ah." The scientist chuckled. "When you put it like that, it makes sense." He stepped back from the weapon. "If you send me your data, I'll get to work on a simpler way to switch between attenuation and augmentation using the same generator. We might even be able to send it out to you as a software change."

Meesh nodded. "We thought a software method might work but we lack an underlying knowledge of the physics behind the whole concept, so we went with a simple hardware switch. We've been hoping we'd get a chance to talk with you ever since, so, when we heard Gleb had liberated the *Harpy*, we figured we'd bring his ship here and kill two cheevers with one boot. I'll send you everything we have before we leave orbit."

"Perhaps a quick tour My Lady?" Gleb suggested. "The crew would be thrilled to rub shoulders with an electress." He grinned. "Seeing as you're already here, slumming it…"

"Ha!" Bau held up her hand, middle finger extended, and Siri was suddenly certain this was all just a foolish dream and she'd wake up in her cot, still aboard the *Deathstalker*. She'd never seen the gesture before, but it just seemed so… un-Quailu.

Except Gleb's face showed unmistakable alarm, so maybe this would end up making sense, somehow.

"Uh, my lady," he began cautiously, "that gesture means…"

"I'm well aware of what it means," she said, chuckling. "Or, rather, from talking with your lord recently, I'm *now* aware. I'm using it in the proper context this time, yes?"

Gleb breathed out a sigh of relief. "Yes, ma'am. I suppose it's entirely appropriate, seeing as I was being a bit cheeky with a princess of the empire."

"Lead on," she gestured for Gleb to show the way.

Siri was about to follow, but Meesh stepped forward, catching both her and Mel's eyes with a nod. "So you're the two new crewmen from Melvin's ship?"

She nodded. "That's right, we're both comms techs, so…"

"We have no real need for comms techs," he cut her off.

Siri felt the bottom drop out of her world. What would they do now if they couldn't join this ship?

"Now that Gleb's back, I'm only double-hatted instead of triple," Meesh went on. "I'm chief engineer for the *Stiletto* and also the XO. We don't need a traditional comms team because we use our own coding to fix up the data automatically.

"No. Where I'm short-handed is right here, in engineering. You two want to work down here for me?"

The bottom returned to Siri's world but she didn't notice. She was soaring high above it. "I would love to work in engineering, Master Warrant!"

"Hells, yeah!" Mel added. "I was so sick of sitting in that comms suite." He frowned. "We'll get some training? We've both done some modules but we're not seasoned, by any stretch."

"That's no problem," Meesh assured him. "We've got a chamber on board. We'll get you up to speed in no time. Gleb said you were both pretty sharp. Chim!" he shouted over his shoulder. "Show these guys to their quarters."

The quarters were small. Chim led them to two doors, each opening on rooms that were two by five meters but, compared to the reeking bunks on the *Deathstalker*, this was an incredible luxury. There were additional doors on either side of the room that could be used to connect to adjacent quarters and she opened the one on Mel's side to find him standing in his room, a huge grin on his face.

She returned to her own quarters and opened a sliding door on the hall-side of the room, staring in amazement at the three under-armor suits that hung there. She reached out and touched one. *Is this supposed to be for me?* She took it from its hanger and held it up. It was clearly meant for a Human.

"Hey!" Mel's voice came through the door. "They gave us under-armor suits!"

She tossed the suit on her bed. *A bed!* She deactivated her EVA suit and stepped out of the footplates. Turning her attention back to the suit, she saw that it opened down the front.

Hopping first on one foot and then the other, she worked her way into the suit and closed it up. The fabric adjusted itself, flowing into a close fit that wouldn't interfere with her armored EVA suit.

She stretched out her arms, marveling at how comfortable it felt. It provided support where needed but didn't restrict movement at all. She turned to see Mel standing in the connecting doorway, a surprised look on his face.

"What?" she asked, dropping her arms.

"That suit," he stammered. "On you, it's…"

"Oh, come on!" she said, disbelieving. "You've seen me naked. You've done far more than just *see* me naked over the last few days."

"Yeah, but this is different," he tried to explain. "It's more exciting, somehow…"

"When I'm covered up?" She wrinkled her nose at him. "Thanks a lot!"

He shook his head. "That's not what I meant! I don't know how to explain it, but hinting at your shape while still concealing it… It engages the mind more.

"Remember how, on the *Deathstalker*, folks would cling to each other just to numb their minds? Here, I don't want to numb my mind and it's running wild right now…"

She was surprised to realize how much sense that made. She had to admit that first time, in their dingy apartment on Henx, had been unlike any experience she'd ever known.

Siri took the time to check out how his own suit fit. The way it clung to his shoulder muscles was surprisingly attractive. Her eyes traveled down his chest, over his flat stomach.

She sucked in a sharp breath. "Oh! You really weren't kidding!"

"Yeah, it kind of caught me off guard," he mumbled, "seeing you in that suit..."

"Well," she said playfully, moving toward him, "we can't have you wandering the corridors like that, now, can we?"

Debrief
The Dibbarra, *Fleet R.V. point #233*

Mishak looked at Eth, seeking some sign that he was joking. He could feel his subordinate's emotions once again, though not as completely as before. Still, there was no deception in the Human's mind.

He could feel Tashmitum's skepticism but she seemed to be keeping an open mind or, at least, trying to.

He leaned on what Oliv had taught him about physical tells but that held no clues either. Eth seemed to believe what he was saying. He looked to the woman who'd come in with him. *Scylla,* he thought.

She was even harder to read. He turned back to Eth. "What?" He knew it sounded stupid but it was definitely appropriate.

"I know this is all hard to believe, Lord," Eth said evenly, "but that makes it no less true." He kept his eyes on Mishak. "Scylla," he said quietly.

Mishak looked to Scylla, wondering why Eth had spoken her name, and his entire body sank into a combat-or-retreat posture. *Where the hells did she go?"*

"I'm right here, lord." The woman's voice brought him spinning to face her. Tashmitum radiated a clear sense of surprise.

Gods! It's all real? Mishak fought to bring his response under control. He came back to a normal standing posture.

"How did you do that?" Tashmitum asked.

"It's not an easy thing to explain," she said. "If I tried right now, I'd be wasting your time, grasping at useless metaphors. If you give me some time to think about it, I can return another time and go through it more effectively."

It sounded reasonable, but Mishak wondered if they might simply be reluctant to give all of their secrets away. He felt a surge of anger at the thought but he beat it down with the practiced ease of a Quailu who's learned to keep his feelings to himself. "Can you do that again?"

"Of course, lord." Again, the voice came from behind him and he still wasn't aware of seeing her disappear. It was more a question of noticing she was no longer there. He didn't know if that was important but it gave him a sense of control over his own reactions.

"And how long has it been since this began?"

Eth frowned. "I first noticed the changes around the time we fought your uncle at Heiropolis."

"Heiropolis," Mishak mused. "Your mind *did* go dark to me after that visit we paid to the Varangian ship, as I recall."

Eth's gaze slipped to the right for a heartbeat, and then he frowned, nodding. "True, Lord. I believe they awakened something in my mind."

"But how do you explain Scylla? She wasn't even at the battle for Heiropolis, was she?"

"I was taken by the Varangians at Kwharaz Station, Lord," she explained. "I was the contraband grown by the Chironians to assassinate you."

The assassin! Mishak thought wildly. *How did I not put something so elementary together? And I think I can rule the HQE?*

His concern must have shown on his face because she smiled at him, reminding him – with a twinge of guilt – of Oliv. "I wasn't exactly Scylla back then, Lord. You would have been briefed on a contraband female, one with no name. And I've managed to remove the Chironian programming, so there's no fear for your safety."

Mishak felt a little less foolish but one thing was nagging at him. "You've been dealing with this, *understanding*, as you call it, for quite some time now. Why are you only coming to me now?"

Eth looked down at the low table between himself and Mishak for a moment. "Lord," he began, looking up to meet Mishak's gaze, "I think you know by now how we all feel about you. We serve you willingly, not out of fear but out of respect and trust."

"I have to admit, Eth, that it's the trust that I'm wondering about right now," Mishak admonished gently.

Eth nodded. "If it were only Scylla and I, we might have handled things differently but there are others."

Mishak felt a shiver run down his spine. "Others?"

"With different degrees of ability, lord, and that is where we foresaw a problem." He paused to marshal his thoughts. "We have a reciprocal duty of protection; the lord must protect his people and the people must defend their lord."

"That only highlights why you should have trusted me earlier than this."

"No, lord. With respect, you also have that same reciprocal bond with the entire empire. You will sit the throne, one day. It's one thing to take a risk within your own fief but a species that could potentially pose a risk to the empire at large?"

Mishak looked down at the hand that had come to lightly grip his forearm, then up at Tashmitum's face. "He's right," she told him. "If you take a moment to consider it, you'll see the truth of it."

Eth set his mug down, still filled with hot coffee. He reached out for Mishak's empty mug and set it down next his own. "If a large enough number of Humans possess the ability to kill with a thought, wouldn't the future emperor feel the need to consider the implications?"

"Kill with a thought?" Mishak fought his emotions. "Aren't you exaggerating a little?"

"Watch your mug, lord."

Mishak looked down at the two mugs. One empty and one emitting a delicious-smelling vapor. He twitched in alarm as the empty mug shattered.

He looked at the pieces, glistening with the remnants of his coffee. *I have to stop taking unannounced meetings just before going to bed,* he thought wryly. He looked up to find Eth watching him calmly.

"Imagine stealthy scout-ships, in the middle of a hostile fleet," Eth said. "Imagine Humans suddenly appearing on the enemy bridges, decapitating their leadership before they're even noticed and then disappearing just as quickly.

"That's a potent weapon, as long as it's at your disposal, but what risk do we pose to the empire at large, an empire you'll rule, one day?"

"I very much doubt you came here to convince us to exterminate all Humans," Mishak said. "You've already worked out a solution. What is it?"

"Tight controls," Eth said immediately. "A small cadre aboard each ship should be enough to handle any special missions. The threat to the empire would be unmanageable, if there were millions of us with this ability, but, if there were only a few hundred, all carefully chosen, the threat becomes manageable."

"You mean it would be easier for me to have your elite group wiped out in one fell swoop," Mishak said, disturbed at the thought but still pleased to note his own success in achieving a dry tone.

"Frankly, yes," Eth admitted. "Some would undoubtedly escape such a fate but they'd be alone and far easier to deal with than an entire species of angry super-Humans!"

Mishak tried out a smile, though it probably looked more like digestive distress. "A species, you said!"

Eth froze for a moment then raised both eyebrows in a grudging nod. "I did say that, didn't I? I suppose I meant it."

"Good! Now, how do we avoid my having to order your elimination someday? I have no doubts about your own loyalty but we're talking about hundreds of Humans that I've never met."

"Which is exactly what we need to change, lord." He shivered. "Pardon, lord, but there wasn't quite enough heat in that coffee to compensate for smashing your mug. Would you mind if I dumped my mug and got another, before we go on?"

"Sit, man!" Mishak waved him toward the couch and picked up the cold mug himself. *It's almost ice!* "Is that what you do?" he asked as he stepped over to the coffee service on the sideboard. "You harvest heat energy and somehow create kinetic energy from it?"

"More like I create the kinetic energy from focused expectation but it requires an energy source. If I don't find it elsewhere, my own core temperature drops to dangerous levels." Eth sat, wrapping his arms around his shivering torso. Scylla sat next to him and draped a warm arm around his shoulders.

"Gleb and I took heat from the Varangians during your mating with the princess. Otherwise, we could never have held them in place for so long."

Mishak cursed mildly as he spilled coffee on his hand. "You were holding them in place?"

"They were moving to intervene, Lord. If they didn't have specific orders from her father to prevent just such a thing, I'd be very surprised." He offered a teeth-chattering grin. "You see? Even back then, we were watching your back!"

Tashmitum let out a deep rumbling chuckle that carried a higher counterpoint. "Given what we were doing, your choice of idiom seems a little too close to home."

Eth joined in the amusement but, though Mishak could feel amusement from Scylla, she displayed none of the usual Human tells.

Almost like a Quailu, that one. He handed the coffee to Eth and sat opposite him.

"So how do we work to ensure loyalty in those we haven't met?"

Eth drained half the cup in one gulp, shuddering with involuntary pleasure as the hot liquid ran down into his chilled core. "This is a good start," he said, hefting the mug toward his lord.

Mishak laughed but then he stopped suddenly. "You're serious!"

"You said it yourself, lord. They haven't met you. Make this a part of the whole package. When they're declared ready for duty, they come to you and sit down for a coffee with the royal couple."

"We're hardly sitting on the throne, just yet," Mishak demurred.

"But you will be," Eth said with an absolute certainty that humbled the Quailu lord. How did he achieve such loyalty from this Human? *Well, he's trying to tell you, isn't he?* "So we just have a coffee with them?"

Eth looked to Scylla. "There should be a bit of ceremony to it, I think."

She nodded. "A touch of formality would increase the value of the experience."

"One of us should present the new member of this... guild?" Eth shook his head ever so slightly. "We'll need a proper name for it. Anyway, one of us brings the new candidate to your door, lord, and your guards challenge us with something formal – *Who comes before the Couple-Royal?* or some such.

"We declare who we are and one of the guards steps aside to reveal a low pedestal with something on it that they have to destroy."

"A mug?" Mishak suggested mischievously.

Eth stopped mid-breath and nodded non-committally. "I'm thinking something that symbolises their new role."

"A clay tablet?" Tashmitum suggested. "Inscribed with a real stylus in court cuneiform. Something like the word 'chaos'. They smash the chaos-tablet using only their own energy, giving their heat as a gesture of fealty."

"And then the shivering new guild member is brought in to us," Mishak continued the thread. "I serve hot coffee and we chat for a while." He had to admit, it was just the sort of thing he loved. Back on Kish, he'd enjoyed the feelings he evoked in his people when he condescended to deal with them on even terms.

"It would become a part of the whole package. Folks would see these people and say 'She's with the guild. She's had coffee with the emperor and empress!'" Eth nodded to himself. "It builds in a degree of respect for them that's tied *directly* to you. That's a good start on binding their loyalty to the throne."

"To the throne?" Scylla asked. "Or to *our* lord and lady, as well as their heirs? The two concepts may not be the same forever and we are, after all, *their* subjects, whether he's the emperor or a one-system minor lord."

Mishak waggled a finger at her. "Now you're *really* selling this!" he said. "Your organisation might be smaller than the Varangians but you could easily rival them in importance. Anyone challenging us or our descendants for the throne would have to give serious thought to your response. Would an emperor from a different family be able to count on guild support or would you maintain the bond with my own family?"

Tashmitum hissed. "That may backfire on us. If the others feel we are too powerful, we might lose votes."

"Most would probably assume that they'd function as an arm of the throne," Mishak countered. "By the time they realize the difference, the vote will be over."

"I would imagine that any support we'd render to an emperor from another lineage would be at your own family's discretion." Eth glanced at Scylla. "As she said, we are your subjects because you're the lord of Kish, not because you're in line for the throne."

"That certainly doesn't hurt our line of succession," Tashmitum said, "and, if we ever lose the throne, it does ensure our family's continued influence." She turned to a holo that had just popped into existence with a light chime.

"Perhaps this is a good moment for us to adjourn," she said. "We should take time to think over what we've discussed so far and we also have someone waiting to speak with us…" She slid the holo over to her husband.

"Gleb!" Mishak leaned forward and set down his mug but then, with a glance at Eth, picked it up and drained the last dregs. "Is he?"

Eth nodded. "No time like the present to start off a new tradition."

Tashmitum touched the orange icon beneath Gleb's name and it turned green. The door to their private lounge opened and the Human walked in.

"Welcome back, lieutenant!" Tashmitum rose from her seat and inclined her head in greeting.

Mishak stood as well. "Who comes before the royal couple?" he boomed formally, startling the poor Human, which Mishak couldn't help but enjoy, especially as it was Gleb. He had a very unsettling effect on most Quailu.

Eth came to his rescue. "We bring Glebkennu of Kish before you. We declare him ready for service in the Guild."

Gleb, reassured that his lord hadn't suddenly lost his wits, looked to the mug that Eth was pointing at.

"You see here… *oh bugger*!" Eth pulled out a marker and scrawled 'CHAOS' in rough cuneiform across one side of the mug

274

before setting it back down. "What is your duty, Glebkennu of Kish, when you find chaos within your lord's domain?"

"I… destroy it?" Gleb raised an eyebrow.

Eth indicated the mug again. "Then do so now, using no external energy."

Gleb widened his eyes at this but he could see that his superior was taking this seriously so, while he was still looking at Eth, the mug shattered.

"It's a good thing we just use cheap mugs from the mess hall," Mishak muttered. He jolted a little from his wife's pinch. "Sorry, dearest," he said, realizing he was jeopardizing what little solemnity the moment possessed.

"Sit, everyone." He turned to the coffee service and poured fresh mugs, bringing the first one to Gleb. "This was our first attempt at a new ceremony," he told the Human as he sat next to his wife. "I'm afraid we're still working out a few bugs."

"You're the first inductee into the…" Eth shook his head. "I don't want us just calling it 'the Guild'. It lacks something."

"This guild is for those of us who possess the understanding?" Gleb asked. "Yeah, Guild doesn't cut it at all. I'd go with something a little scarier like the Nergalihm." He tried to drain his mug but coughed on the last dregs when Eth slapped him on the back.

"You got back just in time!" Eth told him. "Gods only know what kind of lame title me might have settled on, if you weren't here."

Tashmitum stood, reaching down to take Gleb's empty cup.

"This is also a part of the ceremony," Mishak explained, gesturing to the princess. She was refilling the mug with hot coffee. "You're officially the first of the Nergalihm to have coffee with the royal couple."

"And here I thought I was just coming in for a debriefing. Thank-you, your grace." Gleb took the mug back and downed half of it, sighing at the heat.

"Well, things have moved along rather quickly this evening," Mishak told him. He dropped back into his seat. "A half hour ago, I was on my way to bed, no idea what you were up to and now I'm… what… the lord commander of the Nergalihm?"

"Has a good ring to it," Eth said, "and *lord* commander, is a clear reference to your lordship of Kish. Makes us less a fixture of the HQE and more a group loyal to one particular family."

"Good! That's sorted out." Mishak turned back to Gleb. "So, what have you learned while you were away?"

"Well, lord, I've learned that system security is pretty lax out there. Your brother's data was easy enough to steal and even his comms are an open book. Changed his outgoing glyph to read 'Melvin the Bastard'."

"Really?" Mishak laughed. "He must have been livid when he found out!"

"Couldn't say." Gleb cradled the warm mug. "Far as I know, they still hadn't noticed it by the time I left the ship."

"I suppose most folks don't really look at the glyph very closely. They look for the crest to figure out who's calling them, not the cuneiform," Mishak said, still chuckling.

"Your brother won't see it like that," Tashmitum insisted, smiling. "He'll just think of all the nobles he's called with that ridiculous name to announce him and more than a few of them like to have the computer announce the caller by reading that glyph."

"Oh, that is delicious!" Mishak slapped his thigh. "Can you just imagine him wondering at the behavior of those he'd called?" He looked at Gleb. "It's a good thing you left before it was found out." He narrowed his gaze.

"That reminds me, my young Nergalihm, about a rumor that's been circulating. They say that the lord of the underworld paid a visit to Memnon's ship recently…"

"I might have killed a few of his crewmen on my way off his ship," Gleb admitted, "and they might have all been found in the same pose with no discernable cause of death…"

"And a deck officer on the verge of hysteria, shrieking about Nergal wanting to use his entrails for sausage skins," Mishak added. "What was the thought process behind all that?"

"Well, it started out because they were getting in my way but I figured I should make the most of a dicey situation. See if I can get a little panic and fear to spread."

"By posing them?"

Gleb shrugged. "The average Quailu is a fine individual but, with respect, lord, a poorly trained Quailu crew led by a self-absorbed tyro is a panicky herd on the verge of stampeding. I tried giving them a nudge. If you've already heard about it, then I must have met with *some* success."

"True enough." Mishak leaned forward. "So, then you went to my father's ship. He had Humans as well, I take it?"

"Indeed lord, else I'd be dead by now. They're treated slightly better than the ones on Melv… Memnon's ships, but they still only perform the lowest tasks. It seems that the Meleke Corporation is selling them to your father and brother as 'free' Humans, though they have to sign indenture contracts in return for their existence."

"That doesn't sound at all legal," Tashmitum said.

"I don't believe it is, my lady," Gleb confirmed.

"They're just encroaching on the genetic contract to get under my skin," Mishak asserted. "We'll deal with that but, first, have you found anything that explains the influence my father is able to exert over the nobles, even though he can't come through on his threats without plunging everyone into chaos?"

He felt a flicker of unease when he recognized the grimace on Gleb's face.

"You're probably not going to like this, lord. I went there, hoping to uncover your father's clever scheme in all its glory but what I found was alarmingly simple.

"There's no scalpel behind the sledge-hammer. It's all sledge-hammer. He's just riding the threat of exposure until someone dares to stand up to him and then the whole thing comes out. The entire HQE will learn that Meleke has been running a non-extinct slave-trade."

"But that's going to lead to chaos!" Mishak exploded. "He'll... *fornication!*" he said quietly.

"Exactly, lord." Gleb said into the sudden silence. "He wants to carve his own kingdom out of the HQE. What better way to do that than during a time of massive economic and political upheaval?"

"How sure are we about Humans being extinct, Lord?" Eth asked. "Scylla tells me the Chironians only allocated *her* to your assassination. The *other* Humans were destined for something called the Irth project. Why would they need Humans for that?"

"That data I took from your brother's ship wasn't very hard to get, now that I think of it," Gleb warned. "Could he have been waiting for someone like me to come along?"

"I doubt he has the subtlety for that," Mishak said distantly, "but I could see Father putting him up to it. He's probably laughing down his tunic right now, anticipating the scandal it would make if the assumed heirs to the imperial throne were revealed as having contraband wardu!"

"How the hells do we counter that?" Eth asked. "I mean, short of freeing all the Humans on Kish..." He stopped, watching the glint in his lord's eyes. "Lord, that would bankrupt you! The fees to buy out the entire genome from Meleke…"

Mishak looked to his wife. "There's no other option, is there?"

She tilted her head back slightly. Her curiosity was piqued but then it suddenly resolved into certainty. "I know what you're thinking! If we're going to do it, then we'd better do it right now, before events can take this rare opportunity from us."

He nodded. "Computer, prepare to initiate a recording, medium framing on myself and the princess."

A holographic border appeared to show what the system would record. Mishak didn't bother to adjust it. "Initiate."

The border turned green.

"Fellow citizens," he began, "I am Mishak, son of Sandrak and an elector in the Holy Quailu Empire. I hereby announce intent to transition my world of Kish from a wardu economy to a mushkenu economy. I ask all the inhabitants of Kish to remain calm and to continue reporting to your current work assignments, for the time being, in order to avoid undue disruption. In time, you will be able to transfer to new opportunities as you desire, but I must ask you for your patience.

"I extend my congratulations to all the former wardu of Kish! I'm sure you will join me in thanking the Meleke Corporation for so generously waiving the buy-out fee!"

With a gesture, he stopped the recording. "How did I do?" he asked, enjoying the looks on his Humans' faces. He could feel a completely undiluted reaction from Eth – the first he'd noticed in a very long time.

Eth huffed out a half breath, half laugh. "That's great news, lord, but do you think this business about the fee will work?"

"They have to wonder what we know," Mishak reasoned. "Why should my father be the only one to use this indiscriminate threat?" He sat back, relaxed. "No, they don't dare call me on this without risking everything."

"I just came here for a debriefing," Gleb said, "and I end up having a fancy ceremony, getting to watch my species win their freedom..." He drained his cup and then waved it in a vague gesture. "I gotta drop by more often!"

"I've let my father run on long enough," Mishak said as if Gleb hadn't spoken. "He's been arranging his deniable conflicts, chipping away at the empire and at our *own* credibility. It's time to force the issue. He needs to fight or tuck-tail."

"You're not thinking of attacking your father?" Tashmitum demanded, horrified.

"That would be..." Eth looked to the side, clearly searching for a diplomatic word to convey his misgivings. "Hells, lord, it would be gods-damned idiotic!"

Tashmitum nodded emphatically.

Mishak chuckled. "I have no intention of violating the patrilineal statutes. I believe we can draw him into attacking us but I want to deal with my upstart brother first. He's stupid enough to be biddable and, what's more, stupid enough not to realize it.

"I learned the rules, growing up at court, but I learned how to *bend* them from my father."

He turned the full intensity of his personality on Eth. "There's something I need done and your Humans are the perfect instrument for the job!"

Eth opened his eyes. He was safely back in his quarters aboard the *Mouse*. The meeting with Mishak had gone well enough...

"You know, I think I trusted him more when I wasn't dead..." Abdu's voice muttered in Eth's head.

His shoulders drooped. He kicked a chair into alignment with his position and dropped into it. He grabbed a mug on a nearby table, draining the cold remnants of the coffee he'd been drinking when he'd been summoned to the *Dibbarra*.

That business about the Nergalihm would keep things on an even keel for a while but the whole thing seemed hollow and not just because they were pretending to be the servants of the underlord.

I had to tell him, he insisted to himself. *We can't keep our abilities secret forever and the longer we held off revealing it, the worse it would have been.*

If they were going to be a part of the empire, they had to be honest with its future emperor. He frowned at the featureless void outside his window.

If...

Where do we belong? He knew he'd made a good case for telling all to Mishak but it wasn't the real reason, was it? Why did he care what Mishak thought of him?

If Eth was searching for family, he wasn't going to find it in his former owner and current lord.

He wasn't going to find it anywhere, was he...

For once, Abdu's voice remained silent.

He hurled the mug at the aft bulkhead.

Top-up
The Dibbarra, *Fleet RV #233*

"Shiiiiit!" Gleb drew out the imprecation, emptying his lungs to prevent rupture. He squeezed his eyes shut, both to avoid the disturbing sight and to prevent them boiling dry in the zero-pressure environment he'd suddenly found himself in.

His helmet flowed into place but he kept his eyes closed for a few more seconds, waiting for the tissue swelling to go down. His eyelids felt like they'd doubled in thickness but they were slowly coming back to normal and he finally opened them to find himself floating in front of the *Mouse*.

He worked his jaw to get some saliva flowing back into his paper-dry mouth.

Eth's cruiser looked large from this distance. He opened a channel. "*Mouse* ready room," he requested, waiting for the light layer of ambient noise to appear. "Scylla, this is Gleb. I missed."

"Where are you?" she asked him.

"Floating in front of the *Mouse*. I tried but I just couldn't see the bridge of the *Scorpion*."

"The bridge?" Scylla's voice had no edge to it but it still managed to convey disapproval. "What did I just finish telling you?"

"See the bridge?"

"And how were you supposed to do that? If your eyes were on the *Mouse*, how were you supposed to see anything on the *Scorpion*? Did you completely ignore that part?"

"Find someone on the *Scorpion* and use *their* eyes," Gleb answered sheepishly. "I kinda got a little too excited after shifting myself around the ready room. Got used to using my own eyes."

"Well, shut your own eyes and find someone on the *Scorpion*."

Gleb did as he was told, closing his still-tender eyelids, and reached out to the *Scorpion* but he couldn't find anyone.

"Are you reaching back for a common origin?" she asked him as if she were watching from inside his mind.

If she was doing that, Gleb could hardly blame her. I wasn't like he was going to win any student-of-the-year awards today.

"Don't just reach out," she continued, saving him the need to admit he was doing it wrong again. "Reach *back*. Follow the path back up to a higher dimension, find our projections into the space within the *Scorpion*."

Gleb blew out a slow, controlled breath and concentrated. He'd made use of that dimension to move his body – with less than stellar results. He just needed to accept that he, that all of his species, existed there, that life was more than the three-dimensional bodies he was accustomed to seeing.

He could feel his own presence there... He shook his head fractionally, not realizing he was doing it. That wasn't quite right was it? That presence wasn't just his. It was more than just himself. He felt it more like a... shared mind... a homecoming. It stretched away, fading in the distance, but he sensed closer knots of it, surrounding him.

It was the crews of the Human ships.

He focused on the one representing the *Scorpion*. As he moved his mind that way, the presence began resolving into individual concentrations.

Crewmen.

Some seemed more familiar than others. He chose one that seemed the most welcoming to his mind and tried to come closer. He felt like a ghost trying to inhabit a live body. He felt as though he were mentally occupying the same space as the crewmember but he couldn't seem to make the connection.

Don't try to take over, Scylla had told him. *Just use their perception. It flows up to where we all connect.* He considered trying to reach back into the higher level but realized that, if his body was in one place and his perceptions were largely focused on the figure aboard the *Scorpion*, some part of him had to already be in that in-between space.

That did it. He suddenly saw the bridge. Oliv was nodding her assent to him and he turned, heading for the aft exit hatch leading to the central companionway. He'd intended to appear on the bridge but he wasn't willing to give up his connection, not after the difficulty in making this one.

He watched the companionway drift past. Several crewmembers nodded his way and he wondered whose eyes he was looking through. He turned to the left and stopped at the third cabin door. A hand pressed the control panel and the door slid open.

He paid particular attention to the layout of the cabin, not wanting to appear in the middle of a bed or chair. Unfortunately, his host barely glanced at the room before turning to the com panel inside the door to set a wake-up alarm.

The crew-member stepped back, the field of vision rocking oddly from side to side, vaguely focused on a section of the bulkhead separating the cabin from the hallway outside. Gleb didn't think there would be room for him there and so he waited until his visual host turned toward the far end of the small room, calling up a holo-mirror.

It was Eve, her underarmor suit pushed down to her waist while she examined a shrapnel scar on the left side of her abdomen. Gleb realized there was room for him in the space where her holo-projection stood and he flowed into it.

It must have escaped Scylla's attention during the briefing or, more likely, Gleb had missed it, but there are some things you don't quite comprehend while reaching across to another mind.

Gleb had seen Eve examining her scar, but he'd been doing it through her eyes. His perception of what she was doing was heavily influenced by localised biology.

Eve's biology.

From the moment he opened his eyes in the glare of her holo-reflection, he realized that, though she saw nothing amiss in examining her own healing skin, she would definitely see problems with him suddenly intruding on a private moment.

She twitched in alarm, dropping into a combat stance. It was something his mind told him he should regret having seen though his body was playing devil's advocate.

Seeing her, now, through his own male brain, he was acutely aware of her sublime curvature. There was also a great deal of delightful motion involved in her adopting a combat stance so rapidly…

He held up his hands. "Look, I know this looks bad…" He shrugged, grimacing. "I mean it doesn't… That is, you don't look…"

"Gleb!" she yelled. "What the actual shit?" She brought an arm up across her chest. "Hiding in my cabin? Did you think I'd find this amusing?"

"No!" He waggled his hands desperately, still palms out toward her. "I was training…"

"You need training to be a perv?" She looked around the room as if searching for something to hit him with.

"No… no. I was with Scylla, training to shift my location. I was aiming for the bridge. I had to find eyes on the bridge to plot an entry point. I wound up piggybacking on your perceptions because your mind offered the strongest connection."

"That's… kind of nice, I suppose," she said grudgingly, "but why show up here instead of on the bridge?"

"You started moving almost as soon as I started seeing through your eyes. I had to wait till you got here, so I could find a safe spot with no obstructions."

"So, you've been using my eyes since I left the bridge?" she asked, a dangerous tone making the hairs on the back of Gleb's neck stir. "You were watching me undress and examine myself?"

"Yeah, but I didn't realize you were undressing and then when you were looking at the holo-mirror, the only thing on my mind was that the holo was in a good spot to materialise."

She glared at him. "I'm having a hard time deciding why I'm gonna punch you. For one thing, you've been watching me undress; for another, you had no reaction at all to what you saw?"

"Hey! You gotta understand. I was seeing you through your own perceptions, the way *you* see your own body. That's how I goofed. I didn't perceive how good you look until I showed up here and saw you through my *own* eyes. Honestly, you don't give yourself anywhere near enough credit."

Her expression softened a fraction, giving way to mild surprise but she covered it quickly enough. "Aww!" she cooed. "Of all the creepy things I've heard over the years, that's gotta be the sweetest..." Her eyes suddenly grew wide.

"Wait! You actually transitioned here? That's incredible! Do you transition back now or what happens?"

"I hit the EBEA," he gestured to the emergency beacon nodule on his forearm, "and she reaches out to guide me back. They don't want to over-tax me on the first attempt between ships. Seeing as how I missed the first time, I'm not complaining."

"You missed?"

He nodded, grinning now. "Appeared in the black, right in front of the *Mouse*. Still some pain from the tissue swelling."

She grinned. "Well, that's the risk you run as a Nergalihm. She dropped her arm, advancing on him. You end up in the wrong place and you have to deal with swelling." She backed him up to the door.

"I hear the combat EVA suit is a little unforgiving where that kind of thing is concerned," she said, eyes wide in a mockery of innocence. "Have you ever noticed that?"

Gleb grimaced. "I'm noticing that right now, thanks ever so much."

"Oh dear," she mused. "In military terms, I believe we call that being 'caught out of position'. She had to reach down to press the EBEA icon because Gleb was starting to double up.

She reached back up and pressed the control to open her door, shoving him out into the narrow hallway. "Next time, knock, jackass!" She shut her door.

Gleb settled into a seated position against the far bulkhead, chuckling ruefully. "Definitely deserved that," he admitted, then frowned up at her door. *Next time?* Before he could assure himself that she hadn't meant that as some kind of backhanded invitation, he felt Scylla's mind reaching out to him.

Oh gods! He could have used a little more time but he closed his eyes and the ready room on the *Mouse* appeared in his mind almost instantly. He appeared in front of her, still sitting on the deck next to one of the chairs.

Scylla took a step closer. "Are you alright?" She stopped at Gleb's outstretched palm.

"Sure!" he insisted. "No worries. It's just... y'know, a little tiring, first time and all that. He put a hand on the seat and levered himself up awkwardly, remaining in a seated position the whole time. He brought up his right leg and crossed it over his left knee, leaning forward to rest his right elbow on his knee.

"I'll just… catch my breath while we get caught up, if that's ok?"

Scylla stared blankly at him for a moment but that was her normal expression, anyway, so it was hard to tell what she was thinking. Gleb could feel mild amusement coming from her, so he supposed he wasn't being nearly as subtle as he thought.

"Sure," she finally agreed. "Whatever's more comfortable. Let's keep at it, though. We've got a lot of candidates waiting."

"I have to go again?"

"Relax." Scylla took a seat. "The second time won't be nearly so hard."

She frowned at him. "What?"

Choosing the Battle

Goading the Ox
Hab-Ring, Kurnugia 2

"They're coming out," Meesh's voice crackled in Oliv's ear. It had that scratchy quality from the narrow-focus speakers in her stowed helmet. The loss in quality was worth the boost to operational security. Meesh could have been screaming and the other noodle-shop patrons around Oliv wouldn't hear a thing.

She abandoned her bowl and threaded her way through the tables. "I don't think Lord Kittebar cared for the entertainment," Meesh opined. The raucous background noise, partially dampened by the processors in their suits, faded as he reached the sidewalk behind their quarry.

Oliv met the Quailu and his entourage just as they were passing a dark alley tunnel. She felt his alarm as he recognized her species and it threatened to set her adrenaline coursing. She willed herself to remain calm as the guards, picking up on their master's feelings, drew their side-arms.

"This way, my lord," she gestured to the tunnel politely and Kittebar, of course, hesitated. "If we wished you dead, we would at least have had the decency to kill you in orbit and spare you the spectacle inside that... establishment."

289

.G. Claymore

She could feel the anger from him, the outrage to his dignity and to his entire species from what he'd just witnessed. It wasn't why she'd waited until now to approach him but it certainly didn't hurt her chances. What she really needed was the information he'd gone in there to retrieve.

Kittebar brought his feelings back under control. He looked back at his small guard detail and waved their guns down. The four Humans behind them had weapons but they were still holstered.

He couldn't quite say why that galled him.

They moved into the grimy tunnel mouth, taking care not to touch the filthy carbon-crete walls. Oliv stood facing Kittebar.

"Lord Kittebar, I doubt you're keen on meeting Melvin the Bastard, given the lack of respect he's shown so far." She felt a tint of amusement in the anger at this use of Memnon's nickname.

"If you allow us to attend in your place, I can guarantee you he'll be so angry with *our* lord that he'll forget he was even expecting you."

"And how do you propose to find him?" Kittebar was no fool. "He'll have someone watching us. By now, they're reporting this deviation to him."

She nodded, though it was hard to see in the dim light and Kittebar was unlikely to understand it anyway. "He did have you followed. Provost crewmen from his own ships. They're good enough at rounding up drunk crewmen overstaying a ground-leave but they're hardly trained as covert operators."

She activated a light on her left wrist and aimed it at the tunnel floor, a few meters farther in. Three bodies lay there. "Enough to execute a few handoffs," she admitted, "but they were too alert for their own good. A good operator learns how to be alert without *looking* like they're alert."

290

She looked back at the Quailu. "We've got the frequency they're using and we've heard no more chatter from them since these three went dark, aside from their controller at Memnon's location who's, understandably, a little curious."

She stepped in a little closer. "And speaking of Memnon's location..." She ended on an inquisitive intonation, though it was wasted on Kittebar.

He smoldered for a moment, clearly upset at talking to a group of natives who, literally, had Quailu blood on their hands. It was the blood of his enemies, certainly, but they'd still been Quailu and it gnawed at the edges of his customary serenity.

"You can't guarantee Memnon won't retaliate against me," he said evenly.

"True," Oliv admitted, "but the chances of him having the inclination or even the resources to do so will be minimal, if you cooperate." She stepped in again, more suddenly this time, forcing him to retreat a half-step.

"There's always alternatives, my lord. Apsu chose to take orders from Memnon..."

It was best not to push an awilu too hard. Pride made them brittle and they tended to crack in unpredictable ways. She could feel him weighing the possibility of Memnon's revenge against the certainty of Mishak's wrath.

"Menchuru 15 6 63," the Quailu said.

Oliv stared at him, one eyebrow raised. Incredibly, she could sense no attempt to deceive. They already had that address from two other sources but they hadn't really expected Memnon to still be using the same place.

They hadn't even planned to check the address out, in case they tipped Memnon's people that they were here. *Using the same address for multiple meetings? Is he sloppy or is there a trap waiting for us?*

She realized that she was still staring at Kittebar. She composed herself. "My lord and lady have instructed me to express their thanks in the event of your cooperation. If ever you are in need of assistance, you need only ask."

She could feel the hackles of his pride smoothing down in response to her polite message. Pride. Such a useful thing.

Especially when it belonged to someone else.

"I would advise you to leave this planet, my lord," she said earnestly. "The next few hours might go entirely unremarked by what passes for an administration here, or we might stir up a stinger's nest."

Memnon only half watched as a barely clad Human twisted gracefully to the left, ducking her opponent's war-hammer and darting in to slide her dagger between his ribs. She ripped it sideways before pulling it back out and her victim stared down at her in outraged shock, pink froth bubbling from his lips as the heavy weapon fell from nerveless fingers.

Mot cackled in triumph. "I told you she'd win, brother! I suppose you were wise not to take my wager."

"I don't like this," Memnon muttered. "Kittebar is late and we've lost contact with his minders. If he's pulling some sort of..."

He turned his head at the fear coming from the three guards by his elevator. They were terrified but he could tell little beyond that. *Why don't they draw their weapons?*

The elevator sighed open and he watched, rooted to his seat, as five humans in EVA armor strode out. Three of them sauntered over to his guards, one for each, and drew daggers, slicing them casually across the back of each Quailu's neck. *Oh gods!* Memnon thought. *Why did they not draw their weapons?*

The fear was now horror and Memnon was caught in its grip, feeling his retainers' emotions as they went into the final darkness.

His sister was a different matter. She watched the dying guards with fascination, licking her lips as they clutched vainly at their necks. She looked up at the lead Human, not the least concerned for her own safety. She took it as a rule of the universe that none would ever dare to raise a finger against her.

The dying minds faded, leaving Memnon with a heaving chest and a bloodstream filled with adrenaline.

"Sorry for the mess," the female Human offered. She took a holo-ring from a mag pouch at her hip. "I bring a message for Melvin the Bastard. That would refer to you, yes?"

"I've... I've been called that," he said, hating himself for the admission, but he was too unsettled.

"I like this one," Mot purred. "I'll have her fight next."

The Human turned to Mot, her armored head tilting. "I know who you are!" the intruder said, drawing a sidearm and turning to point it at her. "Funny how the universe works, sometimes!"

Memnon jumped in shock as the weapon blasted a slug through Mot's chest. He felt her disbelief, her honest inability to accept what had just happened, but he knew better.

He was a vicious bastard himself but he'd never developed his sister's misplaced sense of invincibility. Watching others die had only reinforced his own sense of vulnerability.

"Hey!"

He recoiled from the muzzle of the pistol when it rapped him on the forehead.

"I'm talking here!" the Human said indignantly. She held up the ring. "I'm going to leave you this message from your brother. You understand?"

"I do," he answered flatly. He turned back to Mot, who was still refusing to believe she'd been shot, even though she was starting to fade. "You killed her," he said, confused.

"I had my reasons," the Human replied curtly. She looked over at the Human who'd just fought for Mot's entertainment – as close to naked as made no difference, a dagger in her hand and more in her eyes.

The blood-soaked young gladiator was staring at Memnon with a frightening intensity, her knuckles white on the weapon's hilt.

"Take her," the 'messenger' ordered.

One of the armored Humans stepped over to the gladiator and convinced her to drop the dagger. He turned for the elevator and their leader rolled her eyes.

"Gods save us, Meesh. You understand that 'take her' means bring her with us, don't you?"

Meesh must have responded but Memnon hadn't caught it.

"Then put something on her, you oaf! We're not going to drag her naked through the streets, are we?" She pointed down at Mot. "Get that dress on her."

Perhaps it was the indignity of having her clothing stolen for a slave or maybe she'd finally reached a point where her self-delusion collapsed, but Mot finally felt the fear she'd savoured from her guards. The same fear she'd inflicted on so many victims, over the years.

The fear kindled a dull anger in Memnon. He'd considered shooting his sister more than once but to have someone else do it went against the grain. He watched the Humans walk out as if they hadn't just shot up his apartment and killed his sister.

The elevator door slid shut behind them.

"Security!" Memnon shouted at the ceiling where the sound pickups were located. "Security!"

There was no response, not even a truncated chime to acknowledge his attempt to communicate. *A jammer!* It made sense, he supposed. If they'd planned on leaving him alive, they would need to keep him from reaching help until they were well away.

He pounded the couch in frustration, making the holo-ring buck up into the air before clattering back onto the cushioned leather. In a rage, he grabbed the ring, certain he was about to toss it over the balcony. He almost laughed at the idea of the damned thing smashing at the feet of the Humans as they exited the building.

He looked down in disbelief at his own mutinous thumb, still on the activation glyph.

Mishak loomed above him, life size and standing on his palm. He tossed the ring to the floor between his and Mot's couches. Mishak landed facing the wrong way but his image rotated to face the only life-sign in the room.

"I freely admit," his brother began without preamble, "that I'm tired of finding your fingerprints all over every silly little plot in the sector. You've been doing my father's bidding, I know, but what has he done for you in return?

"Do your officers call you *lord*? No. They call you *sire* because you don't even have a single system to your name."

The holographic figure leaned forward, thumping at its own chest. "I had Kish because I was his true-born son but I didn't stop there. I took systems by right of conquest. I made myself into an elector by my own exertions."

The figure straightened, the better to glare down at Memnon. "I am done with you. It's beneath the dignity of an elector to waste time on an untitled nobody."

The figure shimmered out of view, leaving Memnon staring at Mot's body.

A nobody? He thought, rage boiling up, displacing the shame. *Perhaps we should change places!*

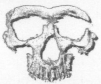

Oliv stepped out onto the sidewalk. "Ok, everyone disperse and make your way back to the shuttle. Meesh, keep an eye on our new friend."

She turned and headed off around the building, following the rim-edge street. Even though it only had buildings on the inward side, it was crowded because it was one of the fast-ways that ran around either edge of the planet-spanning ring. It also had heavy pedestrian traffic because the views from the outer sidewalk were magnificent.

"If the underworld's down below that mess, I hope they keep the roof in good repair," she muttered glancing out at the hellish tableau of lava flows. After a kilometer of walking, she strolled into one of the bastions that jutted out from the edge of the ring every couple of kilometers.

It gave an unobstructed view of the planet below and she walked up to the parapet, leaning over to look straight down. It was quieter out here, as most pedestrians were in a hurry to get wherever they were going. She casually looked around, checking to see if she could spot a tail.

There were three suspicious characters, ex-pat Enibulans, from the look of them. They weren't even trying to conceal their interest in her. They simply swaggered straight up to her.

She pretended to ignore them, still leaning on the parapet as they approached from her left. They should assume she was armed, but she saw no need to advertise the fact.

"Well, well, well," their leader drawled. "What do we have here? A contraband Human! Know what they do to contrabands here, Shegga?"

"Arrest them?"

She felt confusion from his cronies and, making her skin crawl, lustful avarice from the leader. *Well, that's a relief, I suppose,* she thought. At least she wasn't dealing with someone tailing her for Memnon.

Yeah, she added darkly, *they just want me to whore for them.*

"What?" The leader frowned, darting Shegga an irritated glance that he gave up on before it even got halfway there. "No. They sell 'em off at auction, and you wind up with the worst owners at those assizes sales."

He leaned in close, especially for an Enibulan. This one undoubtedly had plenty of experience at intimidating young runaways. "You want to come with us, lass. Stay out here on your own and you're bound to run into someone unsavory."

Oliv snorted. "I can only assume you're being ironic." She was still looking out to the horizon. "And what happens if I decline your generous offer?"

"That isn't really an option," he replied, adding an angry edge to his voice for good measure, "technically speaking."

She could sense his growing frustration at being defied by his own victim. She also sensed that he'd done something she was supposed to take notice of, something that would win this argument for him.

She turned halfway, just enough to face him without revealing her sidearm. He'd pulled back his jacket to reveal the handgrip of a small pistol peeking out of his waistband.

She darted out her left hand, yanking his weapon out, leaving an angry red scar on his abdomen where the back sight had gouged a shallow furrow. "Mihanneh-Hidges-seven," she said, giving a shake of the head to his two henchmen, who were starting to give off a spring-into-action vibe.

"I wouldn't, if I were you," she told them. "I *really* wouldn't."

They held their hands out to the side, an almost universal gesture employed by those who wish to avoid getting shot.

"I commend you," she told her would-be pimp. "Not many males are comfortable enough with their sexuality to be seen with a MH-7."

"Wh… what's wrong with it?" he spluttered, exuding indignation with a strong tracery of fear.

"Oh, nothing," she reassured. "It's just a little dainty for *my* tastes but, if I ever have a little girl, I might get her one of these until she's strong enough to hold something bigger."

She jammed it up under the Enibulan's chin, making him squeak in alarm. "Will a seven even penetrate your skull or is it just good for soft-tissue damage?"

His fear ebbed slightly as she lowered the weapon from his chin but it came roaring back when she whipped out her own weapon.

"The Khesh-fifteen, on the other hand, is more of an all-purpose weapon. This particular one has killed more Quailu than *you* can even count, seeing as Enibulans only have six fingers. It's more than enough to kill some low-level pimp for threatening an officer who was commissioned by our next emperor."

The fear was swamping them now. The three Enibulans now fully understood just how badly they'd judged the power-dynamic of the encounter. She could kill the three of them with impunity.

Oliv sensed the leader's embarrassment and, on a hunch, looked down. A dark patch was spreading down the lead Enibulan's legs. She chuckled. "Let's get you fellas out of those wet clothes."

They stripped down, casting embarrassed glances at the few who wandered into the bastion. Most of them wandered back out, upon seeing the guns. Finally, the three were standing next to piles of clothing, their hands clasped in front of their groins.

"First smart thing you idiots have done, so far," she told them. "None of us want me to see what's behind those hands but you're gonna need them to toss this mess over the side."

"But all our credits are in there!" one of them protested.

"Well, I certainly didn't figure you were using your implant chips on a world like this," she said, grinning. "You can either toss your shit over the edge or I'm gonna toss your brains all over the pavement. Your call…"

They saw the sense in her argument. *Really shouldn't be wasting so much time on this,* she thought, *but I really hate pimps and, now that I think of it, they can serve as a distraction, while I move on.*

"Turn around," she ordered.

"Trackers," she commanded her weapon, feeling the gratifying syntactic vibration as it confirmed the change of ammunition. She lowered the weapon's aim.

"I really hope you boys don't have any explosives stored up your prison wallets."

"Wait, what…?" The one on the left yelped as the tracker round buried itself deep in one of his ass muscles. The entry wound was small enough but it was bleeding freely.

"Hey!" she admonished the other two. "I can just as easily put these in your skulls but you'd end up unfit for anything but government service afterward." She twirled the muzzle at them and they turned away again, shaking with the anticipation of being shot in the ass.

She planted trackers in them, drawing out the time before the last shot. "Fin-stab-guided," she ordered, hefting her pistol.

"You boys understand what I can do with this ammo and your sorry asses?"

They nodded.

"Good! I'm gonna leave now. You're gonna stay here and beat the shit out of each other for at least ten minutes. If I think you're shirking, I pull the trigger. BANG!" she shouted, making them leap in fright.

"I'm tied into the surveillance system," she lied smoothly, "so you boys better put in a good effort or you won't regret it for very long."

She stared at them for a moment, then tilted her head, raising one eyebrow.

One of the henchmen darted a glance at his leader, then slapped him hard on the side of his head. The Enibulan staggered sideways while the other henchman saw an opportunity and darted a left jab at his compatriot's abdomen.

Satisfied, Oliv turned and strolled away, leaving the nude boxing match behind. She tossed the confiscated MH-7 over the parapet and left the bastion through the central arch, noticing on the way out that a small crowd was already starting to gather around the bizarre, naked fight.

"I truly do hate pimps," she said mildly.

The Real Fight
20 light minutes outside the Kish System

"Well," Mishak said, gesturing to the holo in the center of the ready room, "that's our plan. Does anyone have further changes or suggestions?"

Rimush had none and if any of his captains – his Quailu captains – had any, they were probably still too shaken by the unorthodox arrival of the Human captains to realize that some small part of their current apprehension might be due to the plan. He had to make sure.

"Come now, gentlemen," he said gruffly, trying his best to emanate reassurance, "I've never known you to remain so silent at a pre-battle consult."

He could feel something. To his left. "Sargina," he prompted. "You wish to speak?"

Sargina darted a quick look at Eth. "How certain are we that our scouting division will be able to destroy all the debris left in the mine-well?"

Mishak looked to Eth, raising an eye ridge. The Human did him the honor of catching the very un-Quailu gesture and nodded slightly in acknowledgement.

"Not certain at all, Captain Sargina," Eth answered, "but I hardly need to tell you that. I'm sure everyone here has read the collected lectures from your days at the Imperial War College."

Rimush fought to keep his disdain in check. Were his Quailu officers really so easy to manipulate? The warm flow of feeling suffused the room as misgivings fought a hasty rearguard action against this show of Human respect. *He's put them in the palm of his hand and all he did was flatter one blowhard.* He thought it without feeling it, of course, but it was true. His own misgivings about this sudden new power in their midst – this distinctly un-Quailu power – was increased.

They are a danger to us. How does our lord not see it?

"As you have always advised, Captain," Eth continued, "a commander must deal, not in certainty, but in probability, for the *only* certainty in combat is death."

Rimush tamped down the scorn that threatened to emerge as his fellow captains murmured in approval. *At least they're getting over their fear at seeing Humans suddenly appear in front of their eyes!*

"We estimate a high probability of success in eliminating the debris field left in the approach-well by Memnon's forces," Eth continued. "In any event, your phase of the attack won't be trying to path through, unless we transmit a successful clearing phase. If you have to fight your way down-well the old-fashioned way, you should at least have far fewer enemy vessels to fight."

"No increased risks incurred, either way," Sargina grudgingly allowed.

"Indeed," Eth agreed, clearly choosing to overlook Sargina's unthinking insult.

The Humans of the scouting division would be taking on great risks in the opening phase of this fight. If they were going to 'open the door' for Mishak's main force, they'd need to get right in among the enemy.

"With your leave, lord," the Human said, turning to Mishak, "we'll return to our ships and begin?"

"Very well," Mishak answered. "but be careful out there, commander. You're going to be on your own until we can get in there. I don't want to lose my scouting division!"

Rimush, watching Eth closely, saw the corner of his mouth quirk upwards. He knew they relied on physical cues and he was certain he'd just seen one. He looked at his lord, wondering if he'd noticed as well. Mishak had the same up-tilted corner to his mouth. Something had passed between the two.

Perhaps there was more to this gesture-based language than he realized. He twitched slightly, along with the other captains.

The Humans were gone and he couldn't even say he'd noticed when it happened. *This will end badly.*

He wasn't referring to the battle.

He glanced down, surprised to find his right hand patting the tunic pocket where the sealed orders waited. Fifteen sets of orders pressed in court cuneiform and signed by his own hand.

Fifteen of his most trusted captains…

"Full normalization," Hendy advised.

"Secure the path-drive," Oliv ordered, "and bring the cryo-exchangers online."

At a point beneath the engineering spaces, a pair of nano-tubule-coated shields swung out of the way and Noa's latest modification extended into the freezing slipstream of Enlil, the only cold gas giant in the Kish system.

The array of thin lines, bristling with nanite fins, carried a heat-exchange fluid that allowed a more rapid cool-down of the cryo-banks. It was a massive improvement over pumping a gas giant's cold atmosphere into the OEM exchangers that originally came with the cryo-units. It also avoided the risks inherent in a line rupture.

Having the planet's atmosphere accidentally venting into the crew spaces at more than three hundred degrees below comfort levels was always a cause for concern.

"What's our best trade-off velocity with regard to time-on-target?" Eth asked.

"At three eighths," Oliv answered instantly, "We reach the minefield with roughly six hours before the EM systems overload and leave us radiating."

"Time to target?"

"Six and three quarter hours." She'd clearly worked out the scenarios enough times to have it all lodged firmly in her enhanced brain.

"Very well," Eth replied. "Once everyone's out of the atmosphere, I'd be obliged if you could send a narrow beam transmission to each ship with instructions for a three eighths approach."

He stayed long enough to see the first sensor sweep when they emerged from Enlil's outer margins. There was nothing unexpected. Their home was playing host to Memnon's flagship and roughly seventy-five warships – most likely his entire fleet.

He supposed he should feel a chill down his spine at the sight – some kind of existential dread – but he couldn't summon more than a mild annoyance at finding an enemy fleet over his home.

Kish is home for us, so why don't I seem to give a damn? He shrugged. "I'll be in my quarters," he told Oliv, turning for the aft hatch.

We were grown for the lord of Kish. Does that make it our home or just our workplace?

Hela yawned hugely, stretching her arms out and working her shoulders to drive out the kinks. Her cabin had been ripped out to cram more cryo-units into the tiny scout-ship and the crew were expected to just sleep wherever they could find a semi-comfortable perch.

She'd spent the last few hours dozing on top of a weapons locker they'd pulled off the wall to make room for cryo-units. It was brightly-lit, noisy and completely lacking in privacy.

Naturally, she slept far better than she would have in her cabin. She grinned up at Hill, her latest engineer.

There had been so many new positions to fill with the new Scorpion Class ships coming online it seemed as if she lost crew as fast as she could train them.

Gleb, her original ops-rating, was now captain of a shiny, or rather, anti-shiny new scorpion class corvette. She didn't begrudge the mix of circumstances that had elevated him but she was ready for something new herself and she'd made it clear to Eth.

The next corvette was hers; just as soon as they got the time to make one. Assuming she didn't get herself killed in the next few hours, of course.

"Coming up on the debris-field, boss," Hill told her, returning her grin. "You listening for one of us to say that or do you just have a talent for waking up at the right moment?"

"Pure chance," she told him. "Then again; might have caught something in your tone while sleeping." She slid her legs off the side of the locker and stood. "We ready to rig for action?"

"Soon as you say the word."

"She closed up her suit, the helmet flowing into place around her head with a series of chatters and clicks as the various, non-nanite elements were shunted along in the flow, protruding like shards of glass from a lacerated arm.

The HUD came up. Now anything she said was carried by the comms system. It was the best way to avoid missing someone who might not hear her shouting an order this crucial. "All hands prepare to rig the ship for action."

Hill's helmet closed up and he moved over to the weapons locker she'd been sleeping on. He opened it and pulled out a warhead. It was coated with carbon nanotubules everywhere except for the array of handles that both offered a grip and protected the delicate coating from getting crushed.

"Mika, the ship is yours," she announced, barely hearing the answer from the ops station. She tuned out Hill who was moving to the growing opening in the side of the small ship, ready to toss out his first warhead.

Memnon had cluttered the approach through Kish's minefield with large chunks of the planet's defensive ships. It would play havoc with any force attempting an approach through the gap.

She could count on her crew to prep the debris field for demolition. Her task lay ahead of them. She reached out, searching for the faint hint of Quailu consciousness. It was far harder than using Humans to pinpoint a destination. Humans were like different fingers on the same hand but the Quailu were more like a different part of the body entirely.

There was a link, but it was weaker when it was another species. She smiled involuntarily, remembering Scylla's advice.

When there was uncertainty, concentrate instead on what *is* certain.

The control pedestal for the central holo is always clear in the middle. She closed her eyes.

Gleb opened his eyes.

He'd volunteered to go after Memnon. He knew the ship and all of her Human crewmen. He'd seen that they were all in their shared sleeping room and there hadn't been a moment to wait.

One of the Human crewmen was on his knees, waiting in terror for the end to come. A Quailu petty officer was standing over him with his sidearm at the back of the trembling man's head.

The remainder of the Humans were standing in a row, their hands bound by drone-ties. They'd been alarmed to begin with, but they jumped, nonetheless, at Gleb's appearance.

It was if he'd been there all along but they'd failed to notice him, standing there with his knife in the side of the Quailu's head. He had to admit, that could be a startling thing to notice.

He let go of the blade and turned on the second Quailu who'd been standing by the door, clearly radiating his desire to see death. "Haven't I given you what you wished for?" Gleb asked him reasonably.

The Quailu shook his head mutely, more in denial of the situation in general than in any answer to the question.

"No?" Gleb asked. "You wanted to see death. It's disappointing isn't it? Not what you thought it would be."

He could feel the thrill of it. He knew the others he served with didn't take the same pleasure in killing but he saw no reason why he shouldn't enjoy his work.

The guard still hadn't moved but Gleb could feel the impulse bubbling up in the alien's mind. "I'll do you a solid," he told him, conversationally. "I'll help you experience it firsthand."

He felt the alarm in his prey, a sudden flare like a ship exiting path. He reached into the Quailu brain, drawing heat from his cardiac array for the energy required to sever the brainstem.

Gleb turned back to his first victim of the day. This one was still conscious, despite the knife blade in his brain. The fear pulsed out of him like an arterial spray and Gleb soaked it up.

It was a dimension of his violence he'd never fully appreciated until he'd begun his training with Eth and Scylla. He knew Eth tolerated the thoughts of a doomed enemy through sheer force of will but Gleb reveled in it.

"To each his own," he mused quietly, reaching out to grasp the handle of his knife. He yanked it out and the Quailu finally fell, jerking spasmodically on the decking. Gleb savoured the moment before turning to the Humans and opened his helmet.

"Hey, fellas! What did I miss while I was away?" He bent over, retrieving the wrist pad from the Quailu he'd stabbed in the head. He hit the release command and the restraint-drones let go of the prisoner's hands and flew to hover above him in a small crowd.

"Gleb?" one of the engine-room cleaners asked.

"Hey, Mik," Gleb greeted him. "So these two," he nodded vaguely at the corpses, "were planning to kill you all, huh?"

"They were?"

"Oh yeah!" Gleb nodded. "I could see it in their minds." He darted Mik a glance. "Just like I can see you thinking I'm full of dung and did I have anything to do with Siri and Mel disappearing..."

He grinned. "Don't have a lot of time here. I came for my lord's brother. The only reason I came here first is because I need to dock a shuttle with the bridge in order to retrieve him. If you guys want out of here I can offer you a ride and a job on a Human-crewed corvette."

He shifted his gaze to the right. "Yeah, Davu?" He nodded. "Of course I killed him. He was a piece of garbage."

"Gods!" the man he'd addressed this answer to exclaimed in shock. "How did you know?"

"Like I said, I can see what you're thinking. I usually stay out of other people's heads but we're on a tight schedule here and I need to convince you quickly.

"If you want to come then let's go. Just leave the Quailu to me." He turned and walked out the hatch into the main ventral corridor.

There was one senior petty officer walking toward them. "What are you filth doing out here?" he shouted. "You've all been confined to quarters till we sort out who we can trust!"

He slumped to his knees, collapsing sideways against a bulkhead as the animation drained from his body. Gleb shuddered and moved on.

Hela stood over the captain's body, her breath shuddering from the exertion of stabbing so many bridge crewmen in rapid succession. She still didn't trust her ability to focus on something as precise as a cranial nerve while in the middle of a fight and she knew that trying to draw energy from her victims at the same time was asking too much.

Hela *was* very good at projecting herself. She had far more confidence in her ability to appear behind an enemy and knife them. She glanced down at the corpse, realizing that she had no idea which ship this was but it hardly mattered.

The Nergalihm were tasked with disabling as many of Memnon's ships as possible before the scout-ships cleared the approaches of debris.

She keyed in a lockout on the main terminal and closed her eyes, searching out the next bridge crew of unsuspecting Quailu…

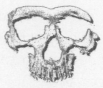

Gleb held up a hand, stopping the gaggle of Humans. He waved them up against the wall and concentrated.

This crew had already been exposed to rumors of the underworld god. They were ripe for more.

He slipped into his alter ego as a servant of Nergal. He reached out, found the nearest Quailu on the bridge and opened his mind to the poor fool.

Gleb was coming to take them all. His master wanted their souls.

He felt the terror swamping back into his own mind. It was reflecting off of the other minds on the bridge as well and, when he could feel them looking at his first victim, he stole his heat.

Heat energy, kinetic, he thought idly as he reached out for the cranial nerve. *Same ingredient, just a different way of cooking it up...*

The first victim's mind went dark but the fear from his crewmates would have been incapacitating for anyone who didn't understand what was happening.

Even Gleb was fighting a feeling of impending doom and he was the *cause* of it all.

He worked his way through the bridge crew, one at a time, pausing in grim amusement when he stumbled into Memnon's mind. The young noble was horrified, unable to understand why his bridge crew was simply dropping dead around him.

Gleb moved on, finishing off the last of the crew before shaking off the mental cobwebs and turning back to the Humans behind him. "Follow me in but stay quiet."

He stepped into the bridge to find Memnon clutching at the central holo-projector with a white-knuckled grip. The Quailu stared blankly, drained by the horror of the last few moments.

"My master," Gleb began calmly, "sent me for you, Memnon, son of Sandrak."

It was like rolling in candy. There was the stunned amazement from his fellow Humans. They'd seen what he'd done to several Quailu already and they had no doubts about who'd wiped out the bridge-crew.

Far more enjoyable was the numb disbelief coming from Memnon's mind.

Gleb walked up to him; halting with the bulk of the central holo projector between them. He felt Memnon's sudden wish to draw his sidearm.

"You don't want to do that," Gleb warned. "You'd be on the floor before your hand reached it." He grinned, reading the Quailu's reaction. "No, but you could say the Underlord lets me know what you're thinking."

He reached up into the interface and set a lockout command. "You're thinking about shooting me again," he said, leaning in so one of the holo panes bisected his face, leaving a bright green line on his skin where the two met.

"Where exactly would you aim?" He asked, gesturing at his chest. "Here?" He pulled back from the three dimensional space and reinserted himself behind the brash young noble. "Or here?"

Memnon let out a deep rumble of alarm and spun around, eyes wide.

"You need to understand," Gleb explained as an opening began to grow on the starboard side of the compartment, "that I'm not letting you keep your weapon because I'm careless. I'm letting you keep it because it poses no threat to me or to those I serve."

He gestured to the opening. "As I said, my master sent me to fetch you."

The thing that surprised Eth the most about being in command was how much he envied those beneath him. Most people he knew wanted advancement.

He wondered if any who'd attained it found themselves missing the old days. He was stuck outside of the minefield entrance in *Bastard Blade,* the newest corvette that he'd kept for himself.

The *Mouse* conveyed a certain prestige in Quailu society – heavy cruisers usually went to senior captains – but it didn't fit in with the nature of the growing Human force.

For one thing, it was inefficient, at least as Eth saw it. For the firepower it delivered, which wasn't negligible, it soaked up a ton of labor.

And it was a huge, easily spotted target. The Quailu might be honor bound to stand toe to toe and slug it out, but Humans didn't care about gaining face from antiquated ideals.

Crushing your foe was a far better way to burnish a reputation and the stealthy corvettes and scout-ships let his Humans get in close. Added to this, the new missile tech gave his smaller ships punch that was way above their weight limit.

But he couldn't take them inside the minefield until the debris had been blown. There were just too many large hull fragments in the approach corridor for his corvettes to slip in unnoticed. They'd be eclipsing the debris, giving their position away to the enemy every time their hulls came between wreckage and enemy sensors.

The scoutships had managed it, but they were smaller and nimbler. That left Eth sitting outside the approach corridor, trying to look calm while his subordinates were taking all the risks.

And having all the fun…

There were seventy-five ships in Memnon's fleet and Mishak had only forty-two. Eth's job was to clear the approach corridor and neutralize as many bridge crews as possible before Mishak could bring his fleet into action.

And here Eth sat. He couldn't go bridge-hopping with the others because his place was aboard the *Bastard Blade*. Someone had to be in charge and that someone happened to be *him*.

"Could be worse," Abdu's voice said and Eth nodded to himself.

"Demo's blowing!" the sensor officer exclaimed.

Finally! "Helm, take us in, full pitch!" Eth commanded. "Comms, bring the signal pair online."

They'd have to use the signal pair to report in to Mishak or the main fleet would never arrive in time for the fight. Light from the explosions would take hours to reach sensors on the *Dibbarra*. Conventional signals would take roughly as long.

Fleet-Captain Rimush shimmered into view.

"The approach is clear," Eth told him.

"Acknowledged," Rimush nodded in confirmation then faded from sight. He understood how much energy the signal pair consumed; how much heat it generated.

Eth stood still for a second. Head tilted to the side. *Rimush just nodded?*

"We're inside the minefield," the helm officer confirmed. "Moving away from the approach zone."

There was no time to waste. The fleet would be hammering through there any minute now and they'd be coming in on path-drives.

If you got in the way of a bow-wave of spatial compression, you'd destroy both ships in spectacular fashion.

The enemy were arrayed around the entry corridor this time. No clever tricks that only served to separate their forces. They'd opted for a simpler plan.

"Deploying missiles," Ops announced.

They would spread their weapons around and then leave them dark for now. Once the fight started, they'd see which ships still posed a threat and task the missiles accordingly.

"Comms drones?" Eth turned to the communications suite.

"Three active so far," the officer replied, sounding a little distracted. "Ejecting number four… now!"

How many ships will still be operational? He wondered. *How many bridge-crews can six of our people kill off in the time they had?* He shook his head. No sense wondering – they'd know soon enough and the plan was as solid as they could make it.

"Path alert! Our fleet is arriving!"

"Send the recall!" Eth ordered urgently.

"Sending the recall," Coms confirmed.

A narrow beam signal lanced out to one of the message drones. The drone immediately sent out two omnidirectional messages, one to query the enemy ships for a lockout command and the other to tell the six Humans to jump back to friendly ships immediately.

Gleb raised an involuntary hand to his right ear as his scout-ship docked with the *Stiletto*. He'd dropped Memnon on the *Bastard Blade* along with the Humans he'd brought from the *Deathstalker*.

He was still looking for a live bridge crew in Memnon's fleet when the recall order came through.

He closed his eyes and found a clear spot on his own bridge.

"Lockout query shows twenty-six enemy ships still active," the ops officer blurted when she suddenly realized he was standing in front of her station. "Our main fleet has just arrived."

The battle had begun. Hundreds of missile traces made the space between the two fleets look like an ancient weaving loom. Most of those traces were outbound from Memnon's remaining ships.

"I don't know what you *magic* Humans have done to my fleet," Memnon said from the entry-hatch of the *Bastard Blade's* bridge, voice dripping with irony, "but it looks like my ships are still putting out more fire…"

He stopped at Eth's raised hand, not understanding the gesture itself but clearly understanding the imperative projected into his own mind. It shook him to have this lowly native inside his mind.

Then his ship icons began showing heavy damages, even though there had been no traces visible. He remembered the 'demonstration' he'd been subjected to. There had been no evidence of the weapons used then either.

They can't even trace their own missiles? he wondered.

Mishak knew he was winning but it wasn't without cost. Four of his ships, two cruisers and two frigates, had taken multiple hits. There was only so much you could do to avoid a swarm of the fast-moving missiles, and the small part of his brother's fleet that remained in action seemed to be coordinating their fire.

He reached into the holo and designated a handful of priority targets, all cruisers. He set them to allocate by division.

Rimush grunted, a wave of approval washing over Mishak. "Looks like someone over there is calling the shots for his brethren."

"And he's probably on a cruiser," Mishak said. "There's the added benefit of taking out ships with larger missile magazines as well…"

316

"Aye, lord," Rimush agreed but with a mildly dubious feeling to it. "Assuming they haven't fired everything off already. That was one hells of a missile storm for only twenty-six hostiles."

Missiles lanced out from Mishak's fleet, punching spears of plasma out through the far sides of their targets. The targets allocated to the scouting division hit from multiple angles simultaneously, looking like the poisonous urchins that inhabited the seas of Kish.

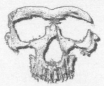

Gillbad leaned over his petty officer's shoulder, gazing at one of the holo-screens. "What am I supposed to see?"

"Here, sir," the NCO pointed. "See how the stars are occluded?"

"Sensor glitch?"

"Perhaps, sir, but the mines are being occluded as well…"

"Nergal's taint! An invisible ship?" Gillbad reared back in denial. "Where's the honor in that?"

"None, sir," the petty officer said patiently, "but they can invent all the honor they want, after we're all dead, can't they?"

"Move," Gillbad ordered, already moving his own posterior into the chair. He set up a target designation, based on occlusion history and projected paths.

His shock escaped before he could control it. The trace didn't just give him the invisible ship. It gave him a small flotilla of ships, at least two different sizes. "Captain!"

"Make it quick," Captain Geshmal said curtly. "I'm trying to coordinate what's left of our fleet."

"Invisible ships, Captain!" Gillbad put the results up on the central holo.

"Yes," the captain said impatiently, already turning back to his holo. "Memnon told us they had something with a special coating."

Gillbad raised his head a fraction. "You knew about them? Sir, we could have been tracking them before this…"

"Let them skulk about like cowards," Geshmal retorted. "What does hiding do for a warrior when there's a battle to be fought?"

"Two thirds of our fleet sits idle, Captain. It may have much to do with these stealth-ships. At least let us validate our tracking. Let me direct fire on…"

"Use one point-defense gun," Geshmal allowed grudgingly. "I need the rest of them to keep enemy missiles off us, assuming we ever see the incoming weapons in the first place…" he trailed off, turning back to face Gillbad.

"Test it," he ordered but with a sudden enthusiasm that hadn't been there before. "If it works, we'll package your tracking parameters for what's left of the fleet."

"Heat-bloom!" Tactical said, just loud enough to make Gleb jump a little. "Picking up debris as well on visible spectra – one-sided debris in line with point-defense fire from a cruiser. It looks like a scoutship, sir."

"Lucky shot?" Gleb asked, more to himself than to the tactical officer. He activated the cruiser's icon. "Helm, bring us bow-on to that target, I want to minimize our cross-section to that ship."

He turned to the tactical officer. "What if…"

He flinched as she disintegrated before his eyes, not two paces away. Then he noticed the shrapnel spraying past, pattering off his armor with inappropriately small sounds, considering the devastation wrought by the blurred path of point-defense rounds.

The incoming rounds seared into the decking a mere step from his feet. The itch in his feet and legs told him his skin was burning from the plasma-spall of the nearby impact.

Definitely not lucky, he thought stupidly as the red haze that had been one of his crewmen spattered accusingly across the remains of the aft bridge bulkhead.

Alarms blared in his helmet, bringing him back to the moment. "Helm, evasive maneuvering! Engineering, damage report!" *Some clever bastard on that cruiser has figured something out.* He opened a new telemetry output on his HUD, watching the cruiser's signal energy.

The helm officer was first to reply. "Captain, she's not answering to the helm! The pitch drives are green across the board but the fields aren't budging her off the current course."

Gleb turned to look at the back of the helmsman's helmet. "Why the hells…"

"Bridge, Engineering," the sudden voice cut Gleb off. "Pitch drives are all active but the path-drive is smashed beyond repair and it gave off an electro-mag wave when it failed. The wave has triggered the MA units in all of our warheads. Those osmium inserts now weigh more than our lord's entire fleet.

"I strongly recommend against any course changes. We're more likely to tear the pitch drives off their mounts than change our heading."

Gleb cursed quietly. "Helm, what's our course?"

"We're headed straight for that cruiser, sir."

Damn your efficiency! He'd been hoping they hadn't managed to execute his earlier order to aim the ship at that cruiser. "Time to impact?"

"Eighty five seconds!"

"All hands, abandon ship!" he shouted. *Good thing these ships are so small!* "Everyone into the scout-ship! She'll auto-separate in seventy seconds!"

He entered a command, cursing at the error message. That EM pulse had done more than turn on the mass augment fields. It had also broken the command link to the warheads.

Evac drills ran in the sixty second range, so he knew they'd all make it. It surprised him to realize what a comfort that was. He would need more than sixty seconds to accomplish his next task but he'd just have to use whatever time he had and hope it was worth it.

He ran aft, heading for the magazine. Siri bumped into him in the central companionway.

"Where are you headed?" she demanded.

"Go!" he shoved her in the direction of the docking hatch. "I'll be right behind you!"

He got to the magazine and ran down the row of warheads, opening their individual holo-menus and setting up a manual link to his own wrist projection.

"Sir, all aboard the scout-ship," Siri called. "Where are you?"

Gleb didn't waste breath on an answer that he knew would be ignored. He simply activated the scout's auto-separate protocol and went back to work, attempting to arm the missiles.

"Shit!" he screamed, suddenly finding himself at the far end of the magazine. How long had he been out this time? There was no chance of... He frowned.

The warheads were all armed.

Good job, other Gleb! He chuckled, confirming that the enemy ship still hadn't sent any priority messages on anything other than their fire-control net.

Of course, now he couldn't transpose himself off the ship. He let out a sharp breath, fogging his visor.

He could have escaped if not for the sudden appearance of his mental roommate. Then again, he'd been thinking only in terms of sacrificing himself to stop that cruiser passing on what it had learned.

Probably wouldn't have even occurred to me if not for the sudden mind-twitch.

And now it was impossible…

A flash of surprise came from Rimush. "There goes Sargina's cruiser!" he said. "Perhaps some old student of his is coordinating the enemy forces."

"One who didn't agree with his grades?"

"Could be. Might even…"

"Holy underworld!" Rimush cut him off. "Something big just impacted that cruiser! Too big for a missile!"

"It must have been one of our corvettes," Mishak fought the dread that threatened to overflow and spread throughout the bridge. *Rimush would definitely not approve,* he thought grimly.

Still, who had he just lost?

"My lord!" the ops officer called out. "They're striking their colors!"

"So they are!" Mishak stared dully at the holo. Inbound missiles were self-destructing in the void between the two fleets. "All ships ceasefire!"

"Hard to keep fighting if two-thirds of your force is sitting quiet," Rimush offered with a mental shrug. He gestured to a blinking icon. "Call from the *Bastard Blade*. They wouldn't risk giving away their location unless they had him…"

Mishak took a moment, stared at the icon while he got his thoughts in order. He'd already run through this conversation a few times in his head but now it was time for the real thing.

He reached out and touched the icon.

Memnon watched his brother shimmer into view. He realized, now, that he'd been played like a zithera. His brother had known how to wind him up and where to point him. He hated him for it but he also had to admit a certain…

Admiration?

"Oddly enough, brother," Mishak's said, "I understand how you must be feeling right now."

Did he just call me brother?

"Nothing I did was ever good enough for the old goat," Mishak continued. "It was pure chance that got me out from under his control."

The hologram leaned in toward Memnon. "What would you do if such a chance ever came your way?"

Why does that sound more like an offer than a question?

"Path alert! Multiple inbounds!"

Mishak turned his head fractionally at this news but he kept his eyes on his brother. "We only need to worry about one of those ships, don't we?" He leaned in toward the holographic Memnon.

"Shall we see how he reacts when we hand him a defeat? A very one-sided defeat that the empire will remember for a very long time?"

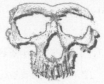

"Should have known the old bastard would stay clear of the approach corridor!" Hela grumbled. "Vel, plot us a direct course but one that brings us in a kilometer aft of Sandrak's flagship."

"Just so we're clear," the pilot answered, "you're asking me to take us *through* the minefield?"

"That's right," she confirmed. "I'd take it as a kindness if you could avoid flying us straight into any mines along the way."

She couldn't see her crew's faces with helmets locked up but she didn't have to in order to know that some reassurance was in order. "The mines lock onto anything that isn't another mine, right? How are they supposed to lock onto a ship with no emissions?"

"S'long as we get through without bleeding off any heat," Hill amended. "I'd been hoping to let off a little as we came out the corridor. Not enough to show at a distance but just to get us a little leeway."

He shrugged when Hela turned to face him. "We can reach him undetected but, after that, I don't know how far we'll get before the EM system overloads and we start radiating like an Enibulan bathhouse."

He cocked his head to the side. "You gonna be a while on Sandrak's bridge; killing crew and such?"

"Most likely."

He nodded, the movement lessened by the helmet. "Might be I can rig a way to dump some heat while you're in there. Just make sure you keep your eyes open once you have His Exaltedness under control.

I'll have a heat vent running into their ship and I'd hate to melt your suits off."

"Taking us in," Vel announced, a faint hint of reproach in her tone. "Velocity at half-pitch."

"Hill, what's our EM profile looking like if we go in at full?" Hela asked.

"Full!" he blurted in surprise. "We'd never make it out of the mines!" He paused for a moment, consulting calculations on his HUD. "At three-quarters, we'd make it there, but we'd be lucky to go half a kilometer before we're lit up like a hearth fire."

"But you've got an idea on how to dump some of that heat, right?"

"Course I do!" The grin wasn't visible but it was definitely audible. "I wouldn't seem nearly as heroic if I just went around telling captains 'no problem'. Gotta make sure they understand just how clever their engineers are being!"

"Three-quarters, Vel," Hela ordered. "Hill, whatever bit of clever you're cooking up better have a short gestation time, cause we're going to be docking very soon!"

Hill gave her an absent wave, already consumed with the details on a holo-screen. Blocks of nanites were already rushing to overhead locations from various damage-control points around the tiny ship.

Hela watched as they began forming a triple-walled tube, roughly a hand's breadth in diameter. It hung from narrow nanite-pylons and it was growing toward the point on the starboard side of the engineering compartment where Hela would be stepping into Sandrak's flagship.

She could see what he was up to and she approved. Still... "Make sure that vents aft, not 'forrard!"

She tore her attention away from Hill's project and moved up to crouch behind her pilot. "I want you to put us at the main companionway, just outside the bridge-entrance. I'll see you there."

She closed her eyes…

Sandrak glared at the central holo. He couldn't understand what he was seeing. There appeared to be losses on both sides but now, both fleets were sitting peaceably inside Kish's protective minefield.

Can't rely on anyone! he fumed. Whatever peace they'd arranged would fall apart pretty damned quickly once his own fleet came into firing range.

His eyes nudged his brain, which protested dumbly at first, but then it threw his body into a half jump backwards. Somebody was crouched in the middle of his holo-table, dappled light playing off matte armor.

Before he could work his way through the sheer impossibility of someone appearing apparently out of the ether, the figure cast him an ironic salute and…

Disappeared!

He saw a warning on his HUD from behind and he spun to find the figure with its dagger embedded in the sensor officer's neck. *A Human!*

Even as he realized this, the Human was gone again, simply gone. He couldn't even put his hand to when the figure had disappeared. He simply came to realize the attacker was gone after the fact.

Another warning and he turned to see the intruder behind the navigation officer, the knife at the Quailu's throat.

Fear had fully infected the bridge crew by now. Death, inexplicable death had been sensed and some had *seen* how it had happened.

Sandrak had seen it as well and he had no way to explain what he was seeing. He could explain the death of the navigation officer, however. One of the junior ops officers had drawn his sidearm and he shot at the intruder, failing to account for the presence of the navigation officer held between them.

The round might have gone through both but the intruder was already gone again. Sandrak spun wildly, catching glimpses of carnage – suits slit, torsos stabbed through armor seals – and he started to back away toward the hatch leading to the main companionway.

He felt a vibration in the deck-plates, felt the brief pulse of outrage and horror and turned to see one of the two guards who stood post outside the entry-hatch lying dead on the ground. The second guard flared a similar mix of emotions and then his mind went silent.

He fell forward, revealing the intruder, knife still held out where it had penetrated the back of the guard's brain. *Or had it just appeared there, inside the guard's head when the Human re-appeared?*

The Human lowered the knife and stepped aside waving toward the exit hatch. "This way, Lord Sandrak."

He was absolutely mystified. He had no explanation for what had just happened but that didn't change the fact that he'd been captured. He couldn't deny it and so there was no advantage to resisting at the expense of his own dignity.

He stepped through the hatch to find a new opening on the port side of the hull where it formed one of the companionway walls. Though the ship was rigged for combat, he could see what looked like atmospheric interference in the light of the curved hallway.

A long tube appeared to have sprouted through the opening and it seemed to be venting air. He had no idea why they'd be doing such a thing, wasting precious atmosphere by pumping it into a combat rigged ship, but it still didn't change the fact of his capture.

An approaching provost *did* seem to have other ideas, however and he came around the corner, weapon up. Sandrak was certain the intruder would appear behind the provost and kill him with his knife but it proved unnecessary.

The approaching security rating passed in front of the tube's end and his helmet seemed to glitch. The nanites realigned to close off the holes that had seemed to appear but the new helmet was now a featureless surface entirely devoid of the various modules that handled the sensors and HUD.

The crewman threw out waves of agony and fell to the deck writhing in pain.

It seemed a strange weapon for a species of the intruder's obvious abilities but he put his thoughts aside for the moment and stepped through the opening and into what looked like a slightly enlarged shuttle's engine-bay.

"How are we looking, Hill?" Hela guided Sandrak over to the locker she'd napped on and motioned him to sit.

"We'll make it back to dock with *Scorpion* at anywhere up to three quarters pitch," Hill told her. "But we don't have any atmo left so we're gonna have to keep the suits buttoned up."

He spread his hands out when she turned her helmeted face to him. "Don't *think* at me like that," he protested. "I needed a heat-transfer medium and our atmo was all we had!"

"We *do* have two-hundred litres of drinking water," she reminded him.

"Yeah, well…" He put a hand to the back of his armored neck. "Actually, that would have worked pretty damned well!"

She laughed. "I'm just tweaking your code. You made a call and it payed off."

She turned to look forward even though it made no difference in audibility. "Vel, get us to the *Dibbarra*, three quarters pitch!"

Mishak gazed calmly at his half-brother. "So, here we all are. Three separate forces and shots fired in anger. You know how that ends."

Memnon reared his holographic head. "It means that two factions will agree and a third will suffer the consequences."

"As it has always been in such a case," Mishak agreed. "Our father arrives late, of course, so that the fighting would be over and his would have likely been the strongest force present when the decisions were made."

He gestured to himself. "In the present scenario, I have the second-strongest position, having emerged as the victor in our skirmish." He paused for a moment.

"What if that were all wrong?"

"You mean to suggest that I'm the strongest?" Memnon quipped.

"Let's not get crazy!" Mishak waved the idea off. "But if I'm the victor here, if we agree to make peace – just a brotherly disagreement – then there's still a third party for us to leave out in the cold…"

"I'm listening."

"Then listen very carefully, brother." Mishak glanced at a boarding notification. Sandrak was already aboard the *Dibbarra*. "We only have time to sketch the rough outline before father steps onto my bridge."

Sandrak was angry but he had to admit he was proud of how Mishak had played this. That didn't mean he would just lie down and take humiliation. Mishak couldn't hold him on the *Dibbarra* for long and, the moment he was back with his fleet, some harsh lessons would be administered.

Magical Humans or not...

He stepped into the bridge to find Mishak standing next to a holo of his brother.

Time to remind them who's in charge. "I don't know what you two fools have been doing but..." He stopped in shock at the sight of Mishak's hand, palm toward him, accompanied by a mental demand for silence.

His attitude was even more shocking. He was displaying his preoccupation with opening another channel rather than attending to his own father's words!

This was unprecedented. Sandrak couldn't remember the last time anyone had ever dared to treat him like this.

And his own son?

He was shaken, confused and that would never do. He had to reassert control. "Did I not teach you the value of loyalty?" he grated.

This time, Mishak did turn to face him but Sandrak didn't like what he felt in him.

"All too well, father," he assured him smoothly. "I'm displaying your particular brand of it right now. My *first* loyalty will always be to the future emperor."

He stepped closer to Sandrak, almost driving him back a pace with the gesture. "You should be pleased to see how well your sons have learned from you."

Sons? Sandrak darted a glance at Memnon's projection. *Sons?*

"You have appeared, unannounced and unexpected," Mishak said gravely. "Your warships sit outside our defensive grid, rigged for combat. I view this as naked aggression from a lord well known for it and I demand mediation."

A second holo appeared, showing a senior Varangian officer.

"You will remain aboard the Dibbarra while Commodore Ingolf..." Mishak gestured toward the new hologram. "... looks into this transgression."

"Insolent young buck!" Sandrak flared with rage. "I'll do no such thing. By all the gods, I'll..."

He froze, but not of his own accord. He knew who was doing this, but he still had no idea how it was being done. He struggled to bring his fear and anger under control. This moment was almost certainly being recorded and he didn't want to appear as helpless as he really was.

"You will do as I have said," Mishak said serenely. He looked past Sandrak, his head bobbling oddly.

Sandrak felt the oppressive control lift away from his body but he remained quiet. To do anything else was to invite further damage to his reputation. *How long until these creatures decide they no longer need your protection, my foolish son?* The Human behind him was not the one who'd captured him. This one was a male. *How many of these abominatinons are there?*

But Mishak had already turned his attention back to Memnon's holo. "A fine skirmish, brother. I do enjoy our little sparring matches."

Memnon bowed politely at this pleasantry. "I should be away, brother. There's much to do."

"Indeed," Mishak agreed. "Before you go; Commodore Ingolf has brought a rather large fleet to this system. It was his intention for some of his ships to embed with local forces. Would you consent to taking a few of them with you?"

"I could be persuaded to take perhaps a dozen small formations," Memnon confirmed. "I'll just jump out to where they're waiting." He shimmered out of view.

Sandrak may have been played by his sons but he wasn't such a fool that he couldn't see what was coming. He thought to voice a protest but he knew it would serve nothing and he could feel a warning in his mind. It came from the Human behind him.

The protest would die before he could give it a voice.

Memnon was taking Varangian ships for one reason. He intended to make himself into an elector and the whole thing would be over and done by the time Sandrak could escape his son's spurious accusations.

He looked down and to the side, simmering with anger. *Not entirely spurious, I suppose.* The difference between the righteous and the wicked is usually a matter of which side has assembled the best lies.

Memnon would be able to snap up enough systems to elevate himself while the arbitration dragged out. As long as Sandrak stood accused of aggression, as long as he was being held by his accuser, his right to dispute Memnon's actions would be severely limited.

To make a fuss about it, weeks after the fact... Well, there was looking weak and then there was looking *weak*.

But how long will Mishak drag this foolish accusation out? He wondered. *When word gets out, there'll be dozens of neighboring lords eyeing my systems.*

Lords with well-honed grudges and impeccable claims…

"Memnon's forces are pathing out of Kish orbit," the sensor officer announced.

"Very well," Rimush said and, after a long pause, he continued. "Signal the fleet. All ships to initiate path-drives at ten percent of threshold and open any sealed orders that may be in their possession.

"*Dibbarra,*" he carried on, "emergency override. Lockout all systems to my voice-print!"

Sandrak looked over his son's fleet-captain. *This has the scent of treachery to it!*

"Rimush?" Mishak turned to face his senior officer. "What the hells are you doing?"

"I don't know," Eth told the assembled holo-Humans. "I'm not holding any sealed orders but let's start recalling the scout-ships back to the corvettes. If the path-drives are online, we may be leaving here in a hurry."

Something was nagging at him. Rimush often delivered orders to the fleet but there had never been sealed orders before. Who was he keeping secrets from?

None of the Human captains had the orders.

"Gods!" he whispered. *It couldn't be!* He knew he couldn't afford to indulge his incredulity. "Recall at maximum possible pitch!" he urged the holographs before him.

The icons in the main holo showed the sudden acceleration of the scout-ships but then Colm turned sideways, throwing out his holographic arms before he shivered out of sight.

On the holo, the *Reason We Can't Have Nice Things* was updated to read 'destroyed'.

"They've turned on us!" He raged. "Don't hang around! Once you've recovered your scouts, jump to the backup RV point."

"Sir," the ops officer called out. "Both of our scouts were already docked."

Dammit! Eth seethed. *I can't run off while my people are being shot at!* He blew out hard from pursed lips. His people were on this ship as well. He had no business risking their lives so he could play the heroic leader.

"*Sometimes, leadership means tucking tail and pulling a skedaddle...*"

"Dammit, old man! I know!" Eth whispered harshly. "Helm," he snapped, "path us out now!"

"We're docked," Chief Warrant Officer Carol announced on the *Falcata's* bridge channel. She could feel the slight vibration caused by the corvette's path-drive as it translated through the nanites connecting to her tiny scout. It was the most reassuring thing she'd ever felt.

The vibrations receded as the *Falcata's* main drive cycled its power level high enough to negate whatever caused the ship's signature quirk.

Carol was just starting to feel the uncomfortable spatial anomalies of path-entry, something the chief-scout would never admit to feeling, when a stream of point-defense rounds lanced past her scout.

It sliced a swath of destruction across the *Falcata's* hull, nearly severing her in half.

Of course our 'own side' would know how to track us, she thought bitterly, reaching past her pilot to stab at the docking release. *They know what they're looking for...*

"Set a course for the bastard who fired on us," she ordered. She touched an icon to show which ship she meant.

"Benk, start tossing warheads their way." She turned to the engineer. "Let's see if we can't do some damage. Might draw attention off the other ships long enough for them to get away."

They all knew the fate they faced. With the Falcata destroyed, they weren't going to ask another corvette crew to risk their lives to save the *four* of them.

Benk dragged a copy of the enemy cruiser's icon to an opening in the hull that was closest to his weapons lockup. Every warhead he tossed out the side had a miniaturised pitch-drive and it would pick up the targeting icon on its way out.

"We'll shift targets now," Carol said. She selected a new cruiser. "Keep your patterns irregular."

"Aye," the pilot confirmed, his voice shaking slightly. "Irregular patterns."

"There goes the Kopis," her ops rating said in disbelief, though it was followed quickly by the destruction of an enemy cruiser.

"That's a start," Carol snarled. "We're the only ones focusing on shooting back, people, so let's make this count!"

She targeted a new cruiser but the destruction of the first had already yielded the desired effects. Someone had identified them as a threat and rounds streaked out from multiple ships at once.

The crew of the *Foot up Your Ass* never even noticed the moment when death came for them.

Mishak was outraged, shaken to his very core, but he couldn't just stand there, spluttering. He forced himself to speak in something close to a normal voice. "Rimush, what in seven hells are you doing?" *Aside from committing treason, that is…*

He darted a quick glance at his father. Were the two colluding against him?

"I am doing what had to be done, lord." Rimush said heavily. "The other electors would never have voted for you if you commanded a native force more potent than even the Varangians.

"And we're kidding ourselves if we say those Humans would have remained loyal indefinitely. They may have been only a few hundred, but they were the sharp point of a wedge that would have cracked the empire into fragments and all under your rule!"

Mishak cast a desperate glance at the central holo. Of the original seven corvettes, only the *Yatagau* remained active in Kish orbit and, as he watched, the icon went red. His shoulders slumped.

All that effort to build a rapport, to build a reciprocal bond of duty and trust. All gone. He was more alone now than he had ever been.

He could only imagine what his Humans thought of him, if any still lived…

"So, you did this for the empire, did you?" he asked, turning back to face Rimush.

"And for my lord," Rimush insisted sadly. "This was a decision you could never have made, not with your honor intact."

Mishak drew his pistol but they were interrupted by a deep, gravelly laugh from Sandrak.

"Unbelievable!" he chortled, looking at his son. "You can't do anything right! Even when your people *betray* you, they do it out of *loyalty*!"

"Well, there's one tough decision made," Mishak told his father.

"What's that?"

"I'm going to put you on a small pension, because I'm not letting you go until your last system is gone and you're nothing but a beggar émigré."

He drew himself up to his full height, reveling in the shock from Sandrak. It gave him the strength to deal with Rimush.

Who, in retrospect, was probably correct in theory, if not in execution.

Mishak frowned.

At least with regard to the votes.

"You did this without my permission," he told his fleet-captain. "I cannot allow my officers to take liberties with my name." *Gods! Did any of them survive? I think I saw the* Bastard Blade *path out...*

Rimush stood formally, arms to the side, hands open and facing his lord. "I am ready to face the consequences, lord." Sadness and pride warred within his heart as he waited for the shot.

Mishak wanted to be angry with Rimush. How many of his trusted Humans had died in this betrayal? Ultimately, it was Mishak who'd betrayed his loyal warriors. It was his own fleet-captain who'd done this and Mishak was responsible for the actions of *everyone* who served him.

But he'd been through too much with Rimush and he'd done it out of a sincere desire to save his lord from his own folly.

And Mishak wasn't entirely certain Rimush was wrong.

He sighed, looking down at the pistol. He reversed the grip and held it out.

The gratitude from Rimush was hard to take but Mishak kept his own feelings under a tight lock. He forced himself to watch impassively as the fleet-captain placed the muzzle against his right temporal plate and pulled the trigger.

Several of the bridge crew were spattered with the senior officer's brains and blood. Though their disgust was palpable, they stayed at their posts.

"Fleet Captain Rimush," the computer voice announced, "is deceased. All lockouts under his voiceprint are now released."

"Fleet-wide! All ships ceasefire immediately!" Mishak ordered. A glance at the central holo told him there was probably nothing left to stop firing at but he had to try. *What a fornicating mess this has turned into.*

He wanted to leave the bridge; work out his anger. *Can't leave Rimush in charge of the fleet if his brains are all over the bridge, can you?*

"I thought I taught you better than this," Sandrak sneered.

"Keep talking, you old goat." Mishak turned slowly to look at his father. "There's no law saying I need to give you that small pension. We could find out how you like begging shelter from obscure relatives."

He grinned bitterly. "You see? You've taught me well enough to know a person's pressure points!"

Lying Low
In Orbit at Babilim Station

Eth stared at the holo. The station was so huge that, from standard orbital altitude, the horizon looked nearly flat.

He felt like they'd already landed on the surface. "Nobody comes to this side?"

Meesh's holographic form shook its head. "Nothing we heard indicated any activity after about ten-thousand clicks from the main city on the other side. Just look at the size of the place. It would take weeks to get around to this side of the station by ground transport, even assuming you could find functioning hyper-loop lines that reached the whole way."

Eth sighed, feeling the heaviness that had been ambushing him at random intervals, when time allowed or reminders intruded.

They'd lost four corvettes and eight scouts; most of that to supposedly 'friendly' forces.

Somehow, in the space of a year, he'd gone from being the second in command of a small unit where he'd known every name to leading a large force where he lamented the deaths of people he couldn't name to save his own life. *Is this what 'success' feels like?*

"We have a theory to test," he declared, "before we can set up shop here." He turned to face 'holo' Meesh who was nodding, opening his mouth to volunteer.

"I'll take a scout down myself," he told him, quickly and finally. He waved his hand in a chopping motion. "I'm going," he insisted.

He turned to the nav station, where Hendy was standing next to the helmsman. "And, no, I don't think it wise to 'take a good pilot along' for what's essentially a test of whether our stealth will get us past the station's defenses, so don't even think of volunteering!"

"Volunteer?" Hendy raised an eyebrow. "For an almost certain-death mission?" He chuckled, strolling over to Eth. "I'll just stay up here and take over my new ship if you happen to get yourself fried." He leaned in closer.

"You don't need to do penance for anything, old friend," Hendy added quietly, "but go ahead and risk your neck if it feels like the thing to do."

Eth's shoulders slumped a fraction. "Is it that obvious?"

Hendy gave a tiny shrug. "You realize we were all grown as combat slaves, right?" He kept his voice low. "We've been getting away with some outrageous shenanigans. The fates were bound to catch up with us and kill off a few hundred of our people at some point."

"Doesn't make them any less dead," Eth countered.

"That's true," Hendy agreed equably, "but they still accomplished ten times more than they were grown for before our lord betrayed them. Not much more a person can ask for in the HQE…"

With that, he strolled back to his station.

Eth sighed again and closed his eyes. When he opened them again, he was between the pilot and co-pilot seats of *Bastard Blade's* scout-ship. He turned to the crewman who he'd positioned in the engineering space with orders to keep an eye on the cockpit.

"Thanks," he told the man, realizing he didn't know his name. "Get back to the *Blade*. I'll take her down alone."

He watched the man leave. *One more person that won't die today over my decisions,* he thought. He strapped into the pilot's seat and initiated the separation sequence.

Nothing to say, old man?

"Nothing that needs saying…"

The coolant umbilicals separated and dissolved into a block of nanites next to the opening in the hull, which was already closing. He caught a faint whiff of whatever fluid Noa was currently using as a heat transfer medium.

"*Blade,* this is *Your Wakeup Call,* umbilicals are retracted and ECM is spooled up." He pressed the final command icon. "Separating now."

He moved away from the hull, but only a few meters, giving time for the corvette to close up the hatch cover that hid the docking ring when there was no scout-ship attached.

Then he moved a hundred meters off and began to rotate the small craft. "*Blade, Wakeup Call,* how do I look?"

"*Wakeup, Blade,* Wish I could tell you," Hendy replied, "but we can't see you. Looks like I'm not getting a shiny new corvette to command any time today. Good luck, going to comms blackout now."

Eth reached up and locked out his auto-transmit functions. The last thing he needed, while sneaking past Babilim Station's vicious security system, was an accidental transmission broadcasting his presence.

"This will work," he told himself. He tilted his head a little. "This will *probably* work." He set a course for the large crater they'd identified from orbital surveys. It stood the best chance of having useful industrial equipment in its cargo handlers.

And it allowed some room to grow.

It would also give them better security. It was never more than a matter of time before one of their own tried selling their secrets but it had still stung Eth when Memnon told them about the traitor.

That, of course, was why Memnon had told him, though he almost certainly regretted it. The Quailu had been alarmed by Eth's subsequent mental incursion and he'd said nothing more until he'd been returned to his own ship.

Memnon had failed to capitalize on the knowledge he'd bought, but that didn't mean it could be safely ignored. They had been betrayed by one of their own people. That would be much harder to do with the last two hundred twenty-six of their people gathered here on Babilim.

Admittedly, the market for such secrets had taken a recent nosedive. Mishak's forces obviously had no trouble coming up with a way to track the stealthy ships, seeing as they knew exactly what they were searching for.

And Eth suspected the path-drive spool-up had been an attempt to prevent his Nergalihm from jumping aboard the bridges of the attacking vessels. He didn't know if it would work, but some tests would have to be made at the earliest opportunity.

He nearly jumped out of his skin at the chime of a second-level alarm. It was just the emissions management system, letting him know he had more than a day of stealth at the current speed.

The crater, looming up around his field of vision told him he'd need far less time than that.

It worked! Their stealth technology was able to slip past the security system! He frowned. *Or the system is inoperable in this region.* Either way, they could use this location as their base of operations.

He settled the small craft inside what looked like the markings for a landing pad and shut down. When he stepped outside, his HUD told him the air was breathable, if slightly higher in nitrogen than he was used to.

The crater's far edge was at least thirty kilometers away, faded slightly by the intervening air. It wasn't even noticeable from orbit.

He retracted his helmet and took a breath, surprised at the pedestrian scent of old dust. *Nothing has moved here for thousands of years,* he reminded himself.

Anything that might off-gas had finished doing so a long time ago.

"It's a gloomy place, isn't it?" Scylla asked, smiling serenely across the massive chasm.

Eth's eyes widened slightly as he realized she was standing there, but a part of him had known she was about to transpose herself down to join him. "Should you be out of sick bay?"

"I'm fine," she assured him. "Just needed fluids and electrolytes. The doc had no excuse to keep me after the last set of scans."

Gleb had connected with her at the time of his death. She'd sensed him, as though he were drifting on a sea, only he'd been swept away by the current before she could reach out…

A crewman had found her curled up in a ball by the serving line in the mess hall, unable to stand.

"You're sure you don't…" Eth trailed off, sensing her preoccupation.

She smiled, something he wasn't used to seeing, and then nodded in confirmation. He tore his gaze away from her as the lighting came on, a warm, slightly-yellow wave of brightness that flowed away from them in both directions. The light raced around the rim of the crater drawing a line between the station and the horizon.

Below, in the depths, harsher lights came on to illuminate the cargo zones. Massive machines lurched into motion for the first time in millennia, but then they slowed to a halt.

"Best to leave everything where it is until we have time to review the cargo manifests," Scylla murmured.

Eth wasn't sure if she was talking to him or to the station itself. He reached out to touch her shoulder, waiting until she looked at him. "While you're communing with the station, can you do anything about the security system in this zone? I'd hate to lose anyone just because the hull coating got scratched off by debris in that last battle."

She nodded. "I'll check."

He walked to the edge of the landing platform, looking down to the cargo complex. The tops of the gantries were more than a kilometer below him and he had no idea how deep they ran.

The smells of lubricating fluid and ozone wafted up from the brief flurry of activity they'd caused. He smiled.

It's not home until it makes its smells known to you...'

"You can start bringing ships down," Scylla said. "And I've found the place you wanted... for the traitor..."

Eth looked back, but only far enough to catch her in his peripheral vision. He was mostly looking at a stack of cargo containers that lay to his left. "How far is it?"

"Just far enough, I'd say." There was no grimace on her face but it made itself known in her voice. "Once those things get a taste for Humans, you don't want them anywhere near here!"

A foggy, glowing blue trail appeared above the floor, leading back into a bank of structures.

"That will show you where to go," she murmured, already forgetting about the path's grisly purpose. "You should take the time to talk to this place. It's really incredible!"

Later, he thought, looking at the wispy path. Before that could happen, one more Human had to die under his watch.

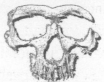

Jay groaned. He rolled over, keeping his eyes closed. He brought a hand up to hold his forehead.

He knew Hela had used her abilities to knock him out. He had seen her coming toward him and he'd known it was all over.

He had also known, even as he approached Memnon, that the Quailu would betray him in a heartbeat, even if just for the amusement it would afford. Still, Jay had sold out his fellow Humans. Whether it had been for the money or just for the rush it afforded, he didn't know.

It was in his nature, beyond that, he couldn't say.

The headache was worse than any he'd ever known. *Bitch must have nearly killed me!* Still, he could hardly blame her. He even disgusted himself.

He jerked his head aside, dislodging his hand as a blade of grass went up his nose.

Grass?

He opened his eyes, slowly, fighting against the searing pain of the light. He lay there, on his side, waiting for his eyes to adjust to the brightness of the… forest meadow?

A small furry creature was sitting up on its little haunches, several meters away, looking at him. It let out warbling squeaks as it angled its head back and forth, examining him from various angles.

He realized the sounds from the creature were part of a larger conversation. The steady, throbbing flow of noise that he'd thought to be a side effect of his incapacitation was actually thousands of the small creatures calling back and forth.

He stared at the small animal, loathing its calm, complacent cuteness. He pushed himself up to a sitting position and his right hand closed on a rock. "Beat it!" he shouted, tossing the rock at it.

It scampered out of the way, not looking at all complacent as it bared its teeth and hissed. It looked past Jay, to his right, and, just as Jay was wondering what it saw, he felt teeth sink into his left forearm.

"Fornication!" He spun around on his buttocks, aiming a kick at another of the small animals but it dodged easily, leaping back nearly two meters in one jump. It landed, filled its little lungs and emitted a piercing shriek from its bloody mouth.

The bite was alarming enough but what made Jay's blood run cold was the sudden, oppressive wall of silence.

He scrambled to his feet, noticing the sea of faces that looked up at him from the grass. The adrenaline was coursing now. He spun, desperately looking for a way out of this place.

There were walls all around him but he was far from all of them. It was hard to evaluate scale without any context but the fact that the nearest structures appeared washed out by the intervening atmosphere told him he'd never make it.

He began running for a nearby tree without any conscious decision. He leapt for the lower branches and clambered up.

He looked back down, sucking in a shuddering breath at the sight of the pursuit. His eyes grew wide. *Why does it smell like dung up here?*

He looked up. *Gods!*

The damned things nested in the trees. Dozens of them fell on him, biting, scrambling to get a secure purchase with surprisingly long claws. He screamed but sharp claws sliced his lower lip and a furry head inserted into his mouth, taking a chunk of his tongue.

He lost his grip and fell from the tree, crushing several of the little bastards when he hit the ground. It was no comfort to Jay, who could feel teeth grating on his ribs.

One bite to his neck struck the same artery that Hela had pinched off to capture him. *Ironic,* he thought, his life pulsing out of his neck, *that the same attack from such an insignificant creature...*

Heavy is the Head
The Dibbarra, *Kish Orbit*

Tashmitum stopped outside the door to the suite she shared with Mishak. She took a deep breath and composed herself before stepping forward.

The door slid out of the way and she entered their sitting room. She could hear Mishak in the bedchamber, feel his mind as he gazed out the portal at the graceful curve of Kish's dayside.

She moved to the chamber door, stepping over the ruins of the coffee table and skirting shards from several coffee mugs on her way.

She came to a stop beside him and looked out the window, saying nothing. It was a beautiful planet, though a bit heavy on desert and tropical climates for a Quailu's liking. There were at least fifty million newly freed Humans down there.

"What will *they* think of us?" Mishak asked, picking up her train of thought. "Eth and his team were heroes to the Humans on Kish. We've had no end of volunteers wanting to serve on our ships, but now…"

He sighed heavily. "It's not right!"

"Welcome to the imperial family," she told him wearily. "Ruling the HQE isn't about doing what's right. It's about managing the wrongs, choosing the least terrible option."

"And turning on Eth, who'd never shown the slightest hint of disloyalty, was the least terrible option?"

"We'll never know," she admitted, "but we'll never *have* to know now. You have to admit, Rimush's reasons were plausible, even if he did take them to a logical extreme. Would we be able to arrange a peaceful transition if the electors are worried about the power the Humans give you?"

"The Varangians give your father a similar power."

346

"And incorporating them in their current role, rather than as ordinary subjects nearly destroyed the empire," she pointed out. "I'm not sure we could have done it again, not when it means *two* very powerful tools at our disposal."

He shook his head, ever so slightly. "That powerful tool is now our enemy. I don't think we ended up with the least terrible option this time."

"They were severely weakened," she replied, not bothering to hide her regret. "I doubt they'll recover for a few generations, especially if they don't have access to Kish to replenish their losses..."

Irth

What is this Comi Conn?

An entire pride of cheevers had taken up residence inside of Gleb's skull.

He knew this for a fact because it felt like they'd been nibbling at his brain and he was pretty sure they were using his sinuses as a latrine.

He wondered, briefly, at his predicament until he remembered the battle. He'd been in the magazine of the *Stiletto*…

He opened his eyes, forgetting about his headache, and saw a sky, reddish blue, and a small building, less than a kilometer in height, to his right. The HUD showed a breathable atmosphere.

Is this some remote colony? He wondered, opening his helmet. *No, not with shiny buildings like that.* It looked wrong somehow.

How did I end up here, wherever here is? He'd reached out at the very last second and he was reasonably sure he'd found Scylla.

There had been no time for fine targeting. He'd simply followed the universe's suggestion and aimed for the first large grouping of Humans he could find.

So why am I not on the Mouse?

A shadow loomed over him. "Hey, buddy," an angry voice growled, "how about you pace the shenanigans? I don't give a bent shit how you managed to do this but I've got a couple hundred guests finishing the breakfast buffet and they're gonna be out here, asking me why the pool is frozen. How do you think that makes me feel, huh?"

Gleb frowned up at him. The man's sentence structure was different from the usual Imperial Standard. Clearly, Gleb's suit had been busy. There was a veritable swamp of signals in the area and they carried a lot of data, including voice. The data was poorly structured but it was easily readable and the suit had done a good job of building a new translation matrix.

Gleb tried to get up, not wanting to deal with this fellow while in such an undignified position, but there was resistance. He looked down.

He was encased in ice, *tons* of it. He was in a large, kidney-shaped, ice-filled depression in the ground.

The energy in the water had saved his life but how to explain that to this angry man? He pushed hard, his suit amplifying his strength, and he broke free, icy shards forcing the man back a step.

He climbed to his feet. "Sorry about that," he said.

"Yeah, yeah," the man waved off the apology as if it was some annoying insect. "Just be glad nobody got hurt or I'd be sitting on your chest until San Diego's finest got here!"

"Ah, yeah," Gleb scratched at the back of his head. "Sorry!"

"Whatever, dude. Next time you feel like pulling a prank, wait till you're inside the convention." He jerked his head toward something behind Gleb. "Go on! Get out of here and take the rest of your nerd-herd with you!"

Gleb turned to find two men and one young woman, wearing what looked like white plastic armor. He couldn't imagine what possible reason anyone would have for such equipment. *Must be ceremonial,* he mused. *It wouldn't stop a strong breeze let alone combat rounds.*

"How did you freeze a whole swimming pool?" the young woman asked, grinning. "Dude, that's epic!"

Her armor, for reasons that Gleb couldn't fathom, exposed her entire midriff. He wasn't complaining, mind you, but that still didn't mean it made sense.

Also, even though she wore the least comprehensive suit, she appeared to be in command of her small team. The two males viewed her with a certain awe and not a little fear.

"Does that mean songs are being composed about it?" he asked her, bewildered.

She rolled her eyes. "Fine! Don't tell me." She looked him up and down. "Sweet suit! Make it yourself?"

"No, but we've made a few tweaks," he admitted wondering what 'sweet' meant in this context. The translation matrix needed a few tweaks itself.

She nodded appreciatively. "Ain't it always the way? They never look that good straight out of the box." She nodded her head toward an awning. A label on it was superimposed by his HUD to read 'BAYSIDE'.

"Better, hurry," she warned. "You don't want to miss the judging!"

So they're cops. That's what this ceremonial armor is for! He took a deep breath. "Very well, officer. Lead on. I shall stand judgement for freezing that man's water!" *Shouldn't be more than a fine…*

She laughed, dragging a stray lock of dark brown hair back over her ear. "Maybe I'll have to punish you, later!"

He fell in beside her. Her attitude seemed to indicate he wouldn't face much trouble at this 'judging' and the feelings he was picking up from her mind indicated an approach to punishment that he heartily approved of.

"What jurisdiction am I in for this judging?"

She grinned. "It's San Diego! You're about to go before the highest court on Earth!"

He stopped walking.

Irth!

350

From the Author

Power, as Mishak has already pointed out, is not a place of comfort. It's a never-ending struggle to hold what you have.

Eth and his Humans have risen high in the HQE and that means new enemies. It was only a matter of time before someone moved against them.

They just never expected it to be their own side.

So now they're forced into exile on the fringe of the empire, cut off from the rest of Humanity on Kish. They should be down for the count but our boy Gleb has stumbled onto a new source of recruits.

He's got a pool of nearly eight Billion potential recruits to work with.

Some interesting things will be happening in book 3.

Meanwhile, I'm outlining book 5 of the 'Black Ships' series. The long range group is planning to cross the great void, sneaking into the Dactari Republic by a back door that nobody thought was even possible.

They're looking to rescue their group's founder, Commander Gabiola. Odin, bored with his role as the law-giver, might be playing a role as well.

I hope you've been enjoying the Human series. I hope to have a third book out this year. If you have a moment, a quick review would be appreciated!

If you like reading shorter stories (less than 50k words) I have a library page where you can download the stores I've done that aren't long enough to actually sell. Mostly, they explore sidelines from the main series.

You can get the link by joining my mailing list (. I figure you should get more for subscribing than just the odd email letting you know I have a new title for sale on Amazon. When you get your welcome email, you'll get the link for the free downloads.

Free eNovellas

You also get my own email when you join so feel free to drop me a line if you have any comments or suggestions.

Thanks for reading and I hope you have a great new year!

 Get Free e-Novellas

When you sign up for my new-release mail list!

Follow this link to get started:
http://eepurl.com/ZCP-z